[See page 48

"I'M CLAUDE. DON'T YOU REMEMBER ME?"

THE SIDE
OF THE ANGELS

A NOVEL

BY

BASIL KING

AUTHOR OF
The Inner Shrine

ILLUSTRATED BY
ELIZABETH SHIPPEN GREEN

HARPER & BROTHERS PUBLISHERS
NEW YORK AND LONDON

THE SIDE OF THE ANGELS

Copyright, 1915, 1916, by Harper & Brothers
Printed in the United States of America
Published February, 1916

B–Q

ILLUSTRATIONS

THE SIDE OF THE ANGELS

THE SIDE OF THE ANGELS

"My lord, I am on the side of the angels."—DISRAELI.

CHAPTER I

THE difficulty was, in the first place, one of date—
not the date of a month or a year, but of a generation
or a century. Had Thorley Masterman found himself
in love with Rosie Fay in 1760, or even in 1860, there
would have been little to adjust and nothing to gainsay.
In 1860 the Fays were still as good as the Thorleys, and
almost as good as the Mastermans. Going back as far
as 1760, the Fays might have been considered better than
the Thorleys had the village acknowledged standards of
comparison, while there were no Mastermans at all. That
is, in 1760 the Mastermans still kept their status as yeo-
men, clergymen, and country doctors among the hills of
Derbyshire, untroubled as yet by that spirit of unrest for
conscience' sake which had urged the Fays and the Thorleys out of the flat farmlands of East Anglia one hundred
and thirty years before.

During the intervening period the flat farmlands remained only as an equalizing symbol. Thorleys, Fays,
Willoughbys, and Brands worked for one another with the
community of interests developed in a beehive, and intermarried. If from the process of intermarriage the Fays

were, on the whole, excluded, the discrimination lay in some obscure instinct for affinity of which no one at the time was able to forecast the significance.

But by 1910 there was a difference, the difference apparent when out of the flat farmlands seismic explosion has thrown up a range of mountain peaks. For the expansion of the country which the middle nineteenth century had wrought, the Thorleys, Mastermans, Willoughbys, and Brands had been on the alert, with eyes watchful and calculations timed. The Fays, on the other hand, had gone on with the round of seed-time and harvest, contented and almost somnolent, awakening to find that the ages had been giving them the chances that would never come again. It was across the wreck of those chances, and across some other obstacles besides, that Thorley Masterman, for the first time since childhood, looked into the gray-green eyes of Rosie Fay and got the thrill of their wide-open, earnest beauty.

He was then not far from thirty years of age, having studied at a great American university, in Paris, Berlin, and Vienna, and obtained other sorts of knowledge of mankind. He knew Rosie Fay, in this secondary, grown-up phase of their acquaintance, as the daughter of his first patient, and he had obtained his first patient through the kindly intervention of Uncle Sim. From February to November, 1910, his "shingle" had hung in one of the two streets of the village without attracting a patient at all. He had already begun to feel his position a trial when his half-brother's daily jest turned it into a humiliation.

"Must be serious matter, Thor," Claude would say, "to be responsible for so many valuable lives."

Mr. Leonard Willoughby, his father's partner in the old "banking-and-broking" house of Toogood & Masterman, enjoyed the same sort of chaff. "Looking pale, Thor. Must be working too hard."

"Never mind, Thor," Mrs. Willoughby would encourage him. "When I'm ill you shall get me—but then I'm never ill."

At such minutes her daughter Lois could only smile sympathetically and talk hurriedly of something else. As he had meant since boyhood to marry Lois Willoughby when the moment for marriage came, Thor counted this tactfulness in her favor.

Nevertheless, he was puzzled. Having disregarded his future possession of money and prepared himself for a useful career with all the thoroughness he could command, nobody seemed to want him. It was not that the village was over-provided with doctors. Every one admitted that it wasn't—otherwise he would not have settled in his native place. The village being really a township with a scattered population—except on the Thorley estate, which was practically part of a great New England city, where there were rows of suburban streets— it was quite insufficiently served by Dr. Noonan at one end and Dr. Hill at the other, for Uncle Sim in the Old Village could scarcely be said to count. No; the opening was good enough. The trouble lay, apparently, in Thorley Masterman himself. Making all allowances for the fact that a young physician must wait patiently, and win his position by degrees, he had reason to feel chagrined. He grew ashamed to pass the little house in the Old Village which he had fitted up as an office. He grew ashamed to go out in his runabout.

The runabout had been worse than an extravagance, since, on the ground that it would take him to his patients the more quickly, he had felt justified in borrowing its price. The most useful purpose it served now was to bring Mr. Willoughby home from town when unfit to come by himself. Otherwise its owner hated taking it out of the garage, especially if Claude were in sight. Claude had envied him the runabout at first, but soon found a way to work his feeling off.

"Anybody dying, old chap?" he would ask, with a

curl of his handsome lip. "Hope you'll get to him in time."

It was while in the runabout, however, in the early part of a November afternoon, that the young doctor met his uncle Sim.

"Hello, Thor!" the latter called. "Where you off to? Was looking for you."

Thor brought the machine to a standstill. Uncle Sim threw a long, thin leg over his mare's back and was on the ground. "Whoa, Delia, whoa! Good old girl!"

He liked to believe that the tall bay was spirited. Standing beside Thor's runabout, he held the reins loosely in his left hand, while the right arm was thrown caressingly over Delia's neck. The outward and visible sign of his eccentricity was in his difference from every one else. In a community—one might say a country—in which each man did his utmost to look like every other man, the fact that Simeon Masterman was willing to look like no one but himself was sufficient to prove him, in the language of his neighbors, "a little off." It was sometimes said that he suggested Don Quixote—he was so tall, so gaunt, and so eager-eyed—and, except that there was no melancholy in his face, perhaps he did.

"Got a job for you." The old man's voice was nasal and harsh without being disagreeable.

Grown sensitive, Thor was on his guard. "Not one of your jobs that are given away with a pound of tea?" he said, suspiciously.

"I don't know about the pound of tea—but it's given away. Giving it away because I can't deal with it myself. Calls for some one with more ingenuity—so I've told 'em about you."

Thor laughed. "Don't wonder you're willing to give it up, Uncle Sim."

"You'll wonder still less when you've seen the patient. By the way, it's Fay's wife. 'Member old Fay, don't you?"

The young man nodded. "Used to be Grandpa Thorley's gardener. Has the greenhouses on father's land north of the pond. Some sort of row going on between him and father now. What's she got?"

"It's not what she's got, poor woman; it's what she hasn't got. That's what's the matter with her."

"I'm afraid it's a variety of symptom I never heard of."

"No; but you'll hear of it soon. Whoa, Delia! Steady! Good girl! If you can treat it you'll be the most distinguished specialist in the country. Whoa, Delia! I'm giving you the chance to begin."

Thor wondered what was at the back of the old fellow's mind. There was generally something in what he said if you could think it out. "Since you've diagnosed the case, Uncle Sim—" he began, craftily.

"Can't I give you a tip for the treatment? No, I can't. And it wouldn't do any good if I did, because she won't take my medicine."

"Perhaps I could make her."

The old man laughed harshly. "You! That's good. Why, you'd be the first to make game of it yourself."

He had his left foot in the stirrup and his right leg over Delia's back before Thor could formulate another question. As with head thrown back he continued his amused chuckling, there was about him, in spite of his sixty years, a something irresponsible and debonair that would have pleased Franz Hals or Simon de Vos.

Within ten minutes Thor was knocking at the door of a small house with a mansard roof, situated in what had once been the apple-orchard of a farm. All but a sparse half-dozen of the trees had given place to lines of hothouses, through the glass of which he could see oblongs of vivid green. He was so preoccupied with the fact of paying his first visit to his first patient as scarcely to notice that the girl who opened the door was pretty. He almost ignored her.

"How do you do, Miss Fay? I'm Dr. Thorley Masterman. I believe your mother would like to see me. May I go to her at once?"

He was in the narrow hallway and at the foot of the stairs when she said: "You can go right up. But perhaps I ought to tell you that she's not—well, she's not very sick."

He looked at her inquiringly, getting the first faint impression of her beauty. "What's the matter, then?"

"That's what we don't know." After a second's hesitation she added, "Perhaps it's melancholy." Another second passed before she said, "We've had a good deal of trouble."

The tone touched him. Her way of holding her head, rather meekly, rather proudly, sufficiently averted to give him the curve of the cheek, touched him, too. "What kind of trouble?"

"Oh, every kind. But she'll tell you about it herself. It's all she'll talk about. That's why we can't do anything for her—and I don't believe you can."

"I'd better see."

Following her directions given from the foot of the stairs, he entered a barely furnished bedroom of which two sides leaned inward, to correspond to the mansard grading of the roof. One window looked out on the greenhouses, another toward Thorley's Pond. Beside the former, in a high, upholstered arm-chair, sat a tall woman, fully dressed in black, with a patchwork quilt of many colors across her knees. In spite of gray hair slightly disheveled, and wild gray eyes, she was a handsome woman who on a larger scale made him think of the girl down-stairs.

"How do you do, Mrs. Fay?" he began, feeling the burden of the situation to be on himself. "I'm Dr. Thor—"

"I know who you are," the woman said, ungraciously. "If you hadn't been a Masterman I shouldn't have sent for you."

He took a small chair, drawing it up beside her. "I know you've been treated by my uncle Sim—"

"He's a fool. Tries to heal a broken heart by feeding it on rainbows."

Thor smiled. "That's like him. And yet rainbows have been known to heal a broken heart before now."

"They won't heal mine. What I want is down on the solid earth." There was a kind of desperate pleading in her face as she added, "Why can't I have it?"

"That depends on what it is. If it's health—?"

"It's better than health."

He smiled. "I've always heard that health is pretty good, as things go—"

"It's good enough. But there's something better, and that's patience. If you've got patience you can do without health."

"I don't think you're much in need of a doctor, Mrs. Fay," he laughed.

"I am," she declared, savagely. "I am, because I 'ain't got either of 'em; and if I had I'd give them both for something else." She held him with her wild gray eyes, as she said: "I'd give 'em both for money. Money's better than patience and better than health. If I had money I shouldn't care how sick I was, or how unhappy. If I had money my son wouldn't be in jail."

Though startled, he knew that, like a confessor, he must show no sign of surprise. He remembered now that there had been a boy in the Fay family, two or three years younger than himself. "I didn't know—" he began, sympathetically.

"You didn't know, because we're not even talked about. If your brother was in jail for stealing money it's the first thing the town would tattle of. But you've been back from your travels for a year or more, and you 'ain't even heard that our Matt is doing three years at Colcord."

"But you'd rather people didn't hear it, wouldn't you?"

"I'd rather that they'd care whether I'm alive or dead," she said, fiercely. "I've lived all my life in this village, and my ancestors before me. Fay's family has done the same. But we're pushed aside and forgotten. It's as much as ever if some one will tell you that Jasper Fay raises lettuce in the winter, and cucumbers in spring, and a few flowers all the year round, and can't pay his rent. I don't believe you've heard that much. *Have* you?"

He dodged the subject by asking the usual professional questions and giving some elementary professional advice. "I'm afraid, Mrs. Fay, you're taking a discouraged view of life," he went on, by way of doing his duty.

She sat still more erect in her arm-chair, her eyes flashing. "If you'd seen yourself driven to the wall for more'n thirty year, and if when you got to the wall you were crushed against it, and crushed again, wouldn't you take a discouraged view of life? I've lived on bread and water, or pretty near it, ever since I was married, and what's come of it? We're worse off than we ever were. Fay's put everything he could scrape together into this bit of land, and now your father is shilly-shallying again about renewing the lease."

"Oh, so that's it!"

"That's it—but it's only some of it. Look out there. All Fay's sweat and blood and all of mine is in those greenhouses and that ground. It's everything we've got to live on, and God knows what kind of a living it is. Your father has never given us more'n a three years' lease, and every three years he's raised the rent on us. He's had us in his power from the first— Oh, he's crafty, getting us to rent the land from him instead of buying it, and Fay that soft that he believed him to be his friend!— he's had us in his power from the first, and he's never spared us. No wonder he's rich! And you're coming in for that Thorley money, too. I know what your grandfather Thorley's will was. Going to get it when you're thirty. Must be pretty nigh that now, ain't you?"

To humor her Thor named the date in the following February when he should reach the age fixed by his grandfather for entering on the inheritance.

"What 'd I tell you? I remember your grandfather as plain as plain. Big, hard-faced man he was, something like you. My folks could remember him when he hawked garden-truck to back doors in the city. Nothing but a farmer's son he was, just like the rest of us—and he died rich. Only difference between the Thorleys and the Fays was that the Thorleys held on to their land and the Fays didn't. Neither did my folks, the Grimeses. If we'd been crafty and hadn't sold till the city was creeping down our chimneys like the Thorleys and the Brands, we should be as rich as them. Cut your father out of his will good and hard, your grandfather did, and now it 'll all come to you. Why, there was a time when the Thorleys hired out to my folks, and so did the Willoughbys! And now—!" She threw the quilt from off her knees and spread her hands outward. "Oh, I'm sick of it! I've spent my life watching every one else go up and me and mine go down—and I'm sick of it. I'm not sick any other way—"

"No, I don't think you are," he said, gently.

"But that's bad enough, isn't it? If I had a fever or a cold you could give me something to take it away. But what can you do for the state of mind I'm in?"

He answered, slowly, "I can't do much just yet—though I can do a little—but by and by, perhaps—when I know more exactly what the trouble is—"

"You can't know it better than I can tell you now. It's just this—that I've all I can do to keep from stealing down to Thorley's Pond, when no one's looking, and throwing myself in. What do you think of that?"

"I think you won't do it," he smiled, "but I wouldn't play with the idea if I were you."

"Look here," she cried, seizing him by the arm and pulling him out of his chair. "Look out of that window." He followed the pointing of her finger to a high bluff covered with oaks, to which the withered brown foliage still clung, though other trees were bare. "That's Duck Rock. Well, there's a spot there where the water's thirty foot deep. What do you think of that?"

He moved back from the window, but remained standing. "I think that it doesn't matter to you and me whether it's thirty foot deep or sixty or a hundred."

"It matters to me. In thirty foot of water I'd go down like a stone; and then it'd be all over. After that nothing but—sleep." Her eyes held him again. "*You* don't believe there'll be anything after it but sleep, do you?"

He dodged that question, too. "But you do."

"I was brought up an orthodox Congregational—but what's the good? All I've ever got out of it was rainbows; and what I've wanted is solid. I've wanted to do something, and be something, and have something—and not be pushed back and trampled out of sight by people who used to hire out to my folks and can treat me like dirt to-day, just because they've got the money. Why haven't I got it, too? I'm fit for it. I had good schooling. Louisa Thorley—your own mother, that is—and me went to school together. Your father ran away with her and she died when you were born. We went to school to old Miss Brand—aunt to Bessie Brand that's now Bessie Willoughby and holds her head so high. Poor as church mice they was in those days. But then every one was poor. We was all poor together—and happy. And now some are poor and some are rich—and there's upper classes and lower classes—and everything's got uneven—and I'm sick of it."

To calm her excitement he talked to her with the inspiration of young earnestness, getting his reward in an attention accorded perhaps for the very reason that the earnestness was young. "I think I must run off now," he finished, when he thought her slightly comforted, "but I'll send you something I want you to take at once. You'll take a tablespoonful in half a glass of water—"

The rebellious spirit revived, though less bitterly. "And it 'll do me as much good as a dose of your uncle's rainbows. What I want is what I shall never get—or sleep."

"Well, you'll get sleep," he said, smiling and holding out his hand. "You'll sleep to-night—and I'll come again to-morrow."

He was at the door when she called out: "Do you know what our Matt got his three years for? It was for stealing money from Massy's grocery-store, where he was book-keeper. And do you know what made him steal it? It was to help us pay the rent the last time your father raised it. I'll bet he's done worse than that twenty times a year; but he's driving round in automobiles, while my poor boy's in Colcord."

CHAPTER II

ON going down-stairs, Thor looked about him for Rosie Fay. She was nowhere to be seen, and the house was cheerless. He could imagine that to an ambitious woman circumscribed by its dreary neatness Duck Rock with its thirty feet of water might be a welcome change.

Continuing his search when he went outside, he gazed round what was left of the old orchard. He remembered Fay—a slim fellow with a gentle, dreamy face and starry eyes. He had seen him occasionally during the past eighteen years, though rarely. As a matter of fact, Fay's greenhouses lay on that part of the shore of Thorley's Pond most out of the way of the pedestrian. Only of late had new roads wormed themselves up the steep northern bank of the pond, bringing from the city well-to-do, country-loving souls who desired space and sunshine. It was a satisfaction to Thor's father, Archie Masterman, that only the best type of suburban residence was going up among these sylvan glades, and that the property was justifying his foresight as an investor.

The young man could understand that it should be so, for the spot was picturesque. Sheltered from the north by a range of wooded hills, it was like a great green cup held out to the sunshine. The region was favorable, therefore, to the raising of early "garden-truck." Whenever the frost was out of the ground, oblongs of green things growing in straight lines gave a special freshness to the landscape, while from any of the knolls over which the township clambered clusters of greenhouses glinted

PAUSING IN HER WORK, THE GIRL LOOKED DOWN THE HALF-LENGTH
OF THE GREENHOUSE AS A HINT FOR HIM TO ADVANCE

like distant sheets of water. One had to get them in contrast to the sparkling blue eye of Thorley's Pond to perceive that they were not tiny lakes. With so pleasing a view, hemmed in by the haze of the city toward the south, and a hint of the Atlantic south of that, there was every reason why Fay's plot of land should appreciate in value.

On these grounds it became comprehensible to Thor that his father might raise the rent and still not be an instrument of oppression. It was consoling to him to perceive this. It helped to allay certain uncomfortable suspicions that had risen in his mind since coming home, and which were not easy to dispel.

He caught sight at last of Rosie's dull-green frock in the one hothouse in which there were flowers. Through the glass roof he could see the red disks of poinsettias and the crimson or white of azaleas coming into bloom. The other two houses sheltered long, level rectangles of tender green, representing lettuce in different stages of the crop. A bow-legged Italian was closing the skylights that had been opened for the milder part of the day; another Italian replaced the covers on hot-beds that might have contained violets. From the high furnace chimney a plume of yellow-brown smoke floated heavily on the windless air. The place looked undermanned and forlorn.

On opening the door he was met by the sweet, warm odor of damp earth and green things growing and blossoming. Pausing in her work, the girl looked down the half-length of the greenhouse as a hint for him to advance. He went toward her between feathery banks of gray-green carnations, on which the long, oval, compact buds were loosening their sheaths to display the dawn-pink within. Half covered up by a coarse apron or pinafore, she stood at a high table, like a counter, against a background of poinsettias.

"We don't go in for flowers, really," she explained to him, after he had given her certain directions concerning her mother. "It would be better if we didn't try to raise them at all."

Thor, whose ear was sensitive, noticed that her voice was pleasant to listen to, and her speech marked by a simple, unaffected refinement. He lingered because he was interested in her work. He found a kind of fascination in watching her as she took a moist red flower-pot from one end of the table, threw in a handful or two of earth from the heap at the other end, then a root that looked like a cluster of yellow, crescent-shaped onions, then a little more earth, after which she turned to place the flower-pot as one of the row on the floor behind her. There was something rhythmic in her movements. Each detail took the same amount of action and time. She might have been working to music. Her left hand made precisely the same gesture with each flower-pot she took from the line in which they lay telescoped together. Her right hand described the same graceful curve with every impatient, petulant handful of earth.

"Why do you raise them, then?" he asked, for the sake of saying something.

She answered, wearily: "Oh, it's father. He can't make up his mind what to do. Or, rather, he makes up his mind both ways at once. Because some people make a good thing out of raising flowers he thinks he'll do that. And because others do a big business in garden-stuff, he thinks he'll do that."

"And so he falls between two stools. I see."

"It's no use being a market-gardener," she went on, disdainfully tossing the earth into another pot, "unless you're a big market-gardener, and it's no use being a florist unless you're a big florist. Everything has to be big nowadays to make it pay. And the trouble with father is that he does so many things small. He sees big," she analyzed, continuing her work—"so big that he goes all to pieces when he tries to carry his ideas out."

"And you think that if he concentrated his forces on raising garden-stuff—"

She explained further: People had to have lettuce and radishes and carrots and cucumbers whatever happened, whereas flowers were a luxury. Whenever money was scarce they didn't buy them. If it were not for weddings and funerals and Christmas and Easter they wouldn't buy them at all. Then, too, they were expensive to raise, and difficult. You couldn't do it by casting a little seed into the ground. Every azalea was imported from Belgium; every lily-bulb from Japan. True, the carnations were grown from slips, but if he only knew the trouble they gave! Those at which he was looking, and which had the innocent air of springing and blooming of their own accord, had been through no less than four tedious processes since the slips were taken in the preceding February. First they had been planted in sand for the root to strike; then transferred to flats, or shallow wooden boxes; then bedded out in the garden; and lastly brought into the house. If he would only consider the labor involved in all that, to say nothing of the incessant watching and watering, and keeping the house at the proper temperature by night and by day—well, he could see for himself.

He did see for himself. He said so absently, because he was noting the fact that her serious, earnest eyes were of the peculiar shade which, when seen in eyes, is called green. It was still absently that he added, "And you have to work pretty hard."

She shrugged her shoulders. "Oh, I don't mind that. Anything to live."

"What are you doing there?"

There was an exasperated note in her voice as she replied: "Oh, these are the Easter lilies. We have to begin on them now."

"And do you do them all?"

"I do, when there's no one else. Father's men keep leaving." She flung him a look he would have thought

15

defiant if he hadn't found it frank. "I don't blame them. Half the time they're not paid."

"I see. So that you fill in. Do you like it?"

"Would you like doing what isn't of any use?—what will never be of any use? Would you like to be always running as hard as you can, just to fall out of the race?"

He tried to smile. "I shouldn't like it for long."

"Well, there's that," she said, as though he had suggested a form of consolation. "It won't be for long. It can't be. Father won't be able to go on like this."

He decided to take the bull by the horns. "Is that because my father doesn't want to renew the lease?"

She shrugged her shoulders again. "Oh no, not particularly. It *is* that—and everything else."

He felt it the part of tact to make signs of going, uttering a few parting injunctions with regard to the mother as he did so.

"And I wouldn't leave her too much alone," he advised. "She could easily slip out without attracting any one's attention. Tell your father I said so. I suppose he's not in the house."

"He's off somewhere trying to engage a night fireman."

He ignored this information to emphasize his counsels. "It's most important that while she's in this state of mind some one should be with her. And if we knew of anything she'd specially like—"

She continued to work industriously. "The thing she'd like best in this world won't do her any good when it happens." She threw in a bulb with impetuous vehemence. "It's to have Matt out of jail. He will be out in the course of a few months. But he'll be—a jail-bird."

"We must try to help him live that down."

She turned her great greenish eyes on him again with that look which struck him as both frank and pitiful. "That's one of the things people in our position can't do. It's the first thing mother herself will think of when she sees Matt hanging about the house—for he'll never get a job."

"He can help your father. He can be the night fireman."

She shrugged her shoulders with the fatalistic movement he was beginning to recognize. "Father won't need a night fireman by that time."

He could only say: "All the same, your mother must be watched. She can't be allowed to throw herself from Duck Rock, now, can she?"

"I don't say allowed. But if she did—"

"Well, what then?"

"She'd be out of it. That would be something."

"Admitting that it would be something for her, what would it be for your father and you?"

She relaxed the energy of her hands. He had time to notice them. It hurt him to see anything so shapely coarsened with hard work. "Wouldn't it be that much?" she asked, as if reaching a conclusion. "If she were out of it, it would be a gain all round."

Never having heard a human being speak like this, he was shocked. "But everything can't be so black. There must be something somewhere."

She glanced up at him obliquely. Months afterward he recalled the look. Her tone, when she spoke, seemed to be throwing him a challenge as well as making an admission. "Well, there *is*—one thing."

He spoke triumphantly. "Ah, there *is* one thing, then?"

"Yes, but it may not happen."

"Oh, lots of things may not happen. We just have to hope they will. That's all we've got to live by."

There was a lovely solemnity about her. "And even if it did happen, so many people would be opposed to it that I'm not sure it would do any good, after all."

"Oh, but we won't think of the people who'd be opposed to it—"

"We should have to, because"—the sweet fixity of her gaze gave him an odd thrill—"because you'd be one."

He laughed as he held out his hand to say good-by. "Don't be too sure. And in any case it won't matter about me."

She declined to take his hand on the ground that her own was soiled with loam, but she mystified him slightly when she said: "It will matter about you; and if the thing ever happens I want you to remember that I told you so. I can't play fair; but I'll play as fair as I can."

CHAPTER III

THOR was deaf to these enigmatic words in the excitement of perceiving that the girl had beauty. The discovery gave him a new sort of pleasure as he turned his runabout toward the town. Beauty had not hitherto been a condition to which he attached great value. If anything, he had held it in some scorn. Now, for the first time in his emotional life, he was stirred by a girl's mere prettiness—a quite unusual prettiness, it had to be admitted; a slightly haggard prettiness, perhaps; a prettiness a little worn by work, a little coarsened by wind and weather; a prettiness too desperate for youth and too tragic for coquetry, but for those very reasons doubtless all the more haunting. He was obliged to remind himself that it was nothing to him, since he had never swerved from the intention to marry Lois Willoughby as soon as he had made a start in practice and come into the money he was to get at thirty; but he could see it was the sort of thing by which other men might be affected, and came to a mental standstill there.

Driving on into the city, he went straight to his father's office in Commonwealth Row. It was already after four o'clock, and except for two young men sorting checks and putting away ledgers, the cagelike divisions of the banking department were empty. One of the men was whistling; the other was calling in a loud, gay voice, "Say, Cheever, what about to-night?"—signs that the enforced decorum of the day was past.

Claude was in the outer office reserved for customers. He wore his overcoat, hat, and gloves. A stick hung over his left arm by its crooked handle. The ticker was silent, but a portion of the tape fluttered between his gloved fingers.

Though his back was toward the door, he recognized his half-brother's step with that mixture of envy and irritation which Thor's presence always stirred in him. He was not without fraternal affection, especially when Thor was away; when he was at home it was difficult for Claude not to resent the elder's superiority. Claude called it superiority for want of a better word, though he meant no more than a combination of advantages he himself would have enjoyed. He meant Thor's prospective money, his good spirits, good temper, and good health. Claude had not good health, which excused, in his judgment, his lack of good spirits and good temper. Neither had Claude any money beyond the fifteen hundred dollars a year he earned in his father's office. He was in the habit of saying to himself, and in confidence to his friends, that it was "damned hard luck" that he should be compelled to live on a pittance like that, when Thor, within a few months, would come into a good thirty thousand a year.

It was some consolation that Thor was what his brother called "an ugly beast"—sallow and lantern-jawed, with a long, narrow head that looked as if it had been sat on. The eyes were not bad; that had to be admitted; they were as friendly as a welcoming light; but the mouth was so big and aggressive that even the mustache Thor was trying to grow couldn't subdue its boldness. As for the nose and chin, they looked—according to Claude's account—as if they had been created soft, and subjected to a system of grotesque elongation before hardening. Claude could the more safely make game of his brother's looks seeing that he himself was notably handsome, with traits as regular as if they had been carved, and a profile so exact that it was frequently exposed in photographers' windows, to the envy of gentlemen gazers. While Thor had once tried to mitigate his features by a beard that had been unsuccessful and had now disappeared, Claude wouldn't disfigure himself by a hair. He was as clean-shaven as a marble Apollo, and not less neatly limbed.

"Gone." Claude raised his eyes just long enough to utter the word.

Thor came to an abrupt stop. "Club?"

"Suppose so." He added, without raising his head, "Wish to God the drunken sot would stay there." He continued, while still apparently reading the tape in his hand, "Father wishes it, too."

Thor was not altogether taken by surprise. Ever since his return from Europe, a year earlier, he had wondered how his father's patience could hold out. He took it that there was a reason for it, a reason he at once expressed to Claude:

"Father can't wish it. He can't afford to."

Claude lifted his handsome, rather insolent face. "Why not?"

"For the simple reason that he's got his money."

"Much you know about it. Len Willoughby hasn't enough money left in Toogood & Masterman's to take him on a trip to Europe."

Thor backed toward the receiving-teller's wicket, where he rested the tips of his elbows on the counter. He was visibly perturbed. "What's become of it, then?"

"Don't ask me. All I know is what I'm telling you."

"Did father say so himself?"

"Not in so many words. But I know it." He tossed the tape from him and began to smooth his gloves. "Father means to ship him."

"Ship him? He can't do that."

"Can't? I should like to know why not."

"Because he can't. That's why. Because he has—"

"Yes? Cough it up. Speak as if you had something up your sleeve."

Thor reflected as to the wisdom of saying more. "Well,

I have," he admitted. "It's something I remember from the time we were kids. You were too young to notice. But *I* noticed—and I haven't forgotten. Father can't ship Len Willoughby without being sure he has enough to live on." He decided to speak out, if for no other reason than that of securing Claude's co-operation. "Father persuaded Mr. Willoughby to put Mrs. Willoughby's money into the business when he didn't want to."

"Ah, shucks!" Claude exclaimed, contemptuously.

"He did," Thor insisted. "It was back in 1892, in Paris, that first time they took us abroad. You were only nine and I was twelve. I heard them. I was hanging round one evening in that little hotel we stayed at in the rue de Rivoli—the Hôtel de Marsan, wasn't it? The Willoughbys had been living in Paris for five or six years, and father got them to come home. I heard him ask mother to talk it up with Mrs. Willoughby. Mother said she didn't want to, but father got round her, and she agreed to try. She said, too, that Bessie might be willing because Len had already begun to take too much and it would brace him up if he got work to do."

"Work!" Claude sniffed. "Him!"

"Father knew he couldn't work—knew he'd tried all sorts of things—first to be an artist, then to write, then to get into the consular service, and the Lord knows what. It wasn't his work that father was after. It was just when the Toogood estate withdrew old Mr. Toogood's money, and father had to have more capital."

"Well, Len Willoughby didn't have any."

"No; but his wife had. It came to the same thing. Suppose she must have had between three and four hundred thousand from old man Brand. I remember hearing father say to mother that Len was making ducks and drakes of it as fast as he could, and that it might as well help the firm of Toogood & Masterman as go to the deuce. Can still hear father feeding the poor fool with bluff about the great banker he'd make and how it was the dead loss of a fortune that he hadn't had a seat on the Stock Exchange years before."

Claude sniffed again. "You'd better carry your load to father himself."

"I will—if I have to." Before Claude had found a rejoinder, Thor went on, changing the subject abruptly, so as not to be led into being indiscreet, "Say, Claude, do you remember Fay, the gardener?"

Claude was still smoothing his gloves, but he stopped, with the thumb and fingers of his right hand grasping the middle finger of the left. More than ever his features suggested a marble stoniness. "No."

"Oh, but you must. Used to be Grandpa Thorley's gardener. Has the greenhouses on father's land north of the pond."

Claude recovered himself slightly. "Well, what about him?"

"Been to see his wife. Patient of Uncle Sim's. Turned her on to me. They're having the deuce of a time."

Claude recovered himself still more. He looked at his brother curiously. "Well, what's it got to do with me?"

"Nothing directly."

"Well, then—indirectly?" Claude asked, defiantly.

"Only this, that it has to do with both of us, since it concerns father."

Claude was by this time master of himself. "Look here, Thor. Are you getting a bee in your bonnet about father?"

"Good Lord! no. But father's immersed in business. He can't be expected to know how all the details of his policy work out. He's not young any longer, and he isn't in touch with modern social and economic ideas."

"Oh, stow the modern social and economic ideas, and let's get to business. What's up with this family—of—of— What-d'you-call-'ems?"

With his feet planted firmly apart, Claude swung his stick airily back and forth across the front of his person, though he listened with apparent attention.

"You know, Thor, as a matter of fact," he explained, when the latter had finished his account, "that the kindest thing father can do for Fay is to let him peter out. Fay thinks that father and the lease are the obstacle he's up against, when in reality it's the whole thing."

"Oh, so you do know about it?"

Claude saw his mistake, and righted himself quickly. "Y-yes. Now that you—you speak of it, I—I do. It comes—a—back to me. I've heard father mention it."

"And what did father say?"

"Just what I'm telling you. That the lease isn't the chief factor in Fay's troubles—isn't really a factor at all. Poor old fellow's a dunderhead. That's where it is in a nutshell. Never could make a living. Never will. Remember him?"

"Vaguely. Haven't seen him for years."

"Well, when you do see him you'll understand. Nice old chap as ever lived. Only impractical, dreamy. Gentle as a sheep—and no more capable of running that big, expensive plant than a motherly old ewe. That's where the trouble is. When father's closed down on him and edged him out—quietly, you understand—it 'll be the best thing that ever happened to them all."

Thor reflected. "I see that you know more about it than you thought. You know all about it."

Again Claude caught himself up, shifting his position adroitly. "Oh no, I don't. Just what I've heard father say. When you spoke of it at first the name slipped my memory."

Thor reverted to the original theme. "The son's in jail. Did you know that?"

But Claude was again on his guard. "Oh, so there's a son?"

"Son about your age. Matt his name is. Surely you must recall him. Used to pick pease with us when Fay'd let us do it."

Claude shook his head silently.

"And there's a girl."

Claude's stick hung limply before him. His face and figure resumed their stony immobility. "Oh, is there? Plain?"

"No; pretty. Very pretty. Very unusually pretty. Come to think of it, I shouldn't mind saying— Yes, I will say it! She's the prettiest girl I've ever seen." The eyes of the two brothers met. "Bar none."

The smile on Claude's lips might have passed for an expression of brotherly chaff. "Go it, old chap. Seem smitten."

"Oh, it isn't that. Nothing of the sort at all. I speak of her only because I'm sorry for her. Brunt of whole thing comes on her."

"Well, what do you propose that we should do?"

"I haven't got as far as proposing. Haven't thought the thing out at all. But I think we ought to do something—you and I."

"We can't do anything without father—and father won't. He simply won't. Fay 'll have to go. Good thing, too; that's what I say. Get 'em all on a basis on which they can manage. Fay 'll find a job with one of the other growers—"

"Yes; but what's to become of the girl?"

Claude stared with a kind of bravado. "How the devil do I know? She'll do the best she can, I suppose. Go into a shop. Lots of girls go into shops."

Thor studied his brother with mild curiosity. "You're a queer fellow, Claude. A minute ago you couldn't remember Fay's name; and now you've got his whole business at your fingers' ends."

But Claude repeated his explanation. "Got father's business at my fingers' ends, if that's what you mean. In such big affairs chap like Fay only a detail. Couldn't recall him at first, but once I'd caught on to him—"

By moving away toward the inner office, where Cheever was still at work, Claude intimated that, as far as he was concerned, the conversation was ended. Thor returned to his runabout.

"Say, Claude," Cheever called, "comin' to see 'The Champion' to-night, ain't you? Countin' on you."

Claude laid a friendly hand on Cheever's arm. He liked to be on easy terms with his father's clerks. "Awfully sorry, Billy, but you must excuse me. Fact is, that damn-fool brother of mine has been putting his finger in my pie. Got to do something to get it out—and do it quick. Awfully sorry. Sha'n't be free."

CHAPTER IV

BESIDE his favorite window at the club, commanding
the movement of the street and the bare trees of the
park, Len Willoughby had got together the essentials to a
pleasant hour. They consisted of the French and English
illustrated papers, two or three excellent Havanas, a
bottle of Scotch whisky, and a siphon of aerated water.
On the table beside him there was also an empty glass
that had contained a cocktail.

It was the consoling moment of the day. After the
strain of a nine-o'clock breakfast and the rush to the city
before eleven, after the hours of purposeless hanging
about the office of Toogood & Masterman, where he could
see he wasn't wanted, he found it restful to retire into his
own corner and sink drowsily into his cups. He did sink
into them drowsily, and yet through well-marked phases
of excitement. He knew those phases now; he could tell
in advance how each stage would pass into another.

There was first the comfort of the big chair and the
friendly covers of *L'Illustration* and the *Graphic*. He
didn't care to talk. He liked to be let alone. When he
came from the office he was generally dispirited. Masterman's queer, contemptuous manner was enough to dis-
courage any one. He was sure, too, that Claude and
Billy Cheever ridiculed his big, fat figure behind his back.
But once he sank into the deep, red-leather arm-chair he
was safe. It was ridiculous that a man of his age should
come to recognize the advantages of such a refuge, but
he laid it to the charge of a mean and spiteful world.

The world did not cease to be mean and spiteful

till after he had had his cocktail. It was wonderful the change that took place then—not suddenly, but with a sweet, slow, cheering inner transformation. It was a surging, a glowing, a mellowing. It was like the readjustment of the eyes of the soul. It was seeing the world as generous, kindly. It was growing generous and kindly himself, with the happy conviction that more remained to be got out of life than he had ever wrung from it.

Still, it was something to be a rich banker. Every one couldn't be that. Archie Masterman had certainly possessed a quick eye when he singled out Len Willoughby as the man who could put the firm of Toogood & Masterman on its feet. Three hundred thousand dollars of Bessie's money had gone into that business in 1892, just in time to profit by the panic of 1893. Lord, how they had bought!—gilt-edged stocks for next to nothing!—and how they had sold, a few years later! Len never knew how much money they made. He supposed Archie didn't, either. There were years when the Stock Exchange had been like a wheat-field, yielding thirtyfold and sixtyfold and a hundredfold for every seed they had sown. He had never attempted to keep a tally on what came in; it was sufficient to know that there was always plenty to take out. Besides, it had been an understanding from the first that Archie was to do the drudgery. Len liked this, because it left him free—free for summers in Europe and winters in Egypt or at Palm Beach.

By degrees reminiscence tended toward somnolence. And yet it couldn't be said that Len slept. He kept sufficiently awake to put out his hand from time to time and seize the tumbler. He could even brew himself another glass. If a brother clubman strolled near enough to say, "Hello, Len!" or, "Hello, Willoughby!" he could respond with a dull, "Hello, Tom!" or, "Hello, Jones!" But he spoke as out of a depth; he spoke with some of that weariness at being called back to life which Rembrandt depicts on the face of Lazarus rising from the tomb.

THE SIDE OF THE ANGELS

It was delicious to sink away from the prosaic and the bore-some, to be so fully awake that he could follow the movement in the street and the hopping of the sparrows in the trees, and yet be, as it were, removed, enchanted, seeing and hearing and thinking and even drinking through the medium of a soothing, slumbrous spell.

It could hardly ever be said that he went beyond this point. Though there were occasions on which he miscalculated his effects, they could generally be explained as accidental. Above all, they didn't rise from an appetite for drink. The phrase was one he was fond of; he often used it in condemning a vice of which he disapproved. He used it on this particular afternoon, when Thor Masterman, who had come to drive him homeward in his runabout, was sitting in the opposite arm-chair, waiting to make the start.

"There's one thing about me, Thor—never had an appetite for drink. Not to say *drink*. Thing I despise. Your father's all wrong about me. Don't know what's got into him. Thinks I take too much. Rot! That's what it is—bally rot! *You* know that, Thor, don't you? Appetite for drink something I despise."

Thor considered the moment one to be made use of. "Has father been saying anything about it?"

"No; but he looks it. Suppose I don't know what he means? Sees double, your father does. Anybody'd think, from the way he treats me, that I was a disgrace to the firm. I'd like to know what that firm 'd be without me."

Thor tried to frame his next question discreetly. "I hope there's been no suggestion of the firm's doing without you, Mr. Willoughby?"

To this Len gave but an indirect reply. "There'll be one soon, if your father doesn't mind himself. I'll retire—and take my money out. Where'll he be then?"

Thor felt his way. "You've taken out a good deal already, haven't you?"

"Not any more than belonged to me. You can bet your boots on that."

"No; not any more than belonged to you, of course. I was only thinking that with the splendid house you've built—and its up-keep—and your general expenses—which are pretty heavy, aren't they?—"

"Not any more than belonged to me, Thor. You can bet your boots on that."

The repetition was made drowsily. The big head of bushy white hair, with its correlative of bushy white beard, swayed with a slow movement that ended in a jerk. It was obvious that the warnings and admonitions to which Thor had been leading up were not for that day. They were useless even when, a half-hour later, the movement of the runabout and the keen air of the high lands as they approached the village roused the big creature to a maudlin cursing of his luck.

On nearing the house, the delicate part of the task which of late Thor had taken almost daily on himself became imminent. It was to get his charge into the house, up to his room, and stretched on a couch without being seen by Lois. Thor had once caught her carrying out this duty unaided. She had evidently called for her father in her mother's limousine, and as Thor passed down the village street she was helping the staggering, ungainly figure toward the door. The next day Thor took his runabout from the garage and went on the errand himself. He was also more ingenious than she in finding a way by which the sorry object could be smuggled indoors. The carriage entrance of the house was too near the street. That it should be so was a trial to Mrs. Willoughby, who would have preferred a house standing in grounds, but there never had been any help for it. When money came in it had been Len's desire to buy back a portion of the old Willoughby farm, and build a mansion on what might reasonably be called his ancestral estate. Of this property there was nothing in the market but a snip along County

Street; and though he was satisfied with the site as enabling him to display his prosperity to every one who passed up and down, his wife regretted the absence of a dignified approach.

By avoiding County Street when he came out from town, and following a road that scrambled over the low hillside till it made a juncture with Willoughby's Lane, by descending that ancient cow-path and bringing Len to the privacy of his side-door, Thor endeavored to keep his father's partner from becoming an object of public scandal. He took this trouble not because he bothered about public scandal in itself, but in order to protect Lois Willoughby.

So far his methods had been successful. They failed to-day only because Lois herself was at the side-door. With a pair of garden shears in her gloved hands she was trimming the leafless vine that grew over the pillars of the portico. Thor could see, as she turned round, that she braced herself to meet the moment's humiliation, speaking on the instant he drew up at the steps.

"So good of you to bring papa out from town! I'm sure he's enjoyed the drive." Her hand was on the lever that opened the door of the machine. "Poor papa! You look done up. I dare say you're not well. Be careful, now," she continued, as he lumbered heavily to his feet. "That's a long step there. Take my hand. I know you must be as tired as can be."

"Dog tired," the father complained, as he lowered himself cautiously. "Dog's life. Tha's wha' I lead. No thanks for it, either. Damn!" The imprecation was necessary because he missed his footing and came down with a jerk. "Can't you see I'm gettin' out?" he groaned, peevishly. "Stan'in' right in my way."

"Better leave him to me," Thor whispered. "I know just what to do with him. One of the advantages of being a doctor."

Willoughby had mind enough to clutch at this suggestion. "Doctor's what I want, hang it all! Sick as a dog. I do' know what 'll happen to me some day. Head aches fit to split. Never had appetite for drink. Tha's one good thing about me."

Lois was still standing near the portico when Thor had assisted his charge to his room, stretched him on a couch, covered him with a rug, left him in a heavy sleep, and crept down the stairs again. It did not escape his eye, quickened by the minutes he had spent with Rosie Fay, that Lois lacked color. For the first time in his life he acutely observed the difference between a plain woman and a pretty one.

"Oh, Thor," she began, as soon as he came out, "I don't know how to thank you for your kindness to papa! How is it to go on? Where is it to end? Oh, Thor, you're a doctor! Tell me what you think. Is there anything I can do?"

His kind, searching eyes, as he stood with one hand on the steering-wheel, rested on her silently. After all, she was twenty-seven, and must take her portion of life's responsibilities. Besides, whatever she might have to bear he meant to share with her. She should not be obliged, like Rosie Fay, for instance, to carry her load alone.

And yet she didn't look as if she would shirk her part. With that tall, erect figure, delicate in outline but strong with the freedom of an open-air life, that proud head which was nevertheless carried meekly, and that straightforward gaze, she gave the impression of being ready to meet anything. The face might be irregular, lacking in many of the tender prettinesses as natural to other girls, even at twenty-seven, as flowers to a field; but no one could deny its force of character.

"I'll tell you something you could do," he said, at last. "You could see—or try to see—that he doesn't spend too much." A slight pause marked his hesitation before adding, "That no one spends too much."

"You mean mamma and me?"

He smiled faintly. "I mean whoever does the spending—but your father most of all, because I'm afraid he's rather reckless. He's spent a good deal during the last twelve or fifteen years, hasn't he?"

She was very quick. "More than he had a right to spend?"

"Well, more than my father," he felt it safe to say.

"But he had more than your father to spend, hadn't he?"

"Do you know that for a certainty?"

"I only know it from papa himself. But, oh, Thor, what is it? Why are you asking?"

He ignored these questions to say: "Couldn't your mother tell us? After all, it was her money, wasn't it?"

She shook her head. "Oh, mamma wouldn't know. If you're in any doubt about it, why don't you ask Mr. Masterman? He could tell you better than any one. Besides, mamma isn't in."

He spoke with a touch of scorn. "I suppose she's in town."

The tone evoked on Lois's part a little smile. They had had battles on the subject before. "That's just where she is."

"That's just where she always is."

"Oh no; not always. Sometimes she stays at home. But she's there pretty often, I admit. She has to make calls, partly because I won't—when I can help it."

He spoke approvingly. "You, at any rate, don't fritter away your time like other women."

"It depends on what other women you mean. I fritter away my time like some women, even though it isn't like the women who make calls. I play golf, for instance, and tennis; I even ride."

"All the same, you don't like the silly thing called society any more than I do."

There was daylight enough to show him the blaze of

bravado in her eyes. Her way of holding her head had a certain daring—the daring of one too frank, perhaps too proud, to shrink at truth. "Oh, I don't know. I dare say I should have liked society well enough if society had liked me. But it didn't. As mamma says, I wasn't a success." To compel him to view her in all her lack of charm, she added, with a persistent smile, "You know that, don't you?"

He did know it, though he could hardly say so. He had heard Claude descant on the subject many a time in the years when Lois was still putting in a timid appearance at dances. Claude was interested in everything that had to do with girls, from their clothes to their complexions.

"Can't make it out," he would say at breakfast, after a party; "dances well; dresses well; but doesn't take. Fellows afraid of her. Everybody shy of a girl who isn't popular. Hasn't enough devil. Girl ought to have some devil, hang it all! Dance with her myself? Well, I do—about three times a year. Have her left on my hands an hour at a time. Fellow can't afford that. Think we have no chivalry? Should come to dances yourself, old chap. You'd be a godsend to the girls in the dump."

Thor's dancing days were over before Lois's had begun, but he could imagine what they had been to her. He could look back over the four or five years that separated her from the ordeal, and still see her in "the dump"— tall, timid, furtively watching the young men with those swimming brown orbs of hers, wondering whether or not she should have a partner; heartsore under her finery, often driving homeward in the weary early hours with tears streaming down her cheeks. He knew as much about it as if he had been with her. He suffered for her retrospectively. He did it to a degree that made his long face sorrowful.

The sorrow caused Lois some impatience. "For

mercy's sake, Thor, don't look at me like that! It isn't as bad as you seem to think. I don't mind it."

"But I do," he declared, with indignation, only to feel that he was slowly coloring.

He colored because the statement brought him within measurable distance of a declaration which he meant to make, but for which he was not ready.

She seemed to divine his embarrassment, speaking with forced lightness. "Please don't waste your sympathy on me. If any one's to be pitied, it's mamma. I'm such a disappointment to her. Let's talk of something else. Where have you been to-day, and what have you been doing?"

He was not blind to her tact, counting it to her credit for the future, and asked abruptly if she knew Fay, the gardener.

"Fay, the gardener?" she echoed. "I know who he is." She went more directly to the point in saying, "I know his daughter."

"Well, she's having a hard time."

"Is she? I should think she might."

His face grew keener. "Why do you say that?"

"Oh, I don't know — she's that sort. At least, I should judge she was that sort from the little I've seen of her."

"How much have you seen of her?"

"Almost nothing; but little as it was, it impressed itself on my mind. I went to see her once at Mr. Whitney's suggestion."

"Whitney? He's the rector at St. John's, isn't he? What had he to do with her? She doesn't belong to his church?"

Lois explained. "It was when we established the branch of the Girl's Friendly Society at St. John's. Mr. Whitney thought she might care to join it."

"And did she?"

"No; quite the other way. When I went to ask her,

she resented it. She had an idea I was patronizing her. That's the difficulty in approaching girls like that."

He looked at her with a challenging expression. "Girls like what?"

"I suppose I mean girls who haven't much money—or who've got to work."

He still challenged her, his head thrown back. "They probably don't consider themselves inferior to you for that reason. It wouldn't be American if they did."

"And it wouldn't be American if I did; and I don't. They only make me feel so because they feel it so strongly themselves. That's what's not American; and it isn't on my part, but on theirs. They force their sentiment back on me. They make me patronizing whether I will or no."

"And were you patronizing when you went to see Miss Fay?"

To conceal the slightly irritated attentiveness with which he waited for her reply he began to light his motor lamps. Condescension toward Rosie Fay suddenly struck him as offensive, no matter from whom it came.

"I'm sure I don't know," she replied, indifferently. "There was something about her that disconcerted me."

"She's as good as we are," he declared, snapping the little door of one of the lanterns.

"I don't deny that."

"A generation or two ago we were all farming people together. The Willoughbys and the Brands and the Thorleys and the Fays were on an equal footing. They worked for one another and intermarried. The progress of the country has taken some of us and hurled us up, while it has seized others of us and smashed us down; but we should try to get over that when it comes to human intercourse."

"That's what I was doing when I asked her to join our Friendly Society."

"Pff! The deuce you were! I know your friendly societies. Keep those who are down down. Help the humble to be humbler by making them obsequious."

"You know nothing at all about it," she declared, with spirit. "In trying to make things better you're content to spin theories, while we put something into practice."

He snapped the door of the second lamp with a little bang. "Put something into practice, with the result that people resent it."

"With the result that Rosie Fay resented it; but she's not a fair example. She's proud and rebellious and intense. I never saw any one just like her."

"You probably never saw any one who had to be like her because they'd had her luck. Look here, Lois," he said, with sudden earnestness, "I want you to be a friend to that girl."

She opened her eyes in mild surprise at his intensity. "There's nothing I should like better, if I knew how."

"But you do know how. It's easy enough. Treat her as you would a girl in your own class—Elsie Darling, for instance."

"It's not so simple as that. When Elsie Darling came back after five or six years abroad mamma and I drove into town and called on her. She wasn't in, and we left our cards. Later, we invited her to lunch or to dinner. I should be perfectly willing to go through the same formalities with Miss Fay—only she'd think it queer. It would be queer. It would be queer because she hasn't got—what shall I say?—she hasn't got the social machinery for that kind of ceremoniousness. The machinery means the method of approach, and with people who have to live as she does it's the method of approach that presents the difficulty. It's not as easy as it looks."

"Very well, then; let us admit that it's hard. The harder it is the more it's the job for you."

There was an illuminating quality in her smile that

atoned for lack of beauty. "Oh, if you put it in that way—"

"I do put it in that way," he declared, with an earnestness toned down by what was almost wistfulness. "There are so many things in which I want help, Lois—and you're the one to help me."

She held out her hand with characteristic frankness. "I'll do anything I can, Thor. Just tell me what you want me to do when you want me to do it—and I'll try."

"Oh, there'll be a lot of things in which we shall have to pull together," he said, as he held her hand. "I want you to remember, if ever any trouble comes, that"—he hesitated for a word that wouldn't say too much for the moment—"that I'll be there."

"Thank you, Thor. That's a great comfort."

She withdrew her hand quietly. Quietly, too, she assured him, as she moved toward the steps, that she would not fail to force herself again on Rosie Fay. "And about that other matter—the one you spoke of first—you'll tell me more by and by, won't you?"

After her capacity for ringing true, his conscientiousness prompted him to let her see that she could feel quite sure of him. "I'll tell you anything I can find out; and one of these days, Lois, I must—I must—say a lot more."

She mounted a step or two without turning away from him. "Oh, well," she said, lightly, as though dismissing a topic of no importance, "there'll be plenty of time."

But her smile was a happy one—so happy that he who smiled rarely smiled back at her from the runabout.

He could scarcely be expected to know as yet that his pleasure was not in any happiness of hers, but in the help she might bring to a little creature whose image had haunted him all the afternoon—a little creature whose desperate flower-like face looked up at him from a background of poinsettias.

CHAPTER V

ON coming to the table that evening Claude begged
his mother to excuse him for not having dressed for
dinner, on the ground that he had an engagement with
Billy Cheever. Mrs. Masterman pardoned him with a
gracious inclination of the head that made her diamond
ear-rings sparkle. No one in the room could be unaware
that she disapproved of Claude's informality. Not only
did it shock her personal delicacy to dine with men who
concealed their shirt-bosoms under the waistcoats they
had worn all day, but it contravened the aims by which
during her entire married life she had endeavored to
elevate the society around her. She herself was one to
whom the refinements were as native as foliage to a tree.
"It's all right, Claudie dear; but you do know I like you
to dress for the evening, don't you?" Without waiting
for the younger son to speak, she continued graciously
to the elder: "And you, Thor. What have you been
doing with yourself to-day?"

Her polite inclusion of her stepson was meant to start
"her men," as she called them, in the kind of conversation
in which men were most at ease, that which concerned
themselves. Thor replied while consuming his soup in
the manner acquired in Parisian and Viennese restaurants
frequented by young men:

"Got a patient."

Hastily Claude introduced a subject of his own. "Ought
to go and see 'The Champion,' father. Hear it's awfully
good. Begins with a prize-fight—"

39

But the father's attention was given to Thor. "Who've you picked up?"

"Fay's wife—Fay, the gardener."

"Indeed? Have to whistle for your fee."

"Oh, I know that—"

"Thor, *please!*" Mrs. Masterman begged. "Don't eat so fast."

"If you know it already," the father continued, "I should think you'd have tried to squeak out of it." He said "know it alweady" and "twied to squeak," owing to a difficulty with the letter *r* which gave an appealing, childlike quality to his speech. "If you start in by taking patients who are not going to pay—"

Claude sought another diversion. "What does it matter to Thor? In three months' time he'll be able to pay sick people for coming to him—what?"

"That's not the point," Masterman explained. "A doctor has no right to pauperize people"—he said "pauperwize people"—"any more than any one else."

"Oh, as to that," Thor said, forcing himself to eat slowly and sit straight in the style commended by his stepmother, "it won't need a doctor to pauperize poor Fay."

"Quite right there," his father agreed. "He's done it himself."

Thor considered the moment a favorable one for making his appeal. "Claude and I have been talking him over—"

"The devil we have!" Claude exclaimed, indignantly.

"What's that?" Masterman's handsome face, which after his day's work was likely to be gray and lifeless, grew sharply interrogative. Time had chiseled it to an incisiveness not incongruous with a lingering air of youth. His hair, mustache, and imperial were but touched with gray. His figure was still lithe and spare. It was the custom to say of him that he looked but the brother of his two strapping sons.

Claude emphasized his annoyance. "Talking him over!
I like that! You blow into the office just as I'm ready to
come home, and begin cross-questioning me about father's
affairs. I tell you I don't know anything about them. If
you call that talking him over—well, you're welcome to
your own use of terms."

The head of the house busied himself in carving the
joint which had been placed before him. "If you want
information, Thor, ask me."

"I don't want information, father; and I don't think
Claude is fair in saying I cross-questioned him. I only
said that I thought he and I ought to do what we could
to get you to renew Fay's lease."

"Oh, did you? Then I can save you the trouble, because I'm not going to."

The declaration was so definite that it left Thor with
nothing to say. "Poor old Fay has worked pretty hard,
hasn't he?" he ventured at last.

"Possibly. So have I."

"But with the difference that you've been prosperous,
and he hasn't."

Masterman laughed good-naturedly. "Which is the
difference between me and a good many other people.
You don't blame me for that?"

"It's not a question of blaming any one, father. I
only supposed that among Americans it was the correct
thing for the lucky ones to come to the aid of the less
fortunate."

"Take it that I'm doing that for Fay when I get him
out of an impossible situation."

Thor smiled ruefully. "When you get him out of the
frying-pan into the fire?"

"Well," Claude challenged, coming to his father's aid,
"the fire's no worse than the frying-pan, and may be a
little better."

"I've seen the girl," Mrs. Masterman contributed to the
discussion. "She's been in the greenhouse when I've gone

to buy flowers. I must say she didn't strike me very favorably." The two brothers exchanged glances without knowing why. "She seemed to me so much—so very much—above her station."

"What *is* her station?" Thor asked, bridling. "Her station's the same as ours, isn't it?"

The father was amused. "The same as *what?*"

"Surely we're all much of a muchness. Most of us were farmers and market-gardeners up to forty or fifty years ago. I've heard," he went on, utilizing the information he had received that afternoon, "that the Thorleys used to hire out to the Fays."

"Oh, the Thorleys!" Mrs. Masterman smiled.

"The Mastermans didn't," Archie said, gently. "You won't forget that, my boy. Whatever you may be on any other side, you come from a line of gentlemen on mine. Your grandfather Masterman was one of the best-known old-school physicians in this part of the country. His father before him was a Church of England clergyman in Derbyshire, who migrated to America because he'd become a Unitarian. Sort of idealist. Lot of 'em in those days. Time of Napoleon and Southey and Coleridge and all that. Thought that because America was a so-called republic, or a so-called democracy, he'd find people living for one another, and they were just looking out for number one like every one else. Your Uncle Sim takes after him. Died of a broken heart, I believe, because he didn't find the world made over new. But you see the sort of well-born, high-minded stock you sprang from."

Thor lifted his big frame to an erect position, throwing back his head. "I don't care a fig for what I sprang from, father. I don't even care much for what I am. It strikes me as far more important to see that our old friends and neighbors—who are just as good as we are—don't have to go under when we can keep them up."

"Yes, when we can," Thor's father said, with unperturbed gentleness; "but very often we can't. In a world where every one's swimming for his own dear life, those who can't swim have got to drown."

"But every one is not swimming for his own dear life. Most of us are safe on shore. You and I are, for example. And when we are, it seems to me the least we can do is to fling a life-preserver to the poor chaps who are throwing up their hands and sinking."

Mrs. Masterman rallied her stepson indulgently. "Oh, Thor, how ridiculous you are! How you talk!"

Claude patted his mother's hand. He was still trying to turn attention from bearing too directly on the Fays. "Don't listen to him, mumphy. Beastly socialist, that's what he is. Divide up all the money in the world so that everybody 'll have thirty cents, and then tell 'em to go ahead and live regardless. That 'd be his way of doing things."

But the father was more just. "Oh no, it wouldn't. Thor's no fool! Has some excellent ideas. A little exaggerated, perhaps, but that 'll cure itself in time. Fault of youth. Good fault, too." He turned affectionately to his elder son. "Rather see you that way, my boy, than with an empty head."

Thor fell silent, from a sense of the futility of talking.

CHAPTER VI

AT the moment when Claude was excusing himself further, begging to be allowed to run away so as not to keep Billy Cheever waiting, Rosie Fay was noticing with relief that her mother was asleep at last. Thor's sedative had taken effect in what the girl considered the nick of time. Having smoothed the pillow, adjusted the patchwork quilt, and placed the small kerosene hand-lamp on a chair at the foot of the bed, so as to shade it from the sleeper's eyes, she slipped down-stairs.

She wore a long, rough coat. Over her hair she had flung a scarf of some gauzy green stuff that heightened her color. The lamplight, or some inner flame of her own, drew opalescent gleams from her gray-greenish eyes as she descended. She was no longer the desperate, petulant little Rosie of the afternoon. Her face was aglow with an eager life. The difference was that between a blossom wilting for lack of water and the same flower fed by rain.

In the tiny living-room at the foot of the stairs her father was eating the supper she had laid out for him. It was a humble supper, spread on the end of a table covered with a cheap cotton cloth of a red and sky-blue mixture. Jasper Fay, in his shirt-sleeves, munched his cold meat and sipped his tea while he entertained himself with a book propped against a loaf of bread. Another small kerosene hand-lamp threw its light on the printed page and illumined his mild, clear-cut, clean-shaven face.

"She's asleep," Rosie whispered from the doorway. "If she wakes while I'm gone you must give her the second dose. I've left it on the wash-stand."

44

The man lifted his starry blue eyes. "You going out?"

"I'm only going for a little while."

"Couldn't you have gone earlier?"

"How could I, when I had supper to get—and everything?"

He looked uneasy. "I don't like you to be running round these dark roads, my dear. You've been doing it a good deal lately. Where is it you go?"

"Why, father, what nonsense! Here I am cooped up all day—"

He sighed. "Very well, my dear. I know you haven't much pleasure. But things will be different soon, I hope. The new night fireman seems a good man, and I expect we'll do better now. He'll be here at ten. Were you going far?"

She answered promptly. "Only to Polly Wilson's. She wants me to" — Rosie turned over in her mind the various interests on which Polly Wilson might desire to consult her—"she wants me to see her new dress."

"Very well, my dear, but I hope after this evening you'll be able to do your errands in the daytime. You know how it was with Matt. If he hadn't gone roaming the streets at night—"

Rosie came close to the table. Her face was resolute. "Father, I'm not Matt. I know what I'm doing." She added, with increased determination, "I'm acting for the best."

He was mildly surprised. "Acting for the best in going to see Polly Wilson's new dress?"

She ignored this. "I'm twenty-three, father. I've got to follow my own judgment. If I've a chance I must use it."

"What sort of a chance, my dear?"

"There's nothing to hope for here," she went on, cruelly, "except from what I can do myself. Mother's no good;

and Matt's worse than if he was dead. I wish to God he would die—before he comes out. And you know what you are, father."

"I do the best I can, my dear," he said, humbly.

"I know you do; but we can all see what that is. Everybody else is going ahead but us."

"Oh no, they're not, my dear. There are lots that fall behind as bad as we do—and worse."

She shook her head fiercely. "No, not worse. They couldn't. And whatever's to be done, I've got to do it. If I don't—or if I can't—well, we might as well give up. So you mustn't try to stop me, father. I know what I'm doing. It's for your sake and everybody's sake as much as for my own."

He dropped his eyes to his book, in seeming admission that he had no tenable ground on which to meet her in a conflict of wills. "Very well, my dear," he sighed. "If you're going to Polly Wilson's you'd better be off. You'll be home by ten, won't you? I must go then to show the new fireman his way about the place."

Outside it was a windy night, but not a cold one. Shreds of dark cloud scudded across the face of a three-quarters moon, giving it the appearance of traveling through the sky at an incredible rate of speed. In the south wind there was the tang of ocean salt, mingled with the sweeter scents of woodland and withered garden nearer home. There was a crackling of boughs in the old apple-trees, and from the ridge behind the house came the deep, soft, murmurous soughing of pines.

If Rosie lingered on the door-step it was not because she was afraid of the night sounds or of the dark. She was restrained for a minute by a sense of terror at what she was about to do. It was not a new terror. She felt it on every occasion when she went forth to keep this tryst. As she had already said to her father, she knew what she was doing. She was neither so young nor so inexperienced as to be unaware of the element of danger that waited on her steps. No one could have told her better than she could have told herself that the voice of wise counsel would have bidden her stay at home. But if she was not afraid of the night, neither was she irresolute before the undertaking. Being forewarned, she was forearmed. Being forearmed, she could run the risks. Running the risks, she could enjoy the excitement and find solace in the romance.

For it was romance, romance of the sort she had dreamed of and planned for and got herself ready to be equal to, if ever it should come. Somehow, she had always known it would come. She could hardly go back to the time when she did not have this premonition of a lover who would appear like a prince in a fairy-tale and lift her out of her low estate.

And he had come. He had come late on an afternoon in the preceding summer, when she was picking wild raspberries in the wood above Duck Rock. It was a lonely spot in which she could reasonably have expected to be undisturbed. She was picking the berries fast and deftly, because the fruitman who passed in the morning would give her a dollar for her harvest. Was it the dollar, or was it the sweet, wandering, summer air? Was it the mingled perfumes of vine and fruit and soft loam loosened as she crept among the brambles, or was it the shimmer of the waning sunlight or the whir of the wings of birds or the note of a hermit-thrush in some still depth of the woodland ever so far away? Or was it only because she was young and invincibly happy at times, in spite of a sore heart, that she sang to herself as her nimble fingers secured the juicy, delicate red things and dropped them into the pan?

He came like Pan, or a faun, or any other woodland thing, with no sound of his approach, not even that of oaten pipes. When she raised her eyes he was standing in a patch of bracken. She had been stooping to gather

47

the fruit that clustered on a long, low, spiny stem. The words on her lips had been:

> At least be pity to me shown
> If love it may na be—

but her voice trailed away faintly on the last syllable, for on looking up he was before her. He wore white flannels, and a Panama hat of which the brim was roguishly pulled down in front to shade his eyes.

He was smiling unabashed, and yet with a friendliness that made it impossible for her to take offense. "Isn't it Rosie?" he asked, without moving from where he stood in the patch of trampled bracken. "I'm Claude. Don't you remember me?"

A Delphic nymph who had been addressed by Apollo, in the seclusion of some sacred grove, could hardly have felt more joyous or more dumb. Rosie Fay did not know in what kind of words to answer the glistening being who had spoken to her with this fine familiarity. Later, in the silence of the night, she blushed with shame to think of the figure she must have cut, standing speechless before him, the pan of red raspberries in her hands, her raspberry-red lips apart in amazement, and her eyes gleaming and wide with awe.

She remained vague as to what she answered in the end. It was confusedly to the effect that though she remembered him well enough, she supposed that he had long ago forgotten one so insignificant as herself. Presently he was beside her, dropping raspberries into her pan, while they laughed together as in those early days when they had picked peas by her father's permission in Grandpa Thorley's garden.

Their second meeting was accidental—if it was accidental that each had come to the same spot, at the same hour, on the following day, in the hope of finding the other. The third meeting was also on the same spot, but by appointment, in secret, and at night. Claude had been careful to impress on her the disaster that would ensue if their romance were discovered.

But Rosie Fay knew what she was doing. She repeated that statement often to herself. Had she really been a Delphic nymph, or even a young lady of the best society, she might have given herself without reserve to the rapture of her idyl; but her circumstances were peculiar. Rosie was obliged to be practical, to look ahead. A fairy prince was not only a romantic dream in her dreary life, but an agency to be utilized. The least self-seeking of drowning maids might expect the hero on the bank to pull her out of the water. The very fact that she recognized in Claude a tendency to dally with her on the brink instead of landing her in a place of safety compelled her to be the more astute.

But she was not so astute as to be inaccessible to the sense of terror that assailed her every time she went to meet him. It was the fright of one accustomed to walk on earth when seized and borne into the air. Claude's voice over the telephone, as she had heard it that afternoon, was like the call to adventures at once enthralling and appalling, in which she found it hard to keep her head. She kept it only by saying to herself: "I know what I'm doing. I know what I'm doing. My father is ruined; my brother is in jail. But I love this man and he loves me. If he marries me—"

But Rosie's thoughts broke off abruptly there. They broke off because they reached a point beyond which imagination would not carry her. If he marries me! The supposition led her where all was blurred and roseate and golden, like the mists around the Happy Isles. Rosie could not forecast the conditions that would be hers as the wife of Claude Masterman. She only knew that she would be transported into an atmosphere of money, and money she had learned by sore experience to be the sovereign palliative of care. Love was much to poor Rosie, but relief from anxiety was more. It had to be so, since both love and light are secondary blessings to the tired creature whose first need is rest. It was for rest that Claude Masterman stood primarily in her mind. He was a fairy prince, of course; he was a lover who might have satisfied any girl's aspirations. But before everything else he was a hero and a savior, a being in whose vast potentialities, both social and financial, she could find refuge and lie down at last.

It needed but this bright thought to brace her. She clasped her hands to her breast; she lifted her eyes to the swimming moon; she drew deep breaths of the sweet, strong air; she appealed to all the supporting forces she knew anything about. A minute later she was speeding through the darkness.

CHAPTER VII

BETWEEN the greenhouses, of which the glass gleamed dimly in the moonlight, Rosie followed a path that straggled down the slope of her father's land to the new boulevard round the pond. The boulevard here swept inland about the base of Duck Rock, in order to leave that wooded bluff an inviolate feature of the landscape. So inviolate had it been that during the months since Rosie had picked wild raspberries in its boskage the park commissioners had seized on it as a spot to be subdued by winding paths and restful benches. To make it the more civilized and inviting they had placed one of the arc-lamps that now garlanded the circuit of the pond just where it would guide the feet of lovers into the alluring shade. Rosie was glad of this friendly light before engaging on the rough path up the bluff under the skeleton-like trees. She was not afraid; she was only nervous, and the light gave her confidence.

But to-night, as she emerged on the broad boulevard from the weedy outskirts of her father's garden, the clatter of horse-hoofs startled her into drawing back. She would have got herself altogether out of sight had there been anything at hand in the nature of a shrub high enough to conceal her. As it was she could only shrink to the extreme edge of the roadside, hoping that the rider, who-ever he was, would pass without seeing her. This he might have done had not the bay mare Delia, unaccus-tomed to the sight of young ladies roaming alone at night, thought it the part of propriety to shy.

"Whoa, Delia! whoa! What's the matter? Steady,

old girl! steady!" There was a flash of the quick, penetrating eyes around the circle made by the arc-light.
"Why, hello, Rosie! 'Pon my soul! Look scared as a
stray kitten. Where you going?"

Rosie could only reply that she wasn't going anywhere.
She was just—out.

"Well, it's a fine night. Everybody seems to be out.
Just met Claude."

The girl was unable to repress a startled "Oh!" though
she bit her tongue at the self-betrayal.

Uncle Sim laughed merrily. "Don't wonder you're
frightened—pretty girl like you. Devil of a fellow,
Claude thinks he is. Suppose you don't know him.
Ah, well, that wouldn't make any difference to him, if he
was to run across you. I'll tell you what! You come
along with me." Chuckling to himself, he slipped from
Delia's back, preparing to lead the mare and accompany
the girl on foot. "We'll go round by the Old Village and
up School-house Lane. The walk 'll do you good. You'll
sleep better after it. Come along now, and tell me about
your mother as we go. Did my nephew, Thor, come to
see her? What did he give her? Did she take it? Did
it make her sleep?"

But Rosie shrank away from him with the eyes of a
terrified animal. "Oh no, Dr. Masterman! Please! I
don't want to take that long walk. I'll go back up the
path—the way I came. I just ran out to—to—"

He looked at her with suspicious kindliness. "Will
you promise me you'll go back the way you came?"

"Yes, yes; I will."

"Then that's all right. It's an awful dangerous road,
Rosie. Tramps—and everything. But if you'll go
straight back up the path I'll be easy in my mind about
you." He watched her while she retreated. "Good
night!" he called.

"Good night," came her voice from half-way up the
garden.

THE SIDE OF THE ANGELS

She was obliged to wait in the shadow of an outlying hothouse till the sound of Delia's hoofs, clattering off toward the Old Village, died away on the night. She crept back again, cautiously. Cautiously, too, she stole across the boulevard and into the wood. Once there, she flew up the path with the frantic eagerness of a hare. She was afraid Claude might have come and gone. She was afraid of the incident with old Sim. What did he mean? Did he mean anything? If he betrayed Claude at home, would it keep the latter from meeting her? She had no great confidence in Claude's ability to withstand authority. She had no great confidence in anything, not even in his love, or in her own. The love was true enough; it was ardently, desperately true; but would it bear the strain that could so easily be put upon it? She felt herself swept by an immense longing to be sure.

She had so many subjects to think of and to dread that she forgot to be frightened as she sped up the bluff. It was only on reaching the summit and discovering that Claude wasn't there that she was seized by fear. There was a bench beside her—a round bench circling the trunk of an oak-tree—and she sank upon it.

The crunching of footsteps told her some one was coming up the slope. In all probability it was Claude; but it might be a stranger, or even an animal. The crunching continued, measured, slow. She would have fled if there had been any way of fleeing without encountering the object of her alarm. The regular beat of the footsteps growing heavier and nearer through the darkness rendered her almost hysterical. When at last Claude's figure emerged into the moonlight, his erect slenderness defined against the sky, she threw herself, sobbing, into his arms.

It was not the least of Claude's attractions that he was so tender with women swept by crises of emotion. Where Thor would have stood helpless, or prescribed a mild sedative, Claude pressed the agitated creature to his breast and let her weep.

When her sobs had subsided to a convulsive clinging to him without tears, he explained his delay in arriving by his meeting with Uncle Sim. They were seated on the bench by this time, his arms about her, her face close to his.

"Awful nuisance, he is. Regular Paul Pry. Can't keep anything from him. Scours the country night and day like the Headless Horseman of Sleepy Hollow. Never know when you'll meet him."

"I met him, too," Rosie said, getting some control of her voice.

"The deuce you did! Did he speak to you? Did he say anything about me?"

"He said he'd seen you."

"Is that all?"

She weighed the possible disadvantages of saying too much, coming to the conclusion that she had better tell him more. "No, it isn't quite all. He seemed to—warn me against you."

"Oh, the devil!" In his start he loosened his embrace, but grasped her to him again. "What's he up to now?"

"Do you think he's up to anything?"

"What else did he say? Tell me all you can think of."

She narrated the brief incident.

"Will it make any difference to us?" she ventured to ask.

"It 'll make a difference to us if he blabs to father. Of course!"

"What sort of difference, Claude?"

"The sort of difference it makes when there's the devil to pay."

She clasped him to her the more closely. "Does that mean that we shouldn't be able to see each other any more?"

The question being beyond him, Claude smothered it under a selection of those fond epithets in which his vocabulary was large. In the very process of enjoying them Rosie was rallying her strength. She was still clasping him as she withdrew her head slightly, looking up at him through the moonlight.

"Claude, I want to ask you something."

With his hand on the knot of her hair, he pressed her face once more against his. "Yes, yes, darling. Ask me anything. Yes, yes, yes, yes."

She broke in on his purring with the words, "Are we engaged?"

The purring ceased. Without relaxing his embrace he remained passive, like a man listening. "What makes you ask me that?"

"It's what people generally are when they're—when they're like us, isn't it?"

Brushing his lips over the velvet of her cheeks, he began to purr again. "No one was every like us, darling. No one ever will be. Don't worry your little head with what doesn't matter."

"But it does matter to me, Claude. I want to know where I am."

"Where you are, dearie. You're here with me. Isn't that enough?"

"It's enough for now, Claude, but—"

"And isn't what's enough for now all we've got to think of?"

"No, Claude dearest. A girl isn't like a man—"

"Oh yes, she is, when she loves. And you love me, don't you, dearie? You love me just a little. Say you love me—just a little—a very little—"

"Oh, Claude, my darling, my darling, you know I love you. You're all I've got in the world—"

"And you're all I've got, my little Rosie. Nothing else counts when I'm with you—"

"But when you're not with me, Claude? What then?

What am I to think when you're away from me? What am I to be?"

"Be just as you are. Be just as you've always been since the day I first saw you—"

"Yes, yes, Claude; but you don't understand. If any one were to find out that I came here to meet you like this—"

"No one must find out, dear. We must keep that mum."

"But if they did, Claude, it wouldn't matter to you at all—"

"Oh, wouldn't it, though? Father'd make it matter, I can tell you."

"Yes, but you wouldn't be disgraced. I should be. Don't you see? No one would ever believe—"

"Oh, what does it matter what any one believes. Let them all go hang."

"We can't let them all go hang. You can't let your father go hang, and I can't let mine. Do you know what my father would do to me if he knew where I am now. He'd kill me."

"Oh, rot, Rosie!"

"No, no, Claude; I'm telling you the truth. He's that sort. You wouldn't think it, but he is. He's one of those mild, dreamy men who, when they're enraged—which isn't often—don't know where to stop. If he thought I'd done wrong he'd put a knife into me, just like that." She struck her clenched hand against his heart. "When Matt was arrested—"

He tore himself from her suddenly. The sensitive part of him had been touched. "Oh, Lord, Rosie, don't let's go into that. I hate that business. I try to forget it."

"No one can forget it who remembers me."

"Oh yes, they can. *I* can—when you don't drag it up. What's the use, Rosie? Why not be happy for the few hours every now and then that we can get together? What's got into you?" He changed his tone. "You hurt me, Rosie, you hurt me. You talk as if you didn't trust me. You seem to have suspicions, to be making schemes—"

"Oh, Claude! For God's sake!" Rosie, too, was touched on the quick, perhaps by some truth in the accusation.

He kissed her ardently. "I know, dear; I know. I know it's all right—that you don't mean anything. Kiss me. Tell me you won't do it any more—that you won't hurt the man who adores you. What does anything else matter? You and I are everything there is in the world. Don't let us talk. When we've got each other—"

Rosie gave it up, for the present at any rate. She began to perceive dimly that they had different conceptions of love. For her, love was engagement and marriage, with the material concomitants the two states implied. But for Claude love was something else. It was something she didn't understand, except that it was indifferent to the orderly procession by which her own ambitions climbed. He loved her; of that she was sure. But he loved her for her face, her mouth, her eyes, her hair, the color of her skin, her roughened little hands, her lithe little body. Of nothing else in her was he able to take cognizance. Her hard life and her heart-breaking struggles were conditions he hadn't the eyes to see. He was aware of them, of course, but he could detach her from them. He could detach her from them for the minutes she spent with him, but he could see her go back to them and make no attempt to follow her in sympathy.

But he loved her beauty. There was that palliating fact. After all, Rosie was a woman, and here was the supreme tribute to her womanhood. It was not everything, and yet it was the thing enchanting. It was the kind of tribute any woman in the world would have put before social rescue or moral elevation, and Rosie was like the rest. She could be lulled by Claude's endearments as a child is lulled by a cradle-song. With this music in her ears doubts were stilled and misgivings quieted and ambitions overruled. Return to the world of care and calculation followed only on Claude's words uttered just as they were parting.

"And you'd better be on your guard against Thor. So long as he's going to your house you mustn't give anything away."

CHAPTER VIII

DRESSED for going out, Mrs. Willoughby was button-ing her gloves as she stood in the square hall hung with tapestries of a late Gobelins period and adorned with a cabinet in the style of Buhl flanked by two decorative Regency chairs. Her gaze followed the action of her fingers or wandered now and then inquiringly up the stairway.

Her broad, low figure, wide about the hips, tapered toward the feet in lines suggestive of a spinning-top. She was proud of her feet, which were small and shapely, and approved of a fashion in skirts that permitted them to be displayed. Being less proud of her eyes, she also approved of a style of hat which allowed the low, sloping brim, worn slantwise across the brows, to conceal one of them.

"You're surely not going in that rag!"

The protest was called forth by Lois's appearance in a walking-costume on the stairs.

"But, mamma, I'm not going at all. I told you so."

"Told me so! What's the good of telling me so? There'll be loads of men there—simply loads. Goodness me! Lois, if you're ever going to know any men at all—"

"I know all the men I want to know."

"You don't know all the men you want to know, and if you do I should be ashamed to say it. A girl who's had all your advantages and doesn't make more show! What on earth are you doing that you don't want to come?"

Lois hesitated, but she was too frank for concealments. "I'm going to see a girl Thor Masterman wants me to look after. He thinks I may be able to help her."

The mother subsided. "Oh, well—if it's that!" She added, so as not to seem to hint too much: "I always like you to do what you can toward uplift. I'll take you as far as the Old Village, if you're going that way."

There had been a time when such concessions at the mention of Thor Masterman would have irritated Lois more than any violence of opposition; but that time was passing. She could hardly complain if others saw what was daily becoming more patent to herself. She could complain of it the less since she found it difficult to conceal her happiness. It was a happiness that softened the pangs of care and removed to a distance the conditions incidental to her father's habits and impending financial ruin.

Nevertheless, the conditions were there, and had to be confronted. She made, in fact, a timid effort to confront them as she sat beside her mother in the admirably fitted limousine.

"Mother, what are we going to do about papa?"

Mrs. Willoughby's indignant rising to the occasion could be felt like an electric wave. "Do about him? Do about what?"

"About the way he is."

"The way he is? What on earth are you talking about?"

"I mean the way he comes home."

"He comes home very tired, if that's what you're trying to say. Any man who works as they work him at that office—"

"Do you think it's work?"

"No, I don't think it's work. I call it slavery. It's enough to put a man in his grave. I've seen him come home so that he could hardly speak; and if you've done the same you may know that he's simply tired enough to die."

Lois tried to come indirectly to her point by saying, "Thor Masterman has been bringing him home lately."

"Oh, well; I suppose Thor knows he doesn't lose anything by that move."

Lois ignored the remark to say, "Thor seems worried."

The mother's alertness was that of a ruffled, bellicose bird defending its mate. "If Thor's worried about your father, he can spare himself the trouble. He can leave that to me. I'll take care of him. What he needs is rest. When everything is settled I mean to take him away. Of course we can't go *this* winter. If we could we should go to Egypt—he and I. But we can't. We know that. We make the sacrifice."

These discreet allusions, too, Lois thought it best to let pass in silence. "It wasn't altogether about papa that Thor was worried. He seems anxious about money."

Bessie tossed her head. "That may easily be. If your father takes our money out of the firm, as he threatens to do, the Mastermans will be—well, I don't know where."

The girl felt it right to go a step further. "He seemed to hint—he didn't say it in so many words—that perhaps papa wouldn't have so very much to take out."

This was dismissed lightly. "Then he doesn't know what's he talking about. Archie's frightfully close in those things, I must say. He's never let either of the boys know anything about the business. He won't even let me. But your father knows. If Thor thinks for a minute the money isn't nearly all ours he may come in for a rude awakening."

Reassured by this firmness of tone, Lois began to take heart. Getting out at the Old Village, she continued her way on foot, and found Rosie among the azaleas and poinsettias.

Thor Masterman met her an hour later, as she returned homeward. He knew where she had been as soon as he saw her turn the corner at which the road descends the hill, recognizing with a curious pang her promptness in carrying out his errand. The pang was a surprise to him

—the beginning of a series of revelations on the subject of himself.

Her desire to please him had never before this instant caused him anything but satisfaction. It had been but the response to his desire to please her. He had not been blind to the goal to which this mutual good-will would lead them, but he had quite made up his mind that she would make him as good a wife as any one. As a preliminary to marriage he had weighed the possibility of falling ardently in love, coming at last to the conclusion that he was not susceptible to that passion.

His long-standing intention to marry Lois Willoughby was based on the fact that besides being sympathetic to him she was plain and lonely. If the motive hadn't taken full possession of his heart it was because the state of being plain and lonely had never seemed to him the worst of calamities, by any means. The worst of calamities, that for which no patience was sufficient, that for which there was no excuse, that which kings, presidents, emperors, parliaments, congresses, embassies, and armies should combine their energies to prevent, was to be poor. He was entirely of Mrs. Fay's opinion, that with money ill-health and unhappiness were details. You could bear them both. You could bear being lonely; you could bear being plain. Consequently, the menace that now threatened Lois Willoughby's fortunes strengthened her claim on him; but all at once he felt, as he saw her descend the hill, that the claim might make complications.

Was it because she was plain? Curious that he had never attached importance to that fact before! But it blinded him now to her graceful carriage as well as to the way she had of holding her head with a noble, independent poise that made her a woman of distinction.

She was smiling with an air at once intimate and triumphant. "I think I've won in the first encounter, at any rate."

In his wincing there was the surprise of a man who in a

SHE WAS SMILING WITH AN AIR AT ONCE INTIMATE AND TRIUMPHANT

moment of expansion has made a sacred confidence only to find it crop up lightly in subsequent conversation. He was obliged to employ some self-control in order to say, with a manner sufficiently offhand, "What happened?"

She told of making her approaches under the plea of buying potted plants. A cold reception had given way before her persistent friendliness, while there had been complete capitulation on the tender of an invitation to County Street to tea. The visit had been difficult to manage, but amusing, and a little pitiful.

To the details that were difficult or pitiful he could listen with calm, but he was inwardly indignant that Lois should find anything in her meeting with Rosie that lent itself to humor. He knew that humor. The superior were fond of indulging in it at the expense of the less fortunate. Even Lois Willoughby had not escaped that taint of class. Fearing to wound her by some impatient word, he made zeal in his round of duties the excuse for an abrupt good-by.

But zeal in his round of duties changed to zeal of another kind as with set face and long, swinging stride he hurried up the hill. The plans he had been maturing for the psychological treatment of Mrs. Fay melted into eagerness to know how the poor little thing had taken Lois's advances. He was disappointed, therefore, that Rosie should receive him coldly.

Within twenty-four hours his imagination had created between them something with the flavor of a friendship. He had been thinking of her so incessantly that it was disconcerting to perceive that apparently she had not been thinking of him at all. He was the doctor to her, and no more. She continued to direct Antonio, the Italian, who was opening a crate of closely packed azalea-plants, while she discussed the effect of his sedative on her mother. Her manner was dry and business-like; her replies to his questions brief and to the point.

But professional duty being done, he endeavored to

raise the personal issue. "What did you mean yesterday when you said that you couldn't play fair, but that you'd play as fair as you could?"

She turned from her contemplation of the stooping Antonio's back. "Did I say that?"

He hardly heeded the question in the pleasure he got from this glimpse of her green eyes. "You said that—or something very much like it."

His uncertainty gave her the chance to correct that which, in the light of Claude's warning, might prove to have been an indiscretion. "I'm sure I can't imagine. You must have—misunderstood me."

He pursued the topic not because he cared, but in order to make her look at him again. "Oh no, I didn't. Don't you remember? It was after you said that there was one thing that might happen—"

She was sure of her indiscretion now. He might even be setting a snare for her. Dr. Sim Masterman might have withdrawn from her mother's case in order to put the one brother on the other's tracks. If Claude was right in his suspicions, there was reasonable ground for alarm. She said, with assumed indifference: "Oh, that! That was nothing. Just a fancy."

He still talked for the sake of talking, attaching no importance to her replies. "Was it a fancy when you said that I would be one of the people opposed to it—if it happened?"

"Well, yes. But you'd only be one among a lot." She shifted to firmer ground. "I wasn't thinking of you in particular—or of any one in particular."

"Were you thinking of any *thing* in particular?"

The question threw her back on straight denial. "N-no; not exactly; just a fancy."

"But I shouldn't be opposed to it, whatever it is—if it was to your advantage."

His persistence deepened her distrust. A man whom she had seen only once before would hardly display such an interest in her and her affairs unless he had a motive, especially when that man was a Masterman. She took refuge in her task with the azaleas. "No, not there, Antonio. Put them there—like this—I'll show you."

The necessity for giving Antonio practical demonstration taking her to the other side of the hothouse, Thor felt himself obliged to go. He went with the greater regret since he had been unable to sound her on the subject of Lois Willoughby's advances, though her skill in eluding him heightened his respect. His disdain for the small arts of coquetry being as sincere as his scorn of snobbery, he counted it to her credit that she eluded him at all. There would be plenty of opportunities for speech with her. During them he hoped to win her confidence by degrees.

In the bedroom up-stairs, where the mother was again seated in her upholstered arm-chair with the quilt across her knees, he endeavored to put into practice his idea of mental therapeutics. He began by speaking of Matt, using the terms that would most effectively challenge her attention. "When he comes back, you know, we must make him forget that he's ever worn stripes."

She eyed him sternly. "What 'd be the good of his forgetting it? He'll have done it, just the same."

"Some of us have done worse than that, and yet—"

"And yet we didn't get into Colcord for them. But that's what counts. You can do what you like as long as you ain't put in jail. Look at your father—"

"So when he comes home—" he interrupted, craftily.

She leaned forward, throwing the quilt from her knees. "See here," she asked, confidentially, "how would you feel if you saw your son coming up out of hell?"

"How should I feel? I should be glad he was coming up instead of going down. You would, too, wouldn't you? And now that he's coming up we must keep him up. That's the point. So many poor chaps that have been in his position feel that because they've once been down they've got to stay down. We must make him see that he's come back among friends — and you must tell us what to do. You must give your mind to it and think it out. He's your boy—so it's your duty to take the lead."

Her cold eye rested on him as if she were giving his words consideration. "Why don't you ask your father to take the lead? He sent him to Colcord."

Thor got no further than this during the hour he spent with her, seeing that Uncle Sim had been right in describing the case as one for ingenuity—and something more. Questioning himself as to what this something more could be, he brought up the subject tentatively with Jasper Fay, whom he met on leaving the house. Thor himself stood on the door-step, while Fay, who wore gardening overalls, confronted him from the withered grass-plot that ended in a leafless hedge of bridal-veil.

"She's never been a religious woman at all, has she?"

Fay answered with a distant smile. "She did go in for religion at one time, sir; but I guess she found it slim diet. It got to seem to her like Thomas Carlyle's hungry lion invited to a feast of chickenweed. After that she quit."

"I had an idea that you belonged to the First Church and were Dr. Hilary's parishioners."

Fay explained. "Dr. Hilary married us, but we haven't troubled the church much since. I never took any interest in the Christian religion to begin with; and when I looked into it I found it even more fallacious than I supposed." To account for this advanced position on the part of a simple market-gardener he added, "I've been a good deal of a reader."

Thor spoke slowly and after meditation. "It isn't so much a question of its being fallacious as of its capacity for producing results."

Fay turned partially round toward the south, where a haze hung above the city. His tone was infused with a mild bitterness. "Don't we see the results it can produce—over there?"

"That's right, too." Thor was so much in sympathy with this point of view that he hardly knew how to go on. "And yet some of us doctors are beginning to suspect that there may be a power in Christianity—a purely psychological power, you understand—that hasn't been used for what it's worth."

Fay nodded. He had been following this current of contemporary thought. "Yes, Dr. Thor. So I hear. Just as, I dare say, you haven't found out all the uses of opium."

"Well, opium is good in its place, you know."

"I suppose so." He lifted his starry eyes with their mystic, visionary rapture fully on the young physician. "And yet I remember how George Eliot prayed that when her troubles came she might get along without being drugged by that stuff—meaning the Christian religion, sir—and I guess I'd kind o' like that me and mine should do the same."

Thor dropped the subject and went his way. As far as he had opinions of his own, they would have been similar to Fay's had he not within a year or two heard of sufficiently authenticated cases in which sick spirits or disordered nerves had yielded to spiritual counsels after the doctor had had no success. He had been so little impressed with these instances that he might not have allowed his speculations with regard to Mrs. Fay to go beyond the fleeting thought, only for the fact that on passing through the Square he met Reuben Hilary. In general he was content to touch his hat to the old gentleman and go on; but to-day, urged by an impulse too vague to take accurate account of, he stopped with respectful greetings.

"I've just been to see an old parishioner of yours, sir," he said, when the preliminaries of neighborly conversation had received their due.

"Have you, now?" was the non-committal response, delivered with a North-of-Ireland intonation.

"Mrs. Fay—wife of Fay, the gardener. I can't say she's ill," Thor went on, feeling his way, "but she's mentally upset." He decided to plunge into the subject boldly, smiling with that mingling of frankness and perplexity which people found appealing because of its conscientiousness. "And I've been wondering, Dr. Hilary, if you couldn't help her."

"Have you, now? And what would you be wanting me to do?"

Thor reflected as to the exact line to take, while the kindly eyes covered him with their shrewd, humorous twinkle. "You see," Thor tried to explain, "that if she could get the idea that there's any other stand to take toward trouble than that of kicking against it, she might be in a fair way to get better. At present she's like a prisoner who dashes his head against a stone wall, not seeing that there's a window by which he might make his escape."

There was renewed twinkling in the merry eyes. "But if there's a window, why don't you point it out to her?"

Thor grinned. "Because, sir, I don't see it myself."

"T't, t't! Don't you, then? And how do you know it's there?"

Thor continued to grin. "To be frank with you, sir, I don't believe it *is* there. But if you can make her believe it is—"

"That is, you want me to deceive the poor creature."

"Oh no, sir," Thor protested. "You wouldn't be deceiving her because you do believe it."

"So that I'd only be deceiving her to the extent that I'm deceived myself."

"You're too many for me," Thor laughed again, preparing to move on. "I didn't know but that if you gave her what are called the consolations of religion—that's the right phrase, isn't it—"

"There is such a phrase. But you can't *give* people the consolations of religion; they've got to find them for themselves. If they won't do that, there's no power in heaven or earth that can force consolation upon them."

"But religion undertakes to do something, doesn't it?"

The old man shook his head. "Nothing whatever—no more than air undertakes that you shall breathe it, or water that you shall drink it, or fire that you shall warm yourself at its blaze."

Thor mused. When he spoke it was as if summing up the preceding remarks. "So that you can't do anything, sir, for my friend, Mrs. Fay?"

"Nothing whatever, me dear Thor—but help her to do something for herself."

"Very well, sir. Will you try that?"

"Sure, I'll try it. I'm too proud of the Word of God to thrust it where it isn't wanted—*margaritas ante porcos*, if you've Latin enough for that—but when any one asks for it as earnestly as you, me dear Thor—"

Having won what he asked, Thor shook the old man's hand and thanked him, after which he hurried off to the garage to take out his runabout and bring Lois's father home from town.

CHAPTER IX

AS November and December passed and the new year came in, small happenings began to remind Thorley Masterman that he was soon to inherit money. It was a fact which he himself could scarcely credit. Perhaps because he was not imaginative the condition of being thirty years of age continued to seem remote even when he was within six weeks of that goal.

He was first impressed with the rapidity of his approach to it on a morning when he came late to breakfast, finding at his plate a long envelope, bearing in its upper left-hand corner the request that in the event of non-delivery it should be returned to the office of Darling & Darling, at 27, Commonwealth Row. A glance, which he couldn't help reading, passed round the table as he took it up. It was not new to him that among the other members of the household, closely as they were united, there was a sense of vague injustice because he was coming into money and they were not.

The communication was brief, stating no more than the fact that in view of the transfer of the estate which would take place a few weeks later, Mr. William Darling, the sole trustee, would be glad to see the heir on a day in the near future, to submit to him the list of investments and other properties that were to make up his inheritance. Thor saw his grandfather's money, so long a fairy prospect, as likely to become a matter of solid cash. The change in his position would be considerable.

As yet, however, his position remained that of a son in his father's family, and, in obedience to what he knew was expected of him, he read the note aloud. Though there was an absence of comment, his stepmother, in passing him his coffee, murmured, caressingly, "Dear old Thor."

"Dear old Thor," Claude mimicked, "will soon be able to do everything he pleases."

Mrs. Masterman smiled. It was her mission to conciliate. "And what will that be?"

"I know what it won't be," Claude said, scornfully. "It won't be anything that has to do with a pretty girl."

Thor flushed. It was one of the minutes at which Claude's taunts gave him all he could do to contain himself. As far as his younger brother was concerned, he meant well by him. It had always been his intention that his first use of Grandpa Thorley's money should be in supplementing Claude's meager personal resources and helping him to keep on his feet. He could be patient with him, too—patient under all sorts of stinging gibes and double-edged compliments—patient for weeks, for months —patient right up to the minute when something touched him too keenly on the quick, and his wrath broke out with a fury he knew to be dangerous. It was so dangerous as to make him afraid—afraid for Claude, and more afraid for himself. There had been youthful quarrels between them from which he had come away pale with terror, not at what he had done, but at what he might have done had he not maintained some measure of self-control.

The memory of such occasions kept him quiet now, though the irony of Claude's speech cut so much deeper than any one could suspect. "Won't be anything that has to do with a pretty girl!" Good God! When he was beginning to feel his soul rent in the struggle between love and honor! It was like something sprung on him—that had caught him unawares. There were days when the suffering was so keen that he wondered if there was no way of lawfully giving in. After all, he had never asked Lois Willoughby to marry him. There had never been more between them than an unspoken intention in his mind which had somehow communicated itself to hers. But that was not a pledge. If he were to marry some one else, she couldn't reproach him by so much as a syllable.

It was not often that he was tempted to reason thus, but Claude's sarcasm brought up the question more squarely than it had ever raised itself before. It was exactly the sort of subject on which, had it concerned any one else, Thor would have turned for light to Lois herself. In being debarred from her counsels, he felt strangely at a loss. While he said to himself that after all these years there was but one thing for him to do, he was curious as to the view other people might take of such a situation. It was because of this need, and with Claude's sneer ringing in his heart, that later in the day he sprang the question on Dearlove. Dearlove was the derelict English butler whom Thor had picked out of the gutter and put in charge of his office so that he might have another chance. He had been summoned into his master's presence to explain the subsidence in the contents of a bottle of cognac that Thor kept at the office for emergency cases and had neglected to put under lock and key.

"That was a full bottle a month ago," Thor declared, holding the accusing object up to the light.

"Was it, sir?" Dearlove asked, dismally. He stood in his habitual attitude, his arms crossed on his stomach, his hands thrust, monklike, into his sleeves.

"And I've only taken one glass out of it—the day that young fellow fell off his bicycle."

Dearlove eyed the bottle piteously. "'Aven't you, sir? Perhaps you took more out that day than you thought."

But Thor broke in with what was really on his mind. "Look here, Dearlove! What would you say to a man who was in love with one woman if he married another?"

Dearlove was so astonished as to be for a minute at a

loss for speech. "What 'd I say to him, sir? I'd say, what did he do it for? If it was—"

"Yes, Dearlove?" Thor encouraged. "If it was for—what?"

"Well, sir, if he'd got money with her, like—well, that 'd be one thing."

"But if he didn't? If it was a case in which money didn't matter?"

Dearlove shook his head. "I never 'eard of no such case as that, sir."

Thor grew interested in the sheerly human aspects of the subject. Romance was so novel to him that he wondered if every one came under its spell at some time—if there was no exception, not even Dearlove. He leaned across the desk, his hands clasped upon it.

"Now, Dearlove, suppose it was your own case, and—"

"Oh, me, sir! I'm no example to no one—not with Brightstone 'anging on to me the way she does. I can't look friendly at so much as a kitten without Brightstone—"

"Now here's the situation, Dearlove," Thor interrupted, while the ex-butler listened, his head judicially inclined to one side: "Suppose a man—a patient of mine, let us say—meant to marry one young lady, and let her see it. And suppose, later, he fell very much in love with another young lady—"

"He'd 'ave to ease the first one off a bit, wouldn't he, sir?"

"You think he ought to."

"I think he'd 'ave to, sir, unless he wanted to be sued for breach."

"It's the question of duty I'm thinking of, Dearlove."

"Ain't it his dooty to marry the one he's in love with, sir? Doesn't the Good Book say as 'ow fallin' in love"—Dearlove blushed becomingly—"as 'ow fallin' in love is the way God A'mighty means to fertilize the earth with people? Doesn't the Good Book say that, sir?"

"Perhaps it does. I believe it's the kind of primitive subject it's likely to take up."

"So that there's that to be thought of, sir. They say the children not born o' love matches ain't always strong." He added, as he shuffled toward the door, "We never had no little ones, Brightstone and me—only a very small one that died a few hours after it was born."

Thor was not convinced by this reasoning, but he was happier than before. Such expressions of opinion, which would probably be indorsed by nine people out of ten, assured him that he might follow the urging of his heart and yet not be a dastard.

He felt on stronger ground, therefore, when he talked with Fay one afternoon in the week following. "Suppose my father doesn't renew the lease—what would happen to you?"

Fay raised himself from the act of doing something to a head of lettuce which was unfolding its petals like a great green rose. His eyes had the visionary look that marked his inability to come down to the practical. "Well, sir, I don't rightly know."

"But you've thought of it, haven't you?"

"Not exactly thought of it. He's said he wouldn t two or three times already, and then changed his mind."

"Would it do you any good if he did? Aren't you fighting a losing battle, anyhow?"

"That's not wholly the way I judge, Dr. Thor. Neither the losing battle nor the winning one can be told from the balance-sheet. The success or failure of a man's work is chiefly in himself."

Thor studied this, gazing down the level of soft verdure to the end of the greenhouse in which they stood. "I can see how that might be in one way, but—"

"It's the way I mostly think of, sir. Every man has his own habit of mind, hasn't he? I agree with the great prophet Thomas Carlyle when he says"—he brought out the words with a mild pomposity—"when he says that a certain inarticulate self-consciousness dwells in us which only our works can render articulate. He speaks of the folly of the precept 'Know thyself' till we've made it 'Know what thou canst work at.' I can work at this, Dr. Thor; I couldn't work at anything else. I know that making both ends meet is an important part of it, of course—"

"But to you it isn't the *most* important part of it."

Fay's eyes wandered to the other greenhouse in which lettuce grew, to the hothouse full of flowers, and out over the forcing-beds of violets. "No, Dr. Thor; not the most important part of it—to me. I've created all this. I love it. It's my life. It's myself. And if—"

"And if my father doesn't renew the lease—?"

"Then I shall be done for. It won't be just going bankrupt in the money sense; it 'll be everything else—blasted." He subjoined, dreamily: "I don't know what would happen to me after that. I'd be—I'd be equal to committing crimes."

Thor couldn't remember ever having seen tears on an elderly's man's cheeks before. He took a turn down half the length of the greenhouse and back again. "Look here, Fay," he said, in the tone of one making a resolution, "supposing my father would give *me* a lease of the place?"

"You, Dr. Thor?"

"Yes, me. Would you work it for me?"

Fay reflected long, while Thor watched the play of light and shadow over the mild, mobile face. "It wouldn't be my own place any more, would it, sir?"

"No, I suppose it wouldn't—not strictly. But it would be the next best thing. It would be better than—"

"It would be better than being turned out." He reflected further. "Was you thinking of taking it over as an investment, sir?"

Not having considered this side of his idea, Thor sought for a natural, spontaneous answer, and was not long in finding one. "I want to be identified with the village industries, because I'm going into politics."

"Oh, are you, sir? I didn't know you was that way inclined."

"I'm not," Thor explained, when they had moved from the greenhouse into the yard. "I only feel that we people of the old stock hang out of politics too much and that I ought to pitch in and make one more. So you get my idea, Fay. It 'll give me standing to hold a bit of property like this, even if it's only on lease."

There was no need for further explanations. Fay consented, not cheerfully, but with a certain saddened and yet grateful resignation, of which the expression was cut short by a cheery, ringing voice from the gateway:

"Hello, Mr. Fay! Hello, Dr. Thor! Whoa, Maud, whoa! Stand, will you? What you thinking of?"

The response to this greeting came from both men simultaneously, each making it according to his capacity for heartiness. "Hello, Jim!" They emphasized the welcome by unconsciously advancing to meet the tall, stalwart young Irishman of the third generation on American soil who came toward them with the long, loose limbs and swinging stride inherited from an ancestry bred to tramping the hills of Connemara. A pair of twinkling eyes and a mouth that was always on the point of breaking into a smile when it was not actually smiling tempered the peasant shrewdness of a face that got further softening, and a touch of superiority, from a carefully tended young mustache.

Thor and Jim Breen had been on friendly terms ever since they were boys; but the case was not exceptional, since the latter was on similar terms with every one in the village. From childhood upward he had been a local character, chiefly because of a breezy self-respect that was as free from self-consciousness as from self-importance. There was no one to whom he wasn't polite, but there had never been any one of whom he was afraid. "Hello,

Mr. Masterman!" "Hello, Dr. Hilary!" "Hello, Father Ryan!" "Hello Dr. Sim!" had been his form of greeting ever since he had begun swaggering around the village, with head up and face alert, at the age of five. No one had ever been found to resent this cheerful familiarity, not even Archie Masterman.

As a man in whom friendliness was a primary instinct, Jim Breen never entered a trolley-car nor turned a street corner without speaking or nodding to every one he knew. Never did he visit a neighboring town without calling on, or calling up, every one he could claim as an acquaintance. He was always on hand for fires, for fights, for fallen horses, for first-aid in accidents, for ball-games, for the outings of Boy Scouts, and for village theatricals and dances. There were rumors that he was sometimes "wild," but the wildness being confined to his incursions into the city—which generally took place after dark—it was not sufficiently in evidence to shock the home community. It was a matter of common knowledge that he used, in village phrase, "to go with" Rosie Fay —the breaking of the friendship being attributed by some of the well-informed to his reported wildness, and by others to differences in religion. As Thor had been absent in Europe during this episode, and was without the native suspicion that would have connected the two names, he took Jim's arrival pleasantly.

Having finished his bit of business, which concerned an order for azaleas too large for his father to meet, and in which Mr. Fay might find it to his advantage to combine, Jim turned blithely toward Thor. "Hear about the town meeting, Dr. Thor?—what old Billy Taylor said about the new bridge? What do you think of that for nerve? Tell you what, there's some things in this town needs clearing up."

The statement bringing out Thor's own intention to run as a candidate for office at the next election, Jim expressed his interest in the vernacular of the hour,

"What do you know about that?" Further discussion of politics ending in Jim's pledging his support to his boyhood's friend, Thor shook hands with an encouraging sense of being embarked on a public career, and went forward to visit his patient in the house.

His steps were arrested, however, by hearing Jim say. with casual light-heartedness, "Rosie anywheres about, Mr. Fay?"

The old man having nodded in the direction of the hothouse, Jim advanced almost to the door, where Thor, on looking over his shoulder, saw him pause.

It was a curious pause for one so self-confident as the young Irishman—a pause like that of a man grown suddenly doubtful, timid, distrustful. His hand was actually on the latch when, to Thor's surprise, he wheeled away, returning to his "team" with head bent and stride slackened thoughtfully. By the time he had mounted the wagon, however, and begun to tug at Maud he was whistling the popular air of the moment with no more than a subdued note in his gaiety.

CHAPTER X

B UT Thor was pleased with the idea that his father could scarcely refuse him the lease. He would in fact make it worth his while not to do so. Rosie Fay and those who belonged to her might, therefore, feel solid ground beneath their feet, and go on working and, if need were, suffering, without the intolerable dread of eviction. It would be a satisfaction to him to accomplish this much, whatever the dictates of honor might oblige him to forego.

He felt, too, that he was getting his reward when, after Jim's departure, Rosie nodded through the glass of the hothouse, giving him what might almost be taken for a smile. He forbore to go to her at once, keeping that pleasure for the end of his visit. After seeing his patient, there were generally small directions to give the daughter which afforded pretexts for lingering in her company. His patient was getting better, not through ministrations of his own, but through some mysterious influence exerted by Reuben Hilary. As a man of science and a skeptic, Thor was slightly impatient of this aid, even though he himself had invoked it.

He was half-way up the stairs on his way to the bedroom in the mansard roof when, on hearing a man's voice, he paused. The voice was saying, with that inflection in which there was no more than a hint of the brogue:

"Now there's what we were talking of the last time I was here: 'Let not your heart be troubled, neither let it be afraid. Ye believe in God; believe also in me.' There's the two great plagues of human existence—fear

79

and trouble—staggered for you at a blow. And you do believe in God, now, don't you?"

Thor had turned to tiptoe down again when he heard the words, spoken in the rebellious tones with which he was familiar, modulated now to an odd submissiveness: "I don't know whether I do or not. Isn't there something in the Bible about, 'Lord, I believe, help thou mine unbelief'?"

"There is, and it's a good way to begin."

Thor was out in the yard before he could hear more. Standing for a minute in the windy sunshine, he wondered at the curious phenomenon presented by men in evident possession of their faculties who relied for the dispersion of human care on means invisible and mystic. The fact that in this case he himself had appealed to the illusion rendered the working of it none the less astonishing. His own method for the dispersion of human care—and the project was dear to him—was by dollars and cents. It was, moreover, a method as to which there was no trouble in proving the efficiency.

He took up the subject of her mother with Rosie, who, with the help of Antonio, was rearranging the masses of azaleas, carnations, and poinsettias after the depletion of the Christmas sales. "She's really better, isn't she?"

Rosie pushed a white azalea to the place on the stand that would best display its domelike regularity. "She seems to be."

"What do you think has helped her?"

She gave him a queer little sidelong smile. "You're the doctor. I should think you'd know."

He adored those smiles—constrained, unwilling, distrustful smiles that varied the occasional earnest looks that he got from her green eyes. "But I don't know. It isn't anything I do for her."

She banked two or three azaleas together, so that their shades of pink and pomegranate-red might blend. "I suppose it's Dr. Hilary."

"I know it's Dr. Hilary. But he isn't working by magic. If she's getting back her nerve it isn't because he wishes it on her, as the boys say."

Suspecting all his approaches, she confined herself to saying, "I'm sure I don't know," speaking like a guilty witness under cross-examination. The assiduity of his visits, the persistency with which he tried to make her talk, kept her the more carefully on her guard against betraying anything unwarily.

But to him the reserve was an added charm. He called it shyness or coyness or maidenly timidity, according to the circumstance that called it forth; but whatever it was, this apathy to his passionate dumb-show piqued him to a frenzy infused with an element of homage. Any other girl in her situation would have come half-way at least toward a man in his. His training having rendered him analytical of the physical side of things, he endeavored, more or less unsuccessfully, to account for the extraordinary transformation in himself, whereby every nerve in his body yearned and strained toward this hard, proud little creature who, too evidently—as yet, at any rate—refused to take him into account. She made him feel like a man signaling in the dark or speaking across a vacuum through which his voice couldn't carry, while he was conscious at the same time of searchings of heart at making the attempts to do either.

He was beset by these scruples when, after taking his runabout from the garage, in order to go to town, he met Lois Willoughby in the Square. On the instant he remembered Dearlove's counsel of a few days earlier—"He'd 'ave to ease the first one off a bit." Whatever was to be his ultimate decision, the wisdom of this course was incontestable. As she paused, smiling, expecting him to stop, he lifted his hat and drove onward. Perhaps it was only his imagination that caught in her great, velvety brown eyes an expression of surprise and pain; but whether his sight was accurate or not, the memory of the moment smote him. The process of "easing the first one off" would probably prove difficult. "I shall have to explain to her that I was in a hurry," he said, to comfort himself, as he flew onward to the town.

The explanation would have been not untrue, since he was already overdue at his appointment with Mr. William Darling, his grandfather's executor.

It was the second of the meetings arranged for giving him a general idea of the estate he was coming into. At the first he had gone over the lists of stocks, mortgages, and bonds. To-day, with a map of the city and the surrounding country spread out, partially on the desk and partially over Mr. Darling's knees as he tilted back in a revolving-chair, Thor learned the location of certain bits of landed property which his grandfather, twenty or thirty years before, had considered good investments. The astuteness of this ancestral foresight was illustrated by the fact that Thor was a richer man than he had supposed. While he would possess no enormous wealth, according to the newer standards of the day, he would have something between thirty and forty thousand dollars of yearly income.

"And that," Mr. Darling explained with pride, "at a very conservative rate of investment. You could easily have more; but if you take my advice you'll not be in a hurry to look for more till you need it. I don't want to hurt any one's feelings. You surely understand that."

Thor was not sure that he did understand it. He was not sure; and yet he hesitated to ask for the elucidation of what was intended perhaps to remain cryptic. In a small chair drawn up beside Mr. Darling's revolving seat of authority, his elbow on his knee, his chin supported by his fist, he studied the map.

"I don't want to hurt any one's feelings," the lawyer declared again, "either before or after the fact."

This time an intention of some sort was so evident that

Thor felt obliged to say, "Do you mean any one in particular, sir?"

The trustee threw the map from off his knees, and, rising, walked to the window. He was a small, neat, sharp-eyed man of fresh, frosty complexion, his exquisite clothes making him something of a dandy, while his manner of turning his head, with quick little jerks and perks, reminded one of a bird. At the window he stood with his hands behind his back, looking over the jumble of nineteenth-century roofs—out of which an occasional "skyscraper" shot like a tower—to where a fringe of masts and funnels edged the bay. He spoke without turning round.

"I don't mean any one in particular unless there should be any one in particular to mean."

With this oracular explanation Thor was forced to be content, and, as the purpose of the meeting seemed to have been accomplished, he rose to take his leave.

Mr. Darling was quick in showing himself not only faithful as a trustee, but cordial as a man of the world. "My wife would like you to come and see her," he said, in shaking hands. "She asked me to say, too, that she hopes you and your brother will come to the dance she's going to give for Elsie in the course of a month or two. You'll get your cards in time."

Warmly expressing the pleasure this entertainment would give him, while knowing in his heart that he wouldn't attend it, the young man took his departure.

But no later than that evening he began to perceive why the oracle had spoken. Claude having excused himself from dressing for dinner on the ground of another mysterious engagement with Billy Cheever, and Mrs. Masterman having retired up-stairs, Thor was alone in the library with his father.

It was a mellow room, in which the bindings of long rows of books, mostly purchased by Grandpa Thorley in "sets," an admirable white-marble chimneypiece in a Georgian style, and a few English eighteenth-century prints added by Archie Masterman himself, disguised the heavy architectural taste of the sixties. Grandpa Thorley had built the house at the close of the Civil War, the end of that struggle having found him—for reasons he was never eager to explain—a far richer man than its beginning. He had built the house, not on his own old farm, which was already being absorbed into the suburban portion of the city, but on a ten-acre plot in County Street, which, with its rich bordering fields, its overarching elms, and its lofty sites, was revealing itself even then as the predestined quarter of the wealthy. So long as there had been no wealthy, County Street had been only a village highway; but the social developments following on the Civil War had required a Faubourg St.-Germain.

In this house Miss Louisa Thorley had grown up and been wooed by Archie Masterman. It had been the wooing of a very plain girl by a good-looking lad, and had received a shock when Grandpa Thorley suspected other motives than love to account for the young man's ardor. Her suitor being forbidden the house, Miss Thorley had no resource but to meet him in the city on the 7th of March, 1880, and go with him to a convenient parsonage. Thor was born on the 10th of February of the year following. Two days later the young mother died.

Grandpa Thorley himself held out for another ten years, when his will revealed the fact that he had taken every precaution to keep Archie Masterman from profiting by a penny of the Thorley money. So strict were the provisions of this document that on the father was thrown the entire cost of bringing up and educating Louisa Thorley's son.

But Archie Masterman was patient. He took a lease of the Thorley house when Darling & Darling as executors put it in the market, and paid all the rent it was worth. Moreover, there had never been a moment in Thor's life when he had been made to feel that his maintenance was a burden unjustly thrown on one who could ill afford to bear it. For this consideration the son had been grateful ever since he knew its character, and was now eager to make due return.

For the minute he was moving restlessly about the room, not knowing what to say. From the way in which his father, who was comfortably stretched in an arm-chair before the fire, dropped the evening paper to the floor, while he puffed silently at his cigar, Thor knew that he was expected to give some account of the interview between himself and the trustee that afternoon. Any father might reasonably look for such a confidence, while the conditions of affectionate intimacy in which the Masterman family lived made it a matter of course.

The son was still marching up and down the room, smoking cigarettes rapidly and throwing the butts into the fire, when he had completed his summary of the information received in his two meetings with the executor.

The father had neither interrupted nor asked questions, but he spoke at last. "What did you say was the approximate value of the whole estate?"

Thor told him.

"And of the income?"

Thor repeated that also.

"Criminal."

Thor stopped dead for an instant, but resumed his march. He had stopped in surprise, but he went on again so as to give the impression of not having heard the last observation.

"It's criminal," the father explained, with repressed indignation, "that money should bring in so trifling a return."

"He said it was very conservatively invested."

"It's damned idiotically invested. Such incompetence deserves an even stronger term. If my own money didn't earn more for me than that—well, I'm afraid you wouldn't have seen Vienna and Berlin."

The remark gave Thor an opening he was glad to seize. "I know that, father. I know how much you've spent for me, and how generous you've always been, with Claude to provide for, too; and now that I'm to have enough of my own I want to repay you every—"

"Don't hurt me, my boy. You surely don't think I'd take compensation for bringing up my own son. It's not in the least what I'm driving at. I simply mean that now that the whole thing is coming into your own hands you'll probably want to do better with it than has been done heretofore."

Thor said nothing. There was a long silence before his father went on:

"Even if you didn't want *me* to have anything to do with it, I could put you in touch with people who'd give you excellent advice."

Thor paced softly, as if afraid to make his footfalls heard. Something within him seemed frozen, paralyzed. He was incapable of a response.

"Of course," the father continued, gently, with his engaging lisp, "I can quite understand that you shouldn't want me to have anything to do with it. The new generation is often distrustful of the old."

Thor beat his brains for something to say that would meet the courtesies of the occasion without committing him; but his whole being had grown dumb. He would have been less humiliated if his father had pleaded with him outright.

"And yet I haven't done so badly," Masterman continued, with pathos in his voice. "I had very little to begin with. When I first went into old Toogood's office I had nothing at all. I made my way by thrift, foresight, and integrity. I think I can say as much as that. Your grandfather Thorley was unjust to me; but I've never resented it, not by a syllable."

It was a relief to Thor to be able to say with some heartiness, "I know that, father."

"Not that I didn't have some difficult situations to face on account of it. When the Toogood executors withdrew the old man's money it would have gone hard with me if I hadn't been able to—to"—Thor paused in his walk, waiting for what was coming—"if I hadn't been able to command confidence in other directions," the father finished, quietly.

Thor hastened to divert the conversation from his own affairs. "Mr. Willoughby put his money in then, didn't he?"

"That was one thing," Masterman admitted, coldly.

Thor could speak the more daringly because his march up and down kept him behind his father's back. "And now, I understand, you think of dropping him."

"I shouldn't be dropping him. That's not the way to put it. He drops himself—automatically." The clock on the mantelpiece ticked a few times before he added, "I can't go on supporting him."

"Do you mean that he's used up all the capital he put in?"

"That's what it comes to. He's spent enormous sums. At times it's been near to crippling me. But I can't keep it up. He's got to go. Besides, the big, drunken oaf is a disgrace to me. I can't afford to be associated with him any longer."

Thor came round to the fireplace, where he stood on the hearth-rug, his arm on the mantelpiece. "But, father, what 'll he do?"

"Surely that's his own lookout. Bessie's got money still. I didn't get all of it, by any means."

"No; but if you've got most of it—"

Masterman shot out of his seat. "Take care, Thor. I object to your way of expressing yourself. It's offensive."

"I only mean, father, that if Mr. Willoughby saved the business—"

"He didn't do anything of the kind," Masterman said, sharply. "No one knows better than he that I never wanted him at all."

But Thor ventured to speak up. "Didn't you tell mother one night in Paris, when we were there in 1892, that his money might as well come to you as go to the deuce? Mother said she hated business and didn't want to have anything to do with it. She hoped you'd let the Willoughbys and their money alone. Didn't that happen, father?"

If Thor was expecting his father to blanch and betray a guilty mind, he was both disappointed and relieved. "Possibly. I've no recollection. I was looking for some one to enter the business. He wasn't my ideal, the Lord knows; and yet I might have said something about it— carelessly. Why do you ask?"

The son tried to infuse his words with a special intensity as, looking straight into his father's eyes, he said, "Because I—I remember the way things happened at the time."

"Indeed? And may I ask what your memories lead you to infer? They've clearly led you to infer something."

During the seconds in which father and son scrutinized each other Thor felt himself backing down with a sort of spiritual cowardice. He didn't want to accuse his father. He shrank from the knowledge that would have justified him in doing so. To express himself with as little stress as possible, he said, "They lead me to infer that we've some moral responsibility toward Mr. Willoughby."

"Really? That's very interesting. Now, I should have said that if I'd ever had any I'd richly worked it off." It was perhaps to glide away from the points already raised that he asked: "Aren't you a little hasty in looking for moral responsibility? Let me see! Who was it the last time? Old Fay, wasn't it?"

Thor flushed, but he accepted the diversion. He even

welcomed it. Such glimpses as he got of his father's mind appalled him. For the present, at any rate, he would force no issue that would verify his suspicions and compel him to act upon them. Better the doubt. Better to believe that Willoughby had been a spendthrift. He would have no difficulty as to that, had it not been for those dogging memories of the little hotel in the rue de Rivoli.

Besides, as he said to himself, he had his own ax to grind. He endeavored, therefore, to take the reference to Fay jocosely. "That reminds me," he smiled, though the smile might have been a trifle nervous, "that if you don't want to renew Fay's lease when it falls in, I wish you'd make it over to me." Disconcerted by the look of amazement his words called up, he hastened to add: "I'd take it on any terms you please. You've only got to name them."

Masterman backed away to the large oblong library table strewn with papers and magazines. He seemed to need it for support. His tones were those of a man amazed to the point of awe. "What in the name of Heaven do you want that for?"

Thor steadied his nerve by lighting a cigarette. "To give me a footing in the village. I'm going into politics."

"O Lord!"

Thor hurried on. "Yes, I know how you feel. But to me it seems a duty."

"Seems a—*what?*"

The son felt obliged to be apologetic. "You see, father, so few men of the old American stock are going into politics nowadays—"

"Well, why should they?"

"The country has to be governed."

"Lots of fools to do that who are no good for anything else. Why should *you* dirty your hands with it?"

"That isn't the way I look at it."

"It's the way you *will* look at it when you know a little

more about it than you evidently do now. Of course, with your money you'll have a right to fritter away your time in anything you please; but as your father I feel that I ought to give you a word of warning. You wouldn't be a Masterman if you didn't need it—on that score?"

"What score?"

"The score of being caught by every humbugging socialistic scheme—"

"I'm not a socialist, father."

"Well, what are you? I thought you were."

"I'm not now. I've passed that phase."

"That's something to the good, at any rate."

"With politics in this country as they are—and so many alien peoples to be licked into shape—it's no use looking for the state to undertake anything progressive for another two hundred years."

"Ah! Want something more rapid-firing."

"Want something immediate."

"And you've found it?"

"Only in the conviction that whatever's to be done must be done by the individual. I've no theories any longer. I've finished with them all. I'm driven back on the conclusion that if anything is to be accomplished in the way of social betterment it must be by the man-to-man process in one's own small sphere. If we could get that put into practice on a considerable scale we should do more than the state will be able to carry out for centuries to come."

"Put what into practice?"

"The principle that no man shall let a friend or a neighbor suffer without relief when he can relieve him."

"Thor, you should have been God."

"I don't know anything about God, father. But if I were to create a God, I should make that his first commandment."

Masterman squared himself in front of his son. "So that's behind this scheme of yours for taking over Fay's lease. You're trying to trick me into doing what you know I won't do of my own accord. What could *you* do with the lease but make a present of it to old Fay? Politics be hanged! Come, now. Be frank with me."

Thor threw back his head. "I can't be wholly frank with you, father; but I'll be as frank as I can. I do want to help the poor old chap; you'd be sorry for him if you'd been seeing him as I have; but that was only one of my motives. Leaving politics out of the question, I have others. But I don't want to speak of them—yet. Probably I shall never need to speak of them at all."

Thor was willing that his father should say, "It's the girl!" but he contented himself with the curt statement: "I'm sorry, Thor; but you can't have the lease. I'm going to sell the place."

"But, father," the young man cried, "what's to become of Fay?"

"Isn't that what you asked me just now about Len Willoughby? Who do you think I am, Thor? Am I in this world to carry every lame dog on my back?"

"It isn't a question of every lame dog, but of an old tenant and an old friend."

"Toward whom I have what you're pleased to call a moral responsibility. Is that it?"

"That's it, father—put mildly."

"Well, I don't admit your moral responsibility; and, what's more, I'm not going to bear it. Do you understand?"

Thor felt himself growing white, with the whiteness that attended one of his surging waves of wrath. He clenched his fists. He drew away. But he couldn't keep himself from saying, quietly, with a voice that shook because of his very effort to keep it firm: "All right, father. If you don't bear it, I will."

He was moving toward the door when Archie called after him, "Thor, for God's sake, don't be a *fool!*"

He answered from the threshold, over his shoulder, "It's no use asking me not to do as I've said, father, because I can't help it." He was in the hall when he added, "And if I could, I shouldn't try."

CHAPTER XI

B Y the time his anger had cooled down, Thor regretted the words with which he had left his father's presence, and continued to regret them. They were braggart and useless. Whatever he might feel impelled to do, for either Leonard Willoughby or Jasper Fay, he could do better without announcing his intentions beforehand. He experienced a sense of guilt when, on the next day, and for many days afterward, his father showed by his manner that he had been wounded.

Lois Willoughby showed that she, too, had been wounded. The process of "easing the first one off," besides affording him side-lights on a woman's heart, involved him in an erratic course of blowing hot and cold that defeated his own ends. When he blew cold the chill was such that he blew hotter than ever to disperse it. He could see for himself that this seeming capriciousness made it difficult for Lois to preserve the equal tenor of her bearing, though she did her best.

He had kept away from her for a week or more, and would have continued to do so longer had he not been haunted by the look his imagination conjured up in her eyes. He knew its trouble, its bewilderment, its reflected heartache. "I'm a damned cad," he said to himself; and whenever he worked himself up to that point remorse couldn't send him quickly enough to pay her a visit of atonement.

He knew she was at home because he met one or two of the County Street ladies coming away from the house. With knowing looks they told him he should find her.

They did not, however, tell him that she had another visitor, whose voice he recognized while depositing his hat and overcoat on one of the Regency chairs in the tapestried square hall.

"Oh, don't go yet," Lois was saying. "Here's Dr. Thor Masterman. He'll want to see you."

But Rosie insisted on taking her departure, making polite excuses for the length of her call.

She was deliciously pretty; he saw that at once on entering. Wearing the new winter suit for which she had pinched and saved, and a hat of the moment's fashion, she easily dazzled Thor, though Lois could perceive, in details of material, the "cheapness" that in American eyes is the most damning of all qualities. Rosie's face was bright with the flush of social triumph, for the County Street ladies had been kind to her, and she had had tea with all the ceremony of which she read in the accredited annals of good society. If she had not been wondering whether or not the County Street ladies knew her brother was in jail, she could have suppressed all other causes for anxiety and given herself freely to the hour's bliss.

But she would not be persuaded to remain, taking her leave with a full command of graceful niceties. Thor could hardly believe she was his fairy of the hothouse. She was a princess, a marvel. "Beats them all," he said, gleefully, to himself, referring to the ladies of County Street, and almost including Lois Willoughby.

He did not quite include her. He perceived that he couldn't do so when, after having bowed Rosie to the door, he returned to take his seat in the drawing-room. There was a distinction about Lois, he admitted to himself, that neither prettiness nor fine clothes nor graceful niceties could rival. He wondered if she wasn't even more distinguished since this new something had come into her life—was it joy or grief?—which he himself had brought there.

Her greeting to him was of precisely the same shade as all her greetings during the past two months. It was like something rehearsed and executed to perfection. When she had given him his tea and poured another cup for herself, they talked of Rosie.

"Do you know," she said, in a musing tone, "I think the poor little thing has really enjoyed being here this afternoon?"

"Why shouldn't she?"

"Yes, but why should she? Apart from the very slight novelty of the thing—which to an American girl is no real novelty, after all—I don't understand what it is she cares so much about?"

He weighed the question seriously. "She finds a world of certain—what shall I say?—of certain amenities to which she's equal—any one can see that!—and which she hasn't got. That's something in itself—to a girl with imagination."

"I think she's in love," Lois said, suddenly.

Thor was startled. "Oh no, she isn't. She can't be. Who on earth could she be in love with?"

"Oh, it's not with you. Don't be alarmed," Lois smiled. It was so like Thor to be shy of a pretty girl. He had been so ever since she could remember him.

"That's good," he managed to say. He regained control of himself, though he tingled all over. "It would have to be with me or Dr. Hilary. We're the only two men, except the Italians, who ever appear on the place."

"Oh, you don't know," Lois said, pensively. "Girls like that often have what they call, rather picturesquely, a fellow."

"Oh, don't!" His cry was instantly followed by a nervous laugh. He felt obliged to explain. "It's so funny to hear you talk like that. It doesn't go with your style."

She took this pleasantly and they spoke of other things; but Thor was eager to get away. A real visit of atonement had become impossible. That must be put off for another day—perhaps for ever. He wasn't sure. He couldn't tell. For the minute his head was in a whirl. He hardly knew what he was saying, except that his rejoinders to Lois's remarks were more or less at random. Vital questions were pounding through his brain and demanding an answer. Who knew but that with regard to Rosie she was right—and yet wrong? Women, with their remarkable powers of divination, didn't always hit the nail directly on the head. It might be the case with Lois now. She might be right in her surmise that Rosie was in love, and mistaken in those light and cruel words: "Oh, not with you!" He didn't suppose it was with him. And yet . . . and yet . . . !

He got away at last, and tore through the winter twilight toward the old apple-orchard above the pond. He knew what he would say. "Rosie, are you in love with any one? If so, for God's sake, tell me." What he would do when she answered him was matter outside his present capacity for thought.

It had begun to snow. By the time he reached the house on the hill his shoulders were white. The necessity for shaking himself in the little entry gave the first prosaic chill to his ardor.

Rosie had returned and was preparing supper. The princess and marvel had resolved herself again into the fairy of the hothouse. Not that Thor minded that. What disconcerted him was her dry little manner of surprise. She had not expected him. There was nothing in her mother's condition to demand his call. She herself was busy. She had come from the kitchen to answer the door. A smell of cooking filled the house.

No one of these details could have kept him from carrying out his purpose; but together they were unromantic. How could he adjure her to tell him for God's sake whether or not she was in love with any one when he saw she was afraid that something was burning on the stove? He could only stammer out excuses for having come. Inventing on the spot new and incoherent directions for the treatment of Mrs. Fay, he took himself away again, not without humiliation.

Being in a savage mood as he stalked down the hill, he was working himself into a rage when an unexpected occurrence gave him other things to think of.

At the foot of the hill, just below the slope of the Square, was the terminus of the electric tram-line from the city. In summer it was a pretty spot, well shaded by ornamental trees, with a small Gothic church and its parsonage in the center of a trimly kept lawn. It was prettier still as Thor Masterman approached it, at the close of a winter's day, with the great soft flakes, heaping their beauty on roof and shrub and roadway, the whole lit up with plenty of cheerful electricity, and no eye to behold it but his own.

Because of this purity and solitude a black spot was the more conspicuous; and because it was a moving black spot it caught the onlooker's glance at once. It was a moving black spot, though it remained in one place—on the cement seat that circled a copper-beech-tree for the convenience of villagers waiting for the cars. It was extraordinary that any one should choose this uninviting, snow-covered resting-place, unless he couldn't do otherwise.

The doctor in Thor was instantly alert, but before advancing many paces he had made his guess. Patients were beginning to take his time, rendering his afternoons less free; and so what might have been expected had happened. Mr. Willoughby had managed to come homeward by the electric car, but was unable to go any farther.

Nevertheless, Thor was startled as he crossed the roadway to hear a great choking sob. The big creature was huddled somehow on the seat, but with face and arms turned to the trunk of the tree, against whose cold bark he wept. He wept shamelessly aloud, with broken exclamations of which "O my God! O my God!" was all that Thor could hear distinctly.

"It's delirium this time, for sure," he said to himself, as he laid his hand on the great snow-heaped shoulder.

He changed his mind on that score as soon as Mr. Willoughby was able to speak coherently. "I'm heartbroken, Thor. Haven't touched a thing to-day—scarcely. But I'm all in."

More sobs followed. It was with difficulty that Thor could get the lumbering body on its feet. "You mustn't stay here, Mr. Willoughby. You'll catch cold. Come along home with me."

"I do' wan' to go home, Thor. Got no home now. Ruined—tha's what I am. Ruined. Your father's kicked me out. All my money gone. No' a cent left in the world."

Thor dragged him onward. "But you must come home just the same, Mr. Willoughby. You can't stay out here. The next car will be along in a minute, and every one will see you."

"I do' care who sees me, Thor. I'm ruined. Father says I'll have to go. Got all the papers ready. O my God! what 'll Bessie say?"

As they stumbled forward through the snow Thor tried to learn what had happened.

"Got all my money and then kicked me out," was the only explanation. "Not a cent in the world. What 'll Bessie say? Oh, what 'll Bessie say? All her money. Hasn't got a hundred thousand dollars left out of tha' grea' big estate. Make away with myself. Tha's what I'll do. O my God! my God!"

On arriving in front of the house Thor saw lights in the drawing-room. Lois was probably still there. It was no more than a half-hour since he had left her, and other callers might have succeeded him. He tried to steer his charge round the corner toward the side entrance in Willoughby's Lane.

But Len grew querulous. "I do' want to go in the side door. Go in the front door, hang it all! Father can't turn me out of my own house, the infernal hound."

The door opened, and Lois stood in the oblong of light. "Oh, what is it?" she cried, peering outward. "Is it you, Thor? What's the matter?"

"Treat me like a servant," Willoughby complained, as, with Thor supporting him, he stumbled up the steps. "I do' want to go in the side door. Front door good enough for me. No confounded kitchen-boy, if I *am* ruined. Look here, Lois," he rambled on, when he had got into the hall and Thor was helping him to take off his overcoat—"look here, Lois; we haven't got a cent in the world. Tha's wha' we haven't got—not a cent in the world. Archie Masterman's got my money, and your money, and your mother's money, and the whole damned money of all of us. Kicked me out now. No good to him any more."

With some difficulty Thor got him to his room, where he undressed him and put him to bed. On his return to the hall he found Lois seated in one of the arm-chairs, her face pale.

"Oh, Thor, is this what you meant a few weeks ago?"

He did his best to explain the situation to her gently. "I don't know just what's happened, but I'm afraid there's trouble ahead."

She nodded. "Yes; I've been expecting it, and now I suppose it's come."

"I shouldn't wonder if it had. But you must be brave, Lois, and not think matters worse than they are."

"Oh, I sha'n't do that," she said, with a hint of haughtiness at his solicitude. "Don't worry about me. I'm quite capable of bearing whatever's to be borne. Please go on."

"If anything has happened," he said, speaking from

where he stood in the middle of the floor, "it's that father wants to dissolve the partnership."

"I've been looking for that. So has mamma."

"And if they do dissolve the partnership, I'm afraid—I'm afraid there'll be very little money coming to Mr. Willoughby."

"Whose fault would that be?"

"Frankly, Lois, I don't know. It might be that of my father or of yours—"

"And I shouldn't think you'd want to find out."

He looked down at her curiously. "Why do you say that? Shouldn't you?"

She seemed to shiver. "Why should I? If the money's gone, it's gone. Whether my father has squandered it or your father has—" She rose and crossed the hall to the stairs, where, with a foot on the lowest of the steps, she leaned on the pilaster of the balustrade. "I don't want to know," she said, with energy. "If the money's gone, they've shuffled it away between them; and I don't see that it would help either you or me to find out who's to blame."

It was a minute at which Thor could easily have brought out the words which for so many years he had supposed he would one day speak to her. His pity was such that it would have been a luxury to tell her to throw all the material part of her care on him. If he could have said that much without saying more he would have had no hesitation. But there was still a chance of the miracle happening with regard to Rosie Fay. Love was love—and sweet. It was first love, and, in its way, it was young love. It was springtide love. The dew of the morning was on it, and the freshness of sunrise. It was hard to renounce it, even to go to the aid of one whose need of him was so desperate that to hide it she turned her face away. Instead of the words of cheer and rescue that were almost gushing to his lips, he said, soberly:

"Has your mother any idea of what's going on?"

She began pacing restlessly up and down. "Oh, she's been worried for the last few weeks. She couldn't help knowing something. Papa's been dropping so many hints that she's been meaning to see your father."

"I suppose it will be very hard for her."

She paused, confronting him. "It will be at first. But she'll rise to it. She does that kind of thing. You don't know mother. Very few people do. She simply adores papa. It's pathetic. All this time that he's been so—so—she won't recognize it. She won't admit for a second—or let me admit it—that he's anything but tired or ill. It's splendid—and yet there's something about it that almost breaks my heart. Mamma has lots of pluck, you know. You mightn't think it—"

"Oh, I know it."

"I'm glad you do. People in general see only one side of her, but it's not the only side. She has her weaknesses. I see that well enough. She's terribly a woman; and she can't grow old. But that's not criminal, is it? There's a great deal in her that's never been called on, and perhaps this trouble will bring it out."

He spoke admiringly. "It will bring out a great deal in you."

She began again to pace up and down. "Oh, me! I'm so useless. I've never been of any help to any one. Do you know, at times, latterly, I've envied that little Rosie Fay?"

"Why?"

"Because she's got duties and responsibilities and struggles. She's got something more to do than dress and play tennis and make calls. There are people who depend on her—"

"She's splendid, isn't she?"

She paused in her restless pacing. "She might be. She is—very nearly."

Though he had taken the opportunity to get further away from the appeal of her distress, he felt a pang of humiliation in the promptness with which she followed his lead.

But he couldn't go on with the discussion. It was too sickening. Every inflection of her voice implied that with her own need he had no longer anything to do—that it was all over—that she recognized the fact—that she was trying her utmost to let him off easily. That she should suspect the truth, or connect the change with Rosie Fay, he knew was out of the question. It was not the way in which her mind would work. If she accounted for the situation at all it would probably be on the ground that when it came to the point he had found that he didn't care for her. The promises he had tacitly made and she had tacitly understood she was ready to give back.

He was quite alive to the fact that her generosity made his impotence the more pitiable. That he should stand tongue-tied and helpless before the woman whom he had allowed to think that she could count on him was galling not only to his manhood, but to all those primary instincts that sent him to the aid of weakness. There was a minute in which it seemed to him that if he did not on the instant redeem his self-respect it would be lost to him for ever. After all, he did care for her—in a way. There was no woman in the world toward whom he felt an equal degree of reverence. More than that, there was no woman in the world whom he could admit so naturally to share his life, whose life he himself could so naturally share. If Rosie were to marry him, the whole process would be different. In that case there would be no sharing; there would be nothing but a wild, gipsy joy. His delight would be to heap happiness upon her, content with her acceptance and the very little which was all he could expect her to give him in return. With Lois Willoughby it would be equality, partnership, companionship, and a life of mutual comprehension and respect. That would be much, of course; it was what a few months ago he would have thought enough; it was plainly that with which he must manage to be satisfied.

He was about to plunge in—to plunge in with one last backward look to the more exquisite joys he must leave behind—and tell her that his strength and loyalty were hers to dispose of as she would when she herself unwittingly balked the impulse.

It was still to hold open to him the way of escape that she continued to speak of Rosie. "If she were to marry some nice fellow, like Jim Breen, for instance—"

Thor bounded. "Like—who?"

She was too deeply preoccupied with her own emotions to notice his. "He was attentive to her for a long time once."

He cried out, incredulously: "Oh no; it couldn't be. She's too—too superior."

"I'm afraid the superiority is just the trouble—though I don't know anything about it, beyond the gossip one hears in the village. Any one who goes to so many of the working people's houses as I do hears it all."

He was still incredulous. "And you've heard—*that*?"

"I've heard that poor Jim wanted to marry her—and she wouldn't look at him. It's a pity, I think. She'd be a great deal happier in marrying a man with the same kind of ways as herself than she'd be with some one—I can only put it," she added, with a rueful smile, "in a way you don't like, Thor—than she'd be with some one of another station in life."

His heart pounded so that he could hardly trust himself to speak with the necessary coolness. "Is there any question of—of any one of another station in life?"

"N-no; only that if she *is* in love—and of course I'm only guessing at it—I think it's very likely to be with some one of that kind."

The statement which was thrown out with gentle indifference affected him so profoundly that had she again declared that it was not with him he could have taken it with equanimity. With whom else could it be? It wasn't with Antonio, and it wasn't with Dr. Hilary. There was the choice. Were there any other rival, he couldn't help knowing it. He had sometimes suspected—no, it was hardly enough for suspicion!—he had sometimes hoped—but it had been hardly enough for hope!—and yet sometimes, when she gave him that dim, sidelong smile or turned to him with the earnest, wide-open look in her greenish eyes, he had thought that possibly—just possibly . . .

He didn't know what answers he made to her further remarks. A faint memory remained with him of talking incoherently against reason, against sentiment, against time, as, with her velvety regard resting upon him sadly, he swung on his overcoat and hurried to take his leave.

CHAPTER XII

HE hurried because inwardly he was running away from the figure he had cut. Never had he supposed that in any one's time of need—to say nothing of hers!—he could have proved so worthless. And he hurried because he knew a decision one way or the other had become imperative. And he hurried because his failure convinced him that so long as there was a possibility that Rosie cared for him secretly he would never do anything for Lois Willoughby. Whatever his sentiment toward the woman-friend of his youth, he was tied and bound by the stress of a love of which the call was primitive. He might be over-abrupt; he might startle her; but at the worst he should escape from this unbearable state of inactivity.

So he hurried. It had stopped snowing; the evening was now fair and cold. As it was nearly six o'clock, his father would probably have come home. He would make him first an offer of new terms, and he would see Rosie afterward. His excitement was such that he knew he could neither eat nor sleep till the questions in his heart were answered.

But on reaching his own gate he was surprised to see Mrs. Willoughby's motor turn in at the driveway and roll up to the door. It was not that there was anything strange in her paying his mother a call, but to-day the circumstances were unusual. Anything might happen. Anything might have happened already. On reaching the door he let himself in with misgiving.

He recognized the visitor's voice at once, but there was

a note in it he had never heard before. It was a plaintive note, and rather childlike:

"Oh, Ena, *what's* become of my money?"

His mother's inflections were as childlike as the other's, and as full of distress. "How do I know, Bessie? Why don't you ask Archie?"

"I have asked him. I've just come from there. I can't make out anything he says. He's been trying to tell me that we've spent it—when I know we haven't spent it."

There were tears in Ena's voice as she said: "Well, I can't explain it, Bessie. *I* don't know anything about business."

From where he stood, with his hand on the knob, as he closed the door behind him, Thor could see into the huge, old-fashioned, gilt-framed mirror over the chimney-piece in the drawing-room. The two women were standing, separated by a small table which supported an azalea in bloom. His stepmother, in a soft, trailing house-gown, her hands behind her back, seemed taller and slenderer than ever in contrast to Mrs. Willoughby's dumpiness, dwarfed as it was by an enormous muff and encumbering furs.

The latter drew herself up indignantly. Her tone changed. "You do know something about business, Ena. You knew enough about it to drag Len and me into what we never would have thought of doing, if you and Archie hadn't—"

"I? Why, Bessie, you must be crazy."

"I'm not crazy; though God knows it's enough to make me so. I remember everything as if it had happened this afternoon."

There was a faint scintillation in the diamonds in Ena's brooch and ear-rings as she tossed her head. "If you do that you must recall that I was afraid of it from the first."

Bessie was quick to detect the admission. "Why?" she demanded. "If you were afraid of it, *why* were you afraid? You weren't afraid without seeing something to be afraid of."

Mrs. Masterman nearly wept. "I don't know anything about business at all, Bessie."

"Oh, don't tell me that," Bessie broke in, fiercely. "You knew enough about it to see that Archie wanted our money in 1892."

"But *I* hadn't anything to do with it."

"Hadn't anything to do with it? Then who had? Who was it suggested to me that Len should go into business?—one evening?—in the Hôtel de Marsan?—after dinner? Who was that?"

"If I said anything at all it was that I hated business and everything that had to do with it."

"Oh, I can understand that well enough," Bessie exclaimed, scornfully. "You hated it because you saw already that your husband was going to ruin us. Come now, Ena! Didn't you?"

Mrs. Masterman protested tearfully. "I didn't know anything about it. I only wished that Archie would let you and your money alone—and I wish it still."

"Very well, then!" Bessie cried, flinging her hands outward dramatically. "Isn't that what I'm saying? You knew something. You knew it and you let us go ahead. You not only let us go ahead, but you led us on. You could see already that Archie was spinning his web like a spider, and that he'd catch us as flies. Now didn't you? Tell the truth, Ena. Wasn't it in your mind from the first? Long before it was in his? I'll say that for Archie, that I don't suppose he really *meant* to ruin us, while you knew he *would*. That's the difference between a man and his wife. The man only drifts, but the wife sees years ahead what he's drifting to. You saw it, Ena—"

When his stepmother bowed her head to sob into her handkerchief Thor ventured to enter the room. Neither of the women noticed him.

"I must say, Ena," Bessie continued, "that seems to me

frightful. I don't know what you can be made of that you've lived cheerfully through these last eighteen years when you knew what was coming. If it had been coming to yourself—well, that might be borne. But to stand by and watch for it to overtake some one else—some one who'd always been your friend—some one you liked, for I do believe you've liked me, in your way and my way—that, I must say, is the limit—*cela passe les bornes*. Now, doesn't it?"

Mrs. Masterman struggled to speak, but her sobs prevented her.

"In a way it's funny," Bessie continued, philosophically, "how bad a good woman can be. You're a good woman, Ena, of a kind. That is, you're good in as far as you're not bad; and I suppose that for a woman that's a very fair average. But I can tell you that there are sinners whom the world has scourged to the bone who haven't *begun* to do what you've been doing these past eighteen years—who wouldn't have had the nerve for it. No, Ena," she continued, with another sweeping gesture. "'Pon my soul, I don't know what you're made of. I almost think I admire you. I couldn't have done it; I'll be hanged if I could. There are women who've committed murder and who haven't been as cool as you. They've committed murder in a frantic fit of passion that went as quick as it came, and they've swung for it, or done time for it. But they'd never have had the pluck to sit and smile and wait for this minute as you've waited for it—when you saw it from such a long way off."

It was the crushed attitude in which his stepmother sank weeping into a chair that broke the spell by which Thor had been held paralyzed; but before he could speak Bessie turned and saw him.

"Oh, so it's you, Thor. Well, I wish you could have come a minute ago to hear what I've been saying."

"I've heard it, Mrs. Willoughby—"

"Then I am sure you must agree with me. Or rather,

you would if you knew how things had been managed in Paris eighteen years ago. I've been trying to tell your dear stepmother that we've been mistaken in her. We haven't done her justice. We've thought of her as just a sweet and gentle ladylike person, when all the while she's been a heroine. She's been colossal—as Clytemnestra was colossal, and Lady Macbeth. She beats them both; for I don't believe either of them could have watched the sword of Damocles taking eighteen years to fall on a friend and not have had nervous prostration—while she's as fresh as ever."

He laid his hand on her arm. "You'll come away now, won't you, Mrs. Willoughby?" he begged.

She adjusted her furs hurriedly. "All right, Thor. I'll come. I only want to say one thing more—"

"No, no; please!"

"I will say it," she insisted, as he led her from the room, "because it 'll do Ena good. It's just this," she threw back over her shoulder, "that I forgive you, Ena. You're so magnificent that I can't nurse a grudge against you. When a woman has done what you've done she may be punished by her own conscience—but not by me. I'm lost in admiration for the scale on which she carries out her crimes."

By the time they were in the porch, with the door closed behind them, Bessie's excitement subsided suddenly. Her voice became plaintive and childlike again, as she said, wistfully:

"Oh, Thor, do you think it's all gone?—that we sha'n't get any of it back? I know we haven't spent it. We *can't* have spent it."

Since Thor was Thor, there was only one thing for him to say. He needed no time to reflect or form resolutions. Whatever the cost to him, in whatever way, he could say nothing else. "You'll get it all back, Mrs. Willoughby. Don't worry about it any more. Just leave it to me."

But Bessie was not convinced. "I don't see how that's

going to be. If your father says the money is gone, it *is* gone—whether we've spent it or not. Trust him!" Nevertheless, she kissed him, saying: "But I don't blame you, Thor. If there were two like you in the world it would be too good a place to live in, and Len and Lois think the same."

He got her into the motor and closed the door upon her. Standing on the door-step, he watched it crawl down the avenue, like a great black beetle on the snow. As it passed the gateway his father appeared, coming on foot from the electric car.

CHAPTER XIII

ON re-entering the house, Thor waited for his father in the hall. Finding the drawing-room empty, and inferring that his mother had gone up-stairs, he decided to say nothing of the scene between her and Mrs. Willoughby. For the time being his own needs demanded right of way. Nothing else could be attended to till they had received consideration.

With that reflection something surged in him—surged and exulted. He was to be allowed to speak of his love at last! He was to be forced to confess it! If he was never to name it again, he would do so this once, getting some outlet for his passion! He both glowed and trembled. He both strained forward and recoiled. Already he felt drunk with a wine that roused the holier emotions as ardently as it fired the senses. He could scarcely take in the purport of his father's words as the latter stamped the snow from his boots in the entry and said:

"Has that poor woman been here? Sorry for her, Thor; sorry for her from the bottom of my heart."

The young man had no response to make. He was in a realm in which the reference had no meaning. Archie continued, while hanging his overcoat and hat in the closet at the foot of the stairs:

"Impossible to make her understand. Women like that can never see why they shouldn't eat their cake and have it, too. Books open for her inspection. But what's one to do?"

When he emerged from the closet Thor saw that his face was gray. He looked mortally tired and sad. He

had been sad for some weeks past—sad and detached—
ever since the night when he had made his ineffectual
bid for the care of Thor's prospective money. He had
betrayed no hint of resentment toward his son—nothing
but this dignified lassitude, this reserved, high-bred,
speechless expression of failure that smote Thor to the
heart. But this evening he looked worn as well, worn
and old, though brave and patient and able to command
a weary, flickering smile.

"But I'm glad it's come. It will be a relief to have it
over. Seen it coming so long that it's been like a nightmare.
Rather have come to grief myself—assure you I would."

"Father, could I speak to you for a few minutes?"

"About this?"

"No, not about this; about something else—something
rather important."

There was a sudden gleam in the father's eyes which
gave Thor a second pang. He had seen it once or twice
already during these weeks of partial estrangement.
It was the gleam of hope—of hope that Thor might have
grown repentant. It had the sparkle of fire in it when,
seated in a business attitude at the desk which held the
center of the library, he looked up expectantly at his son.
"Well, my boy?"

Thor remained standing. "It's about that property
of Fay's, father."

"Oh, again?" The light in the eyes went out with the
suddenness of an electric lamp.

"I only want to say this, father," Thor hurried on, so
as to get the interview over, "that if you want to sell the
place, I'll take it. I'll take it on your own terms. You
can make them what you like."

Archie leaned on the desk, passing his hand over his
brow. "I'm sorry, Thor. I can't."

Thor had the curious reminiscent sensation of being
once more a little boy, with some pleasure forbidden him.
"Oh, father, why? I want it awfully."

"So I see. I don't see why you should, but—"

"Well, I'll tell you. I want to protect Fay, because—"

Masterman interrupted without looking up. "And that's just what I don't want to do. I want to get rid of the lot."

Rid of the lot! The expression was alarming. In his father's mind the issue, then, was personal. It was not only personal, but it was inclusive. It included Rosie. She was rated in—the lot. Clearly the minute had come at which to speak plainly.

"If you want to get rid of them on my account, father, I may as well tell you—"

"No; it's got nothing to do with you." He was still resting his forehead on his hand, looking downward at the blotting-paper on his desk. "It's Claude."

Thor started back. "Claude? What's he got to do with it?"

"I hadn't made up my mind whether to tell you or not; but—"

"He doesn't even know them. Of course he knows who they are. Fay was Grandpa Thorley's—"

Masterman continued to speak wearily. "He may not know them all. It's motive enough for my action that he knows—the girl."

"Oh no, he doesn't."

"You'd better ask him."

"I have asked him."

"Then you'd better ask him again."

"But, father, she couldn't know him without my seeing it. I'm at the house nearly every day. The mother, you know."

"Apparently your eyes aren't sharp enough. You should take a lesson from your uncle Sim."

"But, father, I don't understand—"

"Then I'll tell you. It seems that Claude has known this girl for the past four or five months—"

"Oh no, no! That's all wrong. It isn't three months since I talked to Claude about her. Claude didn't even remember they had a girl. He'd forgotten it."

"I know what I'm talking about, Thor. Don't contradict. Seems your uncle Sim has had his eye on them all along."

Thor smote his side with his clenched fist. "There's some mistake, father. It can't *be*."

"I wish there was a mistake, Thor. But there isn't. If I could afford it I should send Claude abroad. Send him round the world. But I can't just now, with this mix-up in the business. There's no doubt but that the girl is bad—"

"Father!"

If Masterman had been looking up he would have seen the convulsion of pain on his son's face, and got some inkling of his state of mind.

"As bad as they make 'em—" he went on, tranquilly.

"No, no, father. You mustn't say that."

"I can't help saying it, Thor. I know how you feel about Claude. You feel as I do myself. But you and I must take hold of him and save him. We must get rid of this girl—"

"But she's not bad, father—"

Masterman raised himself and leaned back in his chair. He saw that Thor was white, with curious black streaks and shadows in his long, gaunt face. "Oh, I know how you feel," he said, again. "It does seem monstrous that the thing should have happened to Claude; but, after all, he's young, and with a little tact we can pull him out. I've said nothing to your mother, and don't mean to. No use alarming her needlessly. I've not said anything to Claude, either. Only known the thing for four or five days. Don't want to make him restive, or drive him to take the bit between his teeth. High-spirited young fellow, Claude is. Needs to be dealt with tactfully.

Thing will be, to cut away the ground beneath his feet without his knowing it—by getting rid of the girl."

"But I know Rosie Fay, father, and she's not—"

"Now, my dear Thor, what *is* a girl but bad when she's willing to meet a man clandestinely night after night—?"

"Oh, but she hasn't done it."

"And I tell you she has done it. Ever since last summer. Night after night."

"Where?" Thor demanded, hoarsely.

"In the woods above Duck Rock. Look here," the father suggested, struck with a good idea, "the next time Claude says he has an engagement to go out with Billy Cheever, why don't you follow him—?"

There was both outrage and authority in Thor's abrupt cry, "Father!"

"Oh, I know how you feel. You'd rather trust him. Well, I would myself. It's the plan I'm going on. We mustn't be too hard on him, must we? Sympathetic steering is what he wants. Fortunately we're both men of the world and can accept the situation with no Puritanical hypocrisies. He's not the first young fellow who's got into the clutches of a hussy—"

It was to keep himself from striking his father down that Thor got out of the room. For an instant he had seen red; and across the red the word *parricide* flashed in letters of fire. It might have been a vision. It was frightening.

Outside it was a night of dim, spirit-like radiance. The white of the earth and the violet of the sky were both spangled with lights. Low on the horizon the full moon was a glorious golden disk.

The air was sweet and cold. As he struck down the avenue, of which the snow was broken only by his own and his father's footsteps and the wheels of Bessie's car, he bared his head to cool his forehead and the hot masses of his hair. He breathed hard; he was aching; his distress was like that of being roused from a weird, appalling dream. He had not yet got control of his faculties. He scarcely knew why he had come out, except that he couldn't stay within.

On nearing the street the buzzing of an electric car reminded him that Claude was probably coming home. Instinctively he turned his steps away from meeting him, tramping up the long, white, empty stretch of County Street.

At Willoughby's Lane he turned up the hill, not for any particular purpose, but because the tramping there would be a little harder. He needed exertion. It eased the dull ache of confused inward pain. In the Willoughby house there was no light except in the hall and in Bessie's bedroom. Mother and daughter had doubtless taken refuge in the latter spot to discuss the disastrous turn of their fortunes. Ah, well! There would probably be nothing to keep him from going to their rescue now.

Probably! He clung to the faint chance offered by the word. He didn't know the real circumstances—yet. *Probably* his father had been accurate in his statements, even though wrong in what he had inferred. *Probably* Claude and Rosie had met—night after night—secretly—in the woods—in the dark. *Probably!* He stopped dead in his walk; he threw back his head and groaned to the violet sky; he pulled with both hands at his collar as though choking. Secretly—in the woods—in the dark! It was awful—and yet it was entrancing. If Rosie had only come to meet *him* like that!—in that mystery!—in that seclusion!—with that trust!—with that surrender of herself!

"How can I blame Claude?"

It was his first formulated thought. He tramped on again. How could he blame Claude? Poor Claude! He had his difficulties. No one knew that better than Thor. And if Rosie loved the boy . . .

Below the ridge of the long, wooded hill there was a road running parallel to County Street. He turned into that. But he began to perceive to what goal he was tending. He had taken this direction aimlessly; and yet it was as if his feet had acted of their own accord, without the guiding impulse of the mind. From a long, straight stem a banner of smoke floated heavy and luminous against the softer luminosity of the sky. He knew now where he was going and what he had to do.

But he paused at the gate, when he got there, uncertain as to where at this hour he should find her. There was a faint light in the mother's room, but none elsewhere in the house. The moon was by this time high enough to throw a band of radiance across Thorley's Pond and strike pale gleams from the glass of the hothouse roofs.

It required some gazing to detect in Rosie's greenhouse the blurred glow of a lamp. He remembered that there was a desk near this spot at which she sometimes wrote. She was writing there now—perhaps to Claude.

But she was not writing to Claude; she was making out bills. As bookkeeper to the establishment, as well as utility woman in general, it was the one hour in the day when she had leisure for the task. She raised her head to peer down the long, dim aisle of flowers on hearing him open the door.

"It's I, Rosie," he called to her, as he passed between banks of carnations. "Don't be afraid."

She was not afraid, but she was excited. As a matter of fact, she was saying to herself, "He's found out." It was what she had been expecting. She had long ago begun to see that his almost daily visits were not on her mother's account. He had been coming less as a doctor than as a detective. Very well! If his detecting had been successful, so much the better. Since the battle had to be fought some time, it couldn't begin too soon.

She remained seated, her right hand holding the pen, her left lying on the open pages of the ledger. He spoke before he had fully emerged into the glow of the lamp.

"Oh, Rosie! What's this about you and Claude?"

Her little face grew hard and defiant. She was not to be deceived by this wounded, unhappy tone. "Well—what?" she asked, guardedly, looking up at him.

He stooped. His face was curiously convulsed. It frightened her. "Do you *love* him?"

Instinctively she took an attitude of defense, rising and pushing back her chair, to shield herself behind it. "And what if I do?"

"Then, Rosie, you should have told me."

Again the heartbroken cry seemed to her a bit of trickery to get her confidence. "Told you? How could I tell you? What should I tell you for?"

"How long have you loved him?"

Her face was set. The shifting opal lights in her eyes were the fires of her will. She would speak. She would hide nothing. Let the responsibility be on Claude. Her avowal was like that of a calamity or a crime. "I've loved him ever since I knew him."

"And how long is that?"

"It will be five months the day after to-morrow."

"Tell me, Rosie. How did it come about?"

She was still defiant. She put it briefly. "I was in the wood above Duck Rock. He came by. He spoke to me."

"And you loved him from the first?"

She nodded, with the desperate little air he had long ago learned to recognize.

"Oh, Rosie, tell me this. Do you love him—much?"

She was quite ready with her answer. It was as well the Mastermans should know. "I'd die for him."

"Would you, Rosie? And what about him?"

Her lip quivered. "Oh, men are not so ready to die for love as women are."

He leaned toward her, supporting himself with his hands on the desk. "And you are ready, Rosie! You really—would?"

She thought he looked wild. He terrified her. She

"I DON'T WANT TO PART YOU. I WANT TO BRING YOU TOGETHER"

shrank back into the dimness of a mass of foliage. "Oh, what do you mean? What are you asking me for? Why do you come here? Go away."

"I'll go presently, Rosie. You won't be sorry I've come. I only want you to tell me all about it. There are reasons why I want to know."

"Then why don't you ask him?" she demanded, passionately. "He's your brother."

"Because I want you to tell me the story first."

There was such tenderness in his voice that she grew reassured in spite of her alarm. "What do you want me to say?"

"I want you to say first of all that you know I'm your friend."

"You can't be my friend," she said, suspiciously, "unless you're Claude's friend, too; and Claude wouldn't own to a friend who tried to part us."

"I don't want to part you, Rosie. I want to bring you together."

The assertion was too much for credence. She was thrown back on the hypothesis of trickery. "You?"

"Yes, Rosie. Has Claude never told you that he's more to me than any one in the world, except—" He paused; he panted; he tried to keep it back, but it forced itself out in spite of his efforts—"except you." Once having said it, he repeated it: "Except you, Rosie; except—you."

Though he was still leaning toward her across the desk, his head sank. There was silence between them. It was long before Rosie, the light in her eyes concentrated to two brilliant, penetrating points, crept forward from the sheltering mass of foliage. She could hardly speak above a whisper.

"Except—who?"

He lifted his head. She noticed subconsciously that his face was no longer wild, but haggard. He spoke gently: "Except you, Rosie. You're most to me in the world."

As she bent toward him her mouth and eyes betrayed her horror at the irony of this discovery. She would rather never have known it than know it now. It was all she could do to gasp the one word, "Me?"

"I shouldn't have told you," he hurried on, apologetically, "but I couldn't help it. Besides, I want you to understand how utterly I'm your friend. I ask nothing more than to be allowed to help you and Claude in every way—"

She cried out. The thing was preposterous. "You're going to do that—*now?*"

"I'm your big brother, Rosie—the big brother to both of you. That's what I shall be in future. And what I've said will be a dead secret between us, won't it? I shouldn't have told you, but I couldn't help it. It was stronger than me, Rosie. Those things sometimes are. But it's a secret now, dead and buried. It's as if it hadn't been said, isn't it? And if I should marry some one else—"

This was too much. It was like the world slipping from her at the minute she had it within her grasp. The horror was not only in her eyes and mouth, but in her voice. "Are you going to marry some one else?"

"I might have to, Rosie—for a lot of reasons. It might be my duty. And now that I can't marry you—"

She uttered a sort of wail. "Oh!"

"Don't be sorry for me, Rosie dear. I can't stand it. I can stand it better if you're not sorry—"

"But I *am*," she cried, desperately.

"Then I must thank you—only don't be. It will make me grieve the more for saying what I never should have said. But that's a secret between us, as I said before, isn't it? And if I do marry—she'll never find it out, will she? That wouldn't do, would it, Rosie?"

His words struck her as passing all the bounds of practical common sense. They were so mad that she felt herself compelled to ask for more assurance. "Are you—in love—with—with *me?*" If the last syllable had been louder it would have been a scream.

"Oh, Rosie, forgive me! I shouldn't have told you. It was weak. It was wrong. I only did it to show you how you could trust me. But I should have showed you that some other way. You'd already told me how it was between you and Claude, and so it was treachery to him. But I never dreamed of trying to come between you. Believe me, I didn't. I swear to you I only want—"

She broke in, panting. She wouldn't have spoken crudely or abruptly if there had been any other way. But the chance was there. In another minute it might be too late. "Yes; but when I said that about Claude—"

She didn't know how to go on. He encouraged her. "Yes, Rosie?"

She wrung her hands. "Oh, don't you *see?* When I said that about Claude—I didn't—I didn't know—"

He hastened to relieve her distress. "You didn't know I cared for you?"

"No!" The word came out with another long wail.

He looked at her curiously. "But what's that got to do with it?"

Her eyes implored him piteously, while she beat the palm of one hand against the back of the other. It was terrible that he couldn't see what she meant—and the moments slipping away!

"It wouldn't have made you love Claude any the less, would it?"

She had to say something. If she didn't he would never understand. "Not love, perhaps; but—"

The sudden coldness in his voice terrified her again—but differently. "But what, Rosie?"

She cried out, as if the words rent her. "But Claude has no—*money*."

"And I have. Is that it?"

It was no use to deny it. She nodded dumbly. Besides, she counted on his possession of common sense, though his use of it was slow.

He raised himself from his attitude of leaning on the desk. It was his turn to take shelter amid the dark foliage behind him. He couldn't bear to let the lamplight fall too fully on his face. "Is it this, Rosie," he asked, with an air of bewilderment, "that you'd marry me because I have—the money?"

It seemed to Rosie that the question gave her reasonable cause for exasperation. She was almost sobbing as she said: "Well, I can't marry Claude *without* money. He can't marry me." A ray was thrown into her little soul when she gasped in addition, "And there's father and mother and Matt!"

Thor's expression lost some of its bewilderment because it deepened to sternness. "But Claude means to marry you, doesn't he?"

She cried out again, with that strange effect of the words rending her. "I don't—*know*."

He had a moment of wild fear lest his father had been right, after all. "You don't know? Then—what's your relation to each other?"

"I don't know that, either. Claude won't tell me." She crossed her hands on her bosom as she said, desperately, "I sometimes think he doesn't mean anything at all."

The terror of the instant passed. "Oh yes, he does, Rosie. I'll see to that."

"Do you mean that you'll make him marry me?"

He smiled pitifully. "There'll be no making, Rosie. You leave it to me."

He turned from her not merely because the last word had been spoken, but through fear lest something might be breaking within himself. On regaining the white roadway he thought he saw Jasper Fay in the shadow of the house, but he was too deeply stricken to speak to him. He went up the hill and farther from the village. It was not yet eight o'clock, but time had ceased to have measurement. He went up the hill to be alone in that solitude which was all that for the moment he could endure. He climbed higher than the houses and the snow-covered gardens; his back was toward the moon and the glow above the city. The prospect of reaching the summit gave something for his strong body to strain forward to.

The ridge, when he got to it, was treeless, wind-swept, and moon-swept. It was a great white altar, victimless and bare. He felt devastated, weak. It was a relief, bodily and mental, to sink to his knees—to fall—to lie at his length. He pressed his hot face into the cool, consoling whiteness, as a man might let himself weep on a pillow. His arms were outstretched beyond his head. His fingers pierced beneath the snow till they touched the tender, nestling mosses. All round him there was silveriness and silence, and overhead the moon.

CHAPTER XIV

DESCENDING the hill, Thor saw a light in his uncle Sim's stable, and knew that Delia was being settled for the night. Uncle Sim still lived in the ramshackle house to which his father—old Dr. Masterman, as elderly people in the village called him—had taken his young wife, who had been Miss Lucy Dawes. In this house both Sim and Archie Masterman were born. It was the plainest of dwellings, painted by wind and weather to a dovelike silver-gray. Here lived Uncle Sim, cared for in the domestic sense by a lady somewhat older and more eccentric than himself, known to the younger Mastermans as Cousin Amy Dawes.

Thor avoided the house and Cousin Amy Dawes, going directly to the stable. By the time he had reached the door Uncle Sim was shutting it. In the light of a lantern standing in the snow the naked elms round about loomed weirdly. The greetings were brief.

"Hello, Uncle Sim!"

"Hello, Thor!"

Thor made an effort to reduce the emotional tremor of his voice to the required minimum. "Father's been telling me about Claude and Rosie Fay."

Uncle Sim turned the key in the lock with a loud grating. "Father had to do it, did he? Thought you might have caught on to that by yourself. One of the reasons I sent you into the Fay family."

"Did you know it then?—already?"

"Didn't *know* it. Couldn't help putting two and two together."

"You see everything, Uncle Sim."

Uncle Sim stooped to pick up the lantern. "See every-thing that's under my nose. Thought you could, too."

"This hasn't been under my nose."

"Oh, well! There are noses and noses. A donkey has one kind and a dog has another."

Thor was not a finished actor, but he was doing his best to play a part. "Well, what do you think now?"

"What do I think now? I don't think anything—about other people's business."

"I think we ought to do something," Thor declared, with energy.

"All right. Every one to his mind. Only it's great fun to let other people settle their own affairs."

"Settle their own affairs—and suffer."

"Yes, and suffer. Suffering doesn't hurt any one."

"Do you mean to say, Uncle Sim, that I should sit still and do nothing while the people I care for most in the world are in all sorts of trouble that I could get them out of?"

"That little baggage, Rosie Fay, isn't one of the people you care for most in the world, I presume?"

Thor knew that with Uncle Sim's perspicacity this might be a leading question, but he made the answer he considered the most diplomatic in the circumstances. "She is if—if Claude is in love with her. But—but why do you call her that, Uncle Sim?"

"Because she's a little witch. Most determined little piece I know. Hard working; lots of pluck; industrious as the devil. Whole soul set on attaining her ends."

Thor considered it prudent to return to the point from which he had been diverted. "Well, if the people I care for most are in trouble that I can get them out of—"

"Oh, if you can get them out of it—"

"Well, I can."

"Then that's all right. Only the case must be rather rare. Haven't often seen the attempt made except with one result—not that of getting people out of trouble, but of getting oneself in. But every one to his taste, Thor. Wouldn't stop you for the world. Only advise you not to be in a hurry."

"There's no question of being in a hurry when things have to be done *now*."

"All right, Thor. You know better than I. I'm one of those slowpokes who look on the fancy for taking a hand in other people's affairs as I do on the taste for committing suicide—there's always time. If you don't do it to-day, you can to-morrow—which is a reason for putting it off, ain't it?"

There was more than impatience in Thor's protest as he cried, "But how can you put it off when there's some one—some one who's—who's unhappy?"

"I see. Comes back to that. But I don't mind some one's being unhappy. Don't care a tuppenny damn. Do 'em good. I've seen more people unhappy than I could tell you about in a year; and nine out of ten were made men and women by it who before that had been only rags."

"I'm afraid I can't accept that cheerful doctrine, Uncle Sim—"

"All right, Thor. Don't want you to. Wouldn't interfere with you any more than with any one else. Free country. Got your own row to hoe. If you make yourself miserable in the process, why, it 'll do you as much good as it does all the rest. Nothing like it. Wouldn't save you from it for anything. But there's a verse of an old song that you might turn over in your mind—old song written about two or three thousand years ago: 'Oh, tarry thou the Lord's leisure—"

Thor tossed his head impatiently. "Oh, pshaw!"

"But it goes on: 'And be strong.' You can be awful strong when you're tarrying the Lord's leisure, Thor, because then you know you're not making any damn-fool mistakes."

Thor spoke up proudly: "I'd rather *make* mistakes— than do nothing."

"That's all right, Thor; splendid spirit. Don't disapprove of it a mite. Go ahead. Make mistakes. It 'll be live and learn. Not the least afraid. I've often noticed that when young fellows of your sort prefer their own haste to the Lord's leisure there's a Lord's haste that hurries on before 'em, so as to be all ready to meet 'em when they come a cropper in the ditch."

Thor turned away sharply. "I guess I'll beat it, Uncle Sim."

The old man, swinging his lantern, shambled along by his nephew's side, as the latter made for the road again. "Oh, I ain't trying to hold you back, Thor. Now, am I? On the contrary, I say, go ahead. Rush in where angels fear to tread; and if you don't do anything else you'll carry the angels along with you. You may make an awful fool of yourself, Thor—but you'll be on the side of the angels and the angels 'll be on yours."

Though dinner was over by the time Thor reached home, his stepmother sat with him while he ate it. It was a new departure for her. Thor could not remember that she had ever done anything of the sort before. She sat with him and served him, asking no questions as to why he was late. She seemed to divine a trouble on his part beyond her power to console, and for which the only sympathy she dared to express was that of small kindly acts. He understood this and was grateful.

He found her society soothing. This, too, surprised him. He felt so battered and sore that the mere presence of one who approached him from an affectionate impulse had the effect on him of a gentle hand. Never before in his life had he been conscious of woman's genius for comforting, possibly because never before in his life had he needed comfort to the same degree.

No reference was made by his stepmother or himself

to the scene with Mrs. Willoughby in the afternoon, but it was not hard for him to perceive that in some strange way it was stirring the victim of it to newness of life. It was not that she admitted the application of Bessie's charges to herself; they only startled her to the knowledge that there were heights and depths in human existence such as her imagination had never plumbed. Her nature was making a feeble effort to expand, as the petals of a bud that has been kept hard and compact by a backward spring may unfold to the heat of summer.

When he had finished his hasty meal, Thor rose and kissed her, saying, "Thank you, mumphy," using the pet name that had not been on his lips since childhood. She drew his face downward with a sudden sob, a sob quite inexplicable except on the ground that her poor, withered, strangled little soul was at last trying to live.

Having gone up-stairs to his room, Thor shut the door and bolted it in his desire for solitude. He changed his coat and kicked off his boots. When he had lighted a pipe he threw himself on the old sofa which had done duty as couch at the foot of his bed ever since he was a boy. It was the attitude in which he had always been best able to "think things out."

Now that he had eaten a sufficient dinner, he felt physically less bruised, though mentally there was more to torture him. He regretted having seen Uncle Sim. He hated the alternative of letting things alone. There was a sense in which action would have been an anodyne to suffering, and had it not been for Uncle Sim he would have had no scruple in making use of it.

It was all very well to talk of letting people settle their own affairs; but how *could* they settle them, in these particular cases, without his intervention? As far as power went he was like a fairy prince who had only to wave a wand to see the whole scene transfigured. If he hadn't asked Uncle Sim's advice he would be already waving it, instead of lolling on his back, with his right foot poised over his left knee and dangling a heelless slipper in the air. He felt shame at the very attitude of idleness.

True, there were the two distinct lines of action—that of making a number of people happy now, and that of holding back that they might fight their own battles. By fighting their own battles they might emerge from the conflict the stronger—after forty or fifty years! Those who were unlikely to live so long—Len and Bessie Willoughby, for example—would probably go down rebelling and protesting to their graves. But Claude and Rosie and Lois might all grow morally the stronger. There was that possibility. It was plain. Claude and Rosie might marry on the former's fifteen hundred dollars a year, have children, and bring them up in poverty as model citizens; but whatever the high triumph of their middle age, Thor shrank from the thought of the interval for both. And Lois, too, might live down grief, disappointment, small means, and loneliness; might become hardened and toughened and beaten to endurance, and grow to be the best and bravest and kindest old maid in the world. Uncle Sim would probably consider that in these noble achievements the game would be worth the candle; but he, Thor Masterman, didn't. The more he developed the possibilities of this future for every one concerned, himself included, the more he loathed it.

It was past eleven before he reached the point of loathing at which he was convinced that action should begin; but once he reached it, he bounded to his feet. He felt wonderfully free and vigorous. If certain details could be settled there and then—he couldn't wait till the morrow—he thought that, in spite of everything, he should sleep.

He had heard Claude go to his room, which was on the same floor as his own, an hour earlier. Claude was probably by this time in bed and asleep, but the elder brother couldn't hesitate for that. Within less than a minute he had crossed the passage, entered Claude's bedroom, and turned on the electric light.

Claude's profile sunk into the middle of the pillow might have been carved in ivory. His dark wavy hair fell back picturesquely from temple and brow. Under the coverings his slim form made a light, graceful line.

The room was at once dainty and severe. A striped paper, brightened by a design of garlands, knots, and flowers *à la Marie Antoinette*, made a background for white furniture in the style of Louis XVI., modern and inexpensive, but carefully selected by Mrs. Masterman. The walls were further lightened by colored reprints of old French scenes, discreetly amorous, collected by Claude himself.

Thor stood for some seconds in front of the bed before the brother opened his eyes. More seconds passed while the younger gazed up at the elder. "What the dev—!" Claude began, sleepily.

But Thor broke in, promptly, "Claude, why didn't you ever tell me you knew Rosie Fay?"

Claude closed his eyes again. The expected had happened. Like Rosie, he resolved to meet the moment cautiously, creating no more opposition than he could help. "Why should I?" he parried, without hostility.

"Because I asked you, for one thing."

He opened his eyes. "When did you ever ask me?"

"At the bank; one day when I found you there. It must have been two months ago."

Claude stirred slightly under the bedclothes. "Oh, then."

"Yes, then. Why didn't you tell me?"

"I didn't see how I could. What good would it have done, anyhow?"

It was on Thor's tongue to say, "It would have done the good of not telling lies," but he suppressed that. One of his objects was to be conciliating. He had other objects, which he believed would be best served by taking a small chair and sitting on it astride, close to Claude's bed. An easy, fraternal air was maintained by the effect of the pipe still hanging by its curved stem from the corner of his mouth. He began to think highly of himself as a comedian.

"I wish you had told me," he said, quietly, "because I could have helped you."

Claude lay still. His eyes grew brilliant. "Helped me—how?"

"Helped you in whatever it is you're trying to do." He added, with significance, "You are trying to do something, aren't you?"

Claude endeavored to gain time by saying, "Trying to do what?"

"You're—" Thor hesitated, but dashed in. "You're in love with her?"

It was still to gain time that Claude replied, "What do you think?"

Thor's heart bounded with a great hope. Perhaps Claude was not in love with her. He had not been noticeably moved as yet. In that case it might be possible—barely possible—that after Rosie had outlived her disappointment there might be a chance that he . . . But he dared not speculate. Mustering everything that was histrionic within him, he said, with the art that conceals art, "I think you are—decidedly."

Claude rolled partly over in bed. "That's about it."

The confession was as full as one brother could expect from another. Thor's heart sank again. He managed, however, to keep on the high plane of art as he brought out the words, "And what about her?"

Again Claude's avowal was as ardent as the actual conditions called for. "Oh, I guess she's all right."

"So—what now?"

Claude rolled back toward his brother, raising his head slightly from the pillow. "Well—what now?"

"You're going to be married, I suppose?"

Claude lifted himself on his elbow. "Married on fifteen hundred a year?" He went on, before Thor could say anything, "If there was nothing else to consider!"

Thor felt stirrings of hope again. "Then, if you're not going to be married, what do you mean?"

"What do I mean? What can I mean?"

"Oh, come, Claude! You're not a boy any longer. You know perfectly well that a man of honor—with your traditions—can't trifle with a girl like that—or break her heart—or—or ruin her."

"I'm not doing any of the three. She knows I'm not. She knows I'm only in the same box she's in herself."

"That is, you're both in love, without seeing how you're going to—"

Claude lurched forward in the bed. "Look here, Thor; if you want to know, it's this. I've tried to leave the girl alone—and I can't. I'm worse than a damn fool; I'm every sort of a hound. I can't marry her, and I can't give her up. When I haven't seen her for a week, I'm frantic; and when I do see her I swear to God I'll never see her again. So now you know."

Claude threw himself back again on the pillows, but Thor went on, quietly: "Why do you swear to God you'll never see her again?"

"Because I'm killing her. That is, I should be killing her if she wasn't the bravest little brick on earth. You don't know her, Thor. You've seen her, and you know she's pretty; but you don't know that she's as plucky as they make 'em—pluckier."

Thor answered, wearily, "I've rather guessed that, which is one of the reasons why I feel you should be true to her."

"I am true to her—truer than I ought to be. If I was less true it would be better for us both. She'd get over it—"

Again Thor was aware of an up-leaping hope. "And you, too?"

"Oh, I suppose so—in time."

"Yes, but you'd suffer."

Claude gave another lurch forward in the bed. "I couldn't suffer worse than I'm suffering now, knowing I'm an infernal cad—and not seeing how to be anything else."

"But you wouldn't be an infernal cad if you married her."

The young man flung himself about the bed impatiently. "Oh, what's the use of talking?"

"If she had money you could marry her all right."

"Ah, go to the devil, Thor!" The tone was one of utter exasperation.

Thor persisted. "If she had, let us say, four or five thousand dollars a year of her own—"

Claude stretched his person half-way out of bed. "I said—go to the devil!"

"Well, she has."

"Has what?"

"Four or five thousand dollars a year of her own. That is, she *will* have it, if you and she get married."

"Say, Thor, have you got the jimjams?"

"I'm speaking quite seriously, Claude. I've always intended to do something to help you out when I got hold of Grandpa Thorley's money; and, if you like, I'll do it that way."

"Do it what way?"

"The way I say. If you and Rosie get married, she shall have five thousand a year of her own."

"From you?"

Thor nodded.

The younger brother looked at the elder curiously. It was a long minute before he spoke. "If it's to help me out, why don't *I* have it? I'm your brother. I should think I'd be the one."

"Because I'd rather do it that way. It would be a means of evening things up. It would make her more like your equal. You know as well as I do that father and mother will kick like blazes; but if Rosie has money—"

"If Rosie has money they'll know she gets it from somewhere. They won't think it comes down to her out of heaven."

"They can think what they like. They needn't know that I have anything to do with it. They know you haven't got five thousand a year, and if she has—why, there'll be the solid cash to convince them. The whole thing will be a pill for them; but if it's gilded—"

Claude's knees were drawn up in the bed, his hands clasped about them. Thor noticed the strangeness of his expression, but he was unprepared for his words when they came out. "Say, Thor, you're not in love with her yourself, are you?"

Owing to what he believed to be the perfection of his acting, it was the question Thor had least expected to be called on to answer. He knew he was turning white or green, and that his smile when he forced it was nothing but a ghastly movement of the mouth. It was his turn to gain time, but he could think of nothing more forcible than, "What makes you ask me that?"

"Because it looks so funny—so damned funny."

"There's nothing funny in my trying to give a lift to my own brother, is there?"

"N-no; perhaps not. But, see here, Thor—" He leaned forward. "You're *not* in love with her, are you?"

Thor knew the supreme moment of his life had come, that he should never reach another like it. It was within his power to seize the cup and drain it—or thrust it aside. Of all temptations he had ever had to meet none had been so strong as this. It was the stronger for his knowing that if it was conquered now it would probably never return. He would have put himself beyond reach of its returning. That in itself appalled him. There was some joy in feeling the temptation there, as a thing to be dallied with.

He dallied with it now. He dallied with it to the extent
of saying, with a smile he tried to temper to playfulness:

"Well, what if I was in love with her?"

Something about Claude leaped into flame. "Then
I wouldn't touch a cent of your money. I wouldn't let
her touch it. I wouldn't let her look at it. I'd marry
her on my own—I'll be hanged if I wouldn't. I'd marry
her to-morrow. I'd get out of bed and marry her to-night.
I'd—"

Thor forced his smile to a tenderer playfulness, sitting
calmly astride of his chair, his left arm along the back, his
right hand holding his pipe by the bowl. "So you
wouldn't let me have her?"

Claude lashed across the bed. "I'd see you hanged
first. I'd see you damned. I'd see you damned to hell.
She's mine, I tell you. I'm not going to give her up to
any one—and to you least of all. Do you get that?
Now you know."

"All right, Claude. Now I know."

"Yes, but I don't know." Claude wriggled to the side
of the bed, drawing as near to his brother as he could
without getting out. "I don't know. I've asked you a
question, and you haven't answered it. And, by God!
you've got to answer it. Sooner than let any one else
get her, I'll marry her and starve. Now speak."

Thor got up heavily. He had the feeling with which
the ancients submitted when they stood soberly and
affirmed that it was useless to struggle against Fate.
Fate was upon him. He saw it now. He had tried to
elude her, but she had got him where he couldn't move.
She asserted herself again when Claude, hanging half out
of bed, his mouth feverish, his eyes burning, insisted,
imperiously, "Say, you—*speak!*"

Thor spoke. He spoke from the middle of the floor,
his pipe still in his hand. He spoke without premedita-
tion, as though but uttering the words that Destiny had
put into his mouth from all eternity.

"It's all right, Claude. Calm down. I'm—I'm going to be married to Lois Willoughby."

But Claude was not yet convinced. "When?"

"Just as soon as we can fix things up after the tenth of next month—after I get the money."

"How long has that been settled?" Claude demanded, with lingering suspicion.

"It's been settled for years, as far as I'm concerned. I can hardly remember the time when I didn't intend—just what I'm going to do."

Claude let himself drop back again among the pillows.

"So now it's all right, isn't it?" Thor continued, making a move toward the door. "It 'll be Lois and I—and you and Rosie. And the money will go to Rosie. I insist on that. It 'll even things up. Five thousand a year. Perhaps more. We'll see."

He looked back from the door, but Claude, after his excitement, was lying white and silent, his eyes closed, his profile upturned. Thor was swept by compunction. It had always been part of the family tradition to respect Claude's high-strung nerves. Nothing did him more harm than to be thwarted or stirred up. With a murmured good-night Thor tnrned out the light, opening and closing the door softly.

But in the passage he heard the pad of bare feet behind him. Claude stood there in his pajamas.

"Say, Thor," he whispered, hoarsely, "you're top-hole —'pon my soul you are." He caught his brother's hand, pulling it rather than shaking it, like a boy tugging at a bell-rope. "You're a top-hole brother, Thor," he repeated, nervously, "and I'm a beast. I know you don't care anything about Rosie. Of course you don't. But I've got the jumps. I've been through such a lot during the months I've been meeting her that I'm on springs. But with you to back me up—"

"I'll back you up all right, Claude. Just wade in and

get married—and I guess our team will hold its own against all comers. Lois will be with us. She's fond of Rosie—"

With another tug at his brother's arm, and more inarticulate thanks, Claude darted back to his room again.

Thor closed his own door and locked it behind him. He was too far spent for more emotion. He had hardly the energy to throw off his clothes and turn out the light. Within five minutes of his final assurance to Claude he was sleeping profoundly.

10

CHAPTER XV

HAVING slept soundly till after eight in the morning, Thor woke with an odd sense of pleasure. On regaining his faculties he was able to analyze it as the pleasure he had experienced in having Claude tugging at his arm. It meant that Claude was happy, and, Claude being happy, Rosie would be happy. Claude and Rosie were taken care of.

Consequently Lois would be taken care of. Thor turned the idiom over with a vast content. It was the tune to which he bathed and dressed. They would all three be taken care of. Those who were taken care of were as folded sheep. His mind could be at rest concerning them. It was something to have the mind at rest even at the cost of heartache.

There was, of course, one intention that before all others must be carried out. He would have to clinch the statement he had made, for the sake of appeasing and convincing Claude, concerning Lois Willoughby. It was something to be signed and sealed before Claude could see her or betray the daring assertion to his parents. Fortunately, the younger brother's duties at the bank would deprive him of any such opportunity earlier than nightfall, so that Thor himself was free for the regular tasks of the day. He kept, therefore, his office hours during the forenoon, and visited his few patients after a hasty luncheon. There was one patient whom he omitted —whom he would leave henceforth to Dr. Hilary.

It was but little after four when he arrived at the house at the corner of Willoughby's Lane and County Street.

Mrs. Willoughby met him in the hall, across which she happened to be bustling. She wore an apron, and struck him as curiously business-like. As he had never before seen her share in household tasks, her present aspect seemed to denote a change of heart.

"Oh, come in, Thor," she said, briskly. "I'm glad you've come. Go up and see poor Len. He's so depressed. You'll cheer him."

If there was a forced note in her bravery he did not perceive it. "I'm glad to see you're not depressed," he observed as he took off his overcoat.

She shrugged her shoulders. "I'm going to die game."

"Which means—"

"That there's fight in me yet."

"Fight?" His brows went up anxiously.

"Oh, not with your father. You needn't be afraid of that. Besides, I see well enough it would be no use. If he says we've spent our money, he's got everything fixed to make it look so, whether we've spent it or not. No, I'm not going to spare him because he's your father. I'm going to say what I think, and if you don't like it you can lump it. I sha'n't go to law. I'd get the worst of it if I did. But neither shall I be bottled up. So there!"

"It doesn't matter what you say to me—" Thor began, with significant stress on the ultimate word.

"It may not matter what I say to you, but I can tell you it will matter what I say to other people."

Thor took no notice of that. "And if you're not going to law, would it be indiscreet to ask what you are going to do?"

Bessie forced the note of bravery again, with a flash in her little eyes. "I'm going to live on my income; that's what I'm going to do. Thank the Lord I've some money left. I didn't let Archie Masterman get his hands on all of it—not me. I've got some money left, and we've got this house. I'm going to let it. I'm going to let it tomorrow if I get the chance. I'm getting it ready now.

And then we're going abroad. Oh, I know lots of places where we can live—*petits trous pas chers;* dear little places, too—where Len 'll have a chance to—to get better."

Thor made a big resolution. "If you're going to let the house, why not let it to me?"

She knew what was coming, but it made her feel faint. Backing to one of the Regency chairs, she sank into it. It was in mere pretense that she said, "What do you want it for?"

"I want it because I want to marry Lois." He added, with an anxiety that sprang of his declaration to Claude, "Do you think she'll take me?"

Bessie spoke with conviction. "She'll take you unless she's more of a fool than I think. Of course she'll take you. Any woman in her senses would jump at you. I know I would." She dashed away a tear. "But look here, Thor," she hurried on, "if you marry Lois you won't have the whole family on your back, you know. You won't be marrying Len and me. I tell you right now because you're the sort that 'll think he ought to do it. Well, you won't have to. I mean what I say when I tell you we're going to live on our income—what's left of it. We can, and we will, and we're going to."

"Couldn't we talk about all that when—?"

"When you're married to Lois and have more of a right to speak? No. We'll talk about it now—and never any more. Len and I are going to have plenty—plenty. If you think I can't manage—well, you'll see."

"Oh, I know you've got lots of pluck," Mrs. Willoughby—"

She sprang to her feet. With her hands thrust jauntily into the pockets of her apron, she looked like some poor little soubrette, grown middle-aged, stout, and rather grotesque, in a Marivaux play. She acted her part well. "Pluck? Oh, I've got more than that. I've got some ability. If you never knew it before, you'll see it now.

I've spent a lot; but then I've had a lot—or thought I had; and now that I'm going to have little—well, I'll show you I can cut my coat according to my cloth as well as the next one."

"I don't doubt that in the least, and yet—"

"And yet you want us to have all our money back. Oh, I know what you meant yesterday afternoon. I didn't see it at the time—I had so many things to think of; but I caught on to it as soon as I got home. We should get it back, because you'd give it to us. Well, you won't. You can marry Lois, if she'll marry you— and I hope to the Lord she won't be such a goose as to refuse you!—and you can take the house off our hands; but more than that you won't be able to do, not if you were Thor Masterman ten times over."

He smiled. "I shouldn't like to be that. Once is bad enough."

Her little eyes shone tearily. "All the same, I like you for it. I do believe that if you hadn't said it I should have gone to law. I certainly meant to; but when I saw how nice *you* were—" Dashing away another tear, she changed her tone suddenly. "Tell me. What did your mother say after I left yesterday?"

Thor informed her that to the best of his knowledge she hadn't said anything.

Bessie chuckled. "I didn't leave her much to say, did I? Well, I'm glad to have had the opportunity of talking it out with her."

"You certainly talked it out—if that's the word."

"Yes, didn't I? And now, I suppose, she's mad."

Thor was unable to affirm as much as this. In fact, the conversation, since Mrs. Willoughby liked to apply that term to the encounter, had induced in his stepmother, as far as he could see, a somewhat superior frame of mind.

"Well, I hope it 'll do her as much good as it did me," Bessie sighed, devoutly; "and now that I've let off steam

I'll go 'round and make it up. Now go and see Len. He'll want to talk to you."

Thor intimated that he would be glad of a minute with Lois, to which Mrs. Willoughby replied that Lois was having one of her fits of bird-craze. She was in the kitchen at that minute getting suet with which to go up into the woods and feed the chickadees. Good Lord! there had been chickadees since the world began, and they had lived through the winter somehow. Bessie had no patience with what she called "nature-fads," but it was as easy to talk sense into a chickadee itself as to keep Lois from going into the woods with two or three pounds of suet after every snow-storm. She undertook, however, to delay her daughter's departure on this errand till warning had been given to Thor.

Up-stairs Thor found Len sitting in his big arm-chair, clad in a gorgeous dressing-gown. He was idle, stupefied, and woebegone. With his bushy, snow-white hair and beard, his puffy cheeks, his sagging mouth, and his clumsy bulk he produced an effect half spectral and half fleshly, but quite pathetically ludicrous. His hand trembled violently as he held it toward his visitor.

"Not well to-day, Thor," he complained. "Ought to be back in bed. Any other man wouldn't have got up. Always had too much energy. Awful blow, Thor, awful blow. Never could have believed it of your father. But I'm not downed yet. Go to work and make another fortune. That's what I'll do."

Thor sympathized with his friend's intentions, and, having slipped down-stairs again, found Lois in the hall, a basket containing a varied assortment of bird-foods on her arm.

When she had given him permission to accompany her, they took their way up Willoughby's Lane, whence it was possible to pass into the woodland stretches of the hillside. The day was clear and cold, with just enough wind to wake the æolian harp of the forest into sound. Once in the woods, they advanced warily. "Listen to the red-polls," Lois whispered.

She paused, leaning forward, her face alight. There was nothing visible; but a low, continuous warble, interspersed with a sort of liquid rattle, struck the ear. Taking a bunch of millet stalks from her basket, she directed Thor while he tied them to the bough of a birch that trailed its lower branches to the snow. When they had gone forward they perceived, on looking around, that some dozen or twenty of the crimson-headed birds had found their food.

So they went on, scattering seeds or crumbs in sheltered spots, and fixing masses of suet in conspicuous places, to an approving chirrup of *dee-dee, chick-a-dee-dee-dee,* from friendly little throats. The basket was almost emptied by the time they reached the outskirts of the wood and neared the top of the hill.

Lois was fastening the last bunch of millet stalks to a branch hanging just above her head. Thor stood behind her, holding the basket, and noticing, as he had often noticed before, the slim shapeliness of her hands. In spite of the cold, they were bare, the fur of the cuffs falling back sufficiently to display the exquisitely formed wrists.

"Lois, when can we be married?"

She gave no sign of having heard him, unless it was that her hands stopped for an instant in the deft rapidity of their task. Within a few seconds they had resumed their work, though, it seemed to him, with less sureness in the supple movement of the fingers. Beyond the upturned collar of her coat he saw the stealing of a warm, slow flush.

He was moved, he hardly knew how. He hardly knew how, except that it was with an emotion different from that which Rosie Fay had always roused in him. In that case the impulse was primarily physical. He couldn't have said what it was primarily in this. It was perhaps mental, or spiritual, or only sympathetic. But it was an emotion. He was sure of that, though he was less sure that it had the nature of love. As for love, since yesterday the word sickened him. Its association had become, for the present, at any rate, both sacred and appalling. He couldn't have used it, even if he had been more positive concerning the blends that made up his present sentiment.

It was to postpone as long as possible the moment for turning around that Lois worked unnecessarily at the fastening of her millet stalks. They were not yet secured to her satisfaction when, urged by a sudden impulse, he bent forward and kissed her wrist. She allowed him to do this without protest, while she knotted the ends of her string; but she was obliged to turn at last.

"I didn't know you wanted to be married," she said, with shy frankness.

He responded as simply as she. "But now that you do know it—how soon can it be?"

"Why are you asking me?" Before he had time to reply she went on, "Is it because papa has got into trouble?"

He was ready with his answer. "It's because he's got into trouble that I'm asking you to-day; but I've been meaning to ask you for years and years."

She uttered something like a little cry. "Oh, Thor, is that true?"

The fact that he must make so many reservations impelled him to be the more ardent in what he could affirm without putting a strain on his conscience. "I can swear it to you, Lois, if you want me to. It began as long ago as when I was a youngster and you were a little girl."

She clasped her hands tightly. "Oh, Thor!"

"Since that time there hasn't been a—" He was going to say a day, but he made a rapid correction—"there hasn't been a year when I haven't looked forward to your being my wife." He allowed a few seconds to pass before adding, "I should think you'd have seen it."

She answered as well as a joyous distress would let her.

"I did see it, Thor—or thought I did—for a while. Only latterly—"

"You mustn't judge by—latterly," he broke in, hastily. "Latterly I've had a good deal to go through."

"Oh, you poor Thor! Tell me about it."

Nothing would have eased his heart more effectively than to have poured out to her the whole flood of his confidence. It was what he was accustomed to doing when in her company. He could talk to her with more open heart than he had ever been able to talk to any one. It would have been a relief to tell her the whole story of Rosie Fay; and if he refrained from taking this course, it was only because he reminded himself that it wouldn't "do." It obviously wouldn't "do." He was unable to say why it wouldn't "do" except on the general ground that there were things a man had better keep to himself. He curbed, therefore, his impulse toward frankness to say:

"I can't—because there are things I shall never be able to talk about. If I could speak of them to any one it would be to you."

She looked at him anxiously. "It's nothing that I have to do with, is it?"

"Only in as far as you have to do with everything that concerns me."

Tears in her eyes could not keep her face from growing radiant. "Oh, Thor, how can I believe it?"

"It's true, Lois. I can hardly go back to the time when, in my own mind, it hasn't been true."

"But I'm not worthy of it," she said, half tearfully.

"I hope it isn't a question of worthiness on the one side or the other. It's just a matter of—of our belonging together."

It was not in doubt, but with imploring looks of happiness, that she said, "Oh, are you sure we do?"

He was glad she could accept his formula. It not only simplified matters, but enabled him to be sincere. The fact that in his own way he was quite sincere rendered him the more grateful to her for not forcing him, or trying to force him, to express himself insincerely. It was almost as if she divined his state of mind.

"Words aren't of much use between *us*," he declared, in his appreciation of this attitude on her part. "We're more or less independent of them, don't you think?"

She nodded her approval of this sentiment as her eyes followed the action of her fingers in buttoning her gloves.

"But I'll tell you what I feel as exactly as I can put it," he went on. "It's that you're essential to me, and I'm essential to you. At least," he subjoined, humbly, "I hope I'm essential to you."

She nodded again, her face averted, her eyes still following the movements of her fingers at her wrist.

"I can't express it in language very different from that," he stammered, "because—well, because I'm not—not very happy; and the chief thing I feel about you is that you're a kind of—of shelter."

He had found the word that explained his state of mind. It was as a shelter that he was seeking her. If there were points of view from which his object was to protect her, there were others from which he needed protection for himself. In desiring her as his wife he was, as it were, fleeing to a refuge. He did desire her as his wife, even though but yesterday he had more violently desired Rosie Fay. The violence was perhaps the secret of his reaction—not that it was reaction so much as the turning of his footsteps toward home. He was homing to her. He was homing to her by an instinct beyond his skill to analyze, though he knew it to be as straight and sure as that of the pigeon to the cote.

There was a silence following his use of the word shelter —a silence in which she seemed to envelop him with her deep, luminous regard. The still, remote beauty of the winter woods, the notes of friendly birds, the sweet, wild music of the wind in the treetops, accompanied that look, as mystery and incense and organ harmonies go with benedictions.

"Oh, Thor, you're wonderful!" was all she could say, when words came to her. "You make me feel as if I could be of some use in the world. What's more wonderful still, you make me feel as if I had been of use all these years when I've felt so useless."

It was in the stress of the sensation of having wandered into far, exotic regions in which his feet could only stray that he said, simply, "You're home to me."

She was so near to bursting into tears that she turned from him sharply and walked up the hill. He followed slowly, swinging the empty basket. Her buoyant step on the snow, over which the frost had drawn the thinnest of shining crusts, gave a nymphlike smoothness to her motion.

Having reached the treeless ridge, she emerged on that high altar on which, not twenty-four hours earlier, he had sunk face downward in the snow. The snow had drifted again over his footprints and the mark of his form. It was drifting still, in little powdery whirls, across a surface that caught tints of crimson and glints of fire from an angry sunset. It was windy here. As she stood above him, facing the north, her figure poised against a glowering sky, her garments blew backward. Even when he reached her and was standing by her side, she continued to gaze outward across the undulating, snow-covered country, in the folds of which an occasional farm-house lamp shone like a pale twilight star.

"You see, it's this way," he pursued, as though there had been no interruption. "When I'm with you I seem to get back to my natural conditions—the conditions in which I can live and work. That's what I mean by your being home to me. Other places"—he ventured this much of the confession he had at heart—"other places have their temptations; but it's only at home that one lives."

He took courage to go on from the way in which her gloved hand stole into his. "I dare say you think I talk too much about work; but, after all, we can't forget that we live in a country in the making, can we? In a way, it's a world in the making. There's everything to do—and I want to be doing some of it, Lois," he declared, with a little outburst. "I can't help it. I know some people think I'm an enthusiast, and others put me down as a prig—but I can't help it."

"I know you can't, Thor, and I can't tell you how much I—I"—she felt for the right word—"I admire it."

He turned to her eagerly. "You're the only one, Lois, who knows what I mean—who can speak my language. You want to be useful, too."

"And I never have been."

"Nor I. I've known that things were to be done; but I haven't known how to set about them, or where to begin. Don't you think we may be able to find the way together?"

She seemed suddenly to cling to him. "Oh, Thor, if you'd only make me half as good as you are!"

Perhaps the ardor with which he seized her was the unspent force of the longing roused in him by Rosie. Perhaps it blazed up in him merely because she was a woman. For two or three days now his need of the feminine had been acute. Did she minister to that? or did she bring him something that could be offered by but one woman in the world? He couldn't tell. He only knew that he had her in his arms, with his lips on hers, and that he was content. He was content, with a sense of fulfilment and appeasement. It was as if he had been straining for a great prize and won the second—but at a moment when he had expected none at all. There was happiness in it, even if it was a quieter, staider happiness than that of which he now knew himself to be capable.

"You're home to me, Lois," he murmured as he held her. "You're home to me."

He meant that though there were strange, entrancing Edens on which he had not been allowed to enter, there was, nevertheless, a vast peace of mind to be found at the restful, friendly fireside.

"And you're the whole wide world to me, Thor," she whispered, clasping her arms about his neck and drawing his face nearer.

CHAPTER XVI

ON leaving Lois and returning homeward, Thor met his brother at the entrance to the avenue. They had not spoken since the preceding night. On purpose to avoid a meeting, Claude had breakfasted early and escaped to town before Thor had come down-stairs. In the glimpse Thor had caught of his younger brother as the latter left the house he saw that he looked white and worried.

He looked white and worried still under the glare of street electricity. As they walked up the driveway together Thor took the opportunity to put himself right in the matter that lay most urgently on his mind. "Lois and I are to be married on one of the last days of February," he said, with his best attempt to speak casually. "She wants to work it in before Lent, which begins on the first day of March. Have scruples about marrying in Lent in their church. Quiet affair. No one but the two families."

Claude asked the question as to which he felt most curiosity. "Going to tell father?"

"To-night. No use shilly-shallying about things of that sort. Father mayn't like it; but he can't kick."

Claude spoke moodily: "He can't kick in your case."

"We're grown men, Claude. We're the only judges of what's right for us. I don't mean any disrespect to father; but we've got to be free. Best way, as far as I see, is to be open and aboveboard and firm. Then everybody knows where you are."

Claude made no response till they reached the door-step, where he lingered. "Look here, Thor," he said then, "I've got to put this thing through in my own way, you know."

Thor didn't need to be told what this thing was. "That's all right, Claude. I've got nothing to do with it."

"You've got something to do with it when you put up the money. And what I feel," he added, complainingly, "is that my taking it makes me look as if I was bought."

"Oh, rot, Claude!" Thor made a great effort. "Hang it all! when a fellow's in—in love, and going to be married himself, you don't suppose he can ignore his own brother who's in the same sort of box, and can't be married for the sake of a few hundred dollars? That wouldn't be human."

It was not difficult for Claude to take this point of view, but he repeated, tenaciously, "I've got to do it in my own way."

"Good Lord! old chap, I don't care how you do it," Thor declared, airily, "so long as it's done. Just buck up and be a man, and you'll pull it off magnificently. It's the sort of thing you've got to pull off magnificently— or slump."

"That's what I think," Claude agreed, "and so I'm"— he hesitated before announcing so bold a program— "and so I'm going to take her abroad."

"Oh!" Thor gave a little gasp. He had not expected to have Rosie pass out of his ken. He had supposed that he should remain near her, watch over her, know what she was doing and what was being done to her. He was busy trying to readjust his mind while Claude stammered out suggestions for the payment of Rosie's proposed dowry. It was clear without his saying so that he hated doing it; but he did say so, adding that it made him feel as if he was bought.

Thor was irritated by the repetition. "Let's drop that, Claude, if you don't mind. Be satisfied once for all that if you and Rosie accept the money it will be as a favor to

me. I'm so built that I can't be happy in my own marriage without knowing that you and—and she have the
chance to be happy in yours. With all the money that's
coming to me, and that I've never done any more to
deserve than you have, what I'm setting aside will be a
trifle. As to the payments, I'll do just as you say. The
first quarter will be paid to Rosie on the day you're
married—when there'll be a little check for you, for good
luck. So go ahead and make your plans. Go abroad,
if you want to. Dare say it's the best thing you can do."

To escape his brother's shamefaced thanks Thor passed
into the porch. "I'm not going to tell any one about it
till I'm ready," Claude warned as he followed.

Thor turned. "Of course you know that father's on
to the whole business."

"The deuce he is!"

"Father told me. How did you suppose I knew anything about it?"

"So that's it! Been wondering all day who could
have given me away. That's Uncle Sim's tricks. Knew
the old fool had his eye—"

"It was bound to come out somehow, you know, in a
little village like this. Natural enough that Uncle Sim
should want to put father wise to a matter that concerns
the whole family. I thought I'd tell you so that you can
take your line."

"Take what line?"

"How do I know? That's up to you. The line that
will best protect Rosie, I suppose. Remember that that's
your first consideration now. I only want you to understand that you can't keep father in the dark. I should say
it was more dignified, and perhaps better policy, not to try."

An hour later Mrs. Masterman was commenting at the
dinner-table on the pleasing circumstance that invitations
to Miss Elsie Darling's party had come for the entire
family. There were cards not only for the two young men,

but for the father and mother also. Since both the older and the younger members of society were included, it was clear that the function was to pass the limitations of a dance and become a ball.

Neither Mr. nor Mrs. Masterman was superior to this form of entertainment. It was the one above all others that reminded them that they belonged to society in the higher sense. They dined out with tolerable frequency; with tolerable frequency their friends dined with them. As for the afternoon teas to which they were bidden in the course of a season, Mrs. Masterman could scarcely keep count of them. But balls came only once or twice in a winter, and not always so often as that. A ball was a community event. It was an occasion on which to display the fact that the neighborhood could unite in a gathering more socially significant than the mere frolicking of boys and girls. Moreover, it was an opportunity for proving that the higher circles of the village stood on equal terms with those of the city, with the solidarity of true aristocracies all over the world.

On Mrs. Masterman's murmuring something to the effect that Claude would go to the ball, of course, the young man mumbled words that sounded like, "Not for mine." The mother understood the response to be a negative, and replied with a protest.

"Oh, but you must, Claudie dear. It 'll be so nice for you to meet Elsie. She's a charming girl, they say, after her years abroad." She concluded, with a wrinkling of her pretty brow, "It seems to me you don't know many really nice girls."

She had been moved by no more than a mother's solicitude, but Claude kept his eyes on his plate. He knew that his father was probably looking at him, and that Thor was saying, "Now's your chance to speak up and declare that you know the nicest girl in the world." Poor Claude was sensible of the opportunity, and yet felt himself paralyzed with regard to making use of it. In reply he could only say, vaguely, that if he had to go he would have to go, and not long afterward Mrs. Masterman rose.

The sons followed their parents into the library, pausing to light their cigarettes on the way. By the time they had crossed the hall the head of the house had settled himself with the evening paper in his favorite arm-chair before the slumbering wood fire. Mrs. Masterman stooped over the long table strewn with periodicals, turning the pages of a new magazine. Thor advanced to a discreet distance behind his father's chair, where he paused and said, quietly:

"Father, I want to tell you and mother that I'm engaged to Lois Willoughby. We're to be married almost at once—toward the end of next month."

There was dead silence. As far as could be observed, Masterman continued to study his paper, while his wife still stooped over the pages of her magazine. It was long before the father said, with the seeming indifference meant to be more bitter than gall:

"That, I presume, is your answer to my move with regard to the father. Very well, Thor. You're your own master. I've nothing to say."

Before Thor could explain that it was only the carrying out of a long-planned intention, his stepmother looked up and spoke. "I *have* something to say, Thor dear. I hope you're going to be very happy. I'm sure you will be. She's a noble girl."

Her newly germinating vitality having asserted itself to this extent, she stood aghast till Thor strode up and kissed her, saying: "Thank you, mumphy. She is a noble girl—one of the best."

The example had its effect on Claude, who had stood hesitating in the doorway, and now came toward his father's chair, though timidly. "Father, I'm going to be married, too."

His mother uttered a smothered cry. Masterman turned sharply.

"Who? You?"

The implied scorn in the tone put Claude on his mettle. "Yes, father," he tried to say with dignity. It was in search of further support for this dignity that he added, in a manner that he tried to make formal, but which became only faltering, "To — to — to Miss Rosanna Fay."

Masterman shrugged his shoulders and returned to his newspaper. There were full three minutes in which each of the spectators waited for another word. "Have you nothing to say to me, father?" Claude pleaded, in a tone curiously piteous.

The father barely glanced around over his shoulder. "What do you expect me to say?—to call you a damn fool? The words would be wasted."

"I'm a grown man, father—" Claude began to protest.

"Are you? It's the first intimation I've had of it. But I'm willing to take your word. If so, you must assume a grown man's responsibilities—from now on."

Claude's throat was dry and husky. "What do you mean by—from now on?"

"I mean from the minute when you've irrevocably chosen between this woman and us. You haven't irrevocably chosen as yet. You've still time—to reconsider."

"But if I don't reconsider, father?—if I can't?"

"The choice is between her and—us."

He returned to his paper; but again his wife's nascent will to live asserted itself, to no one's astonishment more than to her own. "It's not between her and me, Claude," she cried, casting as she did so a frightened glance at the back of her husband's head. "I'm your mother. I shall stand by you, whoever fails." Her words terrified her so utterly that before she dared to cross the floor to her son she looked again beseechingly at the iron-gray top of her husband's head as it appeared above the back of the arm-chair. Nevertheless, she stole swiftly to her boy and put her hands on his shoulders. "I'm your mother, dear," she sobbed, tremblingly; "and if she's a good girl, and loves you, I'll—I'll accept her."

Masterman turned his newspaper inside out, as though pretending not to hear.

Thor waited till Claude and his mother, clinging to each other, had crept out of the room, before saying, "I'm responsible for this, father."

There was no change in the father's attitude. "So I supposed."

"The girl is a good girl, and I couldn't let Claude break her heart."

"You found it easier to break mine."

"I don't mean that, father—"

"Then I can only say that you're as successful in what you don't mean as in what you do."

"I don't understand."

"No, perhaps not. But it would be futile for me to try to explain to you. Good night."

Thor remained where he was. "It isn't futile for me to try to explain to you, father. I know Rosie Fay, and you don't. She's a beautiful girl, with that strong character which Claude needs to give him backbone. He is in love with her, and he's made her fall in love with him. It wouldn't be decent on his part or honorable on ours—"

The father interrupted wearily. "You'll spare me the sentimentalities. The facts are bad enough. When I want instructions in decency and honor I'll come to you and get them. In the mean time I've said—good night."

"But, father, we *must* talk about it—"

Masterman raised himself in his chair and turned. "Thor," he said, sternly, his words getting increased effect from his childlike lisp, "if you knew how painful your presence is to me—you'd go."

Thor flushed. There was nothing left for him but to turn. And yet he had not gone many steps beyond the library door before he heard his father fling the paper to the floor, uttering a low groan.

THE SIDE OF THE ANGELS

The young man stood still, shifting between two minds. Should he go away and leave his father to the mortifying sense that his sons were setting him at defiance? or should he return and insist on full explanations? He would have done the latter had it not been for the words, "If you knew how painful your presence is to me!" He still heard them. They cut him across the face—across the heart. He went on up-stairs.

As he passed the open door of Mrs. Masterman's room he heard Claude saying: "Oh, mother darling, if you knew her, you'd feel about her just as I do. When she's dressed up as a lady she'll put every other girl in the shade. You'll see she will. After she's had a year or two in Paris—"

Thor entered the room while the mother was crying out: "Paris! Why, Claudie dear, what are you talking about? How are you going to *live?*—let alone Paris!"

"That's all right, mother. Don't fret. I can get money. I'm not a fool. Look here," he added, in a confidential tone, winking at Thor over her shoulder, "I'll tell you something. It's a secret, mind you. Not a word to father! I'm all right for money *now*."

She could only repeat, in a tone of mystification, "All right for money now?"

Claude made an inarticulate sound of assent. "Got it all fixed."

"Oh, but how?"

"I said it was a secret." He winked at his brother again. "I shouldn't tell even you, only you've been such a spanking good mother to back me up that I want to ease your mind."

She threw an imploring look at her stepson, though she addressed her son. "Oh, Claude, you haven't done anything wrong, have you?—forged?—or embezzled?—or whatever it is they do in banks."

"No, mother; it's all on the square." Because of Thor's presence he added: "If it will make you any the more cheerful I'll tell you this, too. It's not going to be my money; it 'll be Rosie's. Strictly speaking, I sha'n't have anything to do with it. She'll have—about *five thousand dollars a year!* When it's all over—and we're married—you can put father wise to that; but not before, mind you."

"But, Claudie darling, I don't understand a bit. How can she have five thousand dollars a year, when they're as poor as poor? And she hasn't a relation who could possibly—"

He, too, threw a glance at Thor. "She may not have a relation, but she might have a—a friend. Now, mother, this is just between you and me. If you hadn't been such a spanking good mother I shouldn't have told you a word of it."

"Yes, but, Claude! Think! What sort of a friend could it possibly be who'd give a girl all that money? Why, it's ridiculous!"

"It isn't ridiculous. Is it, Thor? You leave it to me, mumphy."

"But it is ridiculous, Claudie dear. You'll see if it isn't. No man in the world would settle five thousand dollars a year on a girl like that—without a penny—unless he had a reason, and a very good reason, too. Would he, Thor?" she demanded of her stepson, whom she had not hitherto included. She continued to address him: "I don't care who he is or what he is. Don't you agree with me? Wouldn't anybody agree with me who had his senses?"

Thor's heart jumped. This was a view of his intentions that he had not foreseen. Fortunately he could disarm his stepmother by revealing himself as the god from the machine, for she would consider it no more than just that he should use part of his inheritance for Claude's benefit. He might have made the attempt there and then had not Claude done it for himself.

"Now you leave it to me, mumphy dear. I know

exactly what I'm about. I can't explain. But I'll tell you this much more—it 'll make your mind quite easy—that it's all on my account that Rosie's to have the money." He gave his brother another look. "If she didn't marry me she wouldn't get it. At least," he added, more doubtfully, "I don't think she would. See?"

Mrs. Masterman confessed that she didn't see—quite; but her tone made it clear that she was influenced by Claude's assurances, while Thor felt it prudent to go on his way up the second stairway.

CHAPTER XVII

THERE were both amazement and terror in Rosie's face when, at dusk next day, Claude strolled down the flowery path of the hothouse. Since Thor had turned from her, on almost the same spot, forty-eight hours previously, no hint from either of the brothers had come her way. Through the intervening time she had lived in an anguish of wonder. What was happening? What was to happen still? Would anything happen at all? Had Claude discovered the astounding fact that the elder brother was in love with her? If he had, what would he do? Would he go wild with jealousy? Or would he never have anything to do with her again? Either case was possible, and the latter more than possible if he had received a hint of the degree in which she had betrayed herself to Thor.

As to that, she didn't know whether she was glad or sorry. She knew how crude had been her self-revelation, and how shocking; but the memory of it gave her a measure of relief. It was like a general confession, like the open declaration of what had been too long kept buried in the heart. It had been a shameful thing to own that, loving one man, she would have married another man for money; but a worse shame lay in being driven to that pass. For this she felt herself but partly responsible, if responsible at all. What did she, Rosie Fay, care for money in itself? Put succinctly, her first need was of bread, of bread for herself and for those who were virtually dependent on her. After bread she wanted love and pleasure and action and admiration and whatever else made up life—but only after it. She was craving for them, she was stifling for lack of them, but they were all secondary. The very best of them was secondary. Only one thing stood first—and that was bread.

Undoubtedly her frankness had revolted Thor Masterman. But what did he know of an existence which left the barest possible margin for absolute necessity? What would life have meant to him had he never had a day since he first began to think when he had been entirely free from anxiety as to the prime essentials? Rosie couldn't remember a time when the mere getting of their pinched daily food hadn't been a matter of contrivance, with some doubt as to its success. She couldn't remember a time when she had ever been able to have a new dress or a pair of boots without long calculation beforehand. On the other hand, she remembered many a time when the pinched food couldn't be paid for, and the new dress or the pair of boots had come almost within reach only to be whisked aside that the money might be used for something still more needful. In a world of freedom and light and flowers and abundance her little soul had been kept in a prison where the very dole of bread and water was stinted.

She had never been young. Even in childhood she had known that. She had known it, and been patient with the fact, hoping for a chance to be young when she was older. If money came in then, money for boots and bread, for warm clothes in winter and thin clothes in summer, for fuel and rent and taxes and light, and the pay of the men, and the innumerable details which, owing to her father's dreaminess, she was obliged to keep on her mind—if money were ever to come in for these things, she could be young with the best. She could be young with the intenser happiness that would come from spirits long thwarted. It might never now be a light-hearted happiness, but it would be happiness for all that. It would be the deeper, and the more satisfying, and the more aware of itself for its years of suppression.

To her long experience in denial Rosie could only oppose a heart more imperiously exacting in its demands. Her tense little spirit didn't know how to do otherwise. From lines of ancestry that had never done anything but toil with patient relentlessness to wring from the soil whatever it was capable of yielding, she had inherited no habit of compromise. In them it had been called grit; but a softer generation having let that word fall into disuse, Rosie could only account for herself by saying she "wasn't a quitter." She meant that she could neither forego what she asked for, nor be content with anything short of what she conceived to be the best. Could she have done that, she might have enjoyed the meager "good time" of other girls in the village; she might have listened to the advances of young Breen the gardener, or of Matt's colleague in the grocery-store. But she had never presented such possibilities for her own consideration. She was like an ant, that sees but one object to the errand on which it has set out, disdaining diversion.

And if it had all summed itself up into what looked like a hard, unlovely avariciousness, it was because poor Rosie had nothing to tell her the values and co-relations of the different ingredients in life. For the element that suffuses good-fortune and ill-fortune alike with corrective significance she had imbibed from her mother one kind of scorn, and from her father another. She knew no more of it than did Thor Masterman. Like him, she could only work for a material blessing with material hands, though without his advantages for molding things to his will. He had his advantages through money. Since all things material are measured by that, by that Rosie measured them. The matter and the measure were all she knew. They meant safety for herself and for her parents, and protection for Matt when he came out of jail. How could she do other than spend her heart upon them? What choice had she when the alternative lay between Claude and love on the one side and on the other Thor, with his hands full of daily bread for them all? With Claude and his love there went nothing besides, while with Thor and his daily bread there would be peace and security for life. She asked it of herself; she asked it, in imagination, of him. What else could she do but sell herself when the price on her poor little body had been set so high?

She had spent two burning, rebellious days. All the while she was cooking meals, or setting tables, or washing dishes, or making beds, or selling flowers, or pruning, or watering, or addressing envelopes for the monthly bills, her soul had been raging against the unjust code by which she would have to be judged. Thor would judge her; Claude would judge her, if he knew; any one who knew would judge her, and women most fiercely of all. But what did they know about it? What did they know of twenty-odd years of going around in a cage? What did they know of the terror of seeing the cage itself demolished, and being without a protection? Did they suppose she wouldn't suffer in giving up her love? Of course she would suffer! The very extremity of her suffering would prove the extremity of her need. Passionately Rosie defended herself against her imaginary accusers, because unconsciously she accused herself.

Nevertheless, Claude's sudden appearance startled her, though the set of his shoulders towering through the dusk transported her to the enchanted land. Here were mountains, and lakes, and palaces, and plashed marble steps, and the music of lutes, and banquets of ambrosial things to which daily bread was as nothing. Claude brought them with him. They were the conditions of that glorious life in which he had his being. They were the conditions in which she had her being, too, the minute she came within his sphere.

She passed through some poignant seconds as he approached. For the first time since her idyl had begun to give a new meaning to existence she perceived that if he renounced her it would be the one thing she couldn't bear. She might have the strength to give him up; for him to give her up would be beyond all the limits of endurance. She put it to herself tersely in saying it would break her heart.

But he dispelled her fears by smiling. He smiled from what was really a long way off. Even she could see that he smiled from pleasure, though she couldn't trace his pleasure to his delicious feeling of surprise. If she had ceased to be a dryad in a wood, it was to become the Armida of an enchanted garden. She could have no idea of the figure she presented to a connoisseur in girls as from a background of palms, fern-trees, and banked masses of bloom she stared at him with lips half parted and wide, frightened eyes.

Submitting to this new witchery in the same way. as he was yielding to the heavy, languorous perfumes of the place, Claude smiled continuously. "The fat's all in the fire, Rosie," he said, in a loud whisper, as he drew nearer; "so we've nothing to be afraid of any longer."

It was some minutes before she could give concrete significance to these words. In the mean time she occupied herself with assuring him that there was no one in the hothouse but herself, and that in this gloaming they could not be seen from outside. She even found a spot—a kind of low staging from which foliage plants had recently been moved away—on which they could sit down. They did so, clinging to each other, though—conscious of her coarse working-dress—she was swept by a shameful sense of incongruity in being on such terms with this faultlessly attired man. She did her best to shrink from sight, to blot herself out in his embrace, unaware that to Claude the very roughness, and the scent of growing things, gave her a savage, earthy charm.

He explained the situation to her, word by word. When he told her that their meetings were known to his father, she hid her face on his breast. When he went on to describe how resolute he had been in taking the bull by the horns, she put her hands on his shoulders and looked up into his face with the devotion of a dog. On hearing what a good mother Mrs. Masterman had been, her utterances, which welled up out of her heart as if she had been crying, were like broken phrases of blessing. As a matter of fact, she was only half listening. She was telling herself how mad she had been in fancying for an instant that she could ever have married Thor—that she could ever have married any one, no matter how great the need or how immense the compensation. Having confronted the peril, she knew now, as she had not known it hitherto, that her heart belonged to this man who held her in his arms for him to do with it as he pleased. He might treasure it, or he might play with it, or he might break it. It was all one. It was his. It was his and she was his—to shatter on the wheel or to trample in the mire, just as he was inclined. It was so clear to her now that she wondered she hadn't seen it with equal force in those days when she was so resolute in declaring that she "knew what she was doing."

And yet within a few minutes she saw how difficult it was to surrender herself, even mentally, without reserves. She was still listening but partially. She recognized plainly enough that the things he was saying were precisely those which a month ago would have filled her soul with satisfaction. He loved her, loved her, loved her. Moreover, he had found the means of sweeping all obstacles aside. They were to be married as soon as possible—just as soon as he could "arrange things." Thor and his mother were with them, and his father's conversion would be only a matter of time. These assurances, by which all the calculations of her youth were crowned, found her oddly apathetic. It was not because she had lost the knowledge of their value, but only that they had become subsidiary to the great central fact that she was his—without money or price on his side, and no matter at what cost on hers.

It was only when he began to murmur semi-coherent plans for the future, in which she detected the word Paris, that she was frightened.

"Oh, but, Claude darling, how could I go to Paris when there's so much for me to do here?"

It could not be said that he took offense, but he hinted at reproval. "Here, dearest? Where?"

"Here where we are. I don't see how I could go away."

"But you'd *have* to go away—if we were married."

"Would it be necessary to go so far?"

"Wouldn't it be the farther the better?"

"For some things. But, oh, Claude, I have so many things to consider!"

"But I thought that when a woman married she left.—"

"Her father and mother and everything. Yes, I know. But how can I leave mine—when I'm the only one who has any head? Mother's getting better, but father's not much good except for mooning over books. And then"—she hesitated, but whipped herself on—"then there's Matt. He'll be out before long. Some one must be here to tell them what to do."

He withdrew his arms from about her. "Of course, if you're going to raise so many difficulties—"

"I'm not raising difficulties, Claude darling. I'm only telling you what difficulties there are. God knows I wish there weren't any; but what can I do? If it were just going to Paris and back—"

"Well, why not go—and come back when we're obliged to?"

In the end they compromised on that, each considering it enough for the present. Rosie was unwilling to dampen his ardor when for the first time he seemed able to enter into her needs as a human being with cares and ties. He discussed them all, displaying a wonderful disposition to shoulder and share them. He went so far as to develop a philanthropic interest in Matt. Rosie had never known anything so amazing. She clasped him to her with a kind of fear lest the man should disappear in the god.

"I'll talk to Thor about him," Claude said, confidently. "Got a bee in his bonnet, Thor has, about helping chaps who come out of jail, and all that."

Rosie shuddered. It was curiously distasteful for her to apply to Thor. She felt guilty toward him. If she could do as she chose, she would never see him again. She said nothing, however, while Claude went on: "Thor's a top-hole brother, you know. You'll find that out one of these days. Lots of things I shall have to explain to you." He added, without leading up to it. "He's engaged to Lois Willoughby."

Rosie sprang from his arms. "What? Already?"

She was standing. He looked up at her curiously. "Already? Already—how? What do you mean by that?"

She tried to recapture her position.

"Why, already—right after us."

She reseated herself, getting possession of one of his hands. To this tenderness he made no response. He seemed to ruminate. "Say, Rosie—" he began at last, but apparently thought better of what he had meant to say. "All right," he broke in, carelessly, going on to speak of the wisdom of leaving the public out of their confidence until their plans were more fully matured. "Thor's to be married about the twentieth of next month," he continued, while Rosie was on her guard against further self-betrayal. "After that we'll have Lois on our side, and she'll do a lot for us."

By the time Claude emerged from the hothouse it was dark. Glad of the opportunity of slipping away unobserved, he was hurrying toward the road when he found himself confronted by Jasper Fay. In the latter's voice there was a sternness that got its force from the fact that it was so mild.

"You been in the hothouse, Mr. Claude?"

Claude laughed. In his present mood of happiness he could easily have announced himself as Fay's future son-in-law. Nothing but motives of prudence held him back. He answered, jestingly, "Been in to see if you had any American beauties."

"No, Mr. Claude; we don't grow them; no *kind* of American beauties."

Claude laughed again. "Oh, I don't know about that. Good night, Mr. Fay. Glad to have seen you."

He passed on with spirits slightly dashed because his condescension met with no response. He was so quick to feel that Fay's silence struck him as hostile. It struck him as hostile with a touch of uncanniness. On glancing back over his shoulder he saw that Fay was following him watchfully, like a dog that sneaks after an intruder till he has left the premises. Being sensitive to the creepy and the sinister, Claude was glad when he had reached the road.

CHAPTER XVIII

THE provision that for the moment he was to lead his customary life and Rosie hers made it possible for Claude to attend the ball by which Mrs. Darling drew the notice of the world to her daughter. He did so with hesitations, compunctions, reluctances, and repugnances which in no wise diminished his desire to be present at the event.

It took place in the great circular ball-room of the city's newest and most splendid hotel. The ball-room itself was white-and-gold and Louis Quinze. Against this background a tasteful decorator had constructed a colonnade that reproduced in flowers the exquisite marble circle of the Bosquet at Versailles. An imitation of Girardon's fountain splashed in the center of the room and cooled the air.

Claude arrived late. He did so partly to compromise with his compunctions and partly to accentuate his value. In gatherings at which young men were sometimes at a premium none knew better than he the heightened worth of one who sauntered in when no more were to be looked for, and who carried himself with distinction. Handsome at any time, Claude rose above his own levels when he was in evening dress. His figure was made for a white waistcoat, his feet for dancing-pumps. Moreover, he knew how to enter a room with that modesty which prompts a hostess to be encouraging. As he stood rather timidly in the doorway, long after the little receiving group had broken up, Mrs. Darling said to herself that she had never seen a more attractive young man—whoever he was!

She was glad afterward that she had made this reservation, for without it she might have been prejudiced against him on learning that he was Archie Masterman's son. As it was, she could feel that the sins of the fathers were not to be visited on the children, especially in the case of so delightful a lad. Mrs. Darling had an eye for masculine good looks, particularly when they were accompanied by a suggestion of the thoroughbred. Claude's very shyness—the gentlemanly hesitation which on the threshold of a ball-room has no dandified airs of seeming too much at ease—had this suggestion of the thoroughbred. Mrs. Darling, dragging a long, pink train and waving slowly a bespangled pink fan, moved toward him at once.

"How d'w do? So glad to see you! I'm afraid my daughter is dancing."

There was something in her manner that told him she had no idea who he was—something that could be combined with polite welcome only by one born to be a hostess.

Claude had that ready perception of his rôle which makes for social success. He bowed with the right inclination, and spoke with a gravity dictated by respect. "I'm afraid I must introduce myself, Mrs. Darling. I'm so late. I'm Claude Masterman. My father is—"

"Oh, they're here! So lovely your mother looks! Really there's not a young girl in the room can touch her. Won't you find some one and dance? I'm sorry my daughter— But later on I'll find her and intro— Why, Maidie, there you are! I thought you'd never come. How d'w do, dear?"

A more important guest than himself being greeted, Claude felt at liberty to move on a pace or two and look over the scene. It was easy to do this, for the outer rim of the circle, that which came beneath the colonnade, was raised by two steps above the space reserved for dancing. The *coup d'œil* was therefore extensive.

A mass of color, pleasing and confused, revolved languorously to those strains of the Viennese operetta in which the waltz might be said to have finished the autocracy of its long reign. The rhythm of the dancers was as regular and gentle as the breathing of a child. In glide and turn, in balance and smoothness, in that lift which was scarcely motion, there was the suggestion of frenzy restrained, of passion lulled, which emanates from the barely perceptible heave of a slumbering summer sea. It was dreamy to a charm; it was graceful to the point at which the eye begins to sicken of gracefulness; it was monotonous with the force of a necromantic spell. It was soothing; it also threw a hint of melancholy into a gathering intended to be gay. It was as though all that was most sentimentally lovely in the essence of the nineteenth century had concentrated its strength to subdue the daring spirit of the twentieth, winning a decade of success. Now, however, that the decade was past, there were indications of revolt. On the arc of the circle most remote from the eye of the hostess audacious couples were giving way to bizarre little dips and kicks and attitudes, named by outlandish names, inaugurating a new freedom.

Claude stood alone beneath one of the wide, delicate floral arches—a spectator who was not afraid of being observed. In reality he was noting to himself the degree to which he had passed beyond the merely pleasure-seeking impulse. In Rosie and Rosie's cares he had come to realities. He was rather proud of it. With regard to the young men and young women swirling in this variegated whirlpool, as well as to those who, wearied with the dance, were sitting or reclining on the steps, where rugs and cushions had been thrown for their convenience, he felt a distinct superiority. They were still in the childish stage, while he was grown to be a man. To the pretty girls, with their Parisian frocks and their relatively idle lives, Rosie, with her power of tackling actualities, was as a human being to a race of marionettes. It would be necessary for him, in deference to his hosts, to step down among them in a minute or two and twirl in their company; but he would do it with a certain pity for those to whom this sort of thing was really a pastime; he would do it as one for whom pastimes had lost their meaning and who would be in some sense taking a farewell.

The music breathed out its last drowsy cadence, and the whirlpool resolved itself into a series of shimmering, subsidiary eddies. There was a decentralizing movement toward the rugs and cushions on the steps, or to the seclusion of seats skilfully embowered amid groups of palms. Dowagers sought the rose-colored settees against the walls. Gentlemen, clasping their white-gloved hands at the base of their spinal columns, bent in graceful conversational postures. A few pairs of attractive young people continued to pace the floor. Claude remained where he was. He remained where he was partly because he hadn't decided what else to do, and partly because his quick eye had singled out the one girl in the room who embodied something that was not embodied by every other girl.

When first he saw her she was standing beside the Girardon fountain in conversation with a young man. The fact that the young man was his friend Cheever brought her directly within Claude's circle and stirred that spirit of emulation which five minutes earlier he thought he had outlived. The girl was adjusting something in her corsage, her glance flying upward from the action of her fingers toward Cheever's face, not shyly or coquettishly, but with a perfectly straightforward nonchalance which might have meant anything from indifference to defiance.

Claude knew the precise moment at which she noticed him by the fact that she glanced toward him twice in rapid succession, after which Cheever glanced toward him, too. He understood then that she had been sufficiently struck by him to ask his name, and judged that Billy would treat him to some such pardonable epithet as "awful ass," in order to keep her attention on himself.

In this apparently he didn't succeed, for presently they began to saunter in Claude's direction. The latter stood his ground.

In the knowledge that he could endure scrutiny, he stood his ground with an ease that plainly roused the young lady's interest. With her hand on the arm of her cavalier she sauntered forward, and, swerving slightly, sauntered by. She sauntered by with a lingering look of curiosity that seemed to throw him a challenge. Never in his life had Claude received such a look. It was perhaps the characteristic look of the girl of the twentieth century. It was neither bold nor rude nor self-assertive, but it was unconscious, inquiring, and unabashed. For Claude it was a new experience, calling out in him a new response.

It was a rule with Claude never to take the initiative with girls of his own class, or with those who—because they lived in the city while he lived in the village—felt themselves geographically his superiors. He found it wise policy to wait to be sought, and therefore fell back toward his hostess with compliments for her scheme of decoration. He got the reward he hoped for when Mrs. Darling called to her daughter, saying:

"Elsie dear, come here. I want to introduce Mr. Claude Masterman."

So it happened that when the nineteenth century was putting forth a further effort with the swooning phrases of the barcarolle from the "Contes d'Hoffmann," adapted to the Boston, Claude found himself swaying with the twentieth.

They had not much to say. Whatever interest they felt in each other was guarded, taciturn. When they talked it was in disjointed sentences on fragmentary subjects.

"You've been abroad, haven't you?"

"Yes; for the last five years."

"Do you like being back?"

The answer was doubtful. "Rather. For some things."

Then, as though to explain this lack of enthusiasm, "Everybody looks alike." She qualified this by adding, "You don't."

"Neither do you," he stated, in the matter-of-fact tone which he felt to be suited to the piquantly matter-of-fact in her style.

It was a minute or two before either of them spoke again. "You've got a brother, haven't you? My father's his guardian or something."

Assenting to these statements, Claude said further, "He couldn't come to-night because he's going to be married on Thursday."

"To that Miss Willoughby, isn't it?" A jerky pause was followed by a jerky addition: "I think she's nice."

"Yes, she is; top-hole. So's my brother."

She threw back her head to fling him up a smile that struck him as adorably straightforward. "I like to hear one brother speak of another like that. You don't often."

"Oh, well, every brother couldn't, you know."

They had circled and reversed more than once before she sighed: "I wish I had a brother—or a sister. It's an awful bore being the only one."

"Better to be the only one than one of too many."

More minutes had gone by in the suave swinging of their steps to Offenbach's somnolent measures when she asked, abruptly, "Do you skate?"

"Sometimes. Do you?"

"I go to the Coliseum."

Claude's next question slipped out with the daring simplicity he knew how to employ. "Do you go on particular days?"

"I generally go on Tuesdays." If she was moved by an afterthought it was without flurry or apparent sense of having committed an indiscretion. "Not every Tuesday," she said, quietly, and dropped the subject there.

When, a few minutes later, she was resting on a rug thrown down on the steps, with Claude posed gracefully by her side, Archie Masterman found the opportunity to stroll near enough to his wife to say in an undertone, "Do you see Claude?"

Ena's answer was no more than a flutter of the eyelids, but a flutter of the eyelids quite sufficient to take in the summing up of significant, unutterable things in her husband's face.

CHAPTER XIX

BY the time Thor and Lois had returned from their honeymoon in early May the line of battle in Claude's soul had been extended. The Claude who might be was fighting hard to get the better of the Claude who was. It was, nevertheless, the Claude who was that spoke in response to the elder brother's timid inquiry concerning the situation as it affected Rosie Fay. Hardly knowing how to frame his question, Thor had put it awkwardly.

"Done anything yet?"

"No."

In the little smoking-room that had been Len's and was now Thor's—Mr. and Mrs. Willoughby having retired already to their *petit trou pas cher*—they puffed at their cigars in silence. It had been the wish of both bride and bridegroom that Claude should dine with them on their second evening at home. Thor had manœuvered for these few minutes alone with his brother in order to get the information he was now seeking. For his own assurance there were things he needed to know. He wanted to feel convinced that he hadn't acted hastily, that in marrying he had made no mistake. There would be proof of that when he saw that Claude and Rosie had found their happiness in each other, and that in what he himself had done—there had been no other way! He wished that Uncle Sim's pietistic refrain wouldn't hum so persistently in his memory: "Oh, tarry thou the Lord's leisure!" He didn't believe in a Lord's leisure; but neither did he want to be afraid of his own haste. He had grown so self-conscious on the subject that it took courage for him to say:

"Isn't it getting to be about time?"

Claude drew the cigar from his lips and stared obliquely. "Look here, old chap; I thought I was to put this thing through in my own way?"

"Oh, quite so; quite so."

Claude's thrust went home when he said, "I don't see why *you* should be in such a hurry about it." He followed this by a question that Thor found equally pertinent: "Why the devil are you?"

"Because I thought you were."

"Well, even if I am, I don't see any reason for rushing things."

"Oh, would you call it—rushing?" He threw off, carelessly, "I hear you go a good deal to the Darlings'!"

"Not any oftener than they ask me."

"Well, then, they ask you pretty often, don't they?"

"I suppose they do it when they feel inclined. I haven't counted the number of occasions."

"No; but I dare say Rosie has."

"I'm not a fool, Thor. I don't talk to Rosie about the Darlings."

"Nor to the Darlings about her. That's the point. At least, it's one of the two points; and both are important. It's no more unjust for Rosie Fay to know nothing of Elsie Darling than it is for Elsie Darling to know nothing of Rosie Fay."

"Oh, rot, Thor!" Claude sprang to his feet, knocking off the ash of his cigar into the fireplace. "What do you think I'm up to?"

"I don't know. And what I'm afraid of is that *you* don't know."

"If you think I mean to leave Rosie in the lurch—"

"I don't think you *mean* it—no!"

"Then, if you think I'd do it—"

"The surest way not to do it is to—do the other thing."

"I'll do the other thing when I'm ready—not before."

"Humph! That's just what I thought would happen."

"And this is just what *I* thought would happen—that because you'd put up that confounded money you'd try to make me feel I was bought. Well, I'm not bought. See? Rather than be bribed into doing what I mean to do anyhow I'll not do it at all."

"Oh, if you mean to do it *anyhow*—"

Claude rounded on his brother indignantly. "Say, Thor, do you think I'm going to be a damn scoundrel?"

"Do you think you'd be a damn scoundrel if you didn't put it through?"

"I should be worse. Even a damn scoundrel can be called a man, and I should have forfeited the name. There! Does that satisfy you?"

"Up to a point—yes."

Claude sniffed. "You're such a queer chap, Thor, that if I've satisfied you up to a point I ought to be content."

"Oh, I'm all right, Claude. I only hoped that you'd be able to go on with it for some better reason than just—just not to be a scoundrel."

"Good Lord, old chap! I'm crazy about it. If Rosie wouldn't hum and haw I'd be the happiest man alive."

"Oh? So Rosie hums and haws, does she? What about?"

"About that confounded family of hers. Must do this for the father, and that for the mother, and something else for the beastly cub that's in jail. You can see the position that puts me in."

"But if you're really in love with her—"

"I'm really in love with *her*, I'm not with them. I never pretended to be. But if I have to marry the bunch, the cub and all—"

Thor couldn't help thinking of the opening he would have had here for his own favorite kinds of activity. "Then that 'll give you a chance to help them."

"Not so stuck on helping people as you, old chap. Want help myself."

"But you've got help, whereas they've got no one. You'll be a godsend to them."

"That's just what I'm afraid of. Who wants to be a godsend to people?"

"I should think any one would."

"If I'm a godsend to them, it shows what *they* must be."

"Mustn't undervalue yourself. Besides, you knew what they were when you began—"

"Oh, hang it all, Thor! I didn't begin. It—it happened."

Thor's eyes followed his brother as the latter began moving restlessly about the room. "Well, you're glad it happened, aren't you?"

Claude stopped abruptly. "Of course I am. But what stumps me is why you should be. See here; would you be as keen on it if I were going to marry some one else?"

Before so leading a question Thor had to choose his words. "I'd be just as keen on it; only if you were going to marry some one else, some one in circumstances more like your own, you wouldn't require so much of my—of my sympathy."

"Well, it beats me," Claude admitted, starting for the door. "I know you're a good chap at heart—top-hole, of course!—but I shouldn't have supposed you were as good as all that. I'll be darned if I should!"

Thor thought it best not to inquire too precisely into the suggestions implied by "all that," contenting himself with asking, "When may I tell Lois?"

Claude answered over his shoulder as he passed into the hall. "Tell her myself—perhaps now."

He joined his sister-in-law in the drawing-room, though he didn't tell her. He was on the point of doing so once or twice, but sheered off to something else.

"Awful queer fellow, Thor. Can *you* make him out?"

Lois was doing something with white silk or thread which she hooked in and out with a crocheting implement.

The action, as she held the work up, showed the beauty of her hands. On her lips there was a dim, happy smile. "Making Thor out is a good deal like reading in a language you're just beginning to learn; you only see some of the beauties yet—but you know you'll find plenty more when you get on a bit. In the mean while the idioms may bother you."

Claude, who was leaning forward limply, his elbows on his knees, made a circular, protesting movement of his neck and head, as though his collar fitted him uncomfortably. "Well, he's all Greek to me."

"But they say Greek richly repays those who study it."

"Humph! 'Fraid I'm not built that way. Do you know why he's got such a bee in his bonnet about—?"

He was going to say, in order to lead up to his announcement, "about Fay, the gardener"; but he couldn't. The words wouldn't come out. The prospect of telling any one that he was going to marry little Rosie Fay terrified him. He hardly understood now how he could have told his father and mother. He would never have done it if Thor hadn't been behind him. As it was, both his parents were so discreet concerning his confidence that neither had mentioned it since that night—which made his situation endurable. So he changed the form of his question to—"bee in his bonnet about—helping people?"

"Oh, it isn't a bee in his bonnet. It's just—himself. He can't do anything else."

He said, moodily, "Perhaps he doesn't help them as much as he thinks."

"He doesn't—as much as he wants to. I know that."

"Well, why not?"

She dropped her work to her lap and looked vaguely toward the dying fire. Her air was that of a person who had already considered the question, though to little purpose. "I don't know. Sometimes I think he doesn't go the right way to work. And yet it can hardly be that. Certainly no one could go to work with a better heart."

Claude was referring inwardly to Rosie's five thousand a year, and perceiving that it created as many difficulties as it did away with, when he said, "Thinks everything a matter of dollars and cents."

She received this pensively. "Perhaps."

And yet Thor's warning sent Claude to see Rosie on the following afternoon. It was not his regular day for coming, so that his appearance was a matter of happy terror tempered only by the fact that he caught her in her working-dress. His regular days were those on which Jasper Fay took his garden-truck to town. Fay rarely returned then before six or seven, so that with the early twilights there was time for an enchanted hour in the gloaming. The gloaming and the blossoms and the languorous heat and the heavy scents continued to act on Claude's senses as a love-philter might in his veins.

It was the kind of meeting to be clandestine. Secrecy was a necessary ingredient in its deliciousness. The charm of the whole relation was in its being kept *sub rosa*. *Sub rosa* was the term. It should remain under the rose where it had had its origin. It should be a stolen bliss in a man's life and not a daily staple. That was something Thor would never understand, that a man's life needed a stolen bliss to give it piquancy. There was a kind of bliss which when it ceased to be hidden ceased to be exquisite. Mysteries were seductive because they were mysteries, not because they were proclaimed and expounded in the market-place. Rosie in her working-dress among the fern-trees and the great white Easter lilies was Rosie as a mystery, as a bliss. It was the pity of pities that she couldn't be left so, where she belonged— in the state in which she met so beautifully all the requirements of taste. To drag her out, and put her into spheres she wasn't meant for, and endow her with five thousand dollars a year, was like exposing a mermaid, the glory of her own element, by pulling her from the water.

He grew conscious of this, as he always did the minute they touched on the practical. In general he avoided the practical in order to keep within the range of topics of which his love was not afraid. But at times it was necessary to speak of the future, and when they did the poor mermaid showed her fins and tail. She could neither walk nor dance nor fly; she could only flounder. There was no denying the fact that poor little Rosie floundered. She floundered because she was obliged to deal with life on a scale of which she had no experience, but as to which Claude had keenly developed social sensibilities. Not that she was pretentious; she was only what he called pathetic, with a pathos that would have made him grieve for her if he hadn't been grieving for himself.

He had asked her idea of their married life, since she had again expressed her inability to fall in with his. "Oh, Rosie, let us go and live in Paris!" he had exclaimed, to which she had replied, as she had replied so many times already: "Claude, darling, how *can* I? How can I leave them, when they've no one else?"

"Then if we get married, what do you propose that we should do?"

He had never come to anything so bluntly definite before. With that common sense of hers which was always looking for openings that would lead to common-sense results, Rosie took it as an opportunity. She showed that she had given some attention to the matter, though she expressed herself with hesitation. They were sitting in the most embowered recess the hothouse could afford —in a little shrine she kept free, yet secret, for the purpose of their meetings. She let him hold both her hands, though her face and most of her person were averted from him as she spoke. She spoke with an anxiety to let him see that in marrying her he wouldn't be letting himself down too low.

"There's that little house in Schoolhouse Lane," she faltered. "The Lippitts used to live in it."

"Well?"

"If we lived there, I could manage—with a girl." She brought out the subordinate clause with some confusion, for the keeping of "a girl" was an ambition to which it was not quite easy to aspire. She thought it best, however, to be bold, and stammered on, "We could get one for about four a week."

He let her go on.

"And if we lived in the Lippitt house I could slip across our own yard, and across Mrs. Willert's yard—she wouldn't mind!—and keep an eye on things here. Mother's ever so much better. She's taking hold again—"

"Then why couldn't we go and settle in Paris?"

"Because—don't you see, Claude?—that's not the only thing. There's father and Matt and the business. I must be on hand to—to prop them up. If I were to go, everything would come down with a crash—even if your father didn't make any more trouble about the lease. I suppose if we were married he wouldn't do *that?*"

Though he kept silence, his nervous, fastidious, superfine soul was screaming. Why couldn't he have been allowed to keep the poignant joy of touching her, of breathing her acrid, earthy atmosphere, of kissing her lips and her eyelids, to himself? It was an intoxication—but no one wanted intoxication all the time. It was curious that a life in this delirious state should be forced on him by the brother who wished him well. It was still more curious that he should feel obliged to force it on himself in order not to be a cad.

He didn't despise Rosie for the poverty of her ideals. On the contrary, her ideals were exactly suited to the little rustic thing she was. If he could have been Strephon to her Chloe it would have been perfect. But he couldn't be Strephon; he could be nothing but a neurotic twentieth-century youth, sensitive to such amenities and refinements as he had, and eager to get more. He was the type to go sporting with Amaryllis in the shade—but the shade was what made the exercise enchanting.

His obscure rebellion against the power that forced him to drag his love out into the light impelled him to say, without quite knowing why, "Did Thor ever speak of you and me being married?"

Because he was pressing her to him so closely he felt the shudder that ran through her frame. It seemed to run through his own as he waited for her reply.

"No."

Rosie never told a lie unless she thought she was obliged to. She thought it now because of Claude's jealousy. She had seen flashes of it more than once, and always at some mention of his brother. She was terror-stricken as she felt his arm relax its embrace—terror-stricken lest Thor should have already given the information that would prove she was lying. She asked, trembling, "Did he ever say he had?"

"Do you think he'd say it, if he hadn't?"

"N-no; I don't suppose so."

"Then why should you ask me that?"

She surprised him by bursting into tears. "Oh, Claude, don't be cross with me. Don't say what you said the last time you were cross—that you'd go away and never come back again. If you did that I should die. I couldn't live. I should kill myself."

There followed one of the scenes of soothing in which Claude was specially adept, and which he specially enjoyed. The pleasure was so exquisite that he prolonged it, so that by the time he emerged from the hothouse Jasper Fay was standing in the yard.

As the old man's back was turned, Claude endeavored to slip by, unobserved and silent. He succeeded in the silence, but not in being unobserved. Glancing over his shoulder, he saw the dim figure dogging him as it had dogged him on a former occasion, with the bizarre, sinister suggestion of a beast about to spring.

Claude could afford to smile at so absurd an idea in connection with poor old Fay, but his nerves were shaken by certain passionate, desperate utterances he had just heard from Rosie. She was in general so prudent, so self-controlled, that he had hardly expected to see her give way either in weeping or in words. She had broken down in both respects, while his nature was so responsive that he felt as if he had broken down himself. In the way of emotions it had been delicious, wonderful. It was a revelation of the degree to which the little creature loved him. It was a sensation in itself to be loved like that. It struck him as a strange, new discovery that in such a love there was a value not to be reckoned by money or measured by social refinements. New, strange harmonies swept through the æolian harp of his being—harmonies both tragic and exultant by which he felt himself subdued. It came to him conclusively that if in marrying Rosie there would be many things to forego, there would at least be compensation.

And yet he shivered at the stealthy creeping behind him of the shadowy old man, by whom he felt instinctively that he was hated.

13

CHAPTER XX

CLAUDE found it a vivid and curious contrast to dine that evening with the Darlings and their sophisticated friends. The friends were even more sophisticated than Claude himself, since they had more money, had traveled more, and in general lived in a broader world. But Claude knew that it was in him to reach their standards and go beyond them. All he needed was the opportunity; and opportunity to a handsome young American of good antecedents like himself is rarely wanting. He never took in that fact so clearly as on this night.

He was glad that he had not been placed next to Elsie at table, for the reason that he felt some treachery to Rosie in his being there at all. Conversely, in the light of Thor's judgment, he felt some treachery to Elsie that he should come to her with Rosie's kisses on his lips. Not that he owed her any explanations—from one point of view. Considering the broad latitude of approach and withdrawal allowed to American young people, and the possibility of playing fast and loose with some amount of mutual comprehension, he owed her no explanations whatever; but the fact remained that she was expressing a measure of willingness to be Juliet to his Romeo in braving the mute antagonism that existed between their respective families. As far as that went, he knew he was unwelcome to the Darlings; but he knew, too, that Elsie's favor carried over her parents' heads the point of his coming and going. It was conceivable that she might carry over their heads a point more important still if he were to urge her.

To the Claude who was it seemed lamentable that he

couldn't urge her; but to the Claude who might be there were higher things than the gratification of fastidious social tastes, and for the moment that Claude had some hope of the ascendant. It was that Claude who spoke when, after dinner, the men had rejoined the ladies.

"Your mother doesn't like my coming here."

Elsie threw him one of her frank, flying glances. "Well, she's asked you, hasn't she?"

He smiled. "She only asked me at the last minute. I can see some other fellow must have dropped out."

"You can see it because it's a dinner-party of elderly people to which you naturally wouldn't be invited unless there had been the place to fill. That constantly happens when people entertain as much as we do. But it isn't a slight to be asked to come to the rescue. It's a compliment. You never ask people to do that unless you count them as real friends."

He insisted on his point. "I don't suppose it was her idea."

"You mean it was mine; but even if it was, it comes to the same thing. She asked you. She needn't have done it."

He still insisted. "She did it, but she didn't want to." He added, lowering his voice significantly, "And she was right."

He forced himself to return her gaze, which rested on him with unabashed inquiry. Everything about her was unabashed. She was free from the conventional manners of maidendom, not as one who has been emancipated from them, but as one who has never had them. She might have belonged to a generation that had outgrown the need for them, as perhaps she did. Shyness, coyness, and emphasized reserve formed no part of her equipment; but, on the other hand, she was clear—clear with a kind of crystalline clearness, in eyes, in complexion, and in the staccato quality of her voice.

"She's right—how?"

"Right—because I oughtn't to come. I'm—I'm not free to come."

"Do you mean—?" She paused, not because she was embarrassed, but only to find the right words. She kept her eyes on his with a candor he could do nothing but reciprocate. "Do you mean that you're bound—elsewhere?"

He nodded. "That's it."

"Oh!" She withdrew her eyes at last, letting her gaze wander vaguely over the music-room, about which the other guests were seated. They were lined on gilded settees against the white French-paneled walls, while a young man played Chopin's Ballade in A flat on a grand piano in the far corner. Not being in the music-room itself, but in the large, square hall outside, the two young people could talk in low tones without disturbing the company. If she betrayed emotion it was only in the nervousness with which she tapped her closed fan against the palm of her left hand. Her eyes came back to his face. "I'm glad you've told me."

He took a virtuous tone. "I think those things ought to be—to be open and aboveboard."

"Oh, of course. The wonder is that I shouldn't have heard it. One generally does."

"Oh, well, you wouldn't in this case."

"Isn't it anybody—about here?"

"It's some one about here, but not any one you would have heard of. She lives in our village. She's the daughter of a—well, of a market-gardener."

"How interesting! And you're in love with her?" But because of what she saw in his face she went on quickly: "No; I won't ask you that. Don't answer. Of course you're in love with her. *I* think it's splendid— a man with your"—chances was the word that suggested itself, but she made it future—"a man with your future to fall in love with a girl like that."

There was a bright glow in her face to which he tried

to respond. He said that which, owing to its implications, he could not have said to any other girl in the world, but could say to her because of her twentieth-century freedom from the artificial. "Now you see why I shouldn't come."

She gave a little assenting nod. "Yes; perhaps you'd better not—for a while—not quite so often, at any rate. By and by, I dare say, we shall get everything on another —another basis—and then—"

She rose, so that he followed her example; but he shook his head. "No, we sha'n't. There won't be any other basis."

She took this with her usual sincerity. "Well, perhaps not. I don't suppose we can really tell yet. We must just—see. When he stops," she added, with scarcely a change of tone, as she moved away from him, "do go over and talk to Mrs. Boyce. She likes attentions from young men."

What Claude chiefly retained of his brief conversation was the approval in the words, "*I* think it's splendid." He thought it splendid himself. He felt positive now that if he had pressed his suit—if he had been free to press it—he might one day have been treading this polished floor not as guest, but as master. There were no difficulties in the way that couldn't easily be overcome, if he and Elsie had been of a mind to do it—and she would have a good fifty thousand a year! Yes, it was splendid; there was no other word for it. He was giving up this brilliant future for the sake of little Rosie Fay—and counting the world well lost.

The sense of self-approval was so strong in him that as he traveled homeward he felt the great moment to have come. He must keep his word; he must be a gentleman. He was flattered by the glimpse he had got of Elsie Darling's heart; and yet the fact that she might have come to love him acted on him as an incentive, rather than the contrary, to carrying out his plans. She would see him in a finer, nobler light. As long as she lived, and even when she had married some one else, she would keep her dream of him as the magnificently romantic chap who could love a village maid and be true to her.

And he did love a village maid! He knew that now by certain infallible signs. He knew it by the very meagerness of his regret in giving up Elsie Darling and all that the winning of her would have implied. He knew it by the way he thrilled when he thought of Rosie's body trembling against his, as it had trembled that afternoon. He knew it by the wild tingle of his nerves when she shuddered at the name of Thor. That is, he thought she had shuddered; but of course she hadn't! What had she to shudder at? He was brought up against that question every time the unreasoning fear of Thor possessed him. He knew the fear to be unreasoning. However possible it might be to suspect Rosie—and a man was always ready to suspect the woman he loved!—to suspect Thor was absurd. If in the matter of Rosie's dowry Thor was "acting queerly," there was an explanation of that queerness which would do him credit. Of that no one who knew Thor could have any question and at the same time keep his common sense. Claude couldn't deny that he was jealous; but when he came to analyze his passion in that respect he found it nothing but a dread lest his own supineness might allow Rosie to be snatched away from him. He had been dilly-dallying over what he should have clinched. He had been afraid of the sacrifice he would be compelled to make, without realizing, as he realized to-night, that Rosie would be worth it. No later than to-morrow he would buy a license and a wedding-ring, and, if possible, marry her in the evening. Before the fact accomplished difficulties—and God knew there were a lot of them!—would smooth themselves away.

As he left the tram-car at the village terminus he was

too excited to go home at once, so he passed his own gate and went on toward Thor's. It was not yet late. He could hear Thor's voice reading aloud as the maid admitted him, and could follow the words while he took off his overcoat and silk hat and laid them carefully on one of the tapestried chairs. He still followed them as he straightened his cravat before the glass, pulled down his white waistcoat, and smoothed his hair.

"'Christ's mission, therefore,'" Thor read on, "'was not to relieve poverty, but to do away with it. It was to do away with it not by abolition, but by evolution. It is clear that to Christ poverty was not a disease, but a symptom—a symptom of a sick body politic. To suppress the symptom without undertaking the cure of the whole body would have been false to the thoroughness of His methods.'"

Claude appeared on the threshold. Lois smiled. Thor looked up.

"Hello, Claude! Come in. Just wait a minute. Reading Vibart's *Christ and Poverty*. Only a few lines more to the end of the chapter. 'To the teaching of Christ,'" Thor continued, "'belongs the discovery that the causes of poverty are economic only in the second place, and moral in the first. Economic conditions are shifting, changing vitally within the space of a generation. Nothing is permanent but the moral, as nothing is effectual. Thou shalt love the Lord thy God with all thy heart and with all thy soul and with all thy mind, and thy neighbor as thyself; on these two commandments hang all the law and the prophets. On these two commandments hangs also the solution of the problems of poverty, seeing that a race that obeys them finds no such problems confronting it. In proportion to the spread of moral obedience these problems tend to disappear. They were never so near to disappearing as now, when the moral sense has become alive to them.'"

Claude smoked a cigar while they sat and talked. It

was talk in which he personally took little share, but from which he sought to learn whether or not Thor was satisfied with what he had done. If there was any *arrière pensée*, he thought he might detect it by looking on. It was a pleasant scene, Lois with her sewing, Thor with his book. The library had the characteristic of American libraries in general, of being the most cheerful room in the house.

"What I complain of in all this," Thor said, tossing the book on the table, "is the intermediary suffering. It does no good to the starving of to-day to know that in another thousand years men will have so grasped the principles of Christ that want will be abolished."

Lois smiled over her sewing. "You might as well say that it does no good to the people who have to walk to-day, or travel by trains and motors, to know that in a hundred years the common method of getting about will probably be by flying. This writer lays it down as a principle that there's a rate for human progress, and that it's no use expecting man to get on faster than he has the power to go."

"I don't expect him to get on faster than he has the power to go. I only want him to go faster than he's going."

"Haven't you seen others, who wanted the same thing, dragging people off their feet, with the result that legs or necks were broken?"

"That's absurd, of course; but between that and quickening the stride there's a difference."

"Exactly; which is what Vibart says. His whole argument is that if you want to do away with poverty you must begin at the beginning, and neither in the middle nor at the end. People used to begin at the end when they imagined the difficulty to be met by temporarily supplying wants. Now they're beginning in the middle by looking for social and economic readjustments which won't be effective for more than a few years at a time. To begin at the beginning, as I understand him to say, they must get at themselves with a new point of view, and a new line of action toward one another. They must try the Christian method which they never *have* tried, or put up with poverty and other inequalities. It's futile to expect to do away with them by the means they're using now; and that," she added, in defense of the author she was endeavoring to sum up, "seems to me perfectly true."

Without following the line of argument, in which he took no interest, Claude spoke out of his knowledge of his brother. "Trouble with Thor is that he's in too much of a hurry. Won't let anything take its own pace."

This was so like a paraphrase in Claude's language of Uncle Sim's pietistic ditty that Thor winced. "Take its own pace—and stop still," he said, scornfully.

"And then," Lois resumed, tranquilly, "you've got to remember that Vibart has a spiritual as well as a historical line of argument. The evolution of the human race isn't merely a matter of following out certain principles; it depends on the degree of its conscious association with divine energy. Isn't that what he says? The closer the association the faster the progress. Where there's no such association progress is clogged or stopped. You remember, Thor. It's in the chapter, 'Fellow-workers with God.'"

"I couldn't make it out," Thor said, with some impatience. "'Fellow-workers with God!' I don't see what that means."

"Then, until you do see—"

Apparently she thought better of what she was about to say, and suppressed it. The conversation drifted to cognate subjects, while Claude became merely an observer. He wanted to be perfectly convinced that Thor was happy. That Lois was happy he could see. Happiness was apparent in every look and line of her features and every movement of her person. She was like another woman. All that used to seem wistful in her and unfulfilled had resolved itself into radiant contentment. According to Claude, you could see it with half an eye. She had gained in authority and looks, while she had developed a power of holding her own against her husband that would probably do him good.

As to Thor he was less sure. He looked older than one might have expected him to look. There was an expression in his face that was hardly to be explained by marriage and a two months' visit to Europe. Claude was not analytical, but he found himself saying, "Looks like a chap who'd been through something. What?" Being "through something" meant more than the experience incidental to a wedding and a honeymoon. With that thought torture began to gnaw at Claude's soul again, so that when his brother was called to the telephone to answer a lady who was asking what her little boy should take for a certain pain, he sprang the question on Lois:

"What do you really think of Thor? You don't suppose he has anything on his mind, do you?"

Lois was startled. "Do you?"

"I asked first."

"Well, what made you?"

"Oh, I don't know. Two or three things. I just wondered if you'd noticed it."

Her face clouded. "I haven't noticed that he had anything on his mind. I knew already—he told me before we were married—that there was something about which he wasn't—wasn't quite happy. I dare say you know what it is—"

He shook his head.

"Don't you? Well, neither do I. He may tell me some day; and till then— But I've thought he was better lately—more cheerful." .

"Hasn't he been cheerful?"

"Oh yes — quite — as a rule. But of course I've seen—"

They were interrupted by Thor's return, after which Claude took his departure.

He woke in the morning with a frenzy that astonished himself to put into execution what he had resolved. With his nervous volatility he had half expected to feel less intensely on the subject after having slept on it; but everything that could be called desire in his nature had focused itself now into the passion to make Rosie his own. That first!—and all else afterward. That first!—but he could neither see beyond it nor did he want to see.

The excitement he had been tempted to ascribe on the previous evening to his talk with Elsie Darling, and perhaps in some degree to a glass or two of champagne, having become intensified, it was a proof of its being "the real thing." He was sure now that it was not only the real thing, but that it would be lasting. This was no spasmodic breeze through his æolian harp, but the breath and life of his being. He came to this conclusion as he packed a bag that he could send for toward evening, and made a few other preparations for a temporary absence from his father's house. Putting one thing with another, he had reason to feel sure that he and Rosie would be back there together before long, forgiven and received, so that he was relieved of the necessity of taking a farewell.

"*I* think it's splendid," rang in his heart like a cheer. Any one would think it splendid who knew what he was going to do—and what he was renouncing!

It was annoying that on reaching the spot where he took the electric car to go to town old Jasper Fay should be waiting there. It was still more annoying that among the other intending passengers there should be no one whom Claude knew. To drop into conversation with a friend would have kept Fay at a distance. Just now his appearance—neat, shabby, pathetic, the superior workingman in his long-preserved, threadbare Sunday clothes—introduced disturbing notes into the swelling hymeneal chant to which Claude felt himself to be marching. There were practical reasons, too, why he should have preferred to hold no intercourse with Fay till after he had crossed his

Rubicon. He nodded absently, therefore, and, passing to the far end of the little straggling line, prayed that the car would quicken its speed in coming.

Through the tail of his eye he could see Fay detach himself from the patient group of watchers and shamble in his direction. "What's it to be now?" Claude said to himself, but he stood his ground. He stood his ground without turning, or recognizing Fay's approach. He leaned nonchalantly on his stick, looking wearily up the line for rescue, till he heard a nervous cough. The nervous cough was followed by the words, huskily spoken:

"Mr. Claude!"

He was obliged to look around. There was something about Fay that was at once mild and hostile, truculent and apologetic. He spoke respectfully, and yet with a kind of anger in the gleam of his starry eyes.

"Mr. Claude, I wish you wouldn't hang round my place any more. It don't do any one any good." Claude was weighing the advantages of avowing himself plainly on the spot, when Fay went on, "One experience of that kind has been about enough—in *one* year."

Claude's heart seemed to stop beating. "One experience of what kind?"

"You're all Mastermans together," Fay declared, bitterly. "I don't trust any of you. You're both your father's sons."

"By God! I've got at it!" Claude cried to himself. Aloud he said, with no display of emotion. "I don't understand you. I don't know what you mean."

Fay merely repeated, hoarsely, "I don't want either of you coming any more."

Claude took a tone he considered crafty. "Oh, come now, Mr. Fay. Even if you don't want me, I shouldn't think you'd object to my brother Thor."

"Your brother Thor! You've a nice brother Thor!"

"Why, what's he done?"

"Ask my little girl. No, you needn't ask her. She

wouldn't tell you. She won't tell me. All I know is what I've seen."

If it hadn't been for the decencies and the people standing by, Claude could have sprung on the old man and clutched his throat. All he could do, however, was to say, peacefully, "And what *have* you seen?"

Fay looked around to assure himself that no one was within earshot. The car was bearing down on them with a crashing buzz, so that he was obliged to speak rapidly. "I've seen him creep into my hothouse where my little girl was at work, under cover of the night, and I've seen him steal away. And when I've looked in after he was gone she was crying fit to kill herself."

"What made you wait till he went away?" Claude asked, fiercely. "Why didn't you go in after him and see what they were up to?"

The old man's face expressed the helplessness of the average American parent in conflict with a child. "Oh, she wouldn't let me. She won't have none of my interference. She says she knows what she's about. But I don't know what *you're* about, Mr. Claude; and so I'm beggin' you to keep away. No good 'll come of your actions. I don't trust any Masterman that lives."

The car had stopped and emptied itself. The people were getting in. Fay climbed the high steps laboriously, dropping a five-cent piece into a slot as he rounded a little barrier. Claude sprang up after him, dropping in a similar piece of money. Its tinkle as it fell shivered through his nerves with the excruciating sharpness of a knife-thrust.

CHAPTER XXI

CLAUDE went on to the office as a matter of routine, but when his father appeared he begged to be allowed to go home again. "I'm not well, father," he complained, his pallor bearing out his statement.

Masterman's expression was compassionate. He was very gentle with his son since the latter had been going so often to the Darlings'. "All right, my boy. Do go home. Better drop in on Thor. Give you something to put you to rights."

But Claude didn't drop in on Thor. He climbed the hill north of the pond, taking the direction with which he was more familiar in the gloaming. In the morning sunlight he hardly recognized his surroundings, nor did he know where to look for Rosie at this unusual time of day. He was about to turn into the conservatory in which he was accustomed to find her, when an Italian with beady eyes and a knowing grin, who was raking a bed that had been prepared for early planting, pointed to the last hothouse in the row. Claude loathed the man for divining what he wanted, but obeyed him.

It was a cucumber-house. That is, where two or three months earlier there had been lettuce there were now cucumber-vines running on lines of twine, and already six feet high. It was like going into a vineyard, but a vineyard closer, denser, and more regular than any that ever grew in France. Except for one long, straight aisle no wider than the shoulders of a man it was like a solid mass of greenery, thicker than a jungle, and oppressive from the evenness of its altitude. Claude felt smothered, not only by the heat, but by this compact luxuriance that dwarfed him, and which was climbing, climbing still. It was prodigious. In its way it was grotesque. It was like something grown by magic. But a few weeks previous there had been nothing here but the smooth green pavement of cheerful little plants that at a distance looked like jade or malachite. Now, all of a sudden, as it were, there was this forest of rank verdure, sprung with a kind of hideous rapidity, stifling, overpowering, productive with a teeming, incredible fecundity. Low down near the earth the full-grown fruit, green with the faintest tip of gold, hung heavy, indolent, luscious, derisively cool to touch and taste in this semi-tropical heat. The gherkin a few inches above it defied the eye to detect the swelling and lengthening that were taking place as a man looked on. Tendrils crept and curled and twisted and interlocked from vine to vine like queer, blind, living things feeling after one another. Pale blossoms of the very color of the sunlight made the sunlight sunnier, while bees boomed from flower to flower, bearing the pollen from the males, shallow, cuplike, richly stamened, to the females growing daintily from the end of the embryo cucumber as from a pinched, wizened stem.

Advancing a few paces into this gigantic vinery, Claude found the one main aisle intersected by numerous cross-aisles in any of which Rosie might be working. He pushed his way slowly, partly because the warm air heavy with pollen made him faint, and partly because this close pressure of facile, triumphant nature had on his nerves a suggestion of the menacing. On the pathway of soft, dark loam his steps fell noiselessly.

When he came upon Rosie she was buried in the depths of an almost imperceptible cross-aisle and at the end remote from the center. As her back was toward him and she had not heard his approach, he watched her for a minute in silence. His quick eye noticed that she wore a blue-green cotton stuff, with leaf-green belt and collar, that made her the living element of her background, and that her movements and attitudes were of the kind to display the exquisite lines of her body. She was picking delicately the pale little blossoms and letting them flutter to the ground. Her way was strewn with the frail yellow things already beginning to wither and shrivel, adding their portion of earth unto earth, to be transmuted to life unto life with the next rotation in planting.

"Rosie, what are you doing?"

He expected her to be startled, but he was not prepared for the look of terror with which she turned. He couldn't know the degree to which all her thoughts were concentrated on him, nor the fears by which each of her waking minutes was accompanied. She would have been startled if he had come at one of his customary hours toward night; but it was as death in her heart to see him like this in the middle of the forenoon. The emotion was the greater on both sides because the long, narrow perspective focused the eyes of each on the face of the other, with no possibility of misreading. Claude remained where he was. Rosie clung for support to the feeble aid of the nearest vine.

She began to speak rapidly, not because she thought he wanted his question answered, but because it gave her something to say. It was like the effort to keep up by splashing about before going down. She was picking off the superfluous female flowers, she said, in order that the strength of the plant might go into the remaining ones. One had to do that, otherwise—

He broke in abruptly. "Rosie, why did you tell me Thor never said anything about you and me being married?"

"Oh, what's he been saying?" She clasped her hands on her breast, with a sudden beseeching alarm.

"It's not a matter of what he's been saying. It's only a matter of what you say. And I want you to tell me why he's paying me for marrying you."

He spoke brutally not only because his suffering nerves made him brutally inclined, but in the hope of wringing from her some cry of indignation. But she only said:

"I didn't know he was doing that."

"But you knew he was going to do something."

It seemed useless to poor Rosie to keep anything back now; she could only injure her cause by hedging. "I knew he was going to do something, but he didn't tell me what it would be."

"And why should he do anything at all? What had it to do with him?"

She wrung her hands. "Oh, Claude, I don't know. He came to me. He took me—he took me by surprise. I never thought of anything like that. I never dreamt it."

Claude drew a bow at a venture. "You mean that you never thought of anything like that when he said"—he was obliged to wet his lips with his tongue before he could get the words out—"when he said he was in love with you."

She nodded. "And, oh, Claude, I didn't mean it. I swear to you I didn't mean it. I knew he'd tell you. I was always afraid of him. But I just thought it *then*— just for a minute. I couldn't have done it—"

He had but the dimmest suspicion of what she meant, but he felt it well to say: "You could have done it, Rosie, and you would. You're that kind."

She took one timid step toward him, clasping her hands more passionately. "Oh, Claude, have mercy on me. If you knew what it is to be me! Even if I had done it, it wouldn't have been because I loved *you* any the less. It would have been for father and mother and Matt— and—and everything."

The way in which the words rent her made him the more cruel. They made him the more cruel because they rent him, too. "That doesn't make any difference, Rosie. You would have done it just the same. As it is, you were false to me—"

"Only that once, Claude!"

"And if you want me to have mercy on you, you'll have to tell me everything that happened—the very worst."

"The worst that happened was then."

"Then? When? There were so many times."

"But the other times he didn't say anything at all. He just came. I never dreamt—"

"But if you had dreamt, you would have played another sort of hand. Now, wouldn't you?"

"Claude, if you only knew! If you could only imagine what it is to have nothing at all!—to have to live and fight and scrimp and save!—and no one to help you!—and your brother in jail!—and coming out!—coming out, Claude!—and no one to help *him!*—and everything on you—!"

"That's got nothing to do with it, Rosie—"

"It *has* got something to do with it. It's got everything to do with it. If it hadn't, do you think that I'd have said that I'd marry him?"

Claude felt like a man who knows he's been shot, but as yet is unconscious of the wound. He spoke quietly: "I think I wouldn't have said that I'd marry two men at the same time, and play one off against the other."

There was exasperation in her voice as she cried: "But how could I help it, Claude? Can't you *see?* It wasn't *him.*"

"Oh, I can see that well enough. But do you think it makes it any better?"

"It makes it better if I never would have done it unless I'd been obliged to."

"But you'd have *done* it—"

"No, Claude, I wouldn't—not when it came to the point."

"But why didn't it come to the point? Since you told him you were willing to marry him, why—?"

She implored him. "Oh, what's the use of asking me that, if he's told you already?"

"It's this use, Rosie, that I want to hear it from yourself. You've told me one lie—"

"Oh, Claude!"

"And I want to see if you'll tell me any more."

"I didn't mean it to be a lie, Claude; but what could I say?"

"When we don't mean a thing to be a lie, Rosie, we tell the truth."

"But how *could* I?"

"Well, perhaps you couldn't; but you can now. You can tell me just what happened—and why more didn't happen, since you were willing that it should."

She began with difficulty, wringing her hands. "It was last January—I think it was January—yes, it was—one evening—I was in the other hothouse making out bills—and he came all of a sudden—and he asked me—he asked me—"

"Yes, yes; go on."

"He asked me if I loved you, and I said I did. And he asked me how much I loved you, and I said—I said I'd die for you—and so I would, Claude. I'd do it gladly. You can believe me or not—"

"That's all right. What I want to know is what happened after that."

"And then he said he'd help us. I didn't understand how he meant to help us—and I didn't quite believe him. You see, Claude, even if he is your brother, I never really liked him—or trusted him—not really. There was always something about him I couldn't make out—and now I see what it is. I knew he'd tell. And he made me promise I wouldn't."

"He made you promise you wouldn't tell—what?"

"What he said to me. He said he might go and marry some one else—and then he wouldn't want what he said to me to be known, because it would make trouble."

"But what did he say?"

"Don't you *know* what he said?"

"It doesn't matter whether I know or not, Rosie. It's for you to tell me."

She wrestled with herself. "Oh, Claude, I don't want to. I wish you wouldn't make me."

"Go on, Rosie; go on."

"He said he was in love with me himself—and that if I hadn't been in love with you—"

He was able to help her out. "That he'd have married you."

She nodded, piteously.

"And you said—?"

"Oh, Claude, what's the use?" She gathered her forces together. "I didn't say anything—not then."

"But you told him afterward that you were willing to marry *him* whether you were in love with me or not."

"No; not like that. I—I really didn't say anything at all."

"You just let him see it."

Again she nodded. "He said it himself. He could see —he could see how I felt—that it was like a temptation to me—that it was like bread and water held out to a starving man."

"That is, that the money was?"

She beat one hand against the other as she pressed them against her breast. "Don't you see? It had to be that way. I couldn't see all that money come right— come right into sight—and not wish—just for that minute —that I could have it. Could I, now?"

"No; I don't suppose you could, Rosie—being what you are. But, you see, I thought you were something else."

"Oh no, Claude, you didn't. You've known all along—"

"You mean, I thought I knew all along! But I find I didn't. I find that you're only willing to marry me because Thor wouldn't take you."

"He couldn't take me after I said I'd die for you. How could he?"

"And how can I—after you've said you were willing—!" He threw out his arms with a gesture. "Oh, Rosie, what do you think I feel?"

She crept a little nearer. "I should think you'd feel pity, Claude."

"So I do—for myself. One's always sorry for a fool. But you haven't told me everything yet. You haven't told me what he said about me."

She tried to recollect herself. "About you, Claude? Oh yes. He asked me what our relation was to each other, and I said I didn't know. And then he asked me if you were going to marry me, and I said I didn't know that, either. And then he said not to be afraid, because— because—"

"Because he'd make—"

"No, he didn't say that. I asked him if he'd make you, and he said he wouldn't have to, because you'd do it whether or no, or something like that—I don't just remember what."

"He didn't say I'd do it because he'd give me five thousand dollars a year for the job, did he?"

She shook her head. She began to look dazed. "No, Claude, he didn't say anything like that at all."

"Well, he said it to me. And he was going to do it. He thinks he's going to do it still."

"And isn't he?"

"No, Rosie. I've got better fish to fry than that. If I'm for sale I shall go high."

"Oh, Claude, what do you mean? What are you going to do?"

"I'll tell you, Rosie. It'll give you an idea of the chap I am—of what I was willing to renounce for you. I was talking to a girl last night who let me see that she was all ready to marry me. She didn't say it in so many words, of course; but that's what it amounted to. She lives in a big house, with ten or twelve servants, and is the only child of one of the richest men in the city. She's what you'd call an heiress—and she's a pretty girl, too."

"And what did you say to her, Claude?"

"I told her I couldn't. I told her about you."

"About me? Oh, Claude! And what did she say?"

"She said it was splendid for a chap with my future to fall in love with a girl like you and be true to her. But, you see, Rosie, I thought you were true to me."

"Oh, but I am, Claude!"

He laughed. "True? Why, Rosie, you don't know the meaning of the word! When Thor whistles for you—as he will—you'll go after him like that." He snapped his fingers. "He'll only have to name your price."

She paid no attention to these words, nor to the insult they contained. Her arms were crossed on her breast, her face was turned to him earnestly. "Yes; but what about this other girl, Claude?"

He spoke with apparent carelessness. "Oh, about her?" He nodded in the direction of the door at the end of the hothouse and of the world that lay beyond it. "I'm going to marry her."

She looked puzzled. Her air was that of a person who had never heard similar words before. "You're going to—what?"

"I'm going to marry her, Rosie."

For a few seconds there was no change in her attitude. She seemed to be taking his statement in. When the meaning came to her she withdrew her eyes from his face, and dropped her arms heavily. More seconds passed while she stood like that, meek, crushed, sentenced, her head partially averted, her eyes downcast. Presently she moved, but it was only to begin again, absently, mechanically, to pick the superfluous female blossoms from the nearest vine, letting the delicate, pale-gold things flutter to the ground. It was long before she spoke in a childish, unresentful voice:

"Are you, Claude?"

He answered, firmly, "Yes, Rosie; I am."

She sighed. "Oh, very well."

He could see that for the moment she had no spirit to say more. Her very movements betrayed lassitude, dejection. Though his heart smote him, he felt constrained to speak on his own behalf.

"You'll remember that it wasn't my fault."

She went on with her picking silently, but with a weary motion of the hands. The resumption of the task compelled her to turn her back to him, in the position in which he had found her when he arrived.

"I'm simply doing what you would have done yourself— only Thor wouldn't let you."

She made no response. The picking of the blossoms took her away from him, step by step. He made another effort to let her see things from his point of view.

"It wouldn't be honorable for me now, Rosie, to be paid for doing a thing like that. It *would* be payment to me, though he was going to settle the money on you."

Even this last piece of information had no effect on her; she probably didn't understand its terms. Her fingers picked and dropped the blossoms slowly till she reached the end of her row.

He thought that now she would have to turn. If she turned he could probably wring from her the word of dismissal or absolution that alone would satisfy his conscience. He didn't know that she could slip around the dense mass of foliage and be out of sight. When she did so, amazement came to him slowly.

Expecting her to reappear, he stood irresolute. He could go after her and clasp her in his arms again—or he could steal down the narrow aisle of greenery and pass out of her life for ever. Out of her life, she would be out of his life—and there was much to be said in favor of achieving that condition. There was outraged love in Claude's heart, and also some calculation. It was not all calculation, neither was it all outraged love. If Rosie had flung him one piteous backward look, or held out her hands, or sobbed, he might have melted. But she did nothing. She only disappeared. She was lying like a stricken animal behind the thick screen of leaves, but he didn't know it. In any case, he gave her the option of coming back.

He gave her the option and waited. He waited in the overpowering heat, amid the low humming of bees. The minutes passed; there was neither sound among the vines nor footstep beside him; and so, with head bent and eyes streaming and head aching and nerves unstrung and conscience clamoring reproachfully, he turned and went his way.

He surprised his father by going back to the bank. "Look here, father," he confessed, "I'm not ill. I'm only terribly upset about—about something. Can't you send me to New York? Isn't there any business—?"

Masterman looked at him gravely and kindly. He divined what was happening. "There's nothing in New York," he said, after a minute's thinking, "but there's the Routh matter in Chicago. Why shouldn't you go there? Mr. Wright was taking it up himself. Was leaving by the four-o'clock train this afternoon. Go and tell him I want you to take his place. He'll explain the thing to you and supply you with funds. And," he added, after another minute's thought, "since you're going that far, why shouldn't you run on to the Pacific coast? Do you good. I've thought for some time past that you needed a little change. Take your own time—and all the money you want."

Claude was trying to articulate his thanks when his father cut him short. "All right, my boy. I know how you feel. If you're going to take the four-o'clock you've no time to lose. Good-by," he continued, holding out his hand heartily. "Good luck. God bless you!"

The young man got himself out of his father's room in order to keep from bursting into tears.

LIKE A STRICKEN ANIMAL BEHIND THE THICK SCREEN OF LEAVES

CHAPTER XXII

AS Thor and Lois breakfasted on the following Sunday the former was too busy with the paper to notice that his wife seemed preoccupied. He was made to understand it by her manner of saying, "Thor."

Dropping the paper, he gave her his attention. "Yes?"

Her head was inclined to one side as she trifled with her toast. "You know, Thor, that it's an old custom for newly married people to go to church together on the first Sunday they're at home."

"Oh, Lord!"

She had expected the exclamation. She also expected the half-humorous, half-repentant compliance which ensued.

"All right, I'll go."

It was the sort of yielding that followed on all his bits of resistance to her wishes—a yielding on second thought—a yielding through compunction—as though he were trying to make up to her for something he wasn't giving her. She laughed to herself at that, seeing that he gave her everything; but she meant that if she were not so favored she might have harbored the suspicion that on account of something lacking in their life he fell back on a form of reparation. As it was, she could only ascribe his peculiarity in this respect to the kindness of a nature that never seemed to think it could be kind enough.

It was her turn to feel compunction. "Don't go if you'd rather not. It's only a country custom, almost gone out of fashion nowadays."

But he persisted. "Oh, I'll go. Must put on another suit. Top-hat, of course."

With a good woman's satisfaction in getting her husband to church, if only for once, she said no more in the way of dissuasion. Besides, she hoped that, should he go, he might "hear something" that would comfort this hidden grief of which she no longer had a doubt, since Claude too, was aware of it. It was curious how it betrayed itself—neither by act nor word nor manner, nor so much as a sigh, and yet by a something indefinable beyond all his watchfulness to conceal from her. She couldn't guess at his trouble, even when she tried; but she tried only from inadvertence. When she caught herself doing so she refrained, respecting his secret till he thought it well to tell her.

She said no more till he again dropped the paper to give his attention to his coffee. "Have you been to see the Fays yet?"

He put the cup down without tasting it. He sat quite upright and looked at her strangely. He even flushed.

"Why, no."

The tone appealed to her ear and remained in her memory, though for the moment she had no reason to consider it significant. She merely answered, "I thought I might walk up the hill and see Rosie this afternoon," leaving the subject there.

Thor found the service novel, and impressive from its novelty. Except for the few weddings and funerals he had attended, and the service on the day he married Lois, he could hardly remember when he had been present as a formal participant at a religious ceremony. He had, therefore, no preconceived ideas concerning Christian worship, and not much in the way of prejudice. He had dropped in occasionally on the services of foreign cathedrals, but purely as a tourist who made no attempt to understand what was taking place. On this particular morning, however, the pressure of needs and emotions within his soul induced an inquiring frame of mind.

On reaching the pew to which Lois led him he sat down

awkwardly, looking for a place in which to bestow his top-hat without ruffling its gloss. Lois herself fell on her knees in prayer. The act took him by surprise. It was new to him. He was aware that she said prayers in private, and had a vague idea of the import of the rite; but this public, unabashed devotion gave him a little shock till he saw that others came in and engaged in it. They entered and knelt, not in obedience to any pre-concerted ceremony, but each on his own impulse, and rose, looking, so it seemed to Thor, reassured and stilled.

That was his next impression—reassurance, stillness. There was a serenity here that he had never before had occasion to recognize as part of life. People whom he knew in a commonplace way as this or that in the village sat hushed, tranquil, dignified above their ordinary state, raised to a level higher than any that could be reached by their own attainments or personalities. It seemed to him that he had come into a world of new standards, new values. Lois herself, as she rose from her knees and sat beside him, gained in a quality which he had no capacity to gauge.

He belonged to the new scientific school which studies and co-relates, but is chary of affirmations, and charier still of denials. "Never deny anything—*ne niez jamais rien*"—had been one of the standing bits of advice on the part of old Hervieu, under whom he had worked at the Institut Pasteur. He kept himself, therefore, in a non-hostile attitude toward all theories and systems. He had but a hazy idea as to Christian beliefs, but he knew in a general way that they were preposterous. Preposterous as they might be, it was his place, however, to observe phenomena, and, now that he had an opportunity to do so, he observed them.

"How did you like it?" Lois ventured, timidly, as after service they walked along County Street.

"I liked it."

"Why?"

The answer astonished her. "It was big."

"Big? How?"

"The sweep—the ideas. So high—so universal! Makes a tremendous appeal to—the imagination."

She smiled toward him shyly. "It's something, isn't it, to appeal to the imagination?"

"Oh, lots—since imagination rules the world."

They were on their way to lunch with Thor's father and stepmother. Now that there were two households in the family, the father insisted on a domestic reunion once a week. It was his way of expressing paternal forbearance under the blow Thor had dealt him in marrying Lois Willoughby.

"Where's Claude?"

Thor asked the question on sitting down to table. His father looked at his mother, who replied, with some self-consciousness:

"He's—he's gone West."

"West? Where?"

"To Chicago first, isn't it, Archie?"

Masterman admitted that it was to Chicago first, and to the Pacific coast afterward. Thor's dismay was such that Lois looked at him in surprise. "Why, Thor? What difference can it make to you? Claude's able to travel alone, isn't he?"

The efforts made by both his parents to carry off the matter lightly convinced Thor that there was more in Claude's departure than either business or pleasure would explain. Before Lois, who was not yet in the family secret, he could ask no questions; but it seemed to him that both his father and his mother had uneasiness written in their faces. He could hardly eat. He bolted his food only to put Lois off the scent. The old tumult in his soul which he was seeking every means to still was beginning to break out again. If it should prove that he had given up Rosie Fay to Claude, and that, with his parents' connivance, Claude was trying to abandon her, then, by God . . .

But he caught Lois's eye. She was watching him, not so much in disquietude as with faint amusement. It seemed odd to her that Claude's going away for a holiday should vex him so. Poor Lois! He was already afraid on her account—afraid that if Rosie Fay were left deserted— free!—and a temptation he couldn't resist were to come to him!—Lois would be the one to suffer most.

By the middle of the afternoon, when his father had gone off in one direction and Lois in another, he found an opportunity for the word with his stepmother which he had hung about the house to get.

"There's nothing behind this, is there?"

She averted her head. "How do I know, Thor? *I* had nothing to do with it. All I know is just what happened. Claude came rushing home last Wednesday, and said he had to go right off to Chicago on business. I helped him pack—and he went."

"Why didn't any one tell me?"

"Well, you haven't been at the house. And it didn't seem important enough—"

"But it is important, isn't it? Doesn't father think so?"

She tried to look at him frankly. "Your father doesn't know any more about it than I know—and that's nothing at all. Claude came to him and said—but I really oughtn't to tell you, Thor. Your father would be annoyed with me."

"Then it's something that's got to be kept from me."

"N-no; not exactly. It's only poor Claude's secret. We didn't try to wring it from him because— Oh, Thor, I wish you would let things take their course. I'm sure it would be best."

"Best to let Claude be a scoundrel?"

"Oh, he couldn't be that. I want to be just to that girl, but we both know that there are queer things about her. There's that man who's giving her money—and dear knows what there may be besides. And so if they *have* quarreled—"

But Thor rushed away. Having learned all he needed to know on that side, he must hear what was to be said on the other. He had hoped never again to be brought face to face with Rosie till she was his brother's wife. That condition would have dug such a gulf between them that even nature would be changed. But if she was not to be Claude's wife—if Claude was becoming a brute to her—then she must see that at least she had a friend.

His heart was so hot within him as he climbed the hill that he forgot that Lois would probably be there before him. As a matter of fact, she was talking to Fay in a corner of the yard, standing in the shade of a great magnolia that was a pyramid of bloom. All around it the ground was strewn in a circle with its dead-white petals, each with its flush of red. Near the house there were yellow clumps of forsythia, while the hedge of bridal-veil to the south of the grass-plot seemed to have just received a fall of snow.

Fay confronted him as, slackening his pace, he went toward them; but Lois turned only at his approach. Her expression was troubled.

"Thor, I wish you'd explain to me what Mr. Fay is saying. He doesn't want me to see Rosie."

"Why, what's up?"

Fay's expression told him that something serious was up, for it was ashen. It had grown old and sunken, and the eyes had changed their starry vagueness to a dulled animosity.

"There's this much up, Dr. Thor," Fay said, in that tone of his which was at once mild and hostile, "that I don't want any Masterman to have anything to do with me or mine."

Thor tried to control the sharpness of his cry. "Why not?"

"You ought to know why not, Dr. Thor. And if you don't, you've only to look at my little girl. Oh, why couldn't you leave her alone?"

Lois spoke anxiously. "Is anything the matter with her?"

"Only that you've killed her between you."

Thor allowed Lois to question him. "Why, what *can* you mean?"

"Just what I say, ma'am—that she's done for."

Lois grew impatient. "But I don't understand. Done for—how?" She turned to her husband. "Oh, Thor, do see her and find out what's the matter."

"No, ma'am," Fay said, firmly. "He's seen her once too often as it is."

Lois repeated the words. "'Once too often as it is'! What does that mean?"

"Better ask *him*, ma'am."

"It's no use asking me," Thor declared, "for I've not the slightest idea of what you're driving at."

"Oh, I know you can play the innocent, Dr. Thor; but it's no use keeping up the game. You took me in at first; you took me in right along. You were going to be a friend to me!—and buy the place!—and keep me in it to work it!—and every sort of palaver like that!—when you was only after my little girl."

Thor was dumb. It was Lois who protested. "Oh, Mr. Fay, how can you say such things? It's wicked."

"It may be wicked, all right, ma'am; but ask *him* how I can say them. All I know is what I've seen. If you was going to marry this lady," he went on, turning again to Thor, "why couldn't you have kept away from my little girl? You didn't do yourself any good, and you did her a lot of harm."

It was to come to Thor's aid as he stood speechless that Lois said, soothingly: "But I had nothing to do with that, Mr. Fay. I never wanted anything of Rosie but to be her friend."

"You, ma'am? You're all of a piece. You're all Mastermans together. What had you to do with being a friend to her?—getting her to call!—and have tea!—and putting notions into her head! The rich and the poor can't be friends any longer. If the poor think they can, the more fool they! We've *been* fools in my family, thinking because we were Americans we had rights. There's no rights any more, except the right of the strong to trample on the weak—till some one tramples on *them*. And some one always does. There's that. We're down to-day, but you'll be down to-morrow. Don't forget it, ma'am. America has that kind of justice when it hasn't any other—that it makes everybody take their turn. It's ours now; but you'll get yours as sure as life is life."

Lois looked at Thor. "Can you make out what he means?"

"I can make out that he's very much mistaken—"

"Mistaken, Dr. Thor? I don't see how you can say that. I wasn't mistaken the night I saw you creeping into that hothouse over there, where you knew my little girl was at work. I wasn't mistaken when I saw you creep away. Still less was I mistaken when I stole in after you had gone, and found her with her arms on the desk, and her head bowed down on them, and she crying fit to kill herself. That was just a few days before she heard you was going to marry this lady—and she's never been the same child since. Always troubled—always something on her mind. Not once since that night have you darkened these doors, though you'd had a patient here. Have you, now?"

"I didn't come," Thor stammered, "because Dr. Hilary had done all that was necessary for Mrs. Fay, and—and I've been away."

"But if you didn't come," Fay went on, with the mildness that was more forcible than wrath, "some one else did. You'd left a good substitute. He's finished the work that you began. He was here with her an hour last

Wednesday morning—just after I'd warned him off for good and all."

Thor started. "Let me go to her."

But Fay stood in his way. "No, sir. To see you would be the finishing touch. She can't hear your name without a shiver going through her from head to foot. We've tried it on her. Between the two of you—your brother and you—it's you she's most afraid of." There was silence for a second, while he turned his gray face first to the one and then to the other of his two listeners. "Why couldn't you all have let her be? What were you after? What have you got out of it? *I* can't see."

"Fay, I swear to you that we never wanted anything but her good," Thor cried, with a passion that made Lois turn her troubled eyes on him searchingly. "If my brother hasn't told you what he meant, I'll do it now. He wanted to marry Rosie. He *was* to have married her. If there's trouble between them, it's all a mistake. Just let me see her—"

But Fay dismissed this as idle talk. "No, Dr Thor. Stories of that kind don't do any good. Your brother never wanted to marry her, or meant to, either—not any more than you. What you did want and what you did mean God only knows. It's mystery to me. But what isn't mystery to me is that we're all done for. Now that she's gone, we're all gone—the lot of us. I've kept up till now—"

"If money will do any good, Fay—" Thor began, with a catch in his voice.

"No, Dr. Thor; not now. Money might have helped us once, but I ain't going to take a price for my little girl's unhappiness."

"But what *would* do good, Mr. Fay?" Lois asked. "If you'd only tell us—"

"Then, ma'am, I will. It's to let us be. Don't come near me nor mine any more—none o' you."

She turned to Thor. "Thor, is it true that Claude wanted to marry Rosie? I've never heard of it."

"Oh yes, ma'am, you have," Fay broke in, with irony. "We've all heard of that kind o' marriage. It's as old as men and women on the earth. But it don't go down with me; and if I find that my little girl has been taken in by it, then I sha'n't be to blame if—if some one gets what he deserves."

The words were uttered in tones so mild that, as he shuffled away, leaving them staring at each other, they scarcely knew that there had been a threat in them.

CHAPTER XXIII

IT was an incoherent tale that Thor stammered out to Lois as he and she walked homeward. By trying to tell Claude's story without including his own he was, for the first time since the days of school-boy escapades, making a deliberate attempt at prevarication. He suppressed certain facts, and over-emphasized others. He did it with a sense of humiliation which became acute when he began to suspect that he was not deceiving her. She walked on, saying nothing at all. Now and then, when he ventured to glance at her in profile, she turned to give him a sick, sad smile that seemed to draw its sweetness from the futility of his efforts. "My God, she knows!" were the words actually in his mind while he went floundering on with the explanation of why he couldn't allow Claude to be a cad.

And yet, except for those smiles of an elusiveness beyond him, she betrayed no hint of being stricken in the way he was afraid of. On the contrary, she seemed, when she spoke, to be giving her mind entirely to the course of Claude's romance. "He won't marry her. He'll marry Elsie Darling."

An hour ago the assertion would have angered him. Now he was relieved that she had the spirit to make it at all. He endeavored to imitate her tone. "What makes you think so?"

"I know Claude. She's the sort of girl for him to marry. There's good in him, and she'll bring it out."

"Unfortunately, it's too late to think of Claude's good when he's pledged to some one else."

"Would you make him marry her?"

"I'd make him do his duty."

She gave him another of those faint smiles of which the real meaning baffled him. "I wouldn't lay too much stress on that, if I were you. To marry for the sake of doing one's duty is"—she faltered an instant, but recovered herself—"is as likely as not to defeat its own ends."

He was afraid to pursue the topic lest she should speak more plainly. On arriving home he was glad to see her go to her room and shut the door. It grieved him to think that she might be brooding in silence, but even that was better than speech. As Uncle Sim and Cousin Amy Dawes were coming to Sunday-night supper, the evening would be safe; and to avoid being face to face with her in the meanwhile he went out again.

Having passed an hour in his office, he strolled up into the wood above the village, his refuge from boyhood onward in any hour of trouble. There was space here, and air, and solitude. It was a diversion that was almost a form of consolation to be in touch with the wood's teeming life. Moreover, the trees, with their stately aloofness from mortal cares, their strifelessness and strength, shed on him a kind of benediction. From long association, from days of bird's-nesting in spring, and camping in summer, and nutting in autumn, and snow-shoeing in winter, he knew them almost as individual personalities — the great white oaks, the paper birches, the white pines with knots that were masses of dry resin, the Canada balsams with odorous boughs, the sugar-maples, the silver maples, the beeches, the junipers, the hemlocks, the hackmatacks, with the low-growing hickories, witch-hazels, and slippery-elms. Their green was the green of early May—yellow-green, red-green, bronze-green, brown-green, but nowhere as yet the full, rich hue of summer. Here and there a choke-cherry in full bloom swayed and shivered like a wraith.

In shady places the ferns were unfolding in company with Solomon's-seal, wake-robin, the lady's-slipper, and the painted trillium. There was an abundance of yellow—cinquefoil, crowfoot, ragwort, bellwort, and shy patches of gold-colored violets.

In the sloping outskirts of the wood he stood still and breathed deeply, a portion of his cares and difficulties slipping from his shoulders. Somewhere within him was the sense of kinship with the wilderness that has become atavistic in Americans of six or eight generations on the soil. It was like skipping two centuries and getting back where life was primitive from necessity. There were few if any complications here, nor were there subtleties to consider. As far back as he knew anything of his Thorley ancestors, they had hewed and hacked and delved and tilled on and about this hillside, getting their changes from its seasons, their food from its products, their science from its bird-life and beast-life, their arts and their simples, their dyes and their drinks from its roots and juices. To the extent that men and the primeval could be one, they had been one with the forest of which nothing but this upland sweep remained, treating it as both friend and enemy. As enemy they had felled it; as friend they had lived its life and loved it, transmitting their love to this son, who was now bringing his heartaches, as he was accustomed also to bring his joys, where they had brought their own.

The advantage of the wood to Thor was that once within its shadows he could, to some degree, stop thinking of the life outside. He could give his first attention to the sounds and phenomena about him. As he stood now, listening to the resonant tapping of a hairy woodpecker on a dead tree-trunk he could forget that the world held a Lois, a Rosie, and a Claude, each a storm-center of emotions. It was a respite from emotions—in a measure, a respite from himself. He stepped craftily, following the sound of the woodpecker's tap till he had the satisfaction of seeing a black-and-white back, with a red band across the busily bobbing head. He stopped again to watch a chipmunk who was more sharply watching him. The little fellow, red-brown and striped, sat cocked on a stone, his fore paws crossed on his white breast like the hands of a meek saint at prayer. Strolling on again, he paused from time to time—to listen to a robin singing right overhead, or to catch the liquid, spiritual chant of a hermit-thrush in some stiller thicket of the wood, or to watch a bluebird fly directly into its nest, probably an abandoned woodpecker's hole, in a decaying Norway pine. These small happenings soothed him. Sauntering and pausing, he came up to the high, treeless ridge he had last visited on the day he asked Lois to marry him.

The ridge broke sharply downward to a stretch of undulating farms. Patches of green meadowland were interspersed with the broad, red fields in which as yet nothing had begun to grow. Had it not been Sunday the farmers would have been at work, plowing, sowing, harrowing. As it was, the landscape enjoyed a rich Sabbath peace, broken only by the swooping of birds, out of the invisible, across the line of sight, and on into the invisible again. It was all beauty and promise of beauty, wealth and promise of wealth. The cherry-trees were in bloom; the pear and the apple and the quince would follow soon. Above the farm-houses tall elms rose, fan-shaped and garlanded.

The very charm of the prospect called up those questions he had been trying for a minute to shelve. How was it that in a land of milk and honey men were finding it so hard to live? How was it that with conditions in which every man might have enough and to spare, making it his aim to see that his fellow had the same, there could be greed and ingenious oppression and social crime, with the menace of things graver still? What's the matter with us? he asked, helplessly. Was it something wrong with the American people? or was it something wrong with the whole human race? or was it a condition of permanent strife that the human race could never escape from? Was man a being capable of high spiritual attainment, as he had heard in the church that morning? or was he no better than the ruthless creatures of the woodland, where the weasel preyed on the chipmunk, and the owl on the mouse, and the fox on the rabbit, and the shrike on the phœbe, and the phœbe on the insect, in an endless round of ferocity? Had man emerged above this estate? or was it as foolish to expect him to spare his brother-man as to ask a hawk to spare a hen?

These questions bore on Thor's immediate thoughts and conduct. They bore on his relations with his father and Claude and Lois. Through the social web in which he found himself involved they bore on Rosie Fay; and from the social web they worked out to the great national ideals in which he longed to see his native land a sanctuary for mankind. But could man build a sanctuary? Would he know how to make use of one? Or was he, Thor Masterman, but repeating the error of that great-grandfather who had turned to America for the salvation of the race, and died broken-hearted because its people were only looking out for number one?

Because he couldn't find answers to these questions for himself, he tried, during supper, to sound Uncle Sim, leading up to the subject by an adroit indirectness. "Been to church," he said, after serving Cousin Amy Dawes with lobster à la Newburg.

"Saw you," came from Uncle Sim.

"Did you? What were you doing there? Thought you were a disciple of old Hilary."

"That was the reason. Hilary's idea. Can't go 'round to the different churches himself, so he sends me. Look in on 'em all."

"There's too much sherry in this lobster à la Newburg," Cousin Amy Dawes said, sternly. "I bet she's put in two tablespoonfuls instead of one."

Being stone-deaf, Cousin Amy Dawes took no part in conversation except what she herself could contribute. She was a dignified woman who had the air of being hewn in granite. There was nothing soft about her but three detachable corkscrew curls on each side of an immobile face and a heart that every one knew to be as maternal as milk. Dressed in stiff black silk, a heavy gold chain around her neck, and a huge gold brooch at her throat, and wearing fingerless black-silk mittens, she might have walked out of an old daguerreotype.

"I should think," Thor observed, dryly, "that you'd find your religion growing rather composite."

"No. T'other way 'round. Grows simpler. Get their co-ordinating principle—the common denominator that goes into 'em all."

"That is," Lois said, in the endeavor to be free to think her own thoughts by keeping him on a hobby, "you look for their points of contact rather than their differences."

"Oh, you get beyond the differences. 'Beyond these voices there is peace.' Doesn't some one say that? Well, you get there. If you can stand the clamor of the voices for a while you emerge into a kind of still place where they blend into one. Then you find that they're all trying to say the same thing, which is also the thing you're trying to say yourself."

As he sat back in his chair twisting his wiry mustache with a handsome, sun-burnt hand, Thor felt that he had him where he had been hoping to get him. "But what *do* we want to say, Uncle Sim? What do you want to say? And what do I?"

The old man held his sharp-pointed beard by the tip, eying his nephew obliquely. "That's the great secret, Thor. We're all like little babies, who from the time they begin to hear language are bursting with the desire to say something; only they don't know what it is till they learn to speak. Then it comes to 'em."

"Yes, but what comes to them?"

"Isn't it what comes to all babies—the instinct to say, *Abba—Father?*"

"Say, Lois," Cousin Amy Dawes requested, in her loud, commanding voice, "just save me a mite of this cold duck for old Sally Gibbs. It 'll be tasty for the poor soul. I'll take it to her as we go up the hill. What do you pay your cook?" Without waiting for an answer she continued like an oracle, "I don't believe she's worth it."

Thor leaned across the table. "What I want to know is this: suppose the instinct to say *Abba—Father* does come to us, is there anything there to respond that will show us a better way—personally and nationally, I mean, than the rather poor one we're finding for ourselves?"

"Can't give you any guarantees, Thor, if that's what you're after. Just got to say *Abba—Father*, and see for yourself. Nothing but seeing for oneself is any good when it comes to the personal. And as for the national—well, there was a man once who went stalking through the land crying, 'O Israel, turn thee to the Lord thy God,' and I guess he knew what he was about. It was, 'Turn ye, turn ye! Why will ye die?' They didn't turn and so they died. Inevitable consequence. Same with this people or any other people. In proportion as it turns to the Lord its God it 'll live; and in proportion as it doesn't it 'll go to pot." He veered around to Lois as to one who would agree with him: "Ain't that it?"

She responded with a sweet, absent smile which showed to Thor at least that her thoughts were elsewhere. As a matter of fact, Thor's questions and Uncle Sim's replies, which continued in more or less the same strain, lay in a realm with regard to which she had few misgivings or anxieties. Her heart-searchings being of another nature, she was doing in thought what she had done when in the afternoon she had gone to her room and shut the door. She was standing before her mirror, contrasting the image reflected there with Rosie Fay's worn, touching prettiness.

How awesome, how incredible, that Thor, her great,

noble Thor, should have let his heart go—perhaps the very best of his heart—to anything so insignificant, so unformed, so unequal to himself! It was this awesomeness, this incredibility, that overwhelmed her. Her mind fixed itself on it, for the time being, to the exclusion of other considerations. Thor was like meaner men! He could be caught by a pretty face! He was so big in body and soul that she had thought him free from petty failing —and yet here it was! There was a kind of shame in it. It weakened him, it lowered him.

She had seen it from the minute when he began to tell his halting tale about Claude. It was pitiful the way in which he had betrayed himself. From Fay she had got no more than a hint—a hint she had been quick to collate with her knowledge of some secret grief on Thor's part; but she hadn't been really sure of the truth till she saw he was trying to hide it. That Thor should be trying to hide anything made her burn inwardly with something more poignant than humiliation.

She had smiled when he looked so imploringly toward her, but she hardly knew why. Perhaps it was to encourage him, to give him heart. For the first time in her life she felt the stronger, the superior. She was sorry for him, even though there was something about this new and unexpected phase in him that she despised.

She had got no further than that when the guests came and she had to give them her attention. When they left, and Thor was seeing them to the door, she took the opportunity to slip up to her room again. She locked the door behind her, and locked the door that communicated with his dressing-room. Once more she took her stand before the pier-glass.

Something had come to her; she was sure of it. It had come almost since that afternoon. If it was not beauty, it rendered beauty of no importance. It was a spirit, a fire, that made her a woman who could be proud, a woman a man might be proud of. She had come to her

226

own at last. She could see for herself that there was a subdued splendor about her which raised her in the scale of personality. She had little vanity; hitherto she had had little pride; but she knew now, with an assurance which it would have been hypocritical to disguise, that she was the true mate of the man she had taken Thor to be. She had known it before—diffidently and apologetically. She knew it now calmly, and as a matter of course, in a manner that did away with any necessity for shrinking or self-depreciation.

She moved away from the mirror, taking off the string of small pearls she wore and throwing them on the dressing-table. In the middle of the room she stood with a feeling of helplessness. It was so difficult to see what she ought to do. What was one's duty toward a husband who had practically told her that he had married her only because he couldn't marry a woman he loved better? Other questions began to rise within her, questions and protests and flashes of indignation, but she beat them back, standing in an attitude of reflection, and trying to discern the first steps of her way. She knew that the emotions she was keeping under would assert themselves in time, but just now she wanted only to see what she ought to do during the next half-hour.

There came into her mind what Uncle Sim had said at supper—"Just got to say *Abba—Father*, and see." She shook her head. She couldn't say *Abba—Father* at present. She didn't know why—but she couldn't. Whatever the passion within her, it was nothing she could bring before a Throne of Grace. It crossed her mind that if she prayed at all that night she would pass this whole matter over. And in that case, why pray at all?

And yet the thought of omitting her prayers disturbed her. If she did it to-night, why not to-morrow night? And if to-morrow night, where would it end? It was not a convincing argument, but it drew her toward her bedside.

Even then she didn't kneel down, but clung to one of the tall, fluted posts that supported a canopy. She couldn't pray. She didn't know what to pray for. Conventional petitions would have had no meaning, and for the moment she had no others to offer up. It was but half consciously that she found herself stammering: "*Abba—Father! Abba—Father!*" her lips moving dumbly to the syllables.

It brought her no relief. It gave her neither immediate light on her way nor any new sense of power. She was as dazed as ever, and as indignant. And yet when she raised herself from the weary clinging to the fluted post she went to both the doors she had locked and unlocked them.

CHAPTER XXIV

THE consciousness of something to be suppressed was with Lois when she woke. "Not yet! Not yet!" was the warning of her subliminal self whenever resentments and indignations endeavored to escape control.

With Thor she kept to subjects that had no personal bearing, clearly to his relief. At breakfast they talked of the Mexican rising under Madero, which was discussed in the papers of that morning. She knew that the question in his mind was, "Does she really know?" but she betrayed nothing that would help him to an answer.

When, after having kissed her with a timid, apologetic affection which partly touched and partly angered her, he left for the office, she put on a hat and, taking a parasol, went to see Dr. Hilary.

The First Parish Church, the oldest in the village, stands in a grassy delta where two of the rambling village lanes enter the Square. The white, barn-like nave, with its upper and lower rows of small, oblong windows, retires discreetly within a grove of elms, while a tall, slim spire grows slimmer through diminishing tiers of arches, balconies, and lancet lights till it dwindles away into a high, graceful pinnacle.

Behind the church, in the widest section of the delta, the parsonage, a white wooden box dating from the fifties supporting a smaller box by way of cupola, looks across garden, shrubbery, and lawn to Schoolhouse Lane, from which nothing but the simplest form of wooden rail protects the inclosure.

It was the time for bulbs to be in flower, and the spring

perennials. Tulips in a wide, dense mass bordered the brick pavement that led from the gate to the front door. Elsewhere could be seen daffodils, irises, peonies just bursting into bloom, and long, drooping curves of bleeding-heart hung with rose-and-white pendents. By a corner of the house the ground was indigo-dark with a thick little patch of squills.

It was a relief to Lois to find the old man himself, bareheaded and in an alpaca house-jacket, rooting out weeds on the lawn, his thin, gray locks tossed in the breeze. On seeing her pause and look over the clump of wiegelia, which at this point smothered the rail, he raised himself, dusted the earth from his hands, and went forward. They talked at first just as they stood, with the budding shrubs between them.

"Oh, Dr. Hilary, I'm so anxious about Rosie Fay."

"Are you now?" As neither age nor gravity could subdue the twinkle in his eyes, so sympathy couldn't quench it. "Well, I am meself."

"I think if I could see her I might be able to help her. Or, rather," she went on, nervously, "I think I ought to see her, whether I can help her or not. Have you seen her?"

"I have not," he declared, with Irish emphasis. "The puss takes very good care that I sha'n't, so she does. She's only got to see me coming in the gate to fly off to Duck Rock; and that, so her mother tells me, is all they see of her till nightfall. It's three days now that she's been struck with a fit of melancholy, or maybe four."

"Do you know what the trouble is?"

He evaded the question. "Do you?"

"I do—partly."

"Then you'll be the one to tackle her. As yet I haven't asked. I prefer to know no more about people than what they tell me themselves."

She found it possible to secure his aid on the unexplained ground that there had been a misunderstanding between her husband and herself, on the one side, and Jasper Fay on the other. "I don't *know* that I can help her. I dare say I can't. But if I could only see her—"

"Well, then, you shall see her. Just wait a minute while I change me coat and I'll go along with you."

On the way up the hill Lois questioned him about the Fays. "Did you know much of the boy?"

"Enough to see that he wasn't a thief—not by nature, that is. He's what might have been expected from his parents—the stuff out of which they make revolutionists and anarchists. He came into the world with desires thwarted, as you might say, and a detairmination to get even. He didn't steal; he took money. He took money because they needed it at home, and other people had it. He took it more in protest than in greed, if that's any excuse for him."

"The mother is better, isn't she?"

"She's clothed and in her right mind, if she'll only stay that way. She gets into one of her old tantrums every now and then; but I'm in hopes that the daughter's trouble will end them."

This hope seemed to be partially fulfilled in the welcoming way in which the door was opened to their knock. "I've brought you me friend, Mrs. Thor Masterman," was the old gentleman's form of introduction. "She wants to see Rosie. If Fay makes any trouble, tell him it's my wish."

"I've really only come to see Rosie, Mrs. Fay," Lois explained, not without nervousness, when the two women were alone on the door-step. "No, I won't go in, thank you, not if she's anywhere about the place. I'm really very anxious to have a talk with her."

Having feared a hostile reception, she was relieved to be answered with a certain fierce cordiality. "I'm sure I hope you'll get it. It's more'n her father and I can do."

"Perhaps she'd talk to me. Girls often will talk to a— to a stranger, when they won't to one of their own."

"Well, you can try." In spite of the coldness of the handsome features, something in the nature of a new life, a new softening humanity, was struggling to assert itself. "*We* can't get a word out of her. She'll neither speak, nor sleep, nor eat, nor do a hand's turn. It's the work that bothers me most—not so much that it needs to be done as because it 'd be a relief to her." She added, with a shy wistfulness that contrasted oddly with the hard glint in her eyes, "I've found that out myself."

"Have you any idea where she is?"

She pointed toward Duck Rock. "Oh, I suppose she's over there. She was to have picked the cucumbers this morning, but I see she hasn't done it."

"Has Mr. Fay told you what the trouble is?"

"Well, he has. But then he's so romantic. Always was. Land's sake! I don't pay any attention to young people's goings-on. Seen too much of it in my own day. I don't say that the young fellow hasn't been foolish —and I don't say—you'll excuse me!—that Rosie ain't just as good as he is, even if he *is* Archie Masterman's son—"

"Oh no, nor I," Lois hastened to interpose.

"But there's nothing wrong. I've asked her—and I *know*. I'm sure of it."

Lois spoke eagerly. "Oh yes; so am I."

"So that there's that." She went on with a touch of her old haughtiness of spirit: "And she's every mite as good as he is. It's all nonsense, Fay's talking as if it was some young lord who'd jilted a girl beneath him. Young lord, indeed! I'll young lord him, if he ever comes my way. I tell Rosie not to demean herself to grieve for them that are no better than herself. It's nothing but romantics," she explained further. "I've no patience with Fay—talking as if some one ought to shoot some one or commit murder. That's the way Matt began. Fay ought to know better at his time of life. I declare he has no more sense than Rosie."

THE SIDE OF THE ANGELS

Lois had not expected to be called upon to defend Fay, but she said, "I suppose he naturally feels indignant when he sees—"

"There's a desperate streak in Fay," the woman broke in, uneasily, "and Rosie takes after him. For the matter of that, she takes after us both—for I'm sure I've been gloomy enough. There's been something lacking in us all, like cooking without salt. I see that now as plain as plain, though I can't get Fay to believe me. You might as well talk to a stone wall as talk to Fay when he's got his nose stuck into a book. I hate the very name of that Carlyle; and that Darwin, he's another. They're his Bible, I tell him, and he don't half understand what they mean. It's Duck Rock," she went on, with a quiver of her fine lips, while her hands worked nervously at the corner of her apron—"it's Duck Rock that I'm most afraid of. It kind o' haunted me all the time I was sick; and it kind o' haunts Rosie."

"Then I'll go and see if she's there," Lois said, as she turned away, leaving the austere figure to stare after her with eyes that might have been those of the woman delivered from the seven devils.

It was an easy matter for Lois to find her way among the old apple-trees—of which one was showing an early blossom or two on the sunny side—to the boulevard below, and thence to the wood running up the bluff. Though she had not been here since the berry-picking days of childhood, she knew the spot in which Rosie was likely to be found. As a matter of fact, having climbed the path that ran beneath oaks and through patches of brakes, spleenwort, and lady-ferns, she was astonished to hear a faint, plaintive singing, and stopped to listen. The voice was poignantly thin and sweet, with the frail, melancholy sound she had heard from distant shepherds' pipes in Switzerland. Had she not, after a few seconds, recognized the air, she would have been unable to detect the words:

16   233

THE SIDE OF THE ANGELS

> "Ah, dinna ye mind, Lord Gregory,
>   By bonnie Irvinside,
> Where first I owned the virgin love
>   I long, long had denied?"

Though the singer was invisible, Lois knew she could not be far away, since the voice was too weak to carry. She was about to go forward when the faint melody began again:

> "An exile from my father's ha'
>   And a' for loving thee;
> At least be pity to me shown,
>   If love it may na' be."

Placing the voice now as near the great oak-tree circled by a seat, just below the point where the ascending bluff broke fifty feet to the pond beneath, Lois went rapidly up the last few yards of the ascent.

Rosie was seated with her back to the gnarled trunk, while she looked out over the half-mile of dancing blue wavelets to where, on the other side, the brown, wooden houses of the Thorley estate swept down to the shore. She rose on seeing the visitor approach, showing a startled disposition to run away. This she might have done had not Lois caught her by the hand and detained her.

"I know all about everything, Rosie—about everything."

She meant that she understood the situation not only as regarding one brother, but as regarding both. Rosie's response was without interest or curiosity. "Do you?"

"Yes, Rosie; and I want to talk to you about it. Let us sit down."

Still holding the girl's hands in a manner that compelled her to reseat herself, she examined the little face for the charm that had thrown such a spell on Thor. With a pang she owned to herself that she found it. No one could look at Thor with that expression of entreaty without reaching all that was most tender in his soul.

"WOULD YOU BE HAPPY WITH HIM IF HE CAME BACK?"

For the moment, however, that point must be allowed to pass. "Not yet! Not yet!" something cried to the passion that was trying to get control of her. She went on earnestly, almost beseechingly: "I know just what happened, Rosie dear, and how hard it's been for you; and I want you to let me help you."

There was no light in Rosie's chrysoprase-colored eyes. Her voice was listless. "What can you do?"

Put to her in that point-blank way, Lois found the question difficult. She could only answer: "I can be with you, Rosie. We can be side by side."

"There wouldn't be any good in that. I'd rather be left alone."

"Oh, but there would be good. We should strengthen each other. I—I need help, too. I should find it partly, if I could do anything for you."

Rosie surveyed her friend, not coldly, but with dull detachment. "Do you think Claude will come back to me?"

"What do you think, yourself?"

"I don't think he will." She added, with a catch in her breath like that produced by a sudden, darting pain, "I know he won't."

"Would you be happy with him if he did?"

"I shouldn't care whether I was happy or not—if he'd come."

Lois thought it the part of wisdom to hold out no hope. "Then, since we believe he won't come, isn't it better to face it with—"

"I don't see any use in facing it. You might as well ask a plant to face it when it's pulled up by the roots and thrown out into the sun. There's nothing left to face."

"But you're not pulled up by the roots, Rosie. Your roots are still in the soil. You've people who need you—"

Rosie made a little gesture, with palms outward. "I've given them all I had. I'm—I'm—empty."

"Yes, you feel so now. That's natural. We do feel

empty of anything more to give when there's been a great drain on us. But somehow it's the people who've given most who always have the power to go on giving—after a little while. With time—"

The girl interrupted, not impatiently, but with vacant indifference. "What's the good of time—when it's going to be always the same?"

"The good of time is that it brings comfort—"

"I don't want comfort. I'd rather be as I am."

"That's perfectly natural—for now. But time passes whether we will or no; and whether we will or no, it softens—"

"Time can't pass if you won't let it."

"Why—why, what do you mean?"

"I mean—just that."

Lois clasped the girl's hands desperately. "But, Rosie, you must *live*. Life has a great deal in store for you still—perhaps a great deal of happiness. They say that life never takes anything from us for which it isn't prepared to give us compensation, if we'll only accept it in the right way."

Rosie shook her head. "I don't want it."

Lois tried to reach the dulled spirit by another channel. "But we all have disappointments and sorrows, Rosie. I have mine. I've great ones."

The aloofness in Rosie's gaze seemed to put miles between them. "That doesn't make any difference to me. If you want me to be sorry for them—I'm not. I can't be sorry for any one."

In her desire to touch the frozen springs of the girl's emotions, Lois said what she would have supposed herself incapable of saying. "Not when you know what they are?—when you know what one of them is, at any rate!—when you know what one of them *must* be! You're the only person in the world except myself who can know."

Rosie's voice was as lifeless as before. "I can't be sorry. I don't know why—but I can't be."

"Do you mean that you're glad I have to suffer?"

"N-no. I'm not glad—especially. I just—don't care."

Lois was baffled. The impenetrable iciness was more difficult to deal with than active grief. She made her supreme appeal. "And then, Rosie, then there's—there's God."

Rosie looked vaguely over the lake and said nothing. If she fixed her eyes on anything, it was on the quivering balance of a kingfisher in the air. When with a flash of silver and blue he swooped, and, without seeming to have touched the water, went skimming away with a fish in his bill, her eyes wandered slowly back in her companion's direction.

Lois made another attempt. "You believe in God, don't you?"

There was a second's hesitation. "I don't know as I do."

The older woman spoke with the pleading of distress. "But there *is* a God, Rosie."

There was the same brief hesitation. "I don't care whether there is or not."

Though Lois could get no further, it hurt her to see the look of relief in the little creature's face when she rose and said: "You'd rather I'd go away, wouldn't you? Then I will go; but it won't be for long. I'm not going to leave you to yourself. I'm coming back soon. I shall come back again to-day. If you're not at home, I'll follow you up here."

She waited for some sign of protest, but Rosie sat silent and impassive. Though courtesy kept her dumb, it couldn't conceal the air of resigned impatience with which she awaited her visitor's departure.

Lois looked down at her helplessly. In sheer incapacity to affect the larger issues, she took refuge in the smaller. "Isn't it near your dinner-time? I'm going your way. We could go along together."

"I don't want any dinner. I'll go home—by and by."

Lois felt herself dismissed. "Very well, Rosie. I'll say good-by for now. But it will only be for a little while. You understand that, don't you? I'm not going to let you throw me off. I'm going to cling to you. I've got the right to do it, because—because the very thing that makes you unhappy—makes me."

In the eyes that Rosie lifted obliquely Lois read such unutterable things that she turned away. She carried that look with her as she went down the hill beneath the oaks and between the sunlit patches of brakes, spleenwort, and lady-ferns. What scenes, what memories, had called it up? What part in those scenes and memories had been played by Thor? What had been the actual experience between this girl and him? Would she ever know? Had she better know? What should she do if she were to know? Once more the questions she had been trying to repress urged themselves for answer; but once more she controlled herself through the counsel of the inner voice: "Not yet! Not yet!"

CHAPTER XXV

B UT after Lois had gone Rosie came to life again. That is, she entered once more the conditions in which her mind was free to tread its round of grief. Lois kept her out of them. Her father and mother did the same. Household duties and the tasks of the hothouse and the necessity for eating and sleeping and speaking did the same. She turned from them all with a weariness as consuming as a sickness unto death.

She had done so from the instant when, crouching behind the vines of the cucumber-house, with all her senses strained, she perceived by the mere rustling of the leaves that Claude was making his way down the long, green aisle. She knew then that it was the end. If there had been no other cause of rupture between them, the girl who kept ten or twelve servants would have created it. Rosie knew enough of Claude to be aware that love could not bear down the scale against this princeliness of living. There would be so such repentance and reaction on his part as she had experienced with Thor. Once he was gone, he was gone. It was the end.

The soft opening and closing of the hothouse door as he went out reached her like a sigh, a last sigh, a dying sigh, after which—nothing! Rosie expected nothing—but she waited. She waited as watchers wait round a death-bed for the possibility of one more breath; but none came. She stirred then and rose. She rose mechanically, brushing the earth from her clothing, and began again the interrupted task of picking the superfluous female flowers and letting them flutter downward.

THE SIDE OF THE ANGELS

It was when she had come to the end of her third row and was about to turn into the fourth that the sense of the impossibility of going on swept over her. "Oh, I can't!" She dropped her arms to her side. "I can't. I can't." She meant only that she couldn't go on just then; but in the back of her mind there was the conviction that she would never go on again.

She continued to stand with arms hanging and head drooped to one side, closed in by vines, with flowers of the hue of light around her like a halo, and bees murmuring among them. It was not merely that she was listless and incapable; the world seemed to have dropped away. She was marooned on a rock, with an ocean of nothingness about her. Everything she wanted had gone—sunk, vanished. It had come within sight, like mirage to the shipwrecked, only to torture her with what she couldn't have. It was worse than if it had never shown itself at all. Love had appeared with one man, money with the other. Love and money were two of the three things she cared for; the poor, shiftless family was the third. Since the first two had gone, the last must follow them. Quite consciously and deliberately Rosie lifted her hands with a little lamentable effort, letting them drop again, and so renounced her burden.

She crept back to the spot whence she had risen, and lay down. There was a kind of ritual in the act. It was not now a mere stricken, physical crouching as when she had turned away from Claude. It was something more significant. It was withdrawal from work, from life, from all the demands she had put forth so fiercely.

Renouncing these, Rosie also renounced Claude. It was a proof of the degree to which she had dismissed him that when, a half-hour later, she heard a rustling in the vines behind her it never occurred to her that he might have come back. She knew already that he would never come back. The fatalism of her little soul left her none of those uncertainties which are safeguards against despair. She raised her head and looked; but she saw exactly the person she knew she would see.

Antonio grinned, and announced dinner. The sight of his young mistress half sitting, half lying on the ground struck him as droll.

Rosie got up and brushed herself again. She knew it must be dinner-time. The fact had been at the back of her mind all through these minutes of comforting negation. She should have been in the house laying the table while her mother cooked the meal. It was the first time in years that she had rebelled against a duty. It was not exactly rebellion now. It was something more serious than that. She realized it as she stood where she was, with hands hanging limply, and said to herself, "I've quit."

Nevertheless, she emerged slowly from the jungle of vines and followed Antonio down the long, rustling aisle. There was a compulsion in the day's routine to which she felt the necessity of yielding. She had traversed half the length of the greenhouse before it came to her that it was precisely to the day's routine that she couldn't return. Anything was better than that. Any fate was preferable to the round of cooking and cleaning and seed-time and harvest of which every detail was impregnated with the ambitions she had given up. She had lived through these tasks and beyond them out into something else—into a great emptiness in which her spirit found a kind of ease. She could no more go back to them than a released soul could go back to earth.

In the yard she stood looking at the poor, battered old house. Inside, her father, who had probably by this time returned from town, would be sitting down to table. Antonio—to save the serving of two sets of meals—would be sitting down with him. Her mother would be bringing something from the kitchen, holding a hot platter with the corner of her apron. If she went in her mother would sit down, too, while she herself would do the running to and fro between the table and the pantry or the stove. She would snatch a bite for herself in the intervals of attendance.

Rosie revolted. She revolted not against the drudgery, which was part of the matter-of-course of living unless one "kept a girl"; she revolted against the living itself. It was all over for her. In proof that it was she turned her back on it.

Her moving away was at first without purpose. If her feet strayed into the familiar path that ran down the hill between the hothouses and the apple-trees it was because there was no other direction to take. She hadn't meant to go up through the wood to Duck Rock before she found herself doing it. The newly leafing oaks were a shimmer of bronze-green above her, while she trod on young ferns that formed a carpet such as was never woven by hands. Into it were worked white star-flowers without number, with an occasional nodding trillium. The faint, bitter scent of green things too tender as yet to be pungent rose from everything she crushed. She was not soothed by nature, like Thor Masterman. She had too much to do with the raising of plants for sale to take much interest in what the earth produced without money and without price. If it had not been that her mind was as nearly as possible empty of thought, she wouldn't have paused to watch an indigo-bunting, whose little brown mate was probably near by, hop upward from branch to branch of a solitary juniper, his body like a blue flower in the dark boughs, while he poured forth a song that waxed louder as he mounted. She observed him idly and passed onward because there was nothing but that to do.

Her heart was too dead to feel much emotion when she emerged on the spot where she had been accustomed to keep her trysts with Claude. Her trysts with Claude had been at night; she had other sorts of association with this summit in the daytime. All her life she had been used to come here berrying. Here she came, too, with Polly Wilson and other girl-friends—when she had any—

for strolls and gossiping. Here, too, Jim Breen had made love to her, and Matt's companion of the grocery. The spot being therefore not wholly dedicated to memories of Claude, she could approach it calmly.

She sat down on the familiar seat that circled the oak-tree and gave the best view over the pond. The oak-tree was the last and highest of the wood. Beyond it there was only an upward-climbing fringe of grass, starred with cinquefoil and wild strawberry—and then the precipice. It was but a miniature precipice that broke to a miniature sea, but it gave an impression of grandeur. Sitting on the bench, with one's head against the oak, one could, if one chose, see nothing but sky and water. There was nothing but sky and water and air. In the noon stillness there was not even a boat on the lake nor a bird on the wing. The only sounds were those of a hammering far over on the Thorley estate, the humming of an electric car, which at this distance was no more disturbing than the murmur of a bee, and the song of the indigo-bunting, fluted now from the tree-top. To Rosie it was peace, peace without pleasure, but without pain—as nearly as might be that absorption into nothingness for which she yearned as the Buddhist seeks absorption into God.

She rested, not suffering—at least not suffering anything she could feel. She was beyond grief. The only thing she was not beyond was the horror of returning to the interests that had hitherto made up life.

As for Claude, she could think of him, when she began doing so, with singular detachment. The whole episode with him might have been ended years before. It was like something which no longer perturbs, though the memory of it is vivid. She could go back and reconstruct the experience from the first. Up to the present she had never found any opportunity of doing that, since each meeting with him was so soul-filling in itself. Now that she had the leisure, she found herself using it as the afternoon wore on.

Being on the spot where she had first met him, she could re-enact the scene. She knew the very raspberry-bine at which she had been at work. She went to it and lifted it up. It was a spiny, red-brown, sprawling thing just beginning to clothe itself with leaves. It had been breast-high when she had picked the fruit from it, and Claude had stood over there, in that patch of common brakes which then rose above his knees, but was now a bed of delicate, elongated sprays leaning backward with incomparable grace. She found the heart to sing—her voice, which used to be strong enough, yielding her but the ghost of song, as the notes of an old spinnet give back the ghost of music long ago dead:

> "Oh, mirk, mirk is the midnight hour,
>   And loud the tempest's roar;
> A waeful wanderer seeks thy tower,
>   Lord Gregory ope thy door."

She could not remember having so much as hummed this air since the day Claude had interrupted it; but she went on, unfalteringly, to the lines at which he had broken in:

> "At least be pity to me shown,
>   If love it may na' be—"

She didn't falter even here; she only allowed her voice to trail away in the awed pianissimo into which he had frightened her. She stopped then and went through the conversation that ensued on the memorable day, and of which the very words were imprinted on her heart: "Isn't it Rosie? I'm Claude." She hadn't smiled on that occasion, but she smiled to herself now—a ghost of a smile to match her ghost of a voice—because his tone had been so sweet. She had never heard anything like it before— and since, only in his moments of endearment.

But she went home at last. She went home because the May afternoon grew chilly, and in the gathering of shadows beneath the oaks there was something eery. Expecting a scene or a scolding, she was surprised to find both father and mother calm. They had evidently exchanged views concerning her, deciding that she had better indulge her whims. When she refused to eat they made little or no protest, and only once during the night did her mother cross the passage to ask fretfully why she didn't go to bed. On the following day there was the same silent acknowledgment of her right to refuse to work and of her freedom to absent herself. Rosie was quite clear as to what had taken place. Antonio had betrayed the fact of Claude's visit, and her parents had scented a hopeless love-affair. Rosie was indifferent. Her love-affairs were her own business; she owed neither explanation nor apology to any one. So long as her parents conceded her liberty to come and go, to nibble rather than to eat, and not to speak when spoken to, she was content.

They conceded this all through that week. In her presence they bore themselves with timid constraint, and followed her with stealthy eyes that watched for every shadow that crossed her face; but they let her alone. She was as free as wind all Wednesday, Thursday, Friday, Saturday, and Sunday.

During those days she continued to live in the exultation of the void. There was nothing to fear any more. The worst had happened to her that could happen, and so, in a manner of speaking, she was safe. Never since she had begun to think had she been so free from misgiving and foreboding as to what each new day would bring forth. No day could bring forth anything now that could hurt her.

By Saturday the nerves of sensation began to show signs of recovering themselves and returning to activity. In thinking of Claude, and living through again her meetings with him, there were moments like pangs, of longing, of passion, of despair, as the case might be, that went as quickly as they came. But they didn't frighten her. If they were premonitions of a state of anguish—why, there had been so much anguish in her episode with Claude that there couldn't be much more now. If anything, she welcomed it. It would be more as if he was back with her. The void was peaceful. But the void filled with suffering on his account would be better still. Anything!—anything but to be forced to go back!

But on Monday it was the urgency of going back that confronted her. She had come down in the morning to find her breakfast laid in just the way she liked it—tea, a soft-boiled egg, buttered toast, and, as a special temptation to a capricious appetite, a dab of marmalade. She sat down to the table unwillingly, sipping at the tea and nibbling at the toast, but leaving the egg and the marmalade untouched. In her mother's bustling to and fro she felt the long-delayed protest in the atmosphere. It came while her mother was crossing the room to replace some dishes on the dresser.

"Now, my girl, buck up. Just eat your breakfast and set to work and stop your foolish fancies. If you don't look out you'll get yourself where I was, and I guess it 'll take more than Dr. Hilary to pull *you* out." She added, as she returned to the kitchen: "Your father told me to tell you to get busy on the cucumbers. There's a lot to be picked. He's been spannin' them and finds them ready."

Rosie made use of her privilege of not answering. When she had eaten all she could she took a basket and made her way toward the cucumber-house she had not entered since she had left it with the words, "I've quit." It was like going to the scaffold to drag her feet across the yard; it was like mounting it to lift the latch of the paintless door and feel the stifling, pollen-laden air in her face. Nevertheless, habit took her in. Habit sent her eyes searching among the lowest stretches of the vines, where the cool, green things were hanging. Habit caused her to stoop and span them with her rough little hand. When her father's thumb and fingers met around them they were ready to be picked; they were ready when her own came within an inch of doing so.

But she raised herself with a rebellious impulse of her whole person before she had picked one. She had picked hundreds in her time; she had picked thousands. She couldn't begin again. With the first one she gathered the yoke of the past would be around her neck once more. She couldn't bear it. "I can't. I can't." With the words on her lips she slipped out by the door at the far end of the hothouse and sped toward her refuge on Duck Rock.

She had never felt it as so truly a refuge before. Neither had she ever before needed a refuge so acutely. She needed it to-day because the memory of Claude had at last become a living thing, and every sentient part of her that could be filled with grief was filled with it. Grief had come suddenly; it was creating a new world for her. It was no longer a peaceful void; it was a world of wild passions, wild projects, wild things she would do, wild words she would speak if ever she had the chance to speak them. She would go in search of him! She would find his father and mother! She would appeal to Thor! She would discover the girl with ten or twelve servants who had come between them! She would implore them all to send him back! She would drag him back! She would hang about his neck till he swore never again to leave her! If he refused, she would kill him! If she couldn't kill him, she would kill herself! Perhaps if she killed herself she would inflict on him the worst suffering of all!

She thought about that. After all, it was the thing most practical. The other impulses were not practical. She knew that, of course. She could humiliate herself to the dust without affecting him. Up to to-day she had not wanted him to suffer; but now she did. If she killed herself, he *would* suffer. However long he lived, or however many servants the woman he married would be able to keep, his life would be poisoned by the memory of what he had done to her.

Her imagination reveled in the scenes it was now able to depict. Leaning back with her head resting against the trunk of the old oak, she closed her eyes and viewed the dramatic procession of events that might follow on that morning and haunt Claude Masterman to his grave. She saw herself leaping from the rock; she saw her body washed ashore, her head and hands hanging limp, her long, wet hair streaming; she saw her parents mourning, and Thor remorseful, and Claude absolutely stricken. Her efforts rested there. Everything was subordinate to the one great fact that by doing this she could make the sword go through his heart. She went to the edge of the cliff and peered over. Though it was a sheer fifty feet, it didn't seem so very far down. The water was blue and lapping and inviting. It looked as if it would be easy.

She returned to her seat. She knew she was only playing. It relieved the tumult within her to pretend that she could do as desperately as she felt. It quieted her. Once she saw that she had it in her power to make Claude unhappy, something in her spirit was appeased.

She began the little comedy all over again, from the minute when she started forth from home on the momentous day to fill her pan with raspberries. She traced her steps down the hill and up through the glades of the bluff wherever the ripe raspberries were hanging. She came to the minute when her stage directions called for "Lord Gregory," and she sang it with the same thin, silvery piping which was all she could contribute now to the demand of drama. It was both an annoyance and a surprise to hear a footfall and the swish of robes and to turn and see Lois Willoughby.

Beyond the fact that she couldn't help it, she didn't know why she became at once so taciturn and repellent. "Oh, she'll come again," she said in self-excuse, and with vague ideas of atonement, after Lois had gone away.

Besides, the things that Lois had said in the way of solicitude, sympathy, and God made no appeal to her. If she felt regret it was from obscure motives of compassion, since this woman, too, had missed what was best in love.

She would have returned to her dream had her dream returned to her; but Lois had broken the spell. Rosie could no longer get the ecstasies of re-enactment. Re-enactment itself became a foolish thing, the husk of what had once been fruit. It was a new phase of loss. Everything went but her misery and her desire to strike at Claude—that and the sense that whatever she did, and no matter how elusive she made herself, she would have to go back to the old life at last. She struggled against the conviction, but it settled on her like a mist. She played again with the raspberry-bine, she sang "Lord Gregory," she peered over the brink of the toy precipice—but she evoked nothing. She stood as close to the edge of the cliff as she dared, whipping and lashing and taunting her imagination by the rashness of the act. Nothing came but the commonplace suggestion that even if she fell in, the boat which had appeared on the lake, and from which two men were fishing, would rescue her. The worst she would get would be a wetting and perhaps a cold. She wouldn't drown.

Common sense took possession of her. The thing for her to do, it told her cruelly, was to go back and pick the cucumbers. After that there would be some other job. In the market-garden business jobs were endless, especially in spring. She could set about them with a better heart since, after all that had happened, Archie Masterman couldn't refuse now to renew the lease. He wouldn't have the face to refuse it—so common sense expressed itself—when his son had done her such a wrong. If she had scored no other victory, her suffering would at least have secured that.

It was an argument of which she couldn't but feel the

weight. There would be three more years of just managing to live—three more years of sowing and planting and watering and watching, at the end of which they would not quite have starved, while Matt would have had a hole in which to hide himself on coming out of jail. Decidedly it was an argument. She had already shown her willingness to sell herself; and this would apparently prove to be her price.

Wearily, when noon had passed and afternoon set in, she got herself to her feet. Wearily she began to descend the hill. She would go back again to the cucumbers. She would take up again the burden she had thrown down. She would bring her wild heart into harness and tame it to hopelessness. Common sense could suggest nothing else.

She went now by the path, because it was tortuous and less direct than the bee-line over fern. She paused at every excuse—now to watch a robin hopping, now to look at a pink lady's-slipper abloom in a bed of spleenwort, now for no reason at all. Each step cost her a separate act of renunciation; each act of renunciation was harder than the other. But successive steps and successive acts brought her down the hill at last.

"I can't. I can't."

She dragged herself a few paces farther still.

"I can't! I can't!"

She was in sight of the boulevard, where a gang of Finns were working, and beyond which lay the ragged, uncultivated outskirts of her father's land. Up through a tangle of nettles and yarrow she could see the zigzag path which had been the rainbow bridge of her happiness. She came to a dead stop, the back of her hand pressed against her mouth fearfully. "If I go up there," she said to herself, "I shall never come down again." She meant that she would never come down again in the same spirit. That spirit would be captured and slain. She herself would be captured and slain. Nothing would live of her but a body to drudge in the hothouse to earn a few cents a day.

Suddenly, without forming a resolution or directing an intention, she turned and sped up the hill. At first she only walked rapidly; but the walk broke into a run, and the run into a swift skimming along through the trees like that of a roused partridge.

And yet she didn't know what she was running from. Something within her, a power of guardedness or that capacity for common sense which had made its last desperate effort to get the upper hand, had broken down. All she could yield to was the terror that paralyzed thought; all she could respond to was the force that drew her up the hill with its awful fascination. "I must do it, I must," were the words with which she met her own impulse to resist. If her confused thought could have become explanatory it would have said: "I must get away from the life I've known, from the care, from the hope, from the love. I must do something that will make Claude suffer; I must frighten him; I must wound him; I must strike at the girl who has won him away with her ten or twelve servants. And there's no way but this."

Even so the way was obscure to her. She was taking it without seeing whither it was to lead. If one impulse warned her to stop, another whipped her onward. "I can't stop! I can't stop!" she cried out, when warning became alarm.

For flight gave impetus to itself. It was like release; it was a kind of wild glee. She was as a bird whose wings have been bound, and who has worked them free again. There was a frenzy in sheer speed.

The path was steep, but she was hardly aware of so much as touching it. Fear behind and anguish within her carried her along. She scarcely knew that she was running breathlessly, that she panted, that once or twice she stumbled and fell. Something was beckoning to her from the great, safe, empty void—something that was nothing, unless it was peace and sleep—something that had its abode in the free spaces of the wind and the blue caverns of the sky and the kindly lapping water—something infinite and eternal and restful, in whose embrace she was due.

At the edge of the wood she had a last terrifying moment. The raspberry-bine was there, and the great oak with the seat around it, and the carpet of cinquefoil and wild strawberry. She gave them a quick, frightened look, like an appeal to impede her. If she was to stop she must stop now. "But I can't stop," she seemed to fling to them, over her shoulder, as she kept on to where, beyond the highest tip of greensward, the blue level of the lake appeared.

The boat with the two fishermen was nearer the shore than when she had observed it last. "They'll save me! Oh, they'll save me!" she had time to whisper to herself, at the supreme moment when she left everything behind.

There followed a space which in Rosie's consciousness was long. She felt that she was leaping, flying, out into the welcoming void, and that the promise of rest and peace had not deceived her.

But it was in the shock of falling that sanity returned; and all that the tense little creature had been, and tried to be, and couldn't be, and longed to be, and feared to be, and failed to be broke into a cry at which the fishermen dropped their rods.

CHAPTER XXVI

"THOR, would you mind if I went away for a little while?"

He looked at her across the luncheon-table, but her eyes were downcast. Though she endeavored to maintain the non-committal attitude she had taken up at breakfast, she couldn't meet his gaze.

"If you went away!" he echoed, blankly. "Why should you do that?"

"I've been to see—" She found a difficulty in pronouncing the name—"I've been to see Rosie. She's rather—upset."

Under the swift lifting of her lids he betrayed his self-consciousness. "I suppose so." He kept to the most laconic form of speech in order to leave no opening to her penetration.

"And I thought if I could take her away—"

"Where should you go?"

"Oh, anywhere. That wouldn't matter. To New York, perhaps. That might interest her. But anywhere, so long as—"

He got out his consent while making an excuse for rising from the table. The conversation was too difficult to sustain. It was without looking at him that she said, as he was leaving the room:

"Then I'll go and ask her at once. I dare say she won't come—but I can try. It will give me an excuse for going back. I feel worried at having left her at all."

Between three and four that afternoon she entered her

253

husband's office hurriedly. It was Mrs. Dearlove who received her. "Do you know where Dr. Masterman is? Do you know where he expected to call this afternoon?"

Brightstone consulted a card hanging on the wall. "He was to 'ave seen Mrs. Gibbs, 'm—Number 10 Susan Street—some time through the day."

Lois made no secret of her agitation. "Have they a telephone?"

"Oh, no, 'm; 'ardly. Only a poor charwoman."

"Was he going anywhere at all where they *could* have a telephone?"

Mrs. Dearlove having mentioned the possibilities, Lois rang up house after house. She left the same message everywhere: Thor was to be asked to come directly to his office, where she was awaiting him. It was after four when he appeared.

She met him in the little entry and, taking him by the arm, drew him into the waiting-room. "Come in, Thor dear, come in." She knew by his eyes that he suspected something of what she had to tell.

"Caught me at the Longyears'," he tried to say in a natural voice, but he could hardly force the words beyond his lips.

"It's Rosie, Thor," she said, instantly. "She's *all* right."

He dropped into a chair, supporting himself on the round table strewn with illustrated papers and magazines for the entertainment of waiting patients. His lips moved, but no sound passed them. Long, dark shadows streaked the pallor of his face.

She sat down beside him, covering his hands with her own. "She's all right, Thor dear. . . now . . . and I don't think she'll be any the worse for it in the end. . . . She may be the better. . . . We can't tell yet. . . . But—but you haven't heard it in the village, have you?"

He shook his head, perhaps because he was dazed, perhaps because he didn't trust himself to speak.

"That's good." She spoke breathlessly. "I was so afraid you might . . . I wanted to tell you myself . . . so that you wouldn't—you wouldn't get a shock. . . . There's no reason for a shock—not now, Thor. . . . It's only—it's only . . . just what I was afraid of—what I spoke of at lunch. . . . She—she—she did it."

He found strength to speak. "She did—what?"

Lois continued the same breathless way. "She threw herself into the pond. . . . But she's all right. . . . Jim Breen and Robbie Willert were out in a boat—fishing. . . . They saw her. . . . They got to her just as she went down the second time. . . . Jim Breen dived after her and brought her up. . . . She wasn't unconscious very long . . . and fortunately Dr. Hill was close by—at old Mrs. Jukes's in Schoolhouse Lane. . . . So she's home now and all right, or nearly. . . . I arrived just as they were bringing her ashore. . . . She was breathing then. . . . I went on before them to the house. . . . I told Mrs. Fay . . . and Mr. Fay. . . . I saw them put her to bed. . . . She's all right. . . . And then I came here—to tell you, Thor—"

He struggled to his feet, throwing his head back and clenching his fists. "I swear to God that if I ever see Claude again I'll—I'll kill him!"

Without rising she caught one of his hands and pulled him downward. "Sit down, Thor," she said, in a tone of command. "You mustn't take it like that. You mustn't make things worse than they are. They're bad enough as it is. They're so bad—or at least so hard for—for some of us—that we must do everything we can to make it possible to bear them."

He sat down at her bidding; but with elbows resting on the table he covered his face with his hands. She clasped her own and sat looking at him. That is, she sat looking at his strong knuckles and at the shock of dark hair that fell over the finger-tips where the nails dug into his forehead. She felt a great pity for him; but a pity that permitted her to sit there, watchful, detached, not as if it was Thor—but some one else.

There would be an end now to silences and concealments. She saw that already. He was making no further attempt to keep her in the dark. In the shock of the moment all the barricades he had built around his secret life had fallen like the walls of Jericho. She had nothing to do but walk upward and inward and take possession. All was open. There was neither shrine nor sanctuary any longer. It was no privilege to be admitted thus; anybody would have been admitted who sat beside him as she was sitting now.

But in the end the paroxysm passed and his hands came down.

"I know it's hard for you, Thor—" The eyes he turned on her were full of such unspeakable things that she stopped. She was obliged to wait till he looked away again before she could go on. "I know it's hard for you, Thor. It's hard for—for us all. But my point is that bitterness or violence will only make it worse. You must remember—I feel that I *must* remind you of it—that you're not the—not the only sufferer."

He bowed his head into his hands again, but without the mad anguish of a few minutes earlier.

"Where so much is intolerable," she pursued, "what we have to do—each one of us—is to see how tolerable we can make things for every one else."

He raised his head for one quick, reproachful glance. "Do you mean tolerable for—for Claude?"

"Yes, I do mean for Claude. *We* sha'n't have to punish him."

He gave her another look. "Then what have we got to do?"

"Nothing that isn't kind—and well thought out beforehand. That's really the important thing. When one can't move without hurting some one, isn't it better not to move at all?"

"WE'VE GOT OUR OWN PROBLEMS TO SOLVE, HAVEN'T WE?"

THE SIDE OF THE ANGELS

It was the old doctrine of tarrying the Lord's leisure against which his instincts were still in revolt. His indignation was such that he could partially turn and face her. "Do you mean to say that we should *let* him abandon her—*now?*"

She laid her hand on his arm. "Oh, Thor dear, it isn't for us to let—or prevent—or anything. We can't drive other people—and it's only to a slight degree that we can lead them. Even I know that. What we can do best is to follow—and pick up the pieces."

He shook his head blankly. "I don't understand. What good would that do?"

She rose, saying quietly, "I shall have to let you think it out for yourself."

As he remained seated, his forehead resting on his hand, she passed behind him. With her arm thrown lightly across his shoulders she bent over him till her cheek touched his hair. "Thor dear," she whispered, "we've got our own problems to solve, haven't we? We can't solve Claude's and Rosie's too. No one can do that but themselves. Whatever happens—whether he comes back and marries her, or whether he doesn't—no help would ever come of your interference or mine. If we'd only understood that before—"

"You mean, if I had."

"Well, Thor darling, you haven't. You see, human beings are so terribly free. I say terribly, on purpose—because you can't compel them to be wise and prudent and safe, even when they're making the most obvious mistakes. We must let them make them—and suffer—and learn." She bent closer to his ear. "And it's what we must do, Thor dear, you and I. We've made our mistakes already—though perhaps we didn't know it. Now we must have the suffering — and — and the learning."

She brushed her lips lightly across his hair and left him.

As she walked through the Square, and past the terminus of the tram-line, and on into the beginning of County Street, she was obliged to keep repeating her own words—"Nothing that isn't kind and well thought out beforehand." Having counseled him against bitterness and violence, she saw that her immediate task was not to swallow her own words. Bitterness was beyond suppression, and violence would have been so easy! "*Well thought out beforehand*," she emphasized. "Whatever I do I must keep to that. If *I* don't, God knows where we shall be."

In pursuance of this principle she turned in at her father-in-law's gate. He and Mrs. Masterman must also be warned. Rosie's rash act would touch them so closely that unless they were informed of it gently something regrettable might be said or done.

As to that, however, her fears proved groundless. Masterman himself opened the door for her as she went up the steps. "Saw you coming," he explained. "Just got out from town. Ena's been telling me the most distressing thing—the most damnably theatrical, idiotic thing. Perhaps you've heard of it."

"I know what you mean. I've been there. I was there when they brought her ashore. It may have been idiotic, as you say, but I don't think it was theatrical."

"You will when you know. Ena," he called up the stairs after they had entered the hall; "Lois is here. Come down."

Mrs. Masterman entered the library a minute later with both hands outstretched. "Oh, my dear, what a comedy this is!" It was not often that her manner forsook its ladylike suavity. "*What* a comedy! But of course you don't know. Nobody knows, thank God! But we must tell *you*." She turned to her husband. "Will you tell her, Archie, or shall I?"

"If it's about Claude and Rosie Fay," Lois said, when they had got seated, "I know all that. Thor told me.

He told me yesterday, because—well, because I'd been taking an interest in Rosie for some months past, and when I went to see her yesterday afternoon old Mr. Fay wouldn't let me. He said there'd been trouble—or something—between Claude and Rosie—"

"Oh, he's been so romantic, poor boy," Ena interrupted, "and so loyal. You'd hardly believe. He's been taken in completely. He *did* want to marry her. That's true. There's no use denying it. He told his father and he told me. Oh, you've no idea. We've been *so* worried. But he must have found her out—*simply* found her out."

Lois weighed the wisdom of asking questions or of learning more than Thor chose to tell her, but in the end it seemed reasonable to ask, "Found her out—how?"

Ena threw up her pretty hands. "Oh, well, with a girl of that sort what could you expect? Claude's been completely taken in—or he was. He's so innocent, poor boy. He wouldn't believe—not even when I told him. I tried to stand by him—I really did. Didn't I, Archie? When he said he wanted to marry her I said, said I, 'If she's a good girl, Claude, and loves you, I'll accept her.' I really did, Lois—and you can imagine what it cost me. But I could see at once. Any one who wasn't infatuated as Claude was would have seen at a glance. The girl must be—well, something awful."

Lois spoke warmly. "Oh, I don't think that."

"My dear Lois, I *know*. What's more, Thor knows, too. And I must say I can't help blaming Thor. He's backed Claude up—and backed him up when all the while he's known what she was."

Lois felt obliged to speak. "I don't think he's known anything—anything to her discredit."

"Oh, but he has. I assure you he has. And what amazes me about Thor—simply amazes me—is that he shouldn't see it in the right light. Archie did, as soon as I told him. Didn't you, Archie? And I *didn't* tell him," Ena ran on, excitely, "till I saw what trouble dear

Claudie was in. When Claudie began to see for himself I betrayed his confidence to the extent of telling his father, but not before. You could hardly blame me for that, could you?—his own father. And when I did tell Archie—why, it was so plain that a child could have understood."

The question, "What was plain?" could not but come to Lois's lips, but she succeeded in withholding it. She even rose, with signs of going. It was Archie who responded to his wife, taking a man's view of that which seemed to her so damning.

"We must make allowances, of course, for its being a cock-and-bull story to begin with. Girls like that never know how to tell the truth."

"We couldn't treat it as a cock-and-bull story so long as Claude believed it," the mother declared, in defense of her right to be anxious. "And Thor believed it, too. I know he did. And I *do* blame Thor for not telling Claude—a boy so inexperienced!—that a girl couldn't be getting money from some other man—and go on getting it after she was married—unless there'd been something wrong."

Lois felt as if her blood had been arrested at her heart. "Money from some other man?"

"Money from some other man," Mrs. Masterman repeated, firmly. "I told Claude at the time that no man in his senses would settle money on a girl like that unless there'd been a reason—and a very good reason, too. A very good reason, *too*, I said. But Claude's as ignorant of the world as if he was ten years old. He really is. She took him in completely."

Being too consciously a gentleman to say more in disparagement of a woman's character than he had permitted himself already, Masterman remained in the library while his wife accompanied Lois to the door. The latter had said good-by and was descending the steps when Ena cried out in a tone that was like a confession:

"Oh, Lois, you don't think that poor girl had any *reason* to throw herself into the pond, do you?"

At the foot of the steps Lois turned and looked upward. Ena was wringing her hands, but the daughter-in-law didn't notice it. As a matter of fact, Lois was too deeply sunk into thoughts of her own to have any attention to spare for other people's searchings of heart. Having heard the question, she could answer it, but absently, and as though it were a point of no pressing concern.

"She hadn't the reason you're thinking of. I feel very sure of that. I've asked her mother—and she says she knows it."

Mrs. Masterman was uttering some expression of relief, but Lois could listen to no more. In her heart there was room for only one consideration. "Money! Money!" she was saying to herself as she went down the avenue beneath the leafing elms. "He was going to give her—that."

But Ena returned to the threshold of the library, where her husband, standing with his back to the empty fire-place, was meditating moodily.

"Archie," she faltered, "you do think that girl was only seeking notoriety, don't you?"

He raised his head, which had been hanging pensively. "Certainly. Don't you?"

She tried to speak with conviction. "Oh yes; of—of course."

"That is," Archie analyzed, "she was going in for cheap tragedy in the hope that the sensation would reach Claude. That was her game — quite evidently. Dare say it was a put-up job between her and those two young men. Took very good care, at any rate, to have 'em 'longside."

"But if Claude should hear of it—"

"Must see that he doesn't. Wiring him to-night to go on to Japan, after he's seen California. Let him go to India, if he likes—round the world. Anything to keep him away—and you and I," he added, "had better hook it till the whole thing blows over."

She looked distressed. "Hook it, Archie?"

"Close the house up and go abroad. Haven't been abroad for three years now. Little motor trip through England—and back toward the end of the summer. Fortunately I've sold that confounded property. Good price, too. Hobson, of Hobson & Davies. Going to build for residence. Takes it from the expiration of the lease, which is up in July. He'll clear out the whole gang then, so that by the time we come back they'll be gone. What do you think? Might do Devonshire and Cornwall —always wanted to take that trip—with a few weeks in Paris before we come home."

The suggestion of going abroad came as such a pleasing surprise that Mrs. Masterman slipped into a chair to turn it over in her mind. "Then Claude *couldn't* come back, could he?" expressed the first of the advantages she fore-saw. "He'd have nowhere to go."

"Oh, he'll not be in a hurry to do that," Archie said, confidently.

"And I do want some things," she mused further. "I had nothing to wear for the Darlings' ball—nothing—and you know how long I've worn the dinner-dresses I have. I really couldn't put on the green again." She was silent for some minutes, when another of those queer little cries escaped her such as had broken from her lips when she stood at the door with Lois: "But, oh, Archie, I want to do what's right!—what's right, Archie!"

He looked at her from under his brows as his head again drooped moodily. "What's—*what?*"

"What's right, Archie. Latterly— Oh, I don't know! —but latterly—" She passed her hand across her brow. . . . "Sometimes I feel—I get to be afraid, Archie—as if we weren't—as if we hadn't—as if something were going to happen—to overtake us—"

Crossing the room, he bent back her pretty head and

kissed her. "Nonsense," he smiled, unsteadily. "Nerves, dear. Don't wonder at it—with all we've been through—one way and another. But that's what we'll do. Close the house up and go abroad for three months. Inconvenient just now with the upset in the business—but we'll do it. Get out of the way. See something new. There, now, old girl," he coaxed, patting her on the shoulder, "brace up and shake it off. Nothing but nerves." He added, as he moved back toward his stand by the fireplace, "Get 'em myself."

"Do you, Archie? Like that? Like—like what I said?"

He had resumed his former attitude, his feet wide apart, his hands behind his back, his head hanging, when he muttered, "Like the devil."

She was not sure how much mental discomfort was indicated by the phrase, so she sat looking at him distressfully. Being unused to grappling with grave questions of right and wrong, she found the process difficult. It was like wandering through morasses in which she could neither sink nor swim, till she found herself emerging on solid, familiar ground again with the reconciling observation, "Well, I do need a few things."

CHAPTER XXVII

IT was not till Rosie was well enough to go listlessly back to work, and the Mastermans had sailed, that Lois found her own emotions ripe for speech. During the intervening fortnight she and Thor had lived their ordinary life together, but on a basis which each knew to be temporary. While he kept his office hours in the mornings and visited his patients in the afternoons, and she busied herself with household tasks or superintended the gardener in replanting the faded tulip-beds with phlox and sweet-peas and dahlias; while she sewed or did embroidery in the evenings and listened to him reading aloud, or—since the nights were growing warm—they sat silent on an upper balcony, or talked about the stars, each knew that the inner tension would never be relaxed till it was broken.

If there was any doubt of that it was on Thor's side. Because she said nothing, there were minutes when he hoped she had nothing to say. Unaware of a woman's capacity for keeping the surface unruffled while storm may be raging beneath, he beguiled himself at times into thinking that his fears of her acuteness had been false alarms. If so, he could only be thankful. He wanted to forget. If he had had a prayer to put up on the subject, it would have been that she would allow him to forget. So, as day followed day, regularly, peacefully, with an abstention on her part from comment that could give him pain, he began to indulge the hope—a hope which he knew in his heart to be baseless—that she had nothing to remember.

When he was called on at last to face the realities of the

case the moment was as unexpected to him as it was to her. She had not meant to bring the subject up on that particular evening. She had made no program—not because she was uncertain as to what she ought to say, but because the impulse to say it lagged. In the end it came to her without warning, surprising herself no less than him.

"Thor, were you going to give money to Rosie Fay?"

The croaking of frogs seemed part of the silence in which she waited for his answer. The warm air was heavy with the scents of lilac, honeysuckle, and syringa. As they stood by the railing of the balcony that connected the exterior of their two rooms, she erect, he leaning outward with an arm stretched toward the sky, a great white lilac, whose roots were in the early days of the Willoughby farm, threw up its tribute of blossom almost to their feet. The lights of the village being banked under verdure, the eye sought the stars.

Thor loved the stars. On moonless nights he spent hours in contemplation of their beckoning mystery. From Auriga and Taurus in January, he followed them round to Aries and Perseus in December, getting a beam on his inward way. Just now, with the aid of a pencil, he was tracing for his wife's benefit the lines of the rising Virgin. Lois could almost discern the graceful, recumbent figure, winged, noble, lying on the eastern horizon, Spica's sweet, silvery light a-tremble in her hand. She was actually thinking how white for a star was Spica's radiance, when the words slipped out: "Thor, were you going to give money to Rosie Fay?"

He suppressed the natural question concerning her sources of information in order to say, as quietly as he could, "If—if Claude had married her I was going to—to help them out."

She resented what she considered his evasiveness. "That isn't just what I asked."

"Even so, it tells you what you want to know. Doesn't it?"

"Not everything I want to know."

"Why should you want to know—everything?"

"Because—" It struck her that her reason could be best expressed by shifting her ground. "Thor dear, exactly why did you want to marry me?"

The change in tactics troubled him. "I think I told you that at the time."

"You told me you came to me as to a—to a shelter."

"And as to a home. I said that, too, Lois."

"Yes," she agreed, slowly, "you said that, too." A brief interval gave emphasis to the succeeding words: "But did you think it was enough?"

"I couldn't judge of that. I could only say—what I had to say—truthfully."

"Oh, I know it was—truthfully. It's—it's just the trouble. You see, Thor," she went on, unsteadily, "I thought you were telling me only some of what was in your heart—and it was all."

"I'm not certain that I know what you mean by all. What I felt was—so much." He added, reproachfully, "It's surely a great deal when a man finds a woman his refuge from trouble."

"That's perfectly true, Thor; and there's no one in the world who wouldn't be touched by it. But in the case of a wife, she can hardly help thinking of the kind of trouble he's escaping from."

"But so long as he escapes from it—"

She interrupted quickly: "Yes; so long as he does. But when he doesn't? When, instead of leaving his trouble outside the refuge, he brings it in?"

He took an uneasy turn up and down the balcony. "Look here, Lois; have you any particular motive in bringing this up now?"

"Yes, Thor. It's the same motive I had a few weeks ago, only that I haven't been sure of it till to-night. I want you"—she hesitated, but urged herself on—"I want you—to let me go away."

"Go away?" he cried, sharply. "Go away where?"

"I don't know yet. Anywhere. There are one or two visits I might make—or I could find a place. That part of it doesn't matter."

"But when you wanted to go away a few weeks ago—"

"It was to—to take *her*. I shouldn't need to do that now, because she's better. In a way she's all right—all right, only changed."

It was to make a show of not being afraid to mention Rosie that he said, "Changed in what way?"

"Well, you'll see." She decided that for his own sake it was kindness to be cruel, and so added: "Changed to a healthier frame of mind. She's very much ashamed of what she tried to do, and wants to begin again on a—on a less foolish basis. So," she continued, reverting to her former point, "my going away wouldn't now have anything to do with her. It would be on my own account. I want to—to think."

"Think about what?"

"Well, chiefly about you."

He knew they were nearing the heart of the question, and so went up to it boldly. "To wonder—whether or not—I—love you? Is that it?"

"N-no; not exactly." She allowed a second to pass before letting slip the words: "Rather the other way."

"The other way—how?"

She spoke very softly. "Whether or not—I love *you*."

"Oh!" His tone was as soft as hers, but with the ejaculation he moved his big hands about his body like a man feeling for his wound. "I thought you did."

"Yes, I thought so, too—till—till lately. Perhaps I do, even now. I don't know. It's what I want to get away for—to think—to see. I can't do either when you're so near me. You—you overwhelm me—you crush me. I don't get the free use of my mind."

He turned again to pace the narrow limits of the balcony. "If you ever did love me, Lois," he said, in a voice she hardly recognized because of the new thrill in it, "I've done nothing to deserve the withdrawal of—of your affection."

She answered while still keeping her eyes absently on Spica's white effulgence. "I know you haven't, Thor dear. But that's not the point. It's rather that I have to go back and—and revise everything—form new conceptions."

He paused, standing behind her. "I don't think I get your idea."

"No, probably not. You couldn't without knowing what it all used to mean to me."

"*Used* to mean?"

"Yes, Thor; used to mean in a way that it doesn't now, and never can any more."

There was pain in his voice as he said, "That's hard, Lois—damnably hard."

"I know, Thor dear. I wouldn't say it if I hadn't made up my mind that I must—that I ought to. I've had a great shock—which has been in its way a great humiliation—but I could go on keeping it to myself if I hadn't come to the conclusion that it's best for you to know. Men are so slow to fathom what their wives are thinking of—"

"Well, then, tell me."

She turned slowly round from her contemplation of the stars, a hand on each side grasping the low rail against which she leaned. The spangles on a scarf over her bare shoulders glittered iridescently in the light streaming from her room. Of Thor she could discern little more than the whiteness of his face and of his evening shirt-front from the obscurity in which he kept himself. A minute or more elapsed before she went on.

"You see, Thor, I didn't fall in love with you first of all for your own sake; it was because—because I thought you'd fallen in love with me. That's a sort of confession, isn't it? It may be something I ought to be ashamed of, and perhaps I am—a little. But you'd understand how it could happen if you were to realize what it was to me that a man should fall in love with me at all."

He tried to interrupt her, but she insisted on going on in her own way. "I wasn't attractive. I never had been. During the years when I was going out I never received what people call attentions—not from any one. I don't say that I didn't suffer on account of it. I did—but I'd begun to take the suffering philosophically. I'd made up my mind that no one would ever care for me, and I was getting used to the idea—when—when you came."

Because her voice trembled she pressed her handkerchief against her lips, while Thor stood silent in the darkness of the far end of the balcony.

"And when you did come, Thor dear, it couldn't but seem to me the most amazing thing that ever happened. I didn't allow myself to think that you were in love with me—I didn't dare—at first. It made me happy that you should think it worth while just to come and see me, to talk to me, to tell me some of the things you hoped to do. That in itself—"

She broke off again, losing something of her self-command. In the stress of physical agitation she drew the spangled scarf over her shoulders and stepped forward into the shaft of light that fell through the open French window of her room.

"But, finally, Thor, I came to the conclusion that you must love me. I couldn't explain your kindness in any other way. Believe me, I didn't accept that way till—till it seemed the only one, but when I did, well, it wasn't merely pride and happiness that I felt—it was something more." A sob in her throat obliged her to interrupt herself again, while the croaking of frogs continued. "And so, Thor dear, love came to me, too. It came because I thought you brought it; but now that I see you didn't bring it, you can understand why I should be in doubt as to—as to whether or not—it really did come."

Since he recognized the futility of making an immediate response, they stood confronting each other in silence.

She took another step nearer him. "But what I'm not in any doubt about at all is the scorn I feel for myself for ever having cherished the delusion. If I'd been a woman with—with more claim, let us say, to being loved—"

"Lois, for God's sake, don't say that!"

"But I must say it, Thor. It's at the bottom of all I mean. I was weak and foolish enough to think that in spite of the things I lacked a man had given me his heart —when he hadn't."

"Lois, I can't stand this. Please don't go on."

"But I have to stand it, Thor. I have to stand it day and night, without ever getting away from the thought of it. I have to go back and puzzle and wonder and speculate as to why you did what you've done to me. I see things this way, Thor: There was a time when you thought you might come to care for me. You really thought it. And then—something happened—and you were not so sure. Later, you felt that you couldn't—that you never would. But the something that happened happened the wrong way for you—and papa broke down as he did—and I was in danger of being poor—and you were kind and generous— and—you weren't very happy as things were—you told me so, didn't you? And—and—in short—you thought you might as well. You knew I expected it—or had expected it once—and so—so you did it. Tell me, Thor dear; am I so very far wrong? Wasn't it like that?"

He raised his head defiantly. "And if I admitted that it was like that, what then?"

"Oh, nothing. I should merely ask you the same thing—to let me go away."

"Away for how long?"

She reflected. "Till I could establish a new basis on which to come back."

"I don't know what you mean by a new basis."

"I dare say I don't mean anything very different from

the compromise most people have to make—a little while after marriage; only that in my case the necessity comes more as—a shock. You see, Thor, you're not the man— not the man I thought you were. I must have a little while to get used to that."

He stirred uneasily. "You find I'm—I'm not so good a man."

"Oh, I don't say that. I don't say that at all. You're just as good. Only you're not—" She went up to him, laying her hands on his shoulders—"Oh, you don't under- stand. I loved the other Thor. I'm not sure that I love this one. I don't know. Perhaps I do. I can't tell till I get away from you. Let me go. It may not be for long."

She stepped back from him toward the window of her room, through which she seemed about to pass. He was obliged to speak in order to retain her.

"Look here, Lois," he began, not knowing exactly how he meant to continue. She turned with a foot on the threshold, her hand on the knob of the open window-door. The pose, set off by the simplicity of the old black evening dress she was in the habit of wearing when they were alone, displayed the commanding beauty of her figure to a degree which he had never observed before. He remem- bered afterward that something shot through him, some- thing he had associated hitherto only with memories of little Rosie Fay, but for the minute he was too intensely preoccupied for more than a subconscious attention. She was waiting and he must say something to justify his appeal to her. "It's all right," were the words he found. "I'm willing. That is, I'm willing in principle. Only"— he stammered on—"only I don't want you to go roaming the country by yourself. Why not let me go? I could go away for a while, and you could stay here." He warmed to the idea as soon as he began to express it. "This is your home, rather than mine. It's your father's house. You've lived in it for years. I couldn't stay here without you—while you're used to it without me. I'll go. I'll go—and I'll not come back till you tell me. There. Will that do?"

The advantages of the arrangement were evident. She answered slowly. "It—it might. But what about your patients?"

"Oh, Hill would look after them. He said he would if I wanted to attend the medical congress at Minneapolis. I told him I didn't, but—but"—he tapped the rail to emphasize the timeliness of the idea—"but, by George! I'll do it. You'd have three weeks at least—and as many more as you ask for."

She gave the suggestion a minute's thought. "Very well, Thor. Since the congress is going on—and your time wouldn't be altogether thrown away— You see, all I want is a little quiet—a little solitude, perhaps—just to realize where I am—and to see how—to begin again— if we ever can."

She closed one side of the window, softly and slowly. Her hands were on the other *battant* when he uttered a little throaty cry. "Aren't you going to say good night?"

Standing on the low step of the window, she was sufficiently above him to be able to fold his head in her arms, to pillow it on her breast, while she imprinted a long kiss on the thick, dark mass of his hair. Having released him, she withdrew, closing the window gently and pulling down the blinds.

Outside in the darkness Thor turned once more to where the Virgin, recumbent, noble, outlined and crowned with stars, Spica the wheat-ear in the hand hanging by her side, rose slowly toward mid-heaven. Irrelevantly there came back to his memory something said months before by his uncle Sim, but which he had not recalled since the night he heard it. "You may make an awful fool of yourself, Thor, but you'll be on the side of the angels—and the angels will be on yours."

"Humph!" he snorted to himself. "That's all very fine. But—where are the angels?" And again he sought the stars.

CHAPTER XXVIII

IT was Jim Breen who told Lois that Jasper Fay's tenancy of the land north of the pond was definitely ended. "Want a nice fern-tree, Mrs. Masterman?" he had asked, briskly. "Two or three beauties for sale at Mr. Fay's place. Look dandy in the corner of a big room. Beat palms and rubber-plants like a rose 'll beat a bur. Get a nice one cheap at Mr. Fay's."

Lois wondered. "Is Mr. Fay selling off?"

"Well, not exactly. Father's selling what he don't want to cart over to our place. Didn't you know? Father's bought out Mr. Fay's stock. Mr. Fay's got to beat it by July ninth."

As Lois looked into the honest face she made the reflection with a little jealous pang that Rosie Fay was just the type that men like Jim Breen fell in love with. There was something in men like Jim Breen, in men like Thor Masterman—the big, generous, tender men—that impelled them toward piteous little creatures like Rosie Fay, driven probably by the protective yearning in themselves. It placed the tall women, the strong women, the women whose first impulse was to give to others rather than to get anything for themselves, at a disadvantage. In response to the information just received, she said, anxiously, "Why, Jim, tell me about it."

He drew from the wagon a wooden "flat" filled with zinnia plantlings, like so many little green rosettes. "Hadley B. Hobson owns that property now, Mrs. Masterman," he said, cheerily, depositing the "flat" on the ground. "Going to build. Didn't you know? Have

273

a dandy place there. Had architects and landscape-gardeners prowling 'round for the last two weeks, and old man Fay won't allow one of them on the grounds. You'd die laughing to see him chasing them off with a spade or a rake or whatever he has in his hand. His property till July ninth, he says, and he wouldn't let so much as a crow fly over it if it belonged to Hadley B. Hobson. You'd die laughing."

"I don't see how you can laugh when he's in such trouble, poor man."

"Oh, well," Jim drawled, optimistically, "he won't do so bad. He can always have a job with father. Father's mingled with him ever since the two of them were young. If Mr. Fay hadn't been so moonstruck he'd have had just the same chance as father had."

Lois chose a moment which seemed to be discreet in order to say: "I know Rosie quite well. I've seen a good deal of her during the past few months."

"Rosie's all right, Mrs. Masterman," Jim answered, suddenly and a trifle aggressively. "I don't care what any one says—she's all right."

"I know she's all right, Jim. She's one of the most remarkable characters I've ever met. I often wish she'd let me help her more."

"Well, you hold on to her, Mrs. Masterman," he advised, with a curious, pleading quality in his voice. "You'll find she'll be worth it. And if ever a girl was up against it—she is."

"I will hold on to her, Jim."

"It's all rot what people are saying that she'd gone melancholy because she took that fool jump into the pond. I know how she did it. She'd got to the point where she couldn't help it, where she just couldn't stand any more—with the business all gone to pieces and Matt coming out of jail, and everything else. Who wouldn't have done it? I'd have done it myself, if I'd been a girl. She'd got worked up, Mrs. Masterman, and when girls get worked up, why, they'll do anything. I believe the shock's done her good. Sort of cleared her mind like."

Lois tried to be tactful. "Then you see her?"

"We-ll—on and off." He grew appealing and confidential. "I don't mind telling you, Mrs. Masterman," he began, as if acknowledging an indiscretion, "I went with Rosie once. Went with her for over a year."

"Did you, Jim?"

He leaned nonchalantly against Maud's barrel-shaped body, his face taking on an expressoin of boyish regret. "And I'd have gone on going with her if—if Rosie hadn't —hadn't kind of dropped me."

"Oh, but, Jim, why should she?"

"We-ll, I can understand it. Rosie's high-toned, you know, Mrs. Masterman, and she's got a magnificent education. I guess you wouldn't come across them more refined, not in the most tip-top families. Pretty! My Lord! pretty isn't the word for it. And I think she grows prettier. And work! Why, Mrs. Masterman, if that girl was at the head of a plant like ours there wouldn't be anything for father and me to do but sit in a chair and rock."

"I'm glad she's willing to see you," Lois ventured.

He sprang to his seat behind Maud. "Well, I guess she needs all the friends she's got."

Lois ventured still further. "I'm sure she needs friends like you, Jim."

There was a flare in his eye as he fumbled for the reins. "Well, she's only got to stoop and pick me up. Git along, Maud. Gee!" In obedience to his pull Maud arched her heavy neck and executed a sidewise movement uncertainly. "She knows I'm there," he continued, as the wagon creaked round. "Been there ever since she dropped me. Gee! Maud, gee! What you thinking of? I've never gone with any one else, Mrs. Masterman—not really *gone* with them. Rosie's been the only one so far. Well, good-by. And you *will* hold on to her, Mrs. Masterman, now, won't you?"

"Indeed I will, Jim—and—and you must do the same."

He threw her a rueful look over his shoulder, as Maud paced toward the gate. "Oh, I'm on the job every time."

The visit gave her a number of themes for thought, of which the most insistent was the power some women had of drawing out the love of men. For the rest of the day her gardening became no more than a mechanical directing of the setting out of seedlings, while she meditated on the problem of attractiveness.

How was it that women of small endowments could captivate men at sight, and that others of inexhaustible potentialities—she was not afraid to rank herself among them—went unrecognized and undesired? If Rosie Fay had been content with the honors of a local belle, she could have had her choice among half the young men in the village. What was her gift? What was the gift of that great sisterhood, comprising perhaps a third of the women in the world, to whom the majority of men turned instinctively, ignoring, or partially ignoring, the rest? Was it mere sheep-stupidity in men themselves that sent one where the others went, without capacity for individual discernment?—or was there a secret call that women like Rosie Fay could give which brought them too much of that for which other women were left famishing?

She put the question that evening to Dr. Sim Masterman, who had dropped in to see her, as he not infrequently did after his supper, now that Thor was away. Indeed, his visits were so regular as to make her afraid that with his curious social or spiritual second sight he suspected more in Thor's absence than zeal for the science of medicine.

"Why do men fall in love with inferior women?—become infatuated with them?"

He answered while sprawling before the library fire, his long legs apart, his fingers interlocked over his old tan waistcoat. "No use to discuss love with a woman. She can't get hold of it by the right end."

"Oh, but I thought that was just what she could do—one of the few capabilities universally conceded her."

"All wrong, my dear. A man occasionally understands love, but a woman never—or so rarely that it hardly counts. Gets it backward—wrong end first—nine women out of ten."

She looked up from her sewing. "I do wish you'd tell me what you mean by that."

"Clear enough. Love is in the first place the instinct to love some one else, and only in the second place the desire to be loved in return. Ten to one, the woman puts the cart before the horse. She's thinking of the return before she's done anything to get it. She don't want to love half as much as to be *loved*—and so she finds herself left."

Lois went on with her sewing again, but she was uneasy. She thought of her confession to Thor. Could it be that there was something wrong with her love as well as with his? It was to see what he had to say further that she asked, "Finds herself left in what way?"

"Make 'emselves too sentimental," he grumbled on. "In love with love. They like that expression, and it does 'em harm. Sets 'em to wool-gathering—with the heart. Makes 'em think love more important than it is."

"It's generally supposed to be rather important."

"Rather's the word. But it's not the only thing of which that can be said—and more. Women reason as if it was. Make their lives depend on it. Mistake. If you can get it, well and good; if not—there's compensation."

She lifted her head not less in amazement than in indignation. "Compensation for having to do without *love?*"

"Heaps."

"And may I ask what?"

"No use telling you. Wouldn't believe me. Be like telling a man who's fond of his wine that he'd be just as well off with water."

She said, musingly, "Yes; love *is* the wine of life, isn't it?"

"Wine that maketh glad the heart of man—and can also play the deuce with it."

She sat for some time smiling to herself with faint amusement. "Do you really disapprove of love, Uncle Sim?" she asked, at last.

He yawned loudly and stretched himself. "What 'd be the good of that? Don't disapprove of it any more than I disapprove of the circulation of the blood. Force in life—of course! Treasure to be valued and peril to be controlled. To play with it requires skill; to utilize it calls for wisdom."

She had again been smiling gently to herself when she said, "I doubt if *you* can ever have been in love."

"Got nothing to do with it. Not obliged to have been insane to understand insanity. As a matter of fact, best brain specialists have always kept their senses."

"Oh, then, you rate love with insanity."

"Depends on the kind. Some sorts not far from it. Obsession. Brain-storm. Supernormal excitement. Passing commotion of the senses. Comes as suddenly as a summer tempest—thunder and lightning and rain—and goes the same way."

"Oh, but would you call that love?"

"You bet I'd call it love. Love the poets write about. Grand passion. Whirls along like a tornado—makes a noise and kicks up dust—and all over in an afternoon. That's the real thing. If you can't love like that, you can't love at all—not in the grand manner. The going just as vital as the coming. Very essence of it that it shouldn't last. That's why Shakespeare kills his Romeo and his Juliet at the end of the play—and Wagner his Tristan and his Isolde. Nothing else to do with 'em. People of that kind go through just the same set of high jinks six or eight months later with some one else; and in poetry that wouldn't do. Romantic lovers love by crises, and never pass twice the same way. People who don't do that—and lots of 'em don't—needn't think they can be romantic. They ain't."

"But surely there *is* a love—"

"Of the nice, tame, house-keeping variety. Of course! And it bears the same relation to the other kind as a glass of milk to a bottle of champagne. Mind you, I like milk. I approve of it. In the long run it 'll beat champagne any day—especially where you expect babies. I'm only saying that it doesn't come of the same vintage as Veuve Cliquot. Women often wish it did; and when it doesn't they make things uncomfortable. No use. Can't make a Tristan out of good, honest, faithful William Dobbin, nohow. The thing with the fizz is bound to go flat; and the thing that stands by you, to be relied on all through life, won't have any fizz."

Feeling at liberty to reject these vaporings as those of an eccentric old man who could know little or nothing on the subject, Lois reverted to the aspect of the question which had been in her mind when she started the theme. "You still haven't answered what I asked—as to why men fall in love with inferior women, and often with a kind of infatuation they hardly ever feel for the good ones."

He took longer than usual to reflect. "Part of man's dual nature. Paul knew a good deal about that. Puts the new man in contrast to the old man—the inner man in contrast to the outer man—the spiritual man in contrast to the carnal. The old, outer, carnal man falls in love with one kind of person, and the new, inner, spiritual man with another. Depends on which element is the stronger. The higher falls in love with the higher type; the lower with the lower."

"But suppose neither is stronger than the other?—that they're equally balanced—and—?"

"And in conflict. One of the commonest sights in life. Known fellows in love with two women at the same time— with a good wife at home, mother of the children, and all that—and another kind of woman somewhere else. True, in a way, to 'em both. Struggle of the two natures."

Lois was distressed. "Oh, but that kind of thing can't be love."

"Can't be? 'Tis. Ask any one who's ever felt it—who's been dragged by it both ways at once. He'll tell you whether it's love or not—and each kind the real thing—while it lasts."

It was the expression "while it lasts" that Lois most resented. It reduced love to a phase—to a passing experience that might be repeated on an indefinite number of occasions. It was more than a depreciation; it had the nature of a sacrilege. And yet no later than the following day she received a shock that showed her there was something to be said in its favor.

She had gone nominally to see Rosie, but really to verify for herself Jim Breen's report of the collapse of Jasper Fay's little industry. She found it hard to believe that after Claude's conduct toward Rosie her father-in-law could have the heart to bring further woe upon a family that had already had enough. Nothing but seeing for herself could coerce her incredulity.

She had seen for herself. Over the little place which had always been neat even when it was forlorn there was now the stamp of desolation. The beds which had been seeded or planted a month before, and which should now have been weeded, trimmed, and hoed, were growing with an untended recklessness that had all the proverbial resemblance to moral breakdown. In the cucumber-house the vines had become rusty and limp, sagging from the twines on which they climbed in debauched indifference to sightliness. The roof of the hothouse that had contained the flowers had a deep gash in the glass which it was no longer worth while to mend. There was no yellow-brown plume from the furnace chimney, and the very windows of the old house with the mansard roof had in their stare the glazed, unseeing expression of eyes in which there is death. Inside, Mrs. Fay was packing up. Battered old trunks that had long been stored in some moldy hiding-place stood agape; a packing-case held the place of honor in a forbidding "best room" into which Lois had never looked before. Mrs. Fay had little to say. Tears welled into her cold eyes with the attempt to say anything. Outside, Fay himself had nothing to say at all. Lois had accosted him, and though he had ceased to regard her as an enemy, he stood grimly silent as his only response to her words of consolation.

"I know things will come all right again, Mr. Fay. They must. They look dark now; but haven't you often noticed that after the worst times in our lives we're able to look back and see that the very thing that seemed most cruel was the turning-point at which a change for the better began? You must surely have noticed that—a man with so much experience as you."

He looked vaguely about him, standing in patience till she had said her say, but giving no indication that her words had anything to do with him. The change in his appearance shocked her. Everything in his face had taken on what was to her a terrible significance. The starry mysticism had vanished from the eyes to be re-placed by a look that was at once hunted and searching, vindictive and yet woebegone. The mouth was sunken as the mouths of old men become from the loss of teeth, and the thin lips which used to be kindly and vacillating were drawn with a hard, unflinching tightness. The skin that had long been gray was now ghostly, with the shadowy, not quite earthly, hue of things about to disappear.

She had talked to him for some minutes before he woke to animation. At sight of two young men—surveyor's clerks, perhaps—who had set up in the roadway what might have been a camera on a tripod, or more probably a theodolite, through which they were squinting over the buildings and the slope of the land, he left her abruptly.

With a hoe in his hand he crept forward, taking his place behind a clump of syringa that grew near the gate, ready to strike if either of the lads ventured to put foot on his property. It was the situation at which, according to light-hearted Jim Breen, you would have died laughing; but Lois had difficulty in keeping back her tears.

She found Rosie in the hothouse, of which the interior corresponded to the gash in the roof. All the smaller plants had been removed, disclosing the empty, ugly, earth-stained, water-stained wooden stagings. Only some half-dozen fern-trees remained of all the former beauty.

But even here Rosie was at work, sitting at the old desk, which, deprived of its sheltering greenery, was shabbier than ever, making out bills. There was still money owing to her father, and it was important that it should be collected. Over and over again she wrote her neat "Acct. rendered," while she added as a postscript in every case: "Please remit. Going out of business."

And yet, if there was anything on the dilapidated premises that could cheer or encourage it was Rosie. With the enforced rest and seclusion following on her fruitless dash to escape, her prettiness had become more delicate, less worn. Shame at her folly had put into her greenish eyes a pleading timidity which became a quivering, babyish tremble when it reached the lips. The contrast which the girl thus presented to her parents, as well as something that was visibly developing within her, enabled Lois to affirm that which hitherto she had only hoped or suspected, that the wild leap into the pond had worked some mysterious good.

Like her father and mother, Rosie had little to say. The meeting was embarrassing. There were too many unuttered and unutterable thoughts on both sides to make intercourse easy or agreeable. All they could achieve was to be sorry for each other, in a measure to respect each other, and to make up by an enforced, slightly perfunctory, good will for what they lacked in the way of spontaneity.

Lois took the chair on which Rosie had been seated at the desk, while Rosie leaned against a corner of the empty staging. It furnished the latter with something to say to be able to tell the new plans of the family Her father had taken a job with Mr. Breen. It wouldn't be like managing his own place, but it would be better than nothing. He had also rented a tenement in a "three-family" house on the Thorley estate, to which they would move as soon as possible. It was important to make the change, so as to be settled when Matt came out of jail. Both Rosie and her mother were glad that he wouldn't be free till the 10th of July, because the lease terminated on the 9th. He would return, therefore, to absolutely new conditions, and there would be no necessity of going over any of the old ground again. As far as they were concerned—Rosie and her mother—the sooner they went the better they would like it, since they had to go; but "poor father," Rosie said, with a catch in her voice, "won't leave till the last minute has struck. Even then," she added, "I think they'll have to drive him off. This place has been his life. I don't think he'll last long after he's had to leave it."

Having given sympathetic views on these points as they came up, Lois rose to depart. She had actually shaken hands and turned away when Rosie seemed to utter a little cry. That is, her words came out with the emotion of a cry. "Mrs. Masterman! I want to ask you something!"

Lois turned in surprise. "Yes, Rosie? What?"

With one hand Rosie clung to the staging for support. The back of the other hand was pressed against her lips. She could hardly speak. "Is—is Claude staying away on my account?" Before Lois could answer, Rosie added, "Because he—he needn't."

Lois wondered. "What do you mean by that, Rosie?"

"Only that—that he needn't. I—I don't care whether he stays away or not."

Lois took a step back toward the girl. "You mean that it doesn't make any difference to you what he does?"

She shook her head. "No; not now; not—not any more."

"That is, you've given him up?"

Rosie sought for an explanation. "I haven't given him up. I only—*see*."

"You see what, Rosie?"

"Oh, I don't know. It's—it's like having had a dream —a strange, awful dream—and waking from it."

"Waking from it?"

Rosie nodded. She made a further effort to explain. "After I—I did—what I did—that day at Duck Rock— everything was different. I can't describe it. It was like dying—and coming back. It was like—like waking."

"Do you mean that what happened before seemed— unreal?"

She nodded again. "Yes, that's it. It was like a play." But she corrected herself quickly. "No; it wasn't like a play. It was more than that. It was like a dream—an awful dream—but a dream you like—a dream you'd go through again. No; you wouldn't go through it again—it would kill you." She grew incoherent. "Oh, I don't know—I don't know. It's gone—just gone. I don't say it wasn't real. It *was* real. It was a kind of frenzy. It got hold of me. It got hold of me body and soul. I couldn't think of anything else—while it lasted."

Lois was pained. "Oh, but, Rosie, love can't come and go like that."

"Can't it? Then it wasn't love." But she contradicted herself again. "Yes, it *was* love. It was love—while it lasted."

While it lasted! While it lasted! The phrase seemed to be on every one's lips. There was distress in Lois's voice as she said, "But if it was love, Rosie, it ought to have lasted."

And Rosie seemed to agree with her. "Yes, it ought to have. But it didn't. It went away. No, it didn't go away; it just—it just—*wasn't*." She wrung her hands, struggling with the difficulty she found in explaining herself. "After that day at Duck Rock it was like—it was like the breaking of a spell that was on me. Everything was different. It was like seeing through plain daylight again after looking through colored glass. I didn't want the things I'd been wanting. They were foolish to me— I *saw* they were foolish—and—and impossible. But it wasn't as if they had died; it was as if I had—and come back."

It was on behalf of love that Lois felt driven to make a protest. "And yet, Rosie, if you were to see Claude again—"

"No, no, no," the girl cried, excitedly; "I don't want to see him. He needn't stay away—not on my account— but I sha'n't see him if I can help it. It would be like dying the second time. All the same, he needn't be afraid of me; and his family needn't be afraid of me. I want to—to forget them all."

Enlightenment came slowly to Lois because of her unwillingness to be convinced of the heart's capriciousness. That love could be likened to brain-storm—obsession— the tornado whose rage dies out in an afternoon—was a wound to her tenderest beliefs. That the natural man must be taken into consideration as well as the spiritual also did violence to what she would have liked to make a serene, smooth theory of life. She stood looking long at the girl, studying her subconsciously, before she was able to say, calmly: "Very well, Rosie, dear. I'll let Claude know. I can get his address, and I'll write to him."

But another surprise was in store for her. She was near the door leading from the hothouse when she became aware that Rosie was behind her, and heard the same little gasping cry as before. "Mrs. Masterman! I want to ask you something!" Lois had hardly looked round when the girl went on again. "You know father and mother. They think the world of you—mother especially. Do you suppose they'd mind very much if I—if I turned?"

Lois was puzzled. "If you did what, Rosie?"

"If I turned; if I turned Catholic."

"Oh!"

The reformed tradition was strong in Lois. She was prepared to defend it by argument and with affection. For a minute she was almost on the point of stating the historical Protestant position when she was deterred by the thought of Dr. Sim. What would he have said to Rosie? She remembered suddenly something that he once did say: "If you can seize any one aspect of the Christian religion, do it—for the least of them all will save you."

Remembering this, Lois withheld her arguments, asking the non-committal question, "Why should you think of doing that?"

Rosie flushed. "Oh, I don't know. I've been"—she hung her head—"I've been pretty bad, you know. I've told lies—and I—I tried to kill myself—and everything."

"And you think you'd get more help that way than any other?"

"Oh, I don't know. I went twice lately—not here—in town. It frightened me. I—I liked it."

Had Lois dared she would have asked if Jim Breen had inspired this sudden change, but she said, merely: "Oh, I don't believe your father and mother would feel badly in the end—not if it brought comfort to you, Rosie dear. Is it that you want me to talk to them?—to help you out?"

Rosie nodded silently, and with face averted in a kind of shame.

"Very well, then, I will." She felt it due to her own convictions to add: "Perhaps I can do it all the better because—because my personal opinions are the other way.

They'll see I'm only seeking whatever may make for your happiness." There was silence for a few seconds before she said, in conclusion, "And oh! Rosie dear, I do hope you'll be happy, after all—all that's been so hard for you."

Rosie was too strong and self-contained to cry, but there was a mist in her eyes as they shook hands again and parted.

That night Lois wrote to her husband: "You ask me, dear Thor, if I see my way yet, and frankly I can't say that I do. I begin, however, to wonder if there is not a reason for my remaining puzzled and so long in the dark. I begin to ask if I know what love is—if anybody knows what it is. Do you? If so, what is it? Is it the same thing for every one? or does it differ with individuals? Is it a temporary thing?—or a permanent thing?—or does it matter? Is it one of the highest promptings we have?—or one of the lowest?—or is it that primary impulse of animate nature which when developed and perfected leads to God? Is there a spiritual man and a carnal man, each with a love that can conflict with the love of the other? Is the one man on the side of the angels, as Uncle Sim would say, and the other man on that of the flesh, till the stronger gains the victory? Or is there something in love of the nature of obsession? Does it come and go like the tornado—as violent in its passage, but as quickly passed? Thor, darling, I begin to be afraid of love. If we are to start again I want it to be on some other ground—a new ground—a ground we don't know anything about as yet, but which perhaps we shall discover."

CHAPTER XXIX

THORLEY MASTERMAN pondered on the words Lois had written him as he tramped along the bluffs above the Mississippi, with the towers and spires of Minneapolis looming like battlements through the haze of an afternoon at the end of June. He had left the conference on new methods of treating the thyroid gland which was being held in St. Paul in order to think his position out. Having motored over from his hotel in Minneapolis, he preferred to "tramp it" back. The glorious wooded way on the St. Paul side of the river was in itself an invitation to his strong, striding limbs, while the wine of Western air and the stimulus of Western energy quickened the savage outdoor impulse so ready to leap in his blood. The song of mating birds quickened it, too, and the romance of the river gliding through the gorge below, and the beauty of the cities eying each other like embattled queens from headland across to headland and through the splendor of the promise of a gold-and-purple sunset.

It was a great setting for great thoughts, inspiring ideas so large that when he reached his hotel he found them too big to reduce easily to paper.

"You ask me what love is, and say you don't know. I'm more daring than you in that I think I do know. I know two or three things about it, even if I don't know all.

"For one thing, I know that no one can do more than say what love is for himself. You can't say what it is for me, or isn't, or must be, or ought to be. That's my secret. I can't always share it, or at any rate share it all, even with the person I love. But neither can I say what it is, or isn't, or should be, or must be, for you. You have your secret. No two people love in the same way, or get precisely the same kind of joy or sorrow from loving. Since love is the flower of personality, it has the same infinite variety that personalities possess. We give one thing and we get back another. Do not some of our irritations—I'm not speaking of you and me in particular—arise from the fact that, giving one thing, we expect to get the same thing back, when all the while no one else has that special quality to offer? The flower is different according to the plant that produces it. When the pine-tree loved the palm there was more than the distance to make the one a mystery to the other.

"Of the two things essential to love, the first, so it seems to me, is that what one gives should be one's best—the very blossom of one's soul. It may have the hot luxuriance of the hibiscus, or the flame of the wild azalea in the woods, or no more than the mildly scented, flowerless bloom of the elm or the linden that falls like manna in the roadway. Each has its beauties and its limitations; but it is worth noticing that each serves its purpose in life's infinite profusion as nothing else could serve it to that particular end. The elm lends something to the hibiscus—the hibiscus to the elm. Neither can expect back what it gives to the other. Perfection is accomplished when each offers what it can.

"Which brings me to the remaining thing I know about love—that it exists in offering. Love is the desire to go outward, to pour forth, to express, to do, to contribute. It has no system of calculation and no yard-stick for the little more or the little less. It is spontaneous and irrepressible and overflowing, and loses the extraordinary essence that makes it truly love when it weighs and measures and inspects too closely the quality of its return. It is in the fact that love is its own sufficiency, its own joy, its own compensation for all its pain, that I find it divine.

The one point on which I can fully accept your Christian theology is that your God is love. Given a God who is Love and a Love that is God, I can see Him as worthy to be worshiped. Call Him, then, by any name you please—Jehovah, Allah, Krishna, Christ—you still have the Essence, the *Thing*. Love to be love must feel itself infinite, or as nearly infinite as anything human can be. When I can't pour it out in that way—when I pause to reflect how far I can go, or reach a point beyond which I see that I cannot go any further—I do not truly love."

Having written this much, he laid down his pen and considered. He had said nothing personal, unless it was by implication. It was only after long meditation that he decided to leave the matter there. The prime question was no longer as to whether or not he loved her, but as to whether or not she loved him. That was for her to decide. It was for her to decide without his urging or tormenting. He began to feel not only too sensitive on the subject, but too proud to make appeals to which she would probably listen out of generosity. Since he had been in the wrong, it was for her to make the advances; and so he ended his letter and posted it.

The discussion continued throughout the correspondence that ensued while he migrated from Minneapolis to Milwaukee, from Milwaukee to Denver, and from Denver to Colorado Springs. It was partly from curiosity of travel that he zigzagged in this way across the country, and partly to make it plain to Lois without saying it that he awaited her permission to come home. That he should be obliged to return one day, without her permission if not with it, was a matter of course, but it would make the meeting easier if she summoned him. As a hint that she could do so and have no fear, he asked her in a postscript to one of his letters to tell him, when she next wrote, what was happening to Rosie Fay.

To this she replied as simply and straightforwardly as he had put the question, imparting all that Jim Breen had told her and whatever she had gleaned for herself, adding as a seeming afterthought in the letter she wrote next day:

"If Rosie *could* bring herself to marry Jim it would be the happiest of all solutions, and make things easier for Claude. I think she will. If so, it won't be so much because her heart will have been caught in the rebound as that the poor little thing is mentally and emotionally exhausted, and glad to creep into the arms of any strong, good man who will love her and take care of her. Just to be able to do that much will be enough for Jim. I see a good deal of him; so I know. Every time he brings an order of new plants we have a little talk—always about Rosie. His love is of the kind you wrote about the other day; it has no yard-stick for the little more or the little less in the return. Perhaps men can love like that more easily than women do. Uncle Sim seemed to hint one evening that there is generally a selfish strain in a woman's love, in that what it gets is more precious to it than what it gives. I wonder."

Thor received these two letters together on returning to Colorado Springs from a day's visit to that high wilderness in which John Hay sought freedom from interruption in writing his *Life of Lincoln*. He understood fully that Lois was deliberately being cruel in order to be kind. The very spacing out of her information over two separate days was meant to impress him and at the same time to spare. Things would be easier for Claude, she said, when she meant that they would be easier for him.

But for him it was a matter of indifference. That is, it was the same kind of matter of indifference that pain becomes in a limb that has grown benumbed. For reasons he could hardly explain, that part of his being to which Rosie Fay had made her pathetic appeal couldn't feel any more. It was like something atrophied from over-strain. There was the impulse to suffer, but no suffering. Moreover, he was sure that though these nerves might one day vibrate again, they could never do so otherwise than reminiscently. To the episode he felt as a mother might feel to the dead child she has never been able to acknowledge as her own. It was something buried, and yet sacred—sacred in spite of the fact that it never should have been. As an incident in his life it had brought keen joy and keener pain, but he had already outlived both. He had outlived them as apparently Rosie had outlived them herself—not by the passage of time, but by an intensity of experience which seemed to have covered years.

He came to this conclusion not instinctively, nor all at once, but by dint of reflection, as he sat on the broad terrace of the hotel, watching the transformation scene that takes place in the Rockies during the half-hour before sunset. His pipe was in his mouth; Lois's letters lay open on the little table he had drawn up beside his chair. Other tourists bore him company, scattered singly or in groups, smoking and drinking tea. A mild suggestion of Europe, a suggestion of Cap Martin or of Cannes, was blocked by the domes of the great range and by a shifting interplay of magic lights where his eye was impelled to look for the broad, still levels of Mediterranean blue.

There was a wonder in the moment which the yearning in his spirit was tempted to take as symbolic, and perhaps prophetic, of his future. Where all day long he had seen nothing but hard ridges packed against one another, without water, without snow, without perspective, without a shred of mist, without a hint of mystery, without anything to set the mind to wondering what was above them or beyond them, the dissolving views of late afternoon began to throw up a succession of lovely ranges, pierced by valleys, glens, and gorges. Where the eye had ached with the harsh red of the rocks spread with the harsh green of the scant vegetation, soft vapors rose insensibly— purple, pink, and orange—changing into nameless hues as they climbed into the great clefts and veiled the rolling domes and swathed the pinnacles and furrowed the deep passes and put the horizon infinitely far away. The transmutation from conditions in which Nature herself seemed for once to be barbaric, alien, hostile to civilized man, painted with Cheyenne war-paint and girdled with a belt of scalps, to this breaking up of glory into glory, of color into color, and of form into form, rising, mingling, melting, fading, rising and mingling again, melting again, fading again, passing swiftly in a last brief recrudescence from gold into green and from green into black, with the hurried eclipse and the sudden tranquillity of night—the transmutation which produced all this was to Thor hopeful and in its way inspiriting. In the last rays of light he drew out his fountain-pen and the scribbling-book he kept for notes by the way, writing quickly without preamble or formality.

"Thanks for telling me about Rosie. It is as it should be—as will be best. Jim saved her. Nothing so good could ever happen to her as to marry him.

"As for me, there are two things, Lois, that I can truthfully affirm. I can declare them the more emphatically because I have had time to think them over—to think you over, and myself. If I ever had a doubt about them I haven't now, because leisure and solitude have enabled me to see them clearly. The first is that I have given you my best; and the second, that I have given it without any restriction of which I have been aware. If there was anything I withheld from you, and which you think you should have had, I can only say that it was not of the nature of my best. What it was I make no attempt to say, nor would it do any good to try. Whatever it was, I wish neither to depreciate it nor to deny it. It was something that swept me—like the tornado of which one of your letters speaks—but it passed. It passed, leaving me tired and older—oh, very much older!—and with an intense desire to creep home. As a physicist I know nothing of a carnal man and a spiritual man, so that I cannot enter into your analysis; but I do know that there are higher and lower promptings in the human heart, and that in my case the higher turn to you. As compared with you I'm only as the ship compared to the haven in which it would take refuge. The ship is good for something, but it needs a port."

Again he decided to leave his appeal suspended here, and on the next morning began his preparations for gradually turning homeward.

CHAPTER XXX

I T was William Sweetapple, the gardener's boy, who informed Lois that Claude had come back, throwing the information casually over his shoulder as he watered the lawn.

"Seen Mr. Claude to-day, 'm."

"Oh no, you didn't, Sweetapple," Lois contradicted. "Mr. Claude is in the West."

"He may be in the West now, 'm, but he wasn't at twenty-five minutes past two this afternoon."

Sudden fear brought Lois down a step or two of the portico, over the Corinthian pillars of which roses clambered in early July profusion. In white, with a broad-brimmed Winterhalter hat from which a floating green veil hung over her shoulders and down her back, her strong, slim figure seemed to have gained in fulfilment of herself even in the weeks that Thor had been away.

"Where did you see him, Sweetapple?—or think you saw him?"

Sweetapple turned the nozzle of the hose so as to develop a crown of spray with which he bedewed the roses of all colors grouped in a great central bed. "I didn't think, 'm. It was him."

"Well, where?"

"See him first going into the woods leading up to Duck Rock. That was when I was on my way to Lawyer Petley's."

"Did you see him twice?"

"See him again as I come back. He was down in the road by that time—looking up toward old man Fay's— Hadley B. Hobson's place that is to be. Old man Fay's got to quit. Family moved already. You knew that, didn't you, 'm?"

It was because Lois was really alarmed by this time that she said, "Oh, you must have been mistaken, Sweetapple!"

"Just as you say, 'm," Sweetapple agreed; "but I see him; it was him."

She withdrew again, reseating herself in the shade of the semicircular open porch protecting the side-door, where she had been writing on a pad. Though so near the roadway, a high growth of shrubs screened her from all but the passers up and down Willoughby's Lane. At this time of year they were relatively few, many of the residents of County Street having already gone to the seaside or the mountains. Lois enjoyed the seclusion thus afforded her, and the tranquillity. The garden and her poorer neighbors gave an outlet to her need for physical activity, while in the solitude of the house and in that wider solitude created by the absence of all the Willoughbys and Mastermans something within her was being healed. It was being healed—but healed in a way that left her changed. The change was manifest in what she said when, with the pad on her knee again, she began to write.

"I am deeply moved, dear Thor, by your last letter from Colorado Springs, and would gladly say something adequate in response to it. When I can I will—if I ever can. As to that the decisive word must be with time. I cannot hurry it. I can give you no assurance now. Now I feel—but why should I repeat it? An illusion once dispelled can rarely be brought back. Still less can you replace it by reality. What we are looking for is a substitute for love. You may have found it—but I have not. I can accept your definition of love as a giving out, a pouring forth, a desire to do and to contribute; but it is precisely here that I fail to respond to the test. There is something in me stagnated or dammed up. My heart feels like a well that has gone dry. I have nothing to yield. I understand what Rosie Fay said to me the day when I talked to her on Duck Rock: 'I'm empty; I've given all I had to give.' It was less blameworthy on her part than on mine, because she, poor little thing, had given so much and I so little. And yet my supply seems to be exhausted. It must have been thin and shallow to begin with. As I feel at present it would take a new creation to replenish it.

"With regard to my calling forth what is best in you, dear Thor—well, any one would do that or anything. You're one of those who have nothing but the best to offer. Do you know what Uncle Sim said of you last night?—'Thor is always on the side of the angels—and, though he makes mistakes, they'll rescue him.' They will, dear Thor; I'm sure of it. They may rescue us both—even if at present I don't see how."

Having written this much, she paused to ask what she should say further. Should she speak of his coming home? No. Since the address he had given her indicated that he was on his way, it was best that he should take the responsibility of his own return. Should she tell him that Sweetapple thought he had seen Claude? No. It would alarm him without doing any good. If Claude was back, he was back—besides which, Sweetapple might be wrong. So she signed her name with her usual significant abruptness, sealing the envelope and addressing it.

Her hesitation came in putting on the stamp. Somehow the letter seemed too cold to send. She didn't want to be cold—only to be sincere. Sincerity during these weeks of solitude had become a sort of obsession. She couldn't tell him that she had forgiven him as long as resentment lingered in her heart, and yet she was anxious not to wound him more than she could help. Wounding him she wounded herself more deeply, for in spite of everything his pain was hers.

Slowly she tore the letter open again, to a sunset chorus of birds of whose song she had just become conscious. From tree to tree they fluted to one another and answered back, now with a reckless, passionate warble, now with a long, liquid love-note. It was the voice of the rich world that lay around her—a world of flowers and lawns, and meadows and upland woods, and cool, deep shades and mellowing light. But it was also the voice that had accompanied her into the enchanted land on that winter's day when Thor had kissed her wrist. The day seemed now immeasurably far away in time, and the enchanted land had been left behind her; but the voice was still there, fluting, calling, reminding, entreating, with an insistence that almost made her weep.

She wrote hurriedly in postscript: "If there was ever anything I could do for you, dear Thor, perhaps what I used to feel would come back to me. If it only would! If I could only be great and generous and inexacting as you would be! I want to be, Thor darling; I long to be; but I am like a person paralyzed, whose limbs no longer answer to his will. I pray for recovery and restoration—but will it ever come?"

As encouragement to Thor she was no more satisfied with this than with what she had said earlier, but it expressed all she could allow herself to say. Anything more would have permitted him to infer such things as he had permitted her to infer, an accident that must have no repetition. She ended the note definitely, getting it ready for the post.

She was still engaged in doing so when, the crunching of footsteps causing her to lift her head, she saw Claude. Having come round to the side portico on a hint from William Sweetapple, he stood at a little distance, smiling. He was smiling, but as a dead man might smile. Lois could neither rise nor speak, from awe. Claude himself could neither speak nor advance. He stood like a specter —but a specter who has been in hell. The very smile was that of the specter who has no right to come out of hell, and yet has come.

"THOR IS ALWAYS ON THE SIDE OF THE ANGELS"

Lois was not precisely troubled; she was terrified. If Claude had only spoken a word or taken a step forward it would have broken the spell that held her dazed and dumb. But he did nothing. He only stood and smiled— that awful smile which expressed more anguish than any rictus of pain. He stood just as he came into sight, on turning the corner of the house, with the many colors of the rose-bed at his left hand. It was exactly like this, she had always imagined, that disembodied spirits or astral forms made their appearances to portend death.

She got possession of her faculties at last. "Claude!" She could just whisper it.

He continued to smile as he advanced and came up the steps; but it was not till he was actually beside her that he said, in a voice which might also have been that of a dead man, "You didn't expect me, did you?"

She remembered afterward that they neither shook hands nor exchanged any of the usual forms of greeting, but at the minute it didn't seem natural that they should. Her own tone was as strained as his as she answered, awesomely: "No. Sit down, Claude. When did you come?"

Throwing his hat on the floor, he dropped wearily into a deck-chair and closed his eyes. With the sharp profile grown extraordinarily white and thin, the dead-man expression terrified her again. She wished he would raise his head and look at her—look more like life. All he did was to open his eyes heavily, as he replied, "Got back yesterday."

It was less from interest than from the desire to get on the plane of actual things that she asked, "Where are you staying?"

"Slept at the house last night. Old Maggs, the care-taker, has the key, so I made him let me in."

"But are you going to stay any time?"

"Might as well. Don't see why not."

There was so much to say and so much she was afraid to say that she hardly knew with what to begin. "Weren't you," she ventured, timidly—"weren't you having a good time?"

His answer as he lay back with eyes closed again was another of his smiles, only dimmer now with a faint bitter-sweetness. She knew it was like asking a man if his pain is better when it is killing him. Nevertheless, the ground of common, practical things was the only one to keep to, so she went on: "But you won't like sleeping at the house every night—with no one in it. Don't you want to come here?"

He shook his head. "No, thanks. Mrs. Maggs will make my bed and give me breakfast. That's all I need. Get the rest of my meals in town."

"But you'll stay to dinner now, won't you?"

He lifted himself up in his chair at last, his face taking on its first look of life. "Thor be there?"

"Why, no. Thor's away—in the West. Didn't you know?"

He started nervously. "Away in the West? Not looking for me?"

She tried to smile. "Of course not. He went to attend the medical congress in Minneapolis. He's on his way home now."

"When do you expect him?"

"Oh, not at once. I don't know when. He's taking his time."

He studied her awhile, with eyes that seemed to read her secret. "What for?"

"To see the country, I suppose. My last letter was from Colorado Springs."

He dropped back into the chair with a tired sigh of relief. "All right. I'll stay to dinner. Thanks."

She allowed him to rest, asking no more questions than she could help till dinner was over and they had come out again on the portico, so that he might have his cigar in the cool, scented evening air. She was more at ease with him, too, now that she could no longer see the suffering in his pinched, emaciated face.

"Claude, why did you come home?"

He withdrew the cigar from his lips just long enough to say, "Because I couldn't stay away."

"Why couldn't you?"

"Because I couldn't."

"Don't you think it would have been well to make the effort?"

"What was the good of making the effort when I couldn't keep it up?"

"But you kept it up for a while."

"Not after—after I heard."

"Heard about Rosie?"

He made an inarticulate sound of assent.

"What did you hear?"

"I heard—what she did."

"How? Who told you?"

"That chump Billy Cheever. Wrote me."

"How did he know it had anything to do with you?"

"Oh, I was fool enough to tell him about her once— and so he caught on to it. Put two and two together, I suppose, when he heard that—that—"

She seized the opportunity to make the first incision toward getting in her point. "That she threw herself into the pond? Did he say that Jim Breen dived after her and brought her up?"

He answered indifferently. "He said some one did. He didn't say who."

"It was Jim. He saved her." As the statement evoked no response, she continued, "Claude, what did you come home *for?*"

Again he withdrew his cigar from his mouth, looking at her obliquely. "To marry her."

She allowed some time to elapse before saying, "Claude, I don't think you will."

"Oh yes, I shall."

"What makes you so sure?"

"Because I am."

"I'm not. Or, rather, if I *am* sure—it's the other way."

He sprang up, seizing her by the arm over which there was nothing but a gauze scarf by way of covering. "Lois, for God's sake! What do you mean? You know something. Tell me. She hasn't gone away with Thor, has she?"

She, too, sprang up, shaking off his hand as if it had been a serpent. "You fool! Don't touch me! She'll marry Jim Breen. She'll be in love with him in a week or two."

It was all over in an instant, but the blaze in her eyes seemed literally to knock him down. He fell back into the deck-chair again, though he sat astride on it with his feet on the floor, covering his face with his hands.

"I beg your pardon, Lois," he muttered, humbly. "I don't know what I'm saying."

"No, you don't," she agreed, speaking breathlessly because the leaping of her heart was so wild; "but that's hardly an excuse for taking leave altogether of your senses."

He continued to mutter into his hands. "I'm crazy! I'm drunk! I'm stark mad! But, oh, Lois, if you knew what I've been through you wouldn't mind."

The hot anger that had rolled over her with a wrath such as she had never felt before began to roll away again, leaving her sick and shivering. It was an excuse for going into the house to find a cloak and for getting the minute's respite necessary to self-control. To regain it—to overcome that throb of her being of which the after effect was a faintness unto death—she was obliged to walk steadily, holding her head high. She was obliged, too, to repent of the tigress impulse with which she had turned on Claude, flinging in his face that for which she had meant to prepare him by degrees. The fact that it had seemingly passed over his head was no palliation to the outrage. As she mounted the stairs and went to her room she repeated her own formula: *"Nothing that isn't kind and well thought out beforehand."* What she had said had been neither well thought out nor kind, but the temptation had been overwhelming. For the instant it had seemed secondary that Thor hadn't taken Rosie to the West, since Claude, who knew so much more of the inner history of the episode than she did herself, had thought such an action possible. More clearly than ever before she saw that some appalling struggle for the possession of the little creature must have taken place, and that it had been going on during those months when life was apparently so peaceful and she had been living in her fool's paradise. It was not till he had lost the fight that Thor had come to her in the snow-bound woods with the twitter of birds and the deep music of the tree-tops accompanying those half-truths she had been eager to believe. She herself had been fatuous and vain in assuming that·he could love her; but if there was little to say for her, there was nothing at all to be said for him. He had been the more false for the reason that, as far as he went, he had been sincere. It was his very sincerity that had tricked her. Less than at any time since the day when he had stammered out his futile explanations did she feel it possible to pardon him.

But there was something else. Now, if she chose, she could *know*. In his present state of mind Claude would betray anything. She had only to question him, to throw the emphasis adroitly here or there, and the whole story would come out. It was like having a key come into her hands—a key that would unlock all those mysteries which were her terror. She was still irresolute, however, as to using it after she had taken an old opera-cloak from a wardrobe, thrown it over her shoulders, and gone downstairs again.

She found Claude as she had left him—astride on the deck-chair, his face in his hands, the burning end of the cigar that protruded between his fingers making a point of light. The abject attitude moved her to pity in spite of everything. She herself remained standing, her tall figure thrown into dim relief between two of the white Corinthian pillars of the portico. By standing, it seemed to her obscurely, she could more easily escape if any such awful revelation as she was afraid of were to spring on her against her will. She could almost feel it waiting for her in the depths of the heavy-scented darkness.

For the minute, however, the folly of Claude's return was the matter immediately to be dealt with; to get him to go away again was the end to be attained. It was with this in view, as well as with a measure of compassion, that she said:

"You poor Claude! You *have* been through things, haven't you?"

The answer came laconically: "Been in hell."

"Yes, that's what I thought," she agreed, simply. "I thought it the instant you came round the corner this afternoon. But why? For what reason—exactly?"

He lifted his haunted face, stammering out his recital in a way that reminded her of Thor. She could see that he had profited by his mistake of a few minutes earlier, and that just as Thor had tried to tell Claude's story without involving his own, so Claude was endeavoring to spare her by doing the same thing. Being able to supply the blanks more accurately now than on the former occasion, she found a kind of poignant, torturing amusement in fitting her knowledge in.

He began with his first meeting with Rosie, describing the scene. He had not taken the adventure seriously, not any more than he had taken a dozen similar. Girls like that could generally be thrown off as easily as they were taken on, and they bore you no ill-will for the change. As a matter of fact, a new flirtation generally began where the old one ended, which made part of the fun for the girl as for the man. He was speaking of respectable girls, Lois was to understand—village girls, shop girls, and others of the higher wage-earning variety, who didn't mind showing a spice of devil before they married and settled down. Lots of them didn't, and were no worse for it in the end. It had not occurred to him that Rosie would be different from others of the class, or that she would take in deadly earnest what was no more than play for him.

When he had made this discovery he had tried to withdraw, but only with the result of becoming involved more deeply. Over the processes by which he was led finally to pledge himself he grew incoherent, as also over the signs which caused him to suspect that Rosie was playing fast and loose with him. His mutterings as to "somebody else who was in love with her" and who was "ready to put up money" threw her back on memories of his uneasy questions concerning Thor on the evenings after the return from the honeymoon. It was with a sense of the key slipping into the lock that she said:

"And that made you jealous?"

"As the devil. It was because it did that I knew I couldn't give her up—that I'd never let her go."

There was sincere curiosity in her tone as she asked the question, "But, Claude, why did you?"

"Because she lied to me."

"Oh! And had you never lied to her?"

He mumbled something about that not being the same thing. "She swore to me that there'd never been any put-up job between her and—and—"

She helped him out. "The—the other person." She could hear the key grating as it turned. "And was there?"

He made the impatient, circular movement of his head, as though his collar chafed him, with which she was familiar. He was gaining time in order to use tact. "Oh, I don't know. There was—there was something.

Whatever it was, she denied it, when all the while they were—"

She felt obliged fully to turn the key. She knew how perilous the question might be, but it was beyond her to keep it back. "They were what, Claude?"

"They were trying to catch me in a trap."

It was like the door into the hall of mysteries opening, but only to make disclosures dimmer and more mystifying still. The postponement of dreadful certainties enabled her, however, to say with some slight relief, "But this—this other person couldn't have been very fond of her himself if he—if he gave her up to you."

He bowed his head still lower into his hands, muttering toward the floor: "Oh, I don't know. I don't care—now. Anyhow, she lied to me, and"—he lifted his haggard eyes again—"and I jumped at it. I saw the way out—and I jumped at it. I told her—I told her—I'd go and marry some one else."

"Did you mean Elsie Darling?"

He nodded speechlessly.

It was to come back again to the point which her anger had caused her to miss that she went forward and laid her hand on his shoulder kindly. "I would, Claude, if I were you," she said, in a matter-of-fact voice. "She'd make you a good wife."

"No one will make me a good wife now," he said, hoarsely. "I'm going to marry Rosie. I'll marry her if it puts me in the gutter. I'll marry her if I never have a cent."

She went back to her place between the pillars, leaning against one of them. "But, Claude," she reasoned, "would that do any good? Would it make either of you happy, after all that's been said and done?"

He seemed to writhe. "I don't care anything about that. I've got to do it."

"You haven't got to do it if Rosie doesn't want it."

"It's got nothing to do with her."

She looked at him in astonishment. "Nothing to do with her? What do you mean?"

He tried to explain further. He had not primarily come back to atone for the suffering he had inflicted on Rosie, or because his love for her was such that he couldn't live without her. He had come back to propitiate the demon within himself—the demon or the god, he was not sure which it was, for it possessed the attributes of both. He had come back to escape the chastisement his soul inflicted on itself—because without coming back he could no longer be a man. He had come back because the Furies had driven him with their whip of knotted snakes, and he could do nothing but yield to their hounding. If Lois thought that traveling in the West was beer and skittles when hunted and scourged by yourself like that— well, she had better try it and see.

What she must understand already was that Rosie and happiness had become minor considerations. He would sacrifice both to regain a measure of his self-respect. He had never supposed, and he didn't suppose now, that Rosie would be happy in marrying him, but that was no longer to the point. The demon or the god must be appeased, at no matter what cost to the victim.

He made these explanations not straightforwardly or concisely, but with rambling digressions that took him over half the Middle West. He described, or hinted at, all sorts of scenes, peopled by gay young business men and garnished by pretty girls, in which he could have enjoyed himself had it not been for the enemy in his heart. It wasn't merely that he had thrown over Rosie with a cruelty that made her try to kill herself, and still less was it that he couldn't live down his love when once he set about it. It was that the Claude who might have been was strangled and slain, leaving him no inner fellowship but with the Claude who was. Reviving the Claude who might have been was like reviving a corpse, and yet there was nothing to do but make the attempt.

"I'm a gentlemen—what?" he asked, raising his white face pitifully. "I must act like a gentlemen—what?"

"Yes, but if it's too late, Claude—for that particular thing?"

"Oh, but it isn't—it won't be—not when she sees me."

"It might be; and if she doesn't want it, Claude, I don't see why you—"

"You don't see why because you're not me. If you were, you would. A woman hasn't a man's sense of honor, anyhow."

She let this pass with an inward smile in order to say, "But, Claude, suppose you *can't* do it?"

He twisted his neck, with his customary chafing, irritated movement. "I'll do it—or croak."

"Oh, but that's nonsense!"

"To you—not to me. You haven't been through the mill that I've been ground up in. You don't know what it is to have been born—born a gentleman—and to have blasted yourself into human remains. That's what I am now—not a man—to say nothing of a gentleman—just human remains—too awful to look at."

She tried to reason with him. "But, Claude, you mustn't exaggerate things or put the punishment out of proportion to the crime. Admitting that what you did to Rosie was dishonorable—brutal, if you like—"

"Oh, it isn't that. It's what I did to myself. Can't you see?"

She saw, but not with the intensity of Claude himself. Sitting down at last, she let him talk again. He had felt something shattered in him, so he said, at the very minute when he had turned to leave the cucumber-house on the day of the final rupture. He knew already that he was a cad, and that he was doing what only a cad would have done; but he had expected the remorse to pass. He had known himself for a cad on other occasions, and yet had outlived the sense of shame. That he should outlive it again he had taken for granted, though he knew that this time he couldn't do it without suffering. He was willing to take the suffering. He was not specially unwilling that Rosie should take it, too. In her way she had been as much to blame as he was. Though he didn't question the sincerity of her love for him, she had plotted and schemed to catch him, because from her point of view he was a rich man's son, and even so had had moments of disloyalty. He found it not unreasonable to expect her to share the responsibility for what had overtaken her. But she, too, would outlive the pain of it and follow his example in marrying some one else.

Lois felt her opportunity to have fully come. "I think she will. She'll marry Jim Breen—if you'll only leave her alone."

"Oh, rot!"

The tone expressed the degree of importance he attached to this possibility. He went on again, discursively, incoherently, covering much of the same ground, but with new and illuminating details, details of which the background was still a jumble of suppers and dances and journeys, but in which the god or the demon gave him no rest. His distaste for diversion having declared itself from the day of his starting for Chicago, he had whipped up an appetite to counteract it. Availing himself of the freedom of a young man plentifully supplied with money for the first time in his life, he had made use of all the resources with which strange and exciting cities could furnish him to get back his zest in light-heartedness. The result was not in pleasure, but in disgust, and a horror of himself that grew. It grew from the beginning, like some giant poisonous weed. It grew while he was in Chicago; it grew with each further stage of his journey—in St. Louis, in Cincinnati, in Los Angeles. It was in Los Angeles that he had received Billy Cheever's letter with the news of Rosie's mad leap, and he knew for a certainty that the only thing to be done was to turn his face eastward. Whatever happened, and whoever suffered, he must redeem himself. Redemption had become for him a need more urgent than food, more vital than life. Though he didn't use the word, though his terms were simple and boyish and slangy, Lois could see that his stress was that which sent pilgrims to the Holy Sepulcher, and drove Judas to go and hang himself. Redemption lay in marrying Rosie, and restoring his honor, and bringing the Claude who might have been back to life. Indeed, it was difficult to tell at times which of the two was slain—whether the Claude who might have been, or the other Claude—so distraught and involved were his appeals. But beyond marrying Rosie and keeping his word—being a gentleman, as he expressed it—his outlook didn't extend. "Any damn thing that liked could happen" when that atoning act had been accomplished.

There were so many repetitions in his turns of thought that Lois ended by following them no more than listlessly. Not that she had ceased to be interested, but her mind was occupied with other phases of the drama. She remembered, what she had so often heard, that in the Mastermans there was this extraordinary strain of idealism of which no one could foresee the turn it would take. She knew the traditions of the great-grandfather whose heart had broken on finding that America was not the regenerated land he hoped for. Tales were still current in the village of old Dr. Masterman, his son, who through sheer confidence in his fellow-men never paid any one he owed and never collected money from any one who owed it to him. Archie Masterman, in the next generation, was supposed to have taken the altruistic tendency by the throat in himself and choked it down; but Uncle Sim was a byword of eccentric goodness throughout the countryside. Now the impulse was manifest in Claude, in this revulsion against his own failure, in this marred and broken vision of a Something to which he had not been true. And as for Thor . . .

But here she was tortured and frightened. Who knew what this strange inheritance might be working in him? Who could tell how big and tender and transcending it might become? That it would be transcending and tender and big was certain. If poor, frivolous, futile Claude could feel like this, could feel that he must redeem his soul though "any damn thing that liked" should happen as the price of his redemption, in Thor the yearning would outflank her range. Might not the secret of secrets be in that? Might not that which she had been seeing as treachery to herself be no more than a conflict of aspirations? If Claude, with his blurred distortion of the divine in him, served no other purpose, he at least threw a light on Thor. Thor, too, was a Masterman. Thor, too, was born to the vision—to the longing after the nationally perfect that had become legendary since the time of the great-grandfather—to the sweet, neighborly affection that ran through all the tales of that man's son—to the sturdy righteousness of Uncle Sim—to the standards of honor from which poor Claude had fallen as angels fall—and to God only knew what high promptings strangled and vitiated in his father. Thor was heir to it all, with something of his own to boot, something strong, something patient, something laborious and loyal, something long-suffering and winning and meek, that might have marked the leader of a rebellious people or a pagan, skeptic Christ.

Her mind was so full of this ideal of the man against whom—and also for whom—her heart was hot that she made no effort to detain Claude when, after long silence, he picked up his hat and slipped away into the darkness.

CHAPTER XXXI

HE slipped away into the darkness, but only to do what he had done on the previous evening after making arrangements with old Maggs. He climbed the hill north of the pond, not so much in the hope of seeing Rosie or any one else, as to haunt the scenes so closely associated with his spiritual downfall.

It was a languorous, luscious night, with the scent of new-mown hay mingling with that of gardens. If there was any breeze it was lightly from the east, bringing that mitigation of the heat traditional to the week following Independence Day. As there was no moon, the stars had their full midsummer intensity, the Scorpion trailing hotly on the southern horizon, with Antares throwing out a fire like the red rays in a diamond. Beneath it the city flung up a yellow glow that might have been the smoke of a distant conflagration, while from the hilltop the suburbs were a-sparkle. As, standing in the road, Claude looked through the open gateway down over the slope of land, the hothouse roofs and the distant levels of the pond gleamed with a faint, ghostly radiance like the sheen of ancient tarnished crystal.

The house was dark. It was dark and dead. It was dark and dead and haunted. Everything was haunted; everything was dark. Even the furnace chimney looming straight and black against the stars was plumeless. But in the silence and stillness there was something that drew him on. He crossed the road and went a few paces within the gate. He had not ventured so far on the previous evening, and during the day he had dared no more than to look upward from the boulevard below, after that pilgrimage to Duck Rock on which William Sweet-apple had surprised him. Now in the darkness and quietness he stood, not searching so much as dreaming. He was dreaming of Rosie, dreaming of her with a kind of cheer. After all, he would be bringing joy to her as well as getting peace of spirit for himself. It wouldn't be so hard. She would meet him as she used to meet him here, as she used to let him come and visit her, and then the atonement would be made. The process would be simple, and he should become a man again.

The conviction was so sweet that he lingered to enjoy it, penetrating a few steps farther into the spacious dim-ness of the yard. It was the first minute of inward ease he had known since he had turned his back on it. Now that he was once more on the spot, the Claude who was a devil-of-a-fellow, something of a sport, but a decent chap all the same, began again to run with red blood where there had been nothing but a whining, shriveling apostate. It was like rejuvenescence, like a re-creation.

Suddenly something moved. It moved at first in the shadow of the house, and then out in the starlit spaces. It moved stealthily and creepily and with a grotesque swiftness. Its action seemed irregular and uncertain, like that of some night-marauding animal, till Claude per-ceived that it was stalking him. He waited long enough to get a view that was almost clear of a crouching attitude, the crouching attitude of a beast when it means to spring, whereupon he turned and fled.

That is, he turned and walked away swiftly. He would have run had it not been for his renascent self-respect. He couldn't bring himself to run from poor old Fay even though his nerves were tingling. He tried to reassure himself by saying that it was no more than a repetition of that dogging to which he had been subjected before, and that it would discontinue once he was off the premises.

But when he turned to glance over his shoulder it seemed

to him that the sinister footsteps glided after him. That, he reasoned, might have been no more than fancy. The arc-lights were rare on this rather lonely road, and the enormous shadows they flung lent themselves to the startling of sick imaginations. Nevertheless, as he walked Claude continued to look back over his shoulder, always with renewed impressions of a creepy thing trying to track him down. Having entered the obscurity of their own driveway, he broke at last into a light, soundless trot which was not slackened till he reached the relative protection of the door.

But by morning he had regained a measure of tranquillity. Knowing what he had to do, he was resolved to do it promptly. With sunlight and summer and the sense of being home again to brace him up, the Claude who was a devil-of-a-fellow seemed in a fair way to be reborn. Waiting after breakfast only long enough to be discreet, he took his way up the hill again.

He was confident by this time, and the more so because of his being beyond the need of concealments. There would be no more shrinking into the odorous depths of the hothouse, or hesitancies, or equivocations. He would walk up and avow himself—to father and mother as well as to Rosie. The hero in him was coming to his own at last.

The gash in the hothouse roof which he could see from a distance was what he noticed first. In his two nocturnal visits this had not been apparent. Now that he saw it he stood stock-still. It was something like a gash within himself, a gash in his courage perhaps, or a gash in the dream of a reconstituted self. He knew vaguely that his father had refused the renewal of the lease and that at some time in the near future Fay would have to go; but he had not expected the immediate signs of complete demoralization. Now that they were there they disconcerted him.

He went on till he was in view of the house. It gave him the blind stare with which empty houses respond to interrogation. He continued his way to the gate and into the yard. All was neglected and fantastically overgrown. Vetch, burdock, and yarrow were in luxuriant riot with the planting and seeding of the spring. No living creature was in sight but a dappled mare, whose round body and heavy fetlocks spoke of a Canuck strain, hitched in the shade of the magnolia-tree.

The mare wore a straw hat to which was attached a bunch of artificial roses, and switched her tail to drive away the flies. Harnessed to a light form of dray, the animal suggested business, so that Claude put on a business air, going forward with the assurance of one who has a right to be on the spot. He had not advanced twenty paces before the hothouse door opened to allow the passage of a fern-tree in a giant wooden pot, behind which came the pleasant countenance of Jim Breen, red and perspiring from so much exertion under a July sun. Claude paused till the fern-tree was deposited in the dray, when the two men stared at each other across the intervening space.

For the first time Lois's mention of the young Irishman's name returned to Claude as significant. What the young Irishman thought of him he had no means of knowing, for a sudden eclipse across the cheery face was followed by an equally sudden clearing.

"Hello, Claude!"

Jim threw off the greeting guardedly, and yet with a certain challenge. His very use of the Christian name was meant to be a token of man-to-man equality. Having attended the public school with Claude, and taken part with him in ball-games at an age too early for class distinctions, he was plainly disposed to use that fact as a basis of privilege. He attempted, however, no other advance, remaining sturdily at the tail of his dray, hatless and in his shirt-sleeves, but with head erect and gray eyes set fixedly. The only conciliating feature was his smile, which had come back, not with its native spontaneity, but daringly and aggressively, as a brave man smiles at a foe.

Claude resented the attitude; he resented the smile; he resented the use of his Christian name; but he was resolved to be diplomatic. He went forward a few steps farther still, but in spite of himself his voice trembled when he spoke. "Mr. Fay 'round?"

Jim answered nonchalantly. "No; gone to town. Want a good fern-tree, Claude? Two or three corkers here. Look at that one, now. Get it cheap, too. Dandy in the corner of a big room."

Sickeningly aware of his feebleness in contrast with this easy, honest vigor, Claude made an effort to be manly and matter-of-fact. "Mr. Fay selling off?"

"Not exactly selling off. Fixed things up with father. Father's taken the stock, and Mr. Fay's going in with him. Didn't want this old place any longer," Jim continued, loftily. "Kind o' clung to it because he'd put money into it, like. Money-eater; that's what it was. Make more in a year with father than he would in this old rockery in ten. Hadley B. Hobson's bought the place. Know that, don't you? Come to think of it, it was your old man who owned it. Well, it's Hadley B. Hobson's now—or will be the day after to-morrow. Have a swell residence here. Good enough for that, but too small for a plant like Mr. Fay's."

Claude did his best to digest such details in this information as were new to him while he nerved himself to say, "Is Miss Fay a-about?"

Jim nodded toward the blank windows of the house. "Moved. Better take a fern-tree, Claude. Won't get a bargain like this, not if every florist in the town goes bankrupt. This one's a peach, and yet you'll call it a scream compared to the one I've got inside. Bring it out so as you can get a squint at it. Can't wait, can't you? Well, so long! Got to finish my job. Back, Maud, back! Any time you do want a fern-tree, Claude—"

Claude was obliged to speak peremptorily in order to detain him. "I want to know where the Fays have moved to."

"To town," was the ready answer. "Well, so long! If I don't get on with my job—"

"What part of town?"

Jim turned at the hothouse door. "Oh, a very nice part."

"But that's not telling me."

"No," the young Irishman threw back, with his peculiar smile, "and if you take my advice you won't ask anybody else. If old man Fay was to see you within a mile of the place—"

Claude decided to be confidential. "Old man Fay has no reason to be afraid any longer, Jim—not as far as I'm concerned."

"Oh, it isn't as far as you're concerned; it's as far as he is. The boot's on that foot now."

Claude loathed this discussion with a man so inferior to himself, but he was obliged to get his information somehow. "If he thinks—"

"It's not what he thinks, but what he knows. That's what's the matter with old man Fay. If I was you I'd give him a darned wide berth—from now on."

"Yes, but Jim, you don't understand—"

"I understand what I'm telling you, Claude. If you don't clear out of this village for the next six months—"

Claude was beside himself with exasperation. "But, good God, man, I've come back to marry Rosie! Now don't you see?"

Jim stalked forward from the hothouse door, standing over the smaller, slighter man with a tolerant kindliness which persisted in his sunny, steely smile. "No, I don't see. You clear out. Take a friend's advice. Whether you've come back to marry Rosie or whether you haven't won't make a cent's worth of difference to old man Fay. Clear out, all the same."

In his excitement Claude screamed, shrilly, "Like hell, I will!"

"Like hell, you'll have to. Mind you, Claude, I'm telling you as a friend. And as for marrying Rosie—well, you can't."

Claude became aggressive. "If that's because you think you *can*—"

"Gee! Me! What do you know about that! It's all I can do to get her to look at the same side of the road I'm on—so far. But if I can't, still less can you, and for a very good reason."

"What reason?" Claude demanded, with his best attempt to be stern.

The other became solemn and dramatic. "The reason that—that she's dead."

Claude jumped. "Dead! What in thunder are you talking about? She wasn't dead this afternoon."

"Oh yes, she was, Claude—*that* Rosie. She—she drowned herself. When I dived in after her it was another Rosie altogether that I brought up. Do you get me?"

Claude broke in with smothered objurgations, but Jim, feeling the value of the vein he had started, persisted in going on with it. He did so not bitterly or reproachfully, but with a playful, Celtic sadness in which a misty blinking of the eyes struggled with the smile that continued to hover on his lips.

"The Rosie you knew, Claude, was all limp and white as I held her in my arms while Robbie Willert rowed us ashore. She was gone. The soul was out of her. She was as much in heaven as if she'd been dead a week. Her eyes were shut and her eyelashes wet, just as you might see the fringe of a flower hung with dewdrops of a morning. And her mouth! You know the kind of mouth she's got—a little open when she looks at you, as if you'd taken her by surprise, like. Well, that's the way it was then—a wee little bit open—as if she was going to speak—

but more as if she was going to cry—and her lips that white!—and not a beat to her heart no matter how tight you held her! When Dr. Hill brought the breath into her again it was a different Rosie that came back entirely."

Claude wheeled away in order to hide the spasm that shot across his face. "Ah, shut up, damn you!" was all he had the strength to say, but the tone moved Jim to compunction.

The Irishman in him came out as he tried to make things easier for Claude, without at the same time desisting from his object. "Sure *you* couldn't tell that that was the way she'd take it. You couldn't tell that at all at all. If you'd known it beforehand you'd have acted quite different. We all know that. Any one else might have done the same thing that was—that was"—he sought a consolatory phrase—"that was like you." He plunged still further. "I might have done it myself if I hadn't—hadn't been built the other way 'round. Only that won't matter to old man Fay—nor to Matt, neither."

Claude turned so suddenly pale at the mention of the brother that Jim followed up his advantage. "The old fellow has to be out of this by to-morrow night, and Matt gets his walking-ticket from Colcord the next morning." He laid his strong, earthy hand on the neat summer black-and-white check of Claude's shoulder with the lightest hint of turning him in the direction of the gate. "Now if you'll make yourself scarce for a spell I'll be able to manage them both and coax them back to their senses."

Though he felt himself irresistibly impelled toward the road, Claude made an effort to recover his dignity. "If you think I'm going to run away—"

Jim slipped his arm through his companion's, helping him along. "Sure you're not going to run away. Lay low for a spell, that's all you'll be doing. Old man Fay is crazy—stark, staring, roaring crazy. It isn't you, and it isn't Rosie; it's having to get out of here. It was bluff what I said a minute ago about the place being too small for his plant. He's dotty on these three old hothouses. My Lord! you'd think no one ever had hothouses before and never would again. You'd think it was the end of the world, to hear him talk. You'd die laughing. The fellow he'd like to put it over on is your old man! Gives me a mouthful about him three or four times a day—and it 'd be a barr'l full of buckshot in the back if he could get at *him*. Lucky he's in Europe. But I'll calm him down, don't you fret; and I'll calm down Matt, once I get at him. Let me have two months—let me have a month!—and I'll have 'em coming to you like a gray squirrel comes for nuts."

Out in the roadway Claude made a last effort to react against his humiliation, doing it almost tearfully. "But, look here, Jim, I've got to marry Rosie—I've *got* to."

The Irishman in the young man was still in the ascendant as he wagged his head sympathetically. "Sure you've got to—if she wants it."

"Well, she does want it, doesn't she? She must have told you so, or you wouldn't know so much about it."

"She's told me all about it from seeding to sale, and it's God's truth I'm handing out to you—no bluff at all. This Rosie's another proposition."

"I'll marry her, whatever she is," Claude declared, bravely; "and I've got to see her, too."

Jim looked thoughtful. "It isn't so easy to see her because— Well, now, I'll tell you straight, Claude— because it makes her kind o' sick to think of you. Oh, that's nothing!" he hastened to add, on seeing a second convulsion pass across Claude's face. "Sure she'd feel the same about any one who'd done the like o' that to her, now wouldn't she? It isn't you at all—not any more than it 'd be me or anybody else."

"If I could see her," Claude said, weakly, "I'd—I'd explain."

"Ah, but you couldn't explain quick enough. That's where the trouble about that 'd be. She'd be down on

the floor in a faint before you'd be able to say knife.
You couldn't get near her at all at all—not this Rosie—
not if it was to explain away the ground beneath her feet."

"She'd get over that—" Claude began to plead.

"She'd get over it if it didn't kill her first; but it's my
belief it would. If you could have seen her the night she
told me about you! It was like cutting out her own heart
and picking it to pieces. She's never mentioned you before
nor since—and I don't think ever will again. No, Claude,"
he continued, in a reasoning tone, "there's no two ways
about it, but you've got to get out—for a spell, at any
rate. If you don't, old man Fay 'll be after you with a
gun, and what Matt Fay 'll do may be worse. I can
handle them if you'll keep from hanging yourself out
like a red rag to a bull, like; but if you don't—then the
Lord only knows what 'll happen."

"What 'll happen," Claude cried, with a final up-
leaping of resistance, "is that you'll marry Rosie."

"I'll marry her if she'll have me. Don't you fret about
that. But I won't *try* to marry her—not if I see that she's
got the least little bit of a wish to marry you, Claude.
I'll play fair. If she changes her mind from the way she is
now, and gets so as to be able to think of you again, and
wants you—wants you of her own free will—then I'll put
up the banns for you myself—and that's honest to God."

He offered his hand on the compact, but Claude didn't
take it. He didn't take it because he didn't see it, and he
didn't see it because he looked over it and beyond it, as
over and beyond the young Irishman himself. It was not
that he had any doubt as to Jim's word being honest to
God, or that he questioned Rosie's state of mind as Jim
had sketched it. It was rather that he was seeing the
Claude who was a gentleman and a hero and a devil-of-a-
fellow recede into the ether, while he was left eternally
with the Claude who remained behind.

Jim felt no resentment for the neglect of his proffered
hand, but the long stare of those sick, unseeing eyes made

him uneasy. "Well, I guess I must beat it back to my job," he said, beginning to move away. "So long, Claude, and good luck to you!" He added, in order to return to a colloquial tone, "If you ever want a fern-tree, don't forget that we've got some daisies."

But Claude was still staring at the great blue blank which the fading of his ideal had left behind it.

CHAPTER XXXII

TWENTY-FOUR hours after Claude turned to take
the way of humiliation down the hill, undeceived
by Jim Breen's friendly tone and the hope of future
possibilities held out to him, Thor Masterman found
himself almost within sight of home. On arriving in the
city late in the afternoon he went to a hotel, where he took
a room and dined. When he had devised the means of
letting Lois know that he was camping outside her gates
she might be sufficiently touched to throw them open.
She might never love him again; she might never have
really loved him at all; but he would content himself
with a benevolent toleration. Like her, he was afraid
of love. The word meant too much or too little, he was
not sure which. It was too explosive. Its dynamic
force was at too high a pressure for the calm routine of
married life. If Lois could find a substitute for love, he
was willing to accept it, giving her his own substitute in
return. All he asked was the privilege of seeing her, of
being with her, of proving his devotion, of having her
once more to share his life.

It was not to force this issue, but to play lovingly with
the hope in it, that when dusk had deepened into evening
he took the open electric car that would carry him to the
village. He had no intention beyond that of enjoying the
cool night air and loitering for a few minutes in sight of
the house that sheltered her. She might be on the
balcony outside her room, or beneath the portico of the
garden door, so that he should catch the flutter of her
dress. That would be enough for him—to-night. He

might make it enough for the next night and the next. After absence and distance, it seemed much.

County Street was as he had known it on every warm summer night since he was a boy, and yet conveyed that impression which every summer night conveys, of being the first and only one of its kind. The sky was majestically high and clear and spangled, with the Scorpion and the red light of Antares well above the city's amber glow. Along the streets and lanes dim trees rustled faintly, casting gigantic trembling shadows in the circles of the electric lights. The breeze being from the east and south, the tang of sea-salt mingled with the strong, dry scent of new-mown hay and the blended perfumes of a countryside of gardens. All doors were open as he passed along, and so were all windows. On all verandas and porches and steps faint figures could be discerned, low-voiced for the most part, but sending out an occasional laugh or snatch of song. Thor knew who the people were; many of them were friends; to some of them he was related; there were few with whom he hadn't ties antedating birth. It was soothing to him, as he slipped along in the heavy shadow of the elms, to know that they were near.

On approaching his father's house, which he expected to find dark, he was astonished to see a light. It was a light like a blurred star, on one of the upper floors. From what window it shone he found it difficult to say, the mass of the house being lost in the general obscurity. The strange thing was that it should be there.

He passed slowly within the gate and along the few yards of the driveway, pausing from time to time in order to place the quiet beacon in this room or in that, according to the angle from which it seemed to burn. He was not alarmed; he was only curious. It was no furtive light. Though the curtains were closed, it displayed itself boldly in the eyes of the neighbors and of the two or three ornamental constables who made their infrequent rounds in County Street. He could only attribute it to old Maggs, who lived in the coachman's cottage at the far end of the property, though as to what old Maggs could be doing in the house at this hour in the evening, at a time when the parents were abroad and Claude away on a holiday, he was obliged to be frankly inquisitive. An investigating spirit was further aroused by the fact that in one of his pauses, as he alternately advanced and halted, he was sure he heard a footstep. If it was not a footstep, it was a stirring in the shrubbery, as if something had either moved away or settled into hiding.

He was still unalarmed. Night-crimes were rare in the village, and relatively harmless even when they were committed. The sound he had heard might have been made by some roving dog, or by a cat or a startled bird. Had it not been for the light he would scarcely have noticed it. Taken in conjunction with the light, it suggested some one who had been watching and had slunk away; but even that thought was slightly melodramatic in so well-ordered a community. He went on till he was at the foot of the steps, at a point where he could no longer descry the glow in the upper window, but could perceive through the fanlight over the inner door that, though the lower hall was dark, the electrics were burning somewhere in the interior of the house.

He verified this on mounting the steps and peering into the vestibule through the strip of window at the sides of the outer door. Turning the knob tentatively, he was surprised to find it yield. On entering, he stood in the porch and listened, but no sound reached him from within. Taking his bunch of keys from his pocket, he detached his latch-key softly, and as softly inserted it in the lock. The door opened noiselessly, showing a light down the stairway from the hall above. He could now hear some one moving, probably on the topmost floor, with an opening and shutting of doors that might have been those of closets, followed by a swishing sound like that of the folding or packing of clothes. He entered and closed the door with a distinctly audible bang.

Listening again, he found that the sounds ceased suspiciously. Whoever was there was listening, too. It was easy, by the light streaming from above, to find the button and turn on the electricity in the lower hall, whereupon the movement up-stairs began again. Some one came out of a room and peered downward. He himself went to the foot of the stairs, looking up. When the watcher on the third floor spoke at last it was in a voice he didn't instantly recognize. He would have taken it for Claude's, only that it was so frightened and shrill.

"Who's there?"

"Who are you?" Thor demanded, in tones that rolled and echoed through the house.

There was a long, hesitating silence. Straining his eyes upward, Thor could dimly make out a white face leaning over the highest banister. When the question came at last it was as if reluctantly and shrinkingly.

"Is that you, Thor?"

Thor retreated from the stairs, backing away to the library, of which the door was the nearest open one. He distinctly recorded the words that passed through his mind. He might have uttered them audibly, so indelible was the impression with which they cut themselves in.

"By God! I've got him."

Out of the confused suffering of two months earlier he heard himself saying: "I swear to God that if I ever see Claude again I'll kill him."

He hadn't meant on that occasion deliberately to register a great oath; the oath had registered itself. It was there in the archives of his mind, signed and sealed and waiting for the moment of putting it into execution. He had hardly thought of it since then; and now it urged itself for fulfilment like a vow. It was a vow to cover not merely one offense, but many—all the long years of nameless, unrecorded irritations, ignored but never allayed, culminating in the act by which this man had robbed him; robbed him uselessly, robbed him not to enjoy the spoil, but to fling it away.

It was a moment of seeing red similar to many others in his life. For the instant he could more easily have killed Claude than refrained from doing it. That he should so refrain was a matter of course. Naturally! He still kept a hold on common sense. He would not only refrain, but be civil. If Claude were in need of anything or were short of cash he would probably write him a check. It was the irony of this kind of rage that it was so impotent. It was impotent and absurd. It might shake him to the foundations of his being, but it would come to nothing in the end. It both relieved and embittered him to foresee this result.

From the threshold of the library he called up to Claude, "Come down!" The tone was imperious; it was even threatening. That degree of menace at least he was unable to suppress.

Claude's steps could be heard on the stairs. They were slow and clanking because the carpets were up and the house full of echoes. To Thor's fevered imagination it seemed as if Claude dragged his feet like a man wearing chains, going haltingly and clumsily before some ominous tribunal. The sensation—it was more that than anything else—caused the elder brother to withdraw into the depths of the library, where he turned on a light.

The room, with its bare floors, its shrouded furniture, its screened book cases, its blank pictures swaddled in linen bags, its long, gaunt shadows, and its deadened air, suggested itself horribly and ridiculously as a fitting scene for a crime. He might kill Claude with a blow, and if he turned out the lights and shut the door and stole back to his hotel no one would ever suspect him as the murderer. The idea would have been no more than grotesque had it not acquired a certain terror from the mingling of affection and anger and pity in his heart at the sound of Claude's shrinking, clanking advance. In proportion as Claude seemed to be afraid of him, he was the more aware that he was a man to be afraid of. The consciousness caused him to get deeper into the dimly lighted room, taking his stand at the remotest possible spot, with his back to the empty fireplace.

But when Claude appeared coatless in the doorway, his head was thrown up defiantly in apparent effort to treat Thor's entrance as unwarranted. "What the devil are you doing here?"

Because of the semi-obscurity his face was white with a whiteness that quickened Thor's sympathy into self-reproach.

"What are *you* doing here?"

"That's my business." In making this reply Claude seemed to take it for granted that they met on terms of hostility, though he added, less aggressively: "If you want to know, I'm packing up. Taking the train for New York at one o'clock to-night."

Thor endeavored to speak with casual fraternal interest. "What brought you back?"

Claude took time to light a cigarette, saying, as he blew out the match, "You."

"Me? I thought it might be—might be some one else."

"Then you thought wrong." He walked to a metal ash-tray which helped to keep the covering that protected one of the low bookcases in its place, and deposited the burnt match. He threw off with seeming carelessness as he did so, "I know only one traitor, to make me keep returning on my tracks."

Because the impulse to violence was so terrific, Thor braced himself against it, standing with his feet planted apart and his hands clenched behind him till the nails dug into the flesh. He could not, however, restrain a scornful little grunt which was meant for laughter. "*You* talk of traitors! I'd keep quiet about them,

Claude, if I were you. You make it too easy for an opponent."

"Oh, well," Claude returned, airily, "I'm used to doing that. I made it infernally easy for an opponent —last winter. But, then, sneaking's always easy to a snake, till you get your heel on him."

"And snarling's easy to a puppy, till you've throttled him."

"And bluster's easy to a fool, till you let him see you hold him in contempt."

"As to holding in contempt, two can play at that game, Claude; and you might find the competition dangerous."

Claude came nearer, the lighted cigarette between his fingers. "Not on your life! That's one thing in which I'm not afraid to bet on myself." He came nearer still, planting himself within a few paces of his brother. His smile, his mirthless, dead-man's smile, held Thor's eyes as it had held Lois's a day or two before. He made an effort to speak jauntily. "Why, Thor, a volcano can't belch fire as fast as I can spit contempt on you. There! Take that!"

With a rapid twist of the hand he threw the lighted cigarette into Thor's face, where it struck with a little smarting burn below the eye. Thor held himself in check by clenching his fists more tightly and standing with bowed head. It was a minute or more before he was sufficiently master of himself to loosen the grip with which his fingers dug into one another, and put up his hand to brush the spot of ash from his cheek. Being in so great fear of his passions, he felt the necessity for speaking peaceably.

"What did you do that for, Claude? It's beastly silly."

"Oh no, it isn't—not the way I mean it."

"But why should you mean it that way? What have I ever done to you?"

"Good Lord! what haven't you done? You've— you've ruined me."

22   329

The charge was so unexpected that Thor looked more amazed than indignant. "Ruined you?"

"Yes, ruined me. What else did you set out to do when you began your confounded interference?"

"I didn't mean to interfere—"

Claude might have posed for some symbolical figure of accusation as, with hands in his trousers pockets and classic profile turned in a three-quarter light, he flung his words and directed his glances obliquely and disdainfully at the brother who glowered with bent head. "When you don't mean to go into a thing you keep out. That was your place—out. Do you get that?—out. But you're never satisfied till you've made as vile a mess of every one else's affairs as you've made of your own."

Feeling some justice in the charge, Thor began to excuse himself. "If I've made a mess of my own, Claude, it's because—"

"Because you can't help it. Oh, I know that. No one can be anything but a damn fool if he's born one. All the more reason, then, why you should keep away from where you're not wanted."

By a great effort Thor managed to speak meekly. "How could I keep away when—?"

"When you're a rubber-neck bred in the bone. No, I suppose you couldn't. But you hate a spy and a liar even when he can't be anything else; and the worst of it is—"

"Oh, is there anything worse than that?"

"There's this that's worse, that your spying and your lying weren't bad enough till you got me into a fix where I have to look like a cad, when"—the protest in his soul against the rôle he was compelled to play expressed itself in a little gasp—"when I'm—when I'm not one."

The elder brother found himself unable to resist the opportunity. "If you look like a cad, I suppose it's because you've acted like a cad. It's the usual reason."

"Oh, there's cad and cad. There's a fellow who gets

snarled up in the barbed wire because he runs into it, and there's another who deliberately lays the trap for him. The one can afford to crawl away with a grin on his face, while the other lies scratched and bleeding."

It seemed to Thor that there was an opening here for a timorous attempt to cry quits. "If it comes to the question of suffering, Claude, it isn't all on one side. You may be scratched and bleeding, as you say, and yet you can get over it; whereas I'm lamed for life."

"Ah, don't come the hypocrite! If you're lamed for life, as I hope to God you are, it's because you've got a bullet in the leg—which is what any one hands out to a poacher."

The relatively gentle tone was again the effect of a surprise stimulated to curiosity. "When was I ever a poacher?"

"You were a poacher when you went making love to a woman who belonged to another man, while you belonged to another woman."

"Very well," Thor said, quietly, after a minute's thinking. "I accept the explanation. But I never did it."

"Then you did something so infernally like it that to deny it is mere quibbling with words."

"All the same, I insist on making the denial."

Claude shrugged his shoulders. "I'm not surprised at that. It's exactly what your type of cur would do. Unfortunately for you, I've the proof."

"The proof of what?"

"Of your torturing a poor girl into saying she was willing to marry you—and then throwing the words in her teeth."

It was from the flame in Thor's eyes that Claude leaped back a half-pace, though he steadied himself against a small table covered up from the accumulation of summer's dust by a piece of common calico. Giving himself time enough to have deliberately counted twenty, Thor subdued the impulse of the muscles as well as that of speech. "Who told you that?" he asked, at last, in the tone he might have used of some matter of no importance.

"Who do you think?"

"There's only one person who *could* have told you—"

"Oh, you admit as much as that, do you? There *is* a person who could have told me?"

"Yes, I admit as much as that—but you must have misunderstood her."

Thor's dignity and self-restraint were not without an effect that might eventually have made for peace had not the brother's conscience been screaming for a scapegoat on which to lay a portion of his sins. For him alone the entire weight had become intolerable. Thor had been known to accept such vicarious burdens before now. In the hope that he would do so again, Claude answered, tauntingly:

"I didn't misunderstand her when she said you were making me a cat's-paw to do what you wouldn't do yourself. What kind of stuff are you made of, Thor? You go flaunting your money before a poor little girl who you know can't resist it, and then, when you get her willing to do God knows what, you push her off on me and want to pay me for the job of relieving you of your dirty work. After you've dragged her in the dust she's still considered good enough for me—"

"Stop!"

The roar of the monosyllable echoed through the empty house, while Thor strode forward, the devil in him loose. With the skill of a toreador in throwing his cloak into the eyes of an infuriated bull, Claude snatched the calico strip from the table beside which he stood and flung it in Thor's face. The result was to check the latter in his advance, giving Claude time to dart nimbly to the other side of the room. As Thor stared about him, dazed by his rage, he bore out still further the resemblance to a maddened animal in the bull-ring.

Fear struggled in Claude's heart with the lust for retaliation. Like Thor himself, he knew the minute to be one in which he could work off a thousand unpaid scores that had been heaping themselves up since childhood. For the time being it seemed as if he could not only make the scapegoat bear his sins, but stab him to the heart while he did it.

"Stop?" he laughed, shrilly. "Like hell, I'll stop. Did you stop when you went sneaking after Rosie Fay till you got her in a state where she wanted to kill herself?" The red glare in Thor's eyes was an incentive to going on. "Did you stop when you tried to father your beastly actions off on me, and juggle me into marrying the girl you'd had enough of? Did you stop when you fooled Lois Willoughby into thinking you a saint, and breaking her heart when she found you out? Look at her now—"

With a smothered oath Thor charged as a wounded rhinoceros might charge—in a lunge that would have borne his brother down by sheer force of weight had not Claude eluded him lightly. Once more Thor shook himself, stupefied by his passion, blinded by the blood in his eyes. He needed an instant to place his victim, who, with white face and wild, terrified glances, had found temporary shelter behind the barricade of the heavy library table.

But before renewing his rush Thor marched to the door that led to the hall, the only door to the room, locking it and pocketing the key. The muttered, "By God, I'll have you now!" reached Claude's ears, bringing to his lips a protest which had not burst into words before the huge figure charged again. Behind his fortification Claude was alert, dancing now this way and now that, as Thor brought his strength to bear on the table to wrench it aside. But by the time that was done Claude was already elsewhere, overturning tables and chairs in his flight.

Behind a sofa Claude intrenched himself again, a small chair raised above his head as a weapon of defense. Thor sprang on the sofa, only to receive the weight of the chair in his chest, staggering him backward while Claude bounded off to another refuge. Both were cursing inarticulately; both were panting in broken grunts and sobs; from both the perspiration in that airless room and in the heat of the July night was streaming as rain. The pursuit was like that of a leopard by a lion—the one lithe, agile, and desperate; the other heavy, tremendous, and sure.

In darting from point to point Claude found himself near a window, where he fumbled with the fastening in the hope of throwing up the sash, though wooden shutters defended the outside. Driven from this attempt, he made for the locked door, pulling at it vainly on the chance that it would yield. Seeing Thor bearing down on him with redoubled fury, he obeyed the impulse of the moment and switched off the electricity as he crept swiftly along the wall. In the darkness he stumbled to a corner, where his labored breathing could not but betray his hiding-place. While he crouched in the corner, making himself small, he knew Thor was stalking him by the sound.

He was stalking him, and yet in the inky blackness of the room accurate hunting down was difficult. It was like a duel between blind men. Thor was moving uncertainly, pausing from second to second to fix the object of his search.

In the mad hope of reaching the fireplace and creeping into the chimney, Claude wriggled from his corner along the floor, keeping close to the wainscot. As he did so he touched the legs of a footstool which suggested its use at once. Controlling the thumping of his heart and the pumping of his lungs as best he could, he got noiselessly to his feet. Inch by inch, slinging the footstool by a leg, he moved toward the spot from which Thor's panting breath seemed to proceed. If he could but batter in that long skull he would be acquitted of responsibility on the ground of self-defense. But he was afraid of anything that approached the hand-to-hand. When it seemed to him that he could vaguely make out the swaying of a figure in the darkness, he hurled the missile with all his might—only to hear it crash into one of the covered pictures.

Claude was disappointed, and yet in the din of the shattering glass he was able to escape again. He had lost all sense of direction. Even his touch on the furniture didn't help him, since everything was now displaced. Nevertheless, he continued to duck and dodge, to wriggle and creep and elude. Once Thor's clutch was actually upon him, but he managed to tear himself free with nothing worse than a long rent in his shirt-sleeve. Again Thor seized him, but only to tear his collar from the stud. A third time Thor's strong fingers were closing round his throat, and yet after a momentary choking groan he had been able to slip away. Never before had Claude supposed himself so strong. There was a minute when he had felt Thor's hot breath snorting in his face, and still was able to pick up a small, round table on which his mother sometimes placed her tea-tray, sending it hurtling toward his pursuer, checking him again. With a splutter of stifled oaths, Thor grasped the piece of furniture, throwing it violently back. Claude rejoiced as it crashed into a window and loosened the shutters outside. If he only knew which of the windows it was, there might be a chance of his getting out by it.

With this possibility before him he took heart again. The sound of the breaking of the window enabling him to fix his whereabouts, he began feeling his way toward the unexpected hope of exit. It became the more urgent to reach it as he guessed by the fumbling of Thor's hands along the wall that the latter was trying to find the electric button so as to turn on the light. He groped, therefore, between the tables and overturned chairs, getting as far from his enemy as possible. If only his heart wouldn't pound as though about to burst from his body! If only his breath wouldn't wheeze itself out with the gurgle of water through a bottle-neck! He couldn't last much longer. He was so nearly spent that if Thor kept up the attack he must wear him out. In the end he must let those powerful hands close round his throat, as he had felt them close a few minutes before, while he strangled without further resistance. He felt oddly convinced that it would be by means of strangling that Thor's quiet, awful tenacity of revenge would wreak itself.

During these horrible minutes Thor had the same conviction. All the force of his excited nerves had seemed to be centering in his hands. If he could only tear out that tongue which had hardly ever addressed him except with a sneer since it had begun to lisp! Now that the amazing opportunity was at hand, he wondered how he could have put it off so long. That he should do the thing he was bent on might have been written like a fate. It was like something he had always known, like something toward which he had been always working. The tenderness with which he had yearned over Claude ever since the days when they were children seemed never to have had any other end in view.

So he stalked his prey while the minutes passed—five minutes—ten minutes—perhaps more, perhaps less—he had lost all count of time. So he stalked him—through the darkness, round and round, over tables and chairs, into corners and out of them. The room was sealed; the house was empty; the grounds were large. They might have been in some subterranean vault. When the right moment came he would find the button by which to turn on the light, and then . . .

Revulsion came from the fact that he had accidentally put his hand on the button and lit up the spectacle of the room. At sight of it he could have laughed. Nothing but the big library table and one of the heavy arm-chairs stood on its legs. One of the windows had a gash like a grin on its prim countenance, and one of the pictures sagged drunkenly from its hook, a mere bag of gilded wood and glass. Cowering in a corner, Claude was again arming himself with a chair. It was not his weapon, but his whiteness, that stirred Thor to a pity almost hysterical. One of his arms was bare where the shirt-sleeve had been torn from it; one side of his collar sprang loose where it had been wrested from the stud; his lips were parted in terror, his eyes starting from his head. The thing Thor could have done more easily than anything else would have been to fling himself down and weep.

As it was, he could only hold out his hands with a kind of shamed, broken-hearted appeal, saying, "Claude, come here."

Though his trembling hands dropped the raised chair, Claude shrank more desperately into his corner. When, to reassure him, Thor took a step forward, Claude moved along the wall, with his back to that protection, ready to spring and dodge again. If he understood Thor's advances, he either mistrusted or rejected them.

"Don't be afraid," Thor tried to say, encouragingly, but after the attacks of the past few minutes his voice sounded hollow and unconvincing to himself.

In proportion as he went nearer Claude sidled away, always keeping his back to the wall, with gasps that were like groans. He spoke but once. "Open that door!" It was all he could articulate, but it implied a test of the brother's sincerity.

Thor accepted it, striding to the threshold, turning the key energetically, and flinging the door wide open. The quiet light burning in the quiet hall produced something in the nature of a shock. He stepped into the hall to wipe his brow and curse himself. He could never win his own pardon for the madness of the past quarter of an hour. Neither, probably, could he ever win Claude's, though he must go back and make the attempt.

What happened as he turned again into the library he could never clearly explain, for the reason that he never clearly knew. The minute remained in his consciousness as one unrelated to the rest of life, with nothing to lead up to it and nothing to follow after. Even the savagery of their mutual onslaught had been no adequate preparation for what now took place so rapidly that the mind was unable to record it. As he re-entered the room Claude was standing by one of the low bookcases. So much remained in the elder brother's memory as fact. The vision of Claude raising his arm in a quick, vicious movement was a vision and no more, since on Thor's part it was blurred and then effaced in a sharp, sudden pain accompanied by a blinding light. Of his own act, which must have followed so promptly as to be nearly simultaneous, Thor had no recollection at all. By the time he was able to piece ideas together Claude was senseless on the floor, while he was bending over him with blood streaming down his face.

For the instant the brother was merged in the physician. To bring Claude back to life after the blow that had stunned and felled him was obviously the first thing to be done. Thor worked at the task madly, tearing open the shirt, chafing the hands and the brow, feeling the pulse, listening at the heart. Whether or not there was a response there he couldn't tell; his own emotion was too overpowering. His fingers on Claude's wrist shook as with a palsy; his ear at Claude's heart was deafened by the pounding of his own. Meanwhile Claude lay limp and still, dead-white, with eyes closed and mouth a little open. Thor had seen many a man in a state of syncope, but never one who looked so much like death. Was he dead? Could he be dead? Had the great oath been fulfilled? He worked frantically. Never till that instant had he known what terror was. Never had he beheld so clearly what was in his own soul. As he worked he seemed to be looking in a mirror from which the passion-ridden fratricide whom he had always recognized dimly within himself was staring out. The physician disappeared again in the brother. "O God! O God!" He could hear himself breathing the words. But of what use were they? As he knelt and chafed and rubbed and listened they came out because he couldn't keep them back. And he was accomplishing nothing! Claude was as still and limp as ever. Not a breath!—not a sign!—not a throb at the pulse!—and the minutes going by!

He dropped the poor arm that fell lifeless to the side, and threw back his head with a groan. "O God—if you're anywhere!—give him back to me!"

The broken utterance was the first prayer he had ever uttered in his life, but, having said it, he went on with his work again. He went on with new vigor and perhaps a little hope. He fancied he saw a change. It was not much of a change—a little warmth, a little color, but no more than might have been created by a fancy.

He ran for water to the nearest tap. In returning to the library his foot struck something on the floor. It was the metal ash-tray which had helped to keep the covering in place on one of the bookcases, and into which Claude had thrown a match. The picture of a few minutes earlier reformed itself—Claude standing just there, with the ash-tray under his hand—the rapid motion of the arm—the paralyzing pain—the dazzling light—and then the blow with which he must have hurled himself on Claude, striking him to the floor. There was no time to co-ordinate these memories now or to attend to the wound in his own forehead. The explanation came of its own accord as he touched the ash-tray with his foot while dashing back to Claude's side.

The change continued. There were positive signs of life. The mouth had closed; there was the faintest possible quiver of the lids. When he threw a little water into Claude's face there was a twitching of the muscles and a slight protesting movement of the hand.

"Thank God!"

He couldn't note the involuntary expression of his gratitude, which had nevertheless been audible. Claude had need of air. Taking him in his arms, he lifted him like a baby and staggered to his feet. The body hung loosely over his shoulder as he crossed the room and laid it on the sofa. The broken window served its purpose now, for a little air was coming in by it through the spot where the wooden shutter had given way. Thor succeeded in forcing the shutter altogether, letting the light summer breeze play into the marble face.

If he only had a little brandy! He summed up hurriedly the possibilities in the house, coming to the conclusion that nothing of the sort would have been left within reach. Even the telephone had been disconnected for the summer. It would be, however, an easy thing to run to his office. It would be easier still to run to his house, which was nearer. Claude was breathing freely now. He could be safely left for the few minutes which was all he needed to be away. With a simple restorative the boy would soon be on his feet again.

He pushed the sofa closer to the open window, kneeling once more beside it. Yes, the danger was past. "Thank God! Thank God!" The words were audible again. It was deliverance. It was salvation. There was a positive tinge of color in the cheeks; the eyes opened wearily and closed again. Thor seized the two cold hands in his own and spoke:

"It's all right, old chap. Just lie still for a minute, till I go and get you a taste of brandy. Be back like a shot. Don't move. You'll be all right. Fit as a fiddle when you've had something to brace you up."

No answer came, but Thor sought for none. The worst was past; the danger was averted. With the two cold hands still pressed in his own, he bent forward and kissed the pale lips with a life-giving kiss such as Elijah gave to the Shunamite woman's son. Under the warmth of the imprint Claude stirred again as if making a response.

He ran pantingly like a spent dog—but he ran. He had no idea what time it was. It might have been midnight; it might have been near morning. He was amazed to hear the village clock strike ten. Only ten! and he had lived a lifetime since nine.

He rejoiced to see a light in the house. Lois would be up. As he drew near he saw it was the light streaming from her room to the upper balcony outside it. When nearer still he caught the faint glimmer of a white dress. She was sitting there in the cool of the night, as they had so often sat together in the spring.

He called out as soon as he thought he could make her hear him. "Lois, come down!"

The white figure remained motionless, so that as he ran he called again, "Lois, come down!"

He could see her rise and peer outward. Still running, he called the third time: "Lois, come down! I want something!"

There was a hurried "Oh, Thor, is it you?" after which the figure disappeared in the light from the open window.

She met him at the door as he ran up the steps. There was no greeting between them. He had just breath enough to speak. "It's Claude. He's down there in the house. He's hurt. I want some brandy."

He was in the hall by this time, while she followed. His own appearance, now that he was in the light, drew a cry from her. "But, Thor, you're all cut—and bleeding."

He was now in the dining-room, fumbling at a drawer of the sideboard. "Never mind that now. It doesn't hurt. I'll attend to it by and by. I must get back to Claude. Is it here?"

"No; here." She produced the bottle of cognac from a cupboard, thrusting it into his hands. "Now come. I'm going with you."

They stopped for no further explanation. That could wait. Thor was out of the house, tearing down the empty street, while she followed scarcely less swiftly. At that time of night they were almost sure to have the roadway to themselves.

She lost sight of him as he turned in at the avenue, but continued to press on. That there had been a struggle between the brothers she could guess, though she let the matter pass without further mental comment. The fact that filled her consciousness was that in some strange way Thor was back—wild-eyed and bleeding. Whatever had happened, he would probably need her now, accepting the substitute for love.

Half-way up the avenue she saw that both the inner and outer doors of the house were open and that the electricity from the hall lit up the porch and steps. Thor was still running, but at the foot of the steps he surprised her by coming to a halt instead of leaping up them, two or three at a time. Stopping abruptly, silhouetted in the spot of light, he threw his hands above his head as if he had been shot and were staggering backward. He hadn't been shot, because there was no sound. He hadn't even been wounded, because as she sped toward him she could see him stoop—spring away—return—and stoop again. She was about to call out, "Oh, Thor, what is it?" when, on hearing her footsteps, he bounded to his feet and ran in her direction. "Go back!" he cried, hoarsely. "Go back! Go back, Lois, go back!"

But she hurried on. If there was trouble or danger she must be by his side.

He wheeled around again to that over which he had been stooping, but with a repetition of the movement of flinging up the hands. After that he seemed to crawl away— to crawl away till he reached the steps, where, pulling himself half-way up, he lay with his face hidden. The thing he had seen was something fatal and final, leaving no more to be done. The thought came to her that if there was no more for him to do, it was probable that her work was just beginning and that she must keep herself calm and strong.

THE SIDE OF THE ANGELS

She came to him at last and bent over his long, prostrate form. It was racked and heaving. The sobbing was of a kind she had never heard before—the violent, convulsive sobbing of a man.

Raising herself, she looked about for the cause of this grief, for a second or two seeing nothing. The respite enabled her to renew her sense of the necessity laid upon her to be helpful. Whatever was there, she must neither flinch nor cry out. She must take up the task where he had been forced to lay it down.

It was a bare arm from which the shirt-sleeve had been torn away that caught her attention first—a bare arm with a spatter of blood on it. It lay extended along the grass just beside the driveway. She was obliged to take a step or two toward it before seeing that it was Claude's arm, and that he himself was lying on the sward of the lawn, with a little trickle of blood from his heart.

She was not frightened. She was not even appalled. She understood as readily what she ought to do as if the accident had been part of every day's routine. But as her glance went first to the dead brother and then to the living one she knew that her substitute for love had been found.

CHAPTER XXXIII

WHEN Jasper Fay was tried for the murder of Claude Masterman, and acquitted of the charge, it was generally felt that the ends of justice had been served. No human being, whatever his secret opinion, could have desired the further punishment of that little old man whose sufferings might have expiated any possible crime in advance. The jury having found it improbable that at his age, and with his infirmities, he should have been lurking in the village at ten o'clock at night and waiting in the neighborhood of Colcord jail at dawn of the next morning, the verdict was accepted with relief not only in the little court-house of the county town, but by the outside public. To none was this absolution more nearly of the nature of a joy than to the unfortunate young man's family.

That was in the winter of 1912, and in the mean while Lois had been led so successfully by her substitute for love as to be at times unaware of her lack of the divine original. For she was busy, so it seemed to her, every day of every week and every minute of every day. The first dreadful necessities on that night of the 9th of July having been attended to, her thought flew at once to the father and mother of the dead boy.

"Thor dear, I know exactly what I'm going to do about them, if you'll let me."

It was early morning by the time she said that, and all that was immediately pressing was over. Claude was lying in one of the spare rooms that had been prepared

344

for him, and Dr. Noonan, together with the four or five grave, burly men, Irish-Americans as far as she could judge, who had been in and about the house all night hunting for traces of the crime, had gone away. Those who were still beating the shrubbery and the grounds were not in view from the library windows. Maggs and his wife were in the house, as well as Dearlove and Brightstone, getting it ready for re-occupation, since it was but seemly that the dread guest who had come under its roof should be decently lodged.

Thor, having spent some hours before the stupefied village authorities, was surprised and obscurely disappointed not to be put under arrest. Public disgrace would have appeased in a measure the clamor of self-accusation. To be treated with respect and taken at his word in his account of what had happened between himself and Claude was like an insult to a martyr's memory. When dismissed to his home he found it hard to go.

Having dragged himself back through the gray morning light, it was to discover strange wonders wrought in the immediate surroundings. Lois and her four assistants had whisked the coverings from the furniture and restored something like an air of life. Even the library, having been sufficiently noted and described, had been set in what was approximately order, the broken picture taken from its nail and the broken window hidden by a curtain.

On the threshold of the room Thor paused, shrinking from a spot which henceforth he must regard as cursed. But Lois insisted. "Come in, Thor dear; come in." She felt it imperative that he should overcome on the instant anything in the way of terrible association. He must counteract remorse; he must not let himself be haunted. She herself sat still, therefore, with the restrained demeanor of one who has seen nothing in the circumstances with which she has not been able to cope. Pale, with dark rings under the eyes betraying the inner

23

effect of the night of stress, she nevertheless carried herself as if equal to confronting developments graver still. The strength she inspired came from rising to the facts as to some tremendous matter of course.

Now that there was a lull in the excitement she had been quietly discussing the conditions with Uncle Sim and Dr. Hilary. The latter went forward as Thor, tall, gaunt, red-eyed, the wound in his forehead stanched with plaster, advanced into the room.

"You're face to face with a great moral test, me dear Thor," he said, laying his hands on the young man's shoulders, "but you'll rise to it."

Thor started back, less in indignation than in horror. "Rise? Me?"

"Yes, you, me dear Thor. You'll climb up on it and get it under your feet. The best use we can make of mistake and calamity is to stand on them and be that much higher up. I don't care what your sin has been or what your self-reproach. Now that they're there, you'll utilize them for your spiritual growth. Neither do I say God help you! for I'm convinced in me soul that He's doing it."

Thor moved uneasily from under the weight of the benedictory hands. It was as part of his rejection of mercy that he muttered, "I don't know anything about Him."

"Don't you, now? Well, that's not so important. He knows all about you. It's not what we know about God, but what God knows about us that tells most in the long run."

He passed on into the hall, where he picked up his hat and went out. Uncle Sim, who, with more of Don Quixote in his face than ever, had been pacing up and down the room, threw over his shoulder, "Always said you were on the side of the angels, Thor—and you are."

Thor found his way wearily to the chimney-piece, where he stood with his face buried in his hands and his back to his two companions. He groaned impatiently. "Ah, don't talk about angels!"

Uncle Sim continued his pacing. "But I will. Now's the time. What, after all, are they but the forces in life that make for the best, and who's ever been on their side more than you?"

Thor groaned again. "What good does that do me now?"

"This good, that when you've been with them they'll be with you, and don't you forget it! Life doesn't forsake the children who've been trying to serve it, not even when they lose control of themselves for a few minutes and do—do what they're sorry for afterward."

Thor writhed. "I killed Claude."

"Oh no, you didn't, Thor dear," Lois said, quietly. "It's wrong for you to keep saying so. We can see perfectly well what has happened, can't we, Uncle Sim? If Claude revived while you were away and went out to get more air, and some one, as you think, was lurking in the shrubbery—"

"But if it hadn't been for me—"

"As far as that goes I might as well say, If it hadn't been for me. I've told you how he came to me two days ago and how I discouraged him. We're all involved—you no more than the rest of us."

"If he *is* involved more than the rest of us," Uncle Sim declared, "it's all the more reason why the good forces by which he's stood should now stand by him. It's a matter of common experience to all who've ever made the test that they do." He turned more directly to Thor. "There's a verse in one of those old songs I'm fond of quoting at you—I'll never trouble you with another," he promised, hurriedly, in answer to a movement of protest on his nephew's part, "if you'll only listen to this. It's right to the point, and runs this way: 'The angel of the Lord encampeth round about them that fear Him, and delivereth them.' They're camping round about you now, Thor, as I've always told you they would."

Thor raised his head just enough to say savagely over his shoulder, "But when I never *have* feared Him, in the way you mean—and don't."

"Oh, but you have—and do. There's two types for that sort of thing, both sketched in graphic style by the Master. There's the two sons sent to work in the vineyard, of whom one said to his father, 'I go, sir,' and went not. The other said, 'I will not,' but went. 'Whether of them twain,' the Master asks, 'did the will of his father?' I leave it to yourself, Thor."

Unable to escape from this ingenious pardon that caught and blessed him whether he would or no, Thor remained silent, while the uncle addressed himself to the niece. "I'll be off now, Lois, but I'll come back before long and bring Amy. We'll stay here. The house 'll need to have people in it, to make it look as if it was lived in, till Archie and Ena can be got at and brought home."

Thor turned and looked from the one to the other distressfully. "Poor father and mother! What about them?"

It was then that Lois showed that the matter had already received her attention. "Thor, dear, I know exactly what I'm going to do, if you'll let me."

She had been so efficient throughout the night that both men listened expectantly while she sketched her plan. She would cable the facts as succinctly as she could put them to her own father and mother, who were in their *petit trou pas cher* on the north coast of France. They would then cross to England and break the news to Mr. and Mrs. Masterman. The very fact of the breach between her parents on the one side and the bereaved couple on the other was an additional reason for charging the former with the errand of mercy. Where so much had been taken it was the more necessary to rally what remained.

Having expressed his approval of these suggestions, Uncle Sim took his departure.

"Where is he?" Thor asked at once.

"Come."

Though she rose, she lingered to say, with a manner purposely kept down to the simplest and most matter-of-fact plane: "You'll come up to the house and have breakfast, won't you, Thor? It will be ready about eight." As he began to demur on the ground that he couldn't eat, she insisted. "Oh, but you must. You know that yourself. You'll feel better, too, when you've had a bath. You can't take one here, because Mrs. Maggs hasn't put the towels out. Cousin Amy will attend to that when she comes down."

These and similar maternal counsels having been given and received, she led the way into the hall, only to pause again at the foot of the stairs. "I shall go out now to send my cablegram to mamma. The sooner I get it off the better it will be, so that they can cross from Havre to Southampton to-night. I've got it all thought out and condensed, and I shall write it in French so as to keep it from the people in our own office here. I suppose that everything will be in the papers by the afternoon, and we shall have to accept the publicity." Seeing the pain in his face, she took the opportunity to say: "Oh, we can do that well enough, Thor dear. We mustn't be afraid of it. We mustn't flinch at anything. Whatever has to come out will get its significance only from the way we bear it; and we can bear it well."

Having advanced a few steps up the stairs, she turned again on the first landing, speaking down toward him as he mounted. "If possible, I should like to tell Rosie myself. It will be a shock to her, of course; but I want to be with her when she has to meet it. Don't you think I ought to be?" On his expressing some form of mute agreement, she continued: "Then, if you approve, I shall telephone to Jim Breen, asking him to bring her to see me.

Rosie will guess, by my sending for her, that something strange has happened. I shall word my message to her in that way."

Her last appeal was made to him as she stood with one hand on the knob of the door beyond which Claude was lying. "Thor dear, I hope you get at the truth of the things Uncle Sim and Dr. Hilary have been saying. There's a great message to you there. You *are* on the side of the good things, you know. You always have been, and always will be."

He shook his head. "It's too late to say that to me now."

"Oh no, it isn't! And what's also not too late to say is that you mustn't let yourself be ridden by remorse." His haggard eyes seeming to ask her how he could help it, she continued: "Remorse is one of the most futile things we know anything about. It can't undo the past, while it destroys the present and poisons the future."

He was almost indignant. "But when you've—?"

"When you've given way as you say you gave way last night? You brace yourself against doing it again. You make it a new starting-point. Isn't that it?"

"Yes, but if you're like me!"

With her free hand she brushed back the shock of dark hair from his forehead. It was the first touch of personal contact between them since his sudden reappearance. "If one is like you, Thor, of course it's harder. You're a terrific creature. I begin to see that now. I never took it in before, because in general you're so restrained. I know it's the people who are most restrained who can be swept most terribly by passion—but I hadn't expected it of you. Even so, it's the sort of thing which only goes with something big in the soul—"

He put up a hand protestingly. "Don't!"

"But I must. It ought to be said. You should understand it. Fundamentally—I see it quite plainly now—you're the big primitive creature that's only partially tamed by the tenderest of tender hearts. Do you know what you remind me of?—of a great St. Bernard dog that asks nothing better than to love every one and save life, but which when it's roused . . .! You see what I mean," she went on, with a kind of soothing, serious cajolery. "Thor dear, I was never so afraid of you as I've been this night, and I never"—*loved* was what she was going to say, but, as on the day in the winter woods, she suppressed the word for another—"I never admired you so much. I'm going to make a confession. What you say you felt toward Claude is what I've often felt myself in—in glimpses. God knows I don't say that to malign him. I shouldn't say it at all if it were not to point out that you wouldn't have done him any more harm—not when it came to the act—than I myself. Would you, now?"

He hung his head, murmuring, brokenly, "No."

"What we've got to see is that you're very human, isn't it? and that's what they mean—Uncle Sim and Dr. Hilary—when they say that you're face to face with a great moral test. They mean that after you've used what—what's happened within the last few hours— as you can use it—as you *can* use it, Thor dear—you'll be a far stronger man than you were before—and you were a strong man already."

With eyes downcast he murmured words to the effect that it was difficult to see the way.

"Won't the way be to take each new thing as it comes —and there are some very hard things still to come, you know!—as a step to climb by, to get it under our feet as something that holds us up instead of over our heads as something that crushes us down? Won't that be the way? It may be like climbing a Calvary, but all the same we shall be there—up instead of down—and," she added, with a smile so faint that it was in her eyes rather than on her lips, "and you know, Thor darling, that no one is ever on a Calvary alone."

With these words she turned the handle of the door,

leading him into a room from which the morning light was only partially excluded, and about which vases and bowls of roses had already been set.

Claude was lying naturally, wearing a suit of his own pajamas, white with a little pink stripe, his face turned slightly and, as it were, expectantly toward the two who approached. Having entered the room first, Lois kept to the background, leaving Thor to go to the bedside alone.

The difference between the dead Claude and the sleeping one was in the expression. In the sleeping Claude the features were always as if chiseled in marble, and, like marble, cold. The dead Claude's face, on the contrary, radiated that which might have passed for warmth and life. The look was one he would have worn if mystified and pleased by something he was trying to understand. In any other case Thor would have explained away this phenomenon on grounds purely physiological; but since it was Claude he found himself swept by an invading wonder. He knew what people more credulous than himself would say. They would say that on the instant of the great change toward which he had been so suddenly impelled even poor Claude, with his narrow earthly vision, had been dowered with an increase of perception that bewildered and perhaps rejoiced him. Thor couldn't say this himself; but he could wonder. Was it possible that Claude, with this pleasing, puzzled dawn upon his face, could have entered into phases of life more vivid than any he had left behind? Thor found the question surging within his soul; but before he could silence it with any of his customary answers he heard the counsel of wise old Hervieu of the Institut Pasteur: "*Ne niez jamais rien.*"

But his need was emotional and not philosophical. Stooping, he kissed once more the lips on which there was this quiver of a new life that almost made them move, and sank on his knees beside the bed. Lois, who knew that beyond any subsequent moment this would be the one of last farewell, slipped softly from the room and closed the door behind her. She remembered as she did so that apart from her timid touch on his hair there had been no greeting between her husband and herself since his cry to her as she sat on the balcony in the darkness; but perhaps the substitute for love didn't call for it.

She went down-stairs to carry out her intentions of ringing up Jim Breen and sending her cablegram to France. Since the necessity for doing the former would take her to her own house, she would have the chance of changing her dress before the relative publicity of the telegraph-office in the Square. She would need also to explain the circumstances to her servants, who by this hour would be moving about the house and might be alarmed on finding that her room had not been occupied. The door to the garden portico being that which would probably be unlocked, she turned into Willoughby's Lane, where her attention was caught by the sight of two men coming down the hill.

What she saw was a young man helping an older one. The old man leaned heavily on his companion, hobbling with the weariness of one who can barely drag himself along.

Lois was seized by sudden faintness; but a saving thought restored her. It was no more than the prompting to give this spent wayfarer a cup of coffee as he passed her door, but it met the instant's need. By a deliberate effort of the will she banished every suggestion beyond this kindly impulse. If there were graver arguments to urge themselves, they were for others rather than for her.

That she was not the only person within eight or ten hours to be startled by the sight of that little old man was abundantly evidenced later. John Stanchfield, Elias Palmer, Harold Ormthwaite, and Nathan Ridge, all farmers or market-gardeners of the Colcord district, testified to frights and "spooky feelings" on being accosted by a dim gray figure plodding along the Colcord road in the lonely interval between midnight and morning. The dim gray figure seemed to have recognized the different "teams" by the section of the road through which they jolted or by their flickering lamps.

"That you, 'Lias?"

"Why, yes! Who be you? Darned if it ain't Jasper Fay! What under the everlastin' canopy be you a-doin' this way so late at night?—so early in the mornin', as you might say."

"My poor boy! To be let out at five!"

Grunts of sympathy and inquiries concerning the nature of the "truck" being taken to market made up the rest of the conversation, which ended in a mutual, "So long!"

With John Stanchfield and Harold Ormthwaite the exchange of salutations had been on similar lines. No one but old Nathan Ridge had had the curiosity to ask: "What you trampin' the eight mile for? Could have took the train at Marchfield, and got out at the jail door."

"We-ell, the trains didn't just suit. Marchfield's three mile from my place, and if it comes to trampin' three mile you might as well make it eight."

"Guess you're pretty nigh tuckered out, ain't you?"

"We-ell, I'm some tired. Been takin' it easy, though. Left home about eight o'clock last night and just strolled along. Fact is, Nathan, I had to be out o' my little place last night root and branch, and it's kind of eased my mind like to be footin' it through the dark."

"Guess you feel pretty bad, don't you?"

"Well, I did. Don't so much now."

"Got used to it?"

"No, it ain't that so much. It's just that if I've suffered, others will—" But according to Mr. Ridge further explanation was withheld, the speaker going on disappointingly to say: "Guess I'll be keepin' along. Hope you'll get your price on them pease. Awful sight of them in the market after this last dry spell."

So Jasper Fay trudged on. He trudged on patiently, with the ease of a man accustomed all his life to plodding through the soil, though now and then he paused. He paused for breath or for a minute's repose, and sometimes to listen. He listened most frequently to sounds behind him as if expecting pursuit; he listened to the barking of dogs, the gallop of grazing horses across the dark pastures, or to the occasional bray of a motorist's horn. When nothing happened, he went on again, though with each renewal of the effort his footsteps lagged more wearily.

Dawn was gray by the time he had come face to face with the long, grim house of sorrow. It was grim unintentionally, grim in spite of well-meant efforts to cheer it up and make it alluring, at least to the passer-by. For him ampelopsis had been allowed to clamber over the red-brick walls; for him a fine piece of lawn was kept neatly cut; for him the national flag floated during daylight over a grotesque pinnacle; for him a fountain plashed on feast-days. Neither fountain nor flag nor sward nor vine was visible except to the outsider, but it was for him the effect was planned. For him, too, a little common had been set apart on the other side of the roadway and garnished with a wooden bench under a noble, fan-shaped elm. Jasper Fay sat down on the bench as he had sat down on it many a time before, hunched and weary.

For the three years, or nearly, in which Matt had been shut up here the father had spent with him as many as possible of the minutes allowed for intercourse, prolonging the sense of communion by sitting and staring at the walls. In times past he had stared in patient longing for the moment of the boy's release; but this morning he only stared. Behind the staring, thought was too inactive for either retrospect or forecast; and thought was inactive because both past and future now contained elements too big for the overtaxed mind to deal with. He could only sit wearily and expectantly on the bench, watching, at the end of one of the long wings, a small gray door on which he had been told to keep his eyes.

After the first flicker of light the day came slowly. The lowlands around the prison were shrouded in a thin gray mist, through which Lombardy poplars and warders' cottages and prison walls loomed ghostly. When, a few minutes after the clock in the pinnacle had struck five, the gray door opened soundlessly and a shadowy form slipped out, the effect was like that of a departed spirit materializing within human ken.

The shadowy form shook hands with some one who remained unseen, and after it had taken a step or two forward the soundless door shut it out. It looked timorous and lone in the wide, ghostly landscape, advancing a few paces, stopping, searching, advancing again, but uncertainly. As it emerged more fully into view it disclosed a bundle in the hand, a light gray suit, and a common round straw hat. It moved as though testing ground that might give way beneath it or as trying the conditions of some new and awesome sphere of existence into which it had suddenly been thrust.

With all his remaining forces concentrated into one sharp, eager look, Jasper Fay crept forward. The ground-mist blurring his outlines, the two dim figures were face to face before the son perceived his father's presence or approach. On doing so he started back.

"Why, father! What's the matter? You look"—his voice dropped to faintness—"you look—terrible."

But the father's faculties were already too exhausted to catch the movement and note of dismay. He was drained even of emotion. All he could do was to extend his hand with the casual greeting: "Well, Matt! How are you? Come to meet you."

He explained, however, the immediate program, which was to go by the five-thirty train to Marchfield, whence by taking the short cut through Willoughby's Lane and County Street they could reach home for breakfast by seven. Home, it had to be told, was no longer the little place on the north bank of the pond, but a three-family house on the Thorley estate, with a "back piazza" for yard and nothing at all in the way of garden. A home without a garden to an old man who had lived in gardens all his life was more of an irony than a home without a rooftree, but even this evoked from the sufferer •only a mild statement of the fact. Mildness, resigned and apparently satisfied, marked all the turnings of the narrative unfolded as they plodded to the station, while the son took the opportunity to scan at his leisure those changes in the sunken face that had shocked him at the moment of encounter.

It was no new tale that Matt heard, but it pieced together the isolated facts made known to him in the few letters he had received and the scattered bits of family news he had been able to pick up on visiting-days. For all of it he was prepared. He would have been prepared for it even if he had received no hint in advance, since it was nothing but what the weak must expect from the strong and the poor from the rich. "We'll change all that," was his only comment; but he made it whenever he found an opening.

Only once did he permit himself to go beyond the dogged repetition of this phrase. "Got in with some fellows there"—he jerked his head backward in the direction from which they had come—"who've thought the whole business out. Could always get together—us trusties. Internationals them fellows were—the I. I. A— heard of 'em, haven't you? No bread and treacle in *their* program. Been handing that out too long."

The difference between the face Matt Fay had looked forward to seeing and the one which was now turned up to him was that between a mirror and a pane of glass. In a mirror there would have been reflection and responsiveness. Here there was nothing but a blank, shiny stare, vitreous and unintelligent. Jasper Fay, it seemed to his son, had passed into some pitiful and premature stage of dotage.

To the released prisoner the change was but one more determining factor in his own state of mind. He was prepared to find his mother in worse case than his father, and Rosie in worse case still. Poor little Rosie! She was the traditional victim of the rich man's son. So be it. Since it was for him to see that she was avenged, he asked nothing better. The more wrongs there were besides his own, the more he was justified in joining the campaign of blood and fire, of eloquence and dynamite, to which he felt a call.

He thought sullenly over these things as the train jogged through the rich fields and market-gardens on the way to Marchfield, and the quiet little man with the glassy stare and the gentle, satisfied, senile smile sat silent in the seat beside him. Matt Fay was glad of the silence. It left him the more free to gaze at the meadows and pastures, at the turnips and carrots and cabbages, of which the dewy glimpses fled by in successive visions of wonder. It was difficult not to believe that the sky had grown bluer, the earth greener, and the whole round of nature more productive during the years in which he had been "put away." His surprise in this recognition of the beauty of the world gave a poignant, unexpected blend to his wrath at having been compelled to forfeit it.

He got the same effect from every bird and bee and butterfly that crossed his path between Marchfield and the village. No yellowing spray of goldenrod, no blue-eyed ragged-robin, but symbolized the blessings of which he had been cheated. In proportion as the sun broke through the bank of cloud, burning away the mist and drawing jeweled rays from the dewdrops, the new recruit in revolution found his zeal more eager to begin. The very flagging and stumbling of the steps that tottered beside his own intensified his ardor.

CHAPTER XXXIV

"IT was more strange than I dare tell you, mother dear," Lois added to the letter of details which she wrote at odd minutes during the day, "that that poor old man should have broken down just at our door. There was a kind of fatality in it, as if he had come to throw himself at our feet. The son would have gone on if his father had been able to drag himself another yard; but he wasn't. It was all we could do to get him up the portico steps and into the nearest seat.

"I wonder if you remember him—old Mr. Fay? If so, you wouldn't know him now. I can only compare him to a tree that's been attacked at the roots and shrivels and dries in a season. He seems to have passed from sixty to ninety in the course of a few months, as if the very principle of life had failed him. It would be pitiful if it wasn't worse. I mean that we're afraid it may be worse, though that is a matter which as yet I mustn't write about.

"The son puzzles me—or rather he would if there were not something in him like all the other Fays, desperate and yet attractive, appealing and yet hostile. He looks like his sister, which means that he's handsome, with those extraordinary eyes of the shade of the paler kinds of jade, and a "finish" to the features quite unusual in a man. The prison shows in his pallor, in his cropped hair, and in something furtive in the glance which, Thor says, will probably pass as he gets used again to freedom. I remember that Dr. Hilary once said of him that he's the stuff out of which they make revolutionaries and anar-

359

chists. In that case I should think he might be a valuable addition to the cause, for, as with Rosie, there's a quality in him that wins you at the very moment when you're most repelled. He makes you sorry for him. We're sorry for them all. Even now, with poor Claude lying there, we've no other feeling than that. We've had enough of retaliations and revenges. Nothing could prove their uselessness more thoroughly than what happened here last night. If we could let everything rest where it is, leaving the crime to be its own punishment, God knows we would do it gladly."

Later in the day she continued: "I wish you could have seen the meeting between Thor and that poor fellow who has just come out of jail. Thor was superb—so gentle and kind and tender, and all with an air that tragic sorrow has made noble. There are things I cannot tell you about him—that Thor must tell to his father if they're ever told at all—but this I can say even now, that if any good is to come out of all this it will be through Thor more than any one. He doesn't see his way as yet, but he'll find it. He'll find it by the same impulse that made him march up to Matt Fay, putting his hand on his shoulder and looking him in the eyes with a simple, man-to-man sympathy which no one could resist. The very fact that Thor feels so deeply that he's been to blame—very, very much to blame—gives intensity now to his kindness. As for Matt Fay, he colored and stammered and shuffled, and though he tried to maintain his bravado, it was without much success. He was still more embarrassed when, after the old man had finished his coffee and was able to move again, Thor ordered Sims to bring round the car and drive the two of them home. We said nothing to them about Claude. I couldn't have borne its being mentioned to them here—or to have been obliged to watch the effect. It would be like having to look on at a vivisection. There are things I don't want to see or to know. All that is really imperative is that, whatever the outcome, they should consider us their friends."

The letter was not finished till she was alone that night. She wrote carefully at first, choosing just the right words. "Thor is sleeping at the other house, and may continue to do so for some time. He seems to want to be there— as you can understand. Not only does he make it more bearable for Uncle Sim and Cousin Amy, but he gets a kind of assuagement to his grief in being near Claude. You needn't be surprised, therefore, if he remains a little longer—perhaps longer than you might expect."

Up to this point she had been cautious, but for a minute something less controlled escaped her. "Oh, mother darling, I want to be a good wife to Thor, as you've been a good wife to papa. He needs me, and yet in his inmost heart he's bearing this great trial alone. Don't misunderstand me. I haven't broken down. Perhaps if I could have broken down a little it would have brought me nearer to him. But I'm not near to him. There's the truth. I'm infinitely far away from him. In a sense I'm infinitely below him; for though I've been right in certain matters in which he has been wrong, I feel strangely his inferior. He has things on his conscience for which I know he finds it hard to see the way of repentance—and I have nothing on mine—nothing, that is, but a vague discomfort and a sense of not being wholly right—and yet I feel that he's—how shall I put it?—that he's the nearer to God of us two. He needs me, and I ought to help him; but it's like helping some one who's on a tower while I stay on the ground. Oh, mother darling, why can't I be to him what you've been to papa? What is it that men get from women which *saves* them? Thor needs saving just as much as other men, though you mightn't suppose so. I know you think him perfect, and I used to think the same; but he's not. He has faults—grave ones. I even know that he's weak where I'm strong, and that the thing he needs is the thing I can supply—only I don't supply it. Mother dear, you've given it to papa or he wouldn't be recovering as he is. Why can't I give it, too? He's there in that house, and I'm here in this. His heart is aching for grief, and mine because I don't know how to comfort him—and all because the glimmer of light that leads me on isn't strong enough. It's better than nothing; I don't deny that. I can grope my way by it when I might expect to be utterly bewildered—but, oh, mother dear, it's not love."

But having read this page in the morning, she suppressed and destroyed it. After the night's rest she was more sure of herself. Since she had any clue at all she felt it wise to possess her soul in patience and see to what issue it would lead her. For the passages she withdrew she substituted, therefore, such an account of Rosie as would put her mother in touch with that portion of Claude's life.

"It's hard to know how the little thing feels just now," she went on, when the main facts had been given, "because she's so stunned by dread. It's the same dread that oppresses us all, but which is so much more terrible for them. For poor little Rosie the things that have happened are secondary now to what may happen still. *That* almost blots Claude out of her mind. Luckily she has a great deal of pluck—of what in our old-fashioned New England phrase was called grit. That she'll win in the end, and come out at last to a kind of happiness, I haven't the least doubt, especially as she has that fine fellow, Jim Breen, to turn to. You remember him, don't you? It's touching to see his tenderness to Rosie, now that she has such a need of him. It's the more touching because she doesn't give him anything but the most indirect encouragement. He knows perfectly well that whatever he gets from her now will be only her second best, but he's grateful even for that.

"She came to me yesterday morning of her own accord, before I could get word to her. William Sweetapple had heard the news and told her as he passed the house where they have just gone to live in Susan Street. Rosie had been early to the door to take in the milk, and Sweetapple was going by. She flew here at once. I had expected her to be crushed—but she wasn't. As I've just said, she seemed to be looking forward rather than looking back. She was looking forward to what I've hinted at and dare not say, and setting her face as a flint. That is how I can best describe her—and yet it was as a flint with a wonderful shine on it, as if something had come to her in the way of inner illumination that used not to be in her at all. Jim Breen is fond of saying that this is not the Rosie of a year or two ago, and it isn't. It's not even the Rosie of the episode with Claude. Her face is now like a lighted lamp as compared with the time when it was blank. I'm not enough in her confidence to know exactly what has wrought the change, so that I can only guess. It seems to me the same thing that has given the mother a new view of life, only that Rosie has probably come to it by another way. They're strangely alike, those two—each so tense, so strong, so demanding, each broken on the wheel, and each with that something firm and fine in the grain to which the wheel can do no more than impart a higher *patina* of polishing. They seem to me to bring down into our rather sugary life some of the old, narrow, splendidly austere New England qualities that have almost passed away and to make them bloom—bloom, that is, as the portulacca blooms, in a parched soil where any other plant would bake, and yet with an almost painfully vivid brilliancy. Doesn't George Meredith say in one of his books—is it *The Egoist?*—that the light of the soul should burn upward? Well, that's what it seems to do in them—to burn upward with a persistent glow, in spite of conditions that might reasonably put it out."

"The old man is a mystery to me," she wrote later, "chiefly because it is so impossible to connect him with any of the things we fear. He seemed so small and shrunken and harmless as he sat on the portico yesterday morning, drinking his coffee and munching a slice of toast, that he appealed to me only as something to be taken care of. That sinister element which I've seen in him of late had gone altogether, leaving nothing but his old, faded, dreamy mildness, contented and appeased. That is the really uncanny thing, that he seems *satisfied*. He showed no fear of us at all, nor the slightest nervousness, not even when Thor came. Thor was startled to see him there at first, but I managed to whisper a word or two in French, so that he went straight up to Fay and shook hands. I was glad of that. It put us in the right attitude—that of not trying to find a victim or looking for revenge."

Before adding her next paragraph she weighed its subject-matter pensively. It was not necessary to her letter; it was nothing her mother was obliged to know. She decided to say it, however, from an instinct resembling that of self-preservation. If her mother were ever to *hear* anything....

"Thor saw Rosie, too. He was coming down-stairs from taking a bath just as she was in the hall going away. It was the first time he'd seen her since before we were married. He was so lovely to her!—I wish I could tell you! You know he used to be interested in her in the days when her mother was his only patient. It was through him, if you remember, that Rosie and I came to be friends in the first place. He asked me to go and see her, to be nice to her. He feels very strongly that we people of the old, simple American stock should have held together in a way we haven't done, and that we shouldn't have allowed money to dig the abyss between us which I'm afraid is there now. I know that you personally are not interested in ideals of this kind, and yet Thor wouldn't be the Thor you love unless he had them. So he was lovely with Rosie, holding her hand, and looking down at her with those kind eyes of his, and begging her, whatever happened—*whatever happened*, mind you!—to throw every-

thing on him in the way they would do if he was brother
to them all. People talk about the brotherhood of man;
but there will never be any such thing as the brotherhood
of man till more men, and more women, too, get the spirit
that's in him."

Claude had been a week or more in his grave when the
letters began to arrive from Mrs. Willoughby.

"As to our sailing," she wrote from London, "everything depends on Ena. My cablegrams will have told
you that she's better, but not exactly *how*. She's better
mentally, and very sweet. *I* think it surprising. Now
that the first shock is past, she's calmer, too, and doesn't
say so often that she expected it. Why she should have
expected it I couldn't make out till last night, when Archie
told me that there'd been something between Claude and
a girl named Fay. I remember those Fays; queer people
they always were, and rather uppish. *She* was a big,
handsome girl when I was a little one. Eliza Grimes was
her name, and as long ago as that she couldn't keep her
place. I remember how she came for a while to Aunt
Rachel's school, though not for long. Aunt Rachel
couldn't draw too exclusive a line at first, but she did
drop her in the end. I should never have thought that
Claude would take up with a girl like that—Claude, of all
people. You can't run counter to class distinctions without making trouble, I always say—and you see how it
acts. You and Thor are far too republican, or too
democratic, or whatever it is, but I never thought that of
poor Claude.

"Not that Archie attributes this dreadful thing to the
connection with the Fays. He won't hear of any such
suggestion. Ena seemed to look on it at first as a retribution, but Archie insists that there never was anything to
retribute. There may be two opinions about that, though,
mind you, I'm not saying so. To the best of my ability
I'm letting bygones be bygones, as I think I've shown.

But Ena certainly thought so at first, and it's my belief she does still. She's told me herself that when they were motoring through Devon and Cornwall they never reached their destination for the night without her being afraid of a cablegram awaiting their arrival. She was sure something terrible was going to happen, and knew it before they left home. I asked her in that case why in the name of goodness they should have come, but she couldn't answer me. Or, rather, she did answer me—just the kind of answer you'd expect from her. It was to get some new things, and she's got them. Lovely, some of them are, especially the dinner-gowns from Mariette's—but with their money—*and where it comes from*—it's easy to dress. Retribution indeed! It must be retribution enough for the poor thing just to look at them. She's already had a woman from Jay's to talk over her mourning. Seems heartless, doesn't it? but then, of course, she must have it. Jay's woman had to take her measurements from the gray traveling-suit, for the doctor won't let her get up for another week, not even to be fitted. That will show you how far we are from sailing, and poor Archie has changed the bookings twice.

"As for him, I can't tell, for the life of me, how he feels about being kept here—he's so frightfully the gentleman. I've always said that he wore good manners not as his natural face, but as a mask, and I feel it now more than ever. It's a mask that hides even his tears, though I'm sure, poor man, they flow fast enough beneath it. All the same, I suspect that he finds it something of a relief to be held up here—for a while, at any rate. He wishes he was home, and yet for some reason he's afraid to get there. Terrible as everything is, I know he feels that it will be more terrible still when he's on the spot."

It was in a subsequent letter that Mrs. Willoughby wrote: "I had to scrawl so hurriedly yesterday to catch the first mail that I couldn't begin at the beginning, or get to the point, or anything. I'll try now, though, as for the beginning, it's like going back to the dark ages, it all seems so long ago.

"Your first cablegram giving us the news arrived at Les Dalles in the middle of the afternoon, and such a scramble as we had to get over to Havre in time for the night boat! I can't tell you how we felt, for it was one of those shocks so awful that you don't feel anything. At least I didn't feel anything, though I can't say the same of your father. He, poor lamb, has felt it terribly, so sensitive as he is, and so easily upset. Well, we managed to get to Havre in time, and had a fair crossing. We reached London about ten in the morning, and of course had no notion of where Archie and Ena were. So we drove to their bankers, and, as luck would have it, found they were in London on their way between Cornwall and the north.

"Once we'd learned that, we came straight to this hotel, and sent up our cards. After that we waited. Waited! I should say so. Your father got crosser and crosser, threatening to go away without breaking the news at all. We knew they thought we'd come to make trouble about old scores, and were discussing whether or not to see us. When word came at last that we were to be shown up your father was in such a state that I had to leave him in the public parlor and go and face it alone.

"I wonder if you've ever had the experience of being ushered into a room where you could see you weren't wanted? I don't suppose so. I never had it before, and I hope I never shall again. It was one of those chintzy English sitting-rooms with flowers in every corner. I shall never see Shirley poppies again without thinking of poor Claude. Archie was standing in the middle of the floor, looking more the gentleman than ever, but no Ena!

"'I'm sorry to have kept you waiting, Bessie,' he said, with that frigid sympathy of his which to me is always like iced water down the spine. 'Is there anything I can do for you?'

"We were facing each other, with a round table between us. 'No, Archie,' I said. 'I didn't come on my account, but on yours.'

"I can see him still—the way he stood—with a queer little upward flash of the eyebrows. 'Indeed?'

"'Yes. I had a cablegram yesterday afternoon—from Lois.' I gave him time to take that in. 'We came over at once—Len and I.'

"I had scarcely said this when my heart leaped into my mouth, for Ena cried out from behind the door leading into the bedroom, where I felt sure she was: 'It's about Claude!' It was the strangest sound I ever heard—the kind of sound she might have made if she saw something falling on her that would kill her.

"Archie stood motionless, but he turned a kind of gray-white. 'Is it?' was all he asked.

"I waited again—waited long enough to let them see that what I had to tell was grave. 'It is, Archie,' I said then.

"'Is he—?' Archie began, but I saw he couldn't finish. In fact he didn't need to finish, because Ena cried out again, 'He's dead!'

"Archie could only question me with his eyes, so that I said, 'I'm sorry to have been the one to bring you the news—'

"I got no further than that when a kind of strangling moan came from Ena and a sound as if she was falling. Archie ran into the bedroom, and the first thing I heard was, 'Bessie, for God's sake come here!' When I got there Ena was lying in a little tumbled heap beside the couch. She had on her lilac kimono and could just as well have seen me as not, so I knew that what we had said down-stairs had been true. They did want to give us the cold shoulder.

"Well, you can imagine that it was all over with that. We had everything we could do to bring Ena around and get her on the couch. It took the longest time, and while we were doing it—before she could follow anything we said

—Archie asked me what I knew, and I told him. I was glad to be able to do it in just that way, because I could break it up and get it in by pieces, a fact at a time. There was so much for him to do, too, that he couldn't give his whole mind to it, which was another mercy.

"When I could leave Ena I slipped into the sitting-room, shutting the door behind me, and letting Archie tell her what I had been able to tell him. While he was doing that I scribbled a little note, saying that Len and I were going to Garland's, where they would find us in case we could do anything more to help them. Without waiting for him to come out of the bedroom, I left the note on the table and went away."

In succeeding letters Mrs. Willoughby told how Archie had come to them at Garland's, had insisted on their returning with him to the hotel in Brook Street, and had installed them in a suite of rooms contiguous to his own. Moreover, he clung to them, begging them not to leave him. It was the most extraordinary turning of the tables Bessie had ever known. He produced the impression of a man not only stunned, but terrified. If the hand that had smitten Claude had been stretched right out of heaven he could not have seemed more overawed. He was afraid—that was what it amounted to. If Mrs. Willoughby read him aright, the tragic thing affected him like the first trumpet-note of doom. It was as if he saw the house he had built with so much calculation beginning to tumble down—laid low by some dread power to which he was holding up his hands. He was holding up his hands not merely in petition, but in propitiation. She was not blind to the fact that there was a measure of propitiation in his boarding and lodging her husband and herself. He clung to them because his desolation needed something that stood for old friendship to cling to; but in addition to that he had dim visions of the dread power that had smitten Claude looming up behind them and acting somehow on their behalf.

"It's all very well to insist that there's nothing to retribute," ran a passage in one of the letters, "but the poor fellow is saying one thing with his lips and another in his soul. What's the play in which the ghosts come back? Is it "Hamlet," or "Macbeth," or one of Ibsen's? Well, it's like that. He's seeing ghosts. He wants us to be on hand because we persuade him that they're not there—that they *can't* be there, so long as we're all on friendly terms, and that we're not laying up anything against him. The very fact that he pays our bills makes him hope that the ghosts will keep away."

"We've promised to go back with them," she informed her daughter elsewhere. "For one thing, Ena needs me. If I didn't go she'd have to have a nurse; and I'd rather not leave her till she's safe in your hands. I must say I can't make her out. She puzzles me more than Archie does. Now that a week has gone by and the first shock is over, she's like a person coming out of a trance. She's so sweet and gentle that it's positively weird. Of course she's always been sweet—that's her style—but not in this way. Upon my word, I don't know whether she has a soul or not—whether she never had one, or whether one is being born in her. But she's patient, and you might even say resigned. There's no question about that. She's not a bit hard to take care of, making little or no demand, and just trying to get up strength enough to sail. She's grieving over Claude; and yet her grief has the touching quality in it that you get from a sweet old tune. I must say I don't understand it—*not in her*."

It was when she was able to announce that Mrs. Masterman was well enough to sail that Mrs. Willoughby acknowledged the first letters from her daughter. "We go by the *Ruritania* on the 3rd. Archie is simply furious at the hints you're all throwing out about that old man Fay. Perfectly preposterous, is what he calls them. He seems to think that, once he is on the spot, he'll be able to show every one that Fay had no possible reason to want to avenge himself, and must therefore be beyond suspicion. I must say Archie doesn't strike me as vindictive, which is another surprise, if one could ever be surprised in a Masterman. They're all queer, Thor as much as any of them, though he's queer in such lovable ways. I mean that you never can tell what freaks they'll take, whether for evil or for good. Nothing would astonish me less than to see Archie himself in sackcloth and ashes one of these days, and I do believe that it's the thing he's afraid of himself. What he's fighting in all this business about Fay is his own impulse to do penance. He's thinking of the figure he'll cut, wearing a shroud and carrying a lighted candle. Of course it interests us because—well, because it may turn out to be a matter of dollars and cents. Not that I count on it. I've put all that behind me, and I must say that your father and I have never been so happy together as during these last few months. We get along perfectly on what we have, and we don't lack for anything. Of course the way in which your father, the sweet lamb, is improving makes all the difference in the world to me. So Archie needn't repent on our account. We've let all that go. It only strikes me as funny the way he can't do enough for us—taxis at the door the minute we put our noses out—flowers in the sitting-room— and everything. I know perfectly well what it means. It isn't *us*. He's simply sacrificing to the hoodoo or the voodoo that he sees behind us—just like any other Masterman."

She added in a postscript: "You can read Thor as much or as little of my letters as you choose. I don't care —not a bit! I told him before you were married that I always intended to speak my mind about his father, like it or lump it who would."

CHAPTER XXXV

THE rest of that year became to Archie Masterman a period of popularity and triumph, in so far as such terms could be used of a man so sorely bereaved. Nothing ever sat on him with finer effect than the air of dignity, charity, and sorrow with which he returned from Europe, while his stand toward poor old Jasper Fay brought him a degree of sympathy new even to one whose personality had been sympathetic at all times. The letter he wrote to Eliza Fay when her husband was put under arrest, dissociating himself from the act of the guardians of the law and protesting his belief in his former tenant's innocence, was conceived in a spirit so noble as to raise the estimate of human nature in the minds of all who knew its contents. Whatever the inner convictions of the much-tried woman to whom it was addressed, the document was too precious to her husband's cause not to be exhibited, though in the matter of inner convictions Lois was obliged to caution her.

"I wouldn't put it beyond him, not a mite," Mrs. Fay had confessed, with tragic matter-of-fact; "not after the way he's talked, I wouldn't, and Matt don't, either."

"Has your son said so?"

"He's said worse. He's said that if he didn't do it, he ought to have. That's the way he talks. Oh, he's no comfort to me! I knew he wouldn't be, after that awful place, but I didn't look for him to be quite what he is, wanting to kill and blow up everything. An I. I. A. is what he calls himself, and the Lord only knows what that is. I blame myself," she went on, with dry, unrelenting statement of the case. "I didn't bring them up right. I was discontented—"

"Oh, but there's a discontent that's divine," Lois broke in, consolingly.

"Well, this wasn't it. It was 'hateful and hating one another,' as Paul says. I put it into their heads—I mean Fay's and the children's. Matt 'd commit murder now as quick as a kitten 'll lap milk—or he says he would; and as for Fay—"

Lois interrupted, hurriedly, "We shouldn't do him the injustice of condemning him in advance, should we?"

The woman held herself erect, her hard, uncompromising eyes, in which there was nevertheless an odd suffusion of softness, looking straight over her companion's head. "I can't help what I know."

"And *I* can't help what *I* know, which is that you and I have nothing to do with judgment, still less with condemnation. There are others to attend to that, while we try to bring"—she uttered the word with diffidence—"try to bring love."

"Oh, love!" The tone was that of one who had long ago given up anything so illusory.

"Then whatever we can find that will take the place of love," Lois replied, with relief at getting back to ground of which she was more sure. "Let us call it good will."

Good will was, in fact, what Reuben Hilary had called it, and it was from him she was quoting. Having gone to him for the analysis of her own state of mind, she had been comforted to learn that she placed no impediment in the way of public justice through being privately merciful.

"The mission of Christ, me dear Mrs. Thor, was salvation. And what do we mean by salvation? Isn't it the state of being saved? And what do we want to be saved from? Isn't it from trouble and evil of all kinds? And where and when do we want to be saved from them? Isn't it right here and right now? And who are the people that need most to be saved? Isn't it those that are threatened with danger? And who is to save them? Isn't it you and I? What more do you ask?"

"So that when it comes to justice—"

"Ah, now, I'm not botherin' about justice. Justice has her sword and her scales. Let her look after her own affairs. What you and I are out after is good will."

So Lois got further light upon her way and followed it. She followed it the more easily because her father-in-law seemed willing to follow it, too. He could do this with a touching grace since more fully than by letter she assured him that Claude had come back to redeem his word.

"Oh, thank God!" Ena had exclaimed, on hearing this information emphasized. "The darling boy was always the soul of honor."

An ethereal vision in black, she was having a cup of tea in the library before going up-stairs to take off her traveling-dress. Thor, who had met the party at the dock, had accompanied Mr. and Mrs. Willoughby to their own house, so that Lois was able to get a few words with the sorrowing parents alone, giving them in fuller detail that which her letters had only sketched. She had assumed the privilege of the daughter of the house to sit at the tea-table, while for the minute the returned voyagers took their place as guests.

There were reasons now why Archie was able to echo his wife's rejoicing in Claude's change of heart. In this new turn to the situation, which he had but imperfectly seized from what had been written, he could get the same kind of consolation that a father draws from the death of a son in a war with which he has no sympathy. It was the death of a brave man, when all was said and done. It was also death in conditions that made his own position the stronger, since it was an aid to the clearing of his conscience. It detracted nothing from his grief that he should use Claude's yearning for redemption as a fresh proof that Jasper Fay had not even a shadowy motive for revenge; and with the elimination of Fay's motive for revenge, he,

Archie Masterman, was more amply acquitted at the bar before which the hereditary Masterman impulse summoned him. Lois had the greater confidence, therefore, in making her appeals.

"If they do imprison him, you see, the family will be left without means. One of these days I think Rosie will marry Jim Breen—"

Ena gave a little cry of disapproval. "What? After *Claude!*"

"Oh, it won't be for a long time yet; and while this trouble is hanging over her father she won't listen to any suggestion of the kind, little as she would before. Still— in the end—it will be only natural—" She left Rosie there. "And Thor's been so good about the son—only— well, the I. I. A., whatever that is, have got hold of him, so that we can't count on him to do anything for the poor mother, if she's left alone, or for Rosie—"

"I'll take care of them." It was probable that Archie Masterman had never in his life said anything that gave him so complete a satisfaction. Before Lois could respond to his generosity he went on to add: "I needn't appear in the matter. I'll leave it to your ingenuity to find the way to take care of them without mentioning me at all—unless you think it would be a comfort to them, as a sign of my confidence in poor old Fay. *That* I should like to have generally known—that I absolve him entirely."

By sheer force of will Lois refused to see him as sacrificing to the hoodoo or the voodoo of which her mother's letters had apprised her. If she had nothing to do with condemnation in the case of Jasper Fay, she had nothing to do with it, she reminded herself, in that of Archie Masterman. Her part in life was to accept every one at his nominal face value, for only so could she put good will into effective operation.

Tea was over and they were on their feet when she felt her own need demanding consideration. It was not without nervousness that she said, "You know Thor has been staying here with Cousin Amy and Uncle Sim."

"So we understood."

"Well, I think he might like to stay a little longer."

"That's not necessary on our account," Masterman said, promptly.

"It wouldn't be on your account, but on his own. That is," she explained, "he might think it was on your account, but in reality to feel that he was comforting you would be a comfort to him."

Claude's mother gave way to the first little sob since entering the house, while the father's face settled to the stoniness that masked his suffering. "Wouldn't it look very queer?" was all he said. "People might not understand it."

"Oh, they haven't understood it as it is; but does that matter? I know there's been talk in the village during the past few weeks, but surely we're in a position to ignore it." In the hope of opening up the way for Thor in what he had to make clear, she decided to go further. While speaking she kept her eyes on Masterman. "You may not need him, but he may need you. As a matter of fact, he has still something to explain to you which I may as well tell you now. On that night—the night of the ninth of July—Thor and Claude were here in the house together. There was trouble between them."

Mrs. Masterman gasped; her husband breathed hard, saying, merely, "Go on."

"I don't know what the quarrel was exactly, but—but—there were blows."

"Not the blow—?" Masterman began, with horror in his tone.

"Oh no, not that," Lois interposed, hastily, going on to explain briefly the incidents of the struggle between the brothers, as far as she knew them. "That part of it was all over," she continued, eagerly, before either of the parents could comment on this new phase of the event.

"Claude wasn't much hurt. You can see that from the way he was able to get up and come out into the air while Thor was running up to our house for brandy. If there hadn't been some one lurking in the shrubbery—"

"He's been a terrible son to me," Masterman broke in, wrathfully. "When it isn't in one way it's in another. What have I done to deserve—?"

"He *is* terrible," Lois admitted, soothingly; "but, oh, Mr. Masterman, he's terrible in such splendid ways! He hasn't found himself yet; but he will if you'll give him time. Whatever he's done wrong he'll atone for nobly. You'll see!"

The mother's intervention came to Lois as a new surprise. "Whatever he's done wrong he's sorry for. We can be sure of that." She turned to her husband. "Archie, Claude was my son; and I want to tell you now, before we go any further, that no matter what happened between Thor and him, I forgive it, if there's anything to forgive."

"I know Thor feels there was something to forgive," Lois confessed on her husband's behalf, "whether there was or not."

"Then tell him to come to me," Ena commanded, in a tone such as Lois had never heard from her.

"I'll tell him to go to you, if you'll ask him to stay here with you a little longer."

"I sha'n't ask him; Archie will, won't you, Archie?" She laid her hand on his arm, pleadingly. "If you do, it will mean that you and I are not trying to judge our two boys, or take sides between them"—she gave a little sob— "now when it's no use. They quarreled, as brothers will, but they were fond of each other, for all that."

"Thor adored Claude," Lois said, simply. "I think he cared for him more than for any one in the world that— that I know of."

Masterman wheeled suddenly and walked away, while his wife made signs to Lois that they had won.

But it was in another frame of mind that Thor's wife said to herself, as she saw him coming toward her along County Street: "Now I shall see! I shall see if he will!"

She meant that now he might return to her, that he might return as a matter of course. If he came of his own accord, something within her would leap to greet him. So much she knew; but beyond it she would not trust herself to go. "I shall see if he will!" she repeated, with emphasis, throwing the responsibility of taking the first step on him. It was on him, she felt, that it lay. She had asked him to leave her until she was prepared to call him back, and she was not prepared. If he were to ask to be taken back, her attitude could lawfully be different. Since it was he who had made void the union she had supposed to be based on love, it was for him to suggest another built on whatever they could find as a substitute. Great as her pity for him was, she could not by so much as a glance or a smile relieve him from that necessity.

As they drew near each other she recognized the minute as one that would be decisive, if not for the rest of life, yet for a long time to come. She could look ahead and select the very tree under which they would meet. As a result of the few words that would be then exchanged their lives would blend again—or he would go to the one house and she to the other, and they would be further apart than they had ever been before. He might not think it or see it, because men were so dense; but she would be as quick to read the signs of which he would remain unconscious as à bird to scent a storm.

For this very reason she reduced her manner, when they came face to face, to the simplest and most casual. It was a matter of pride with her to exert no influence, to leave him free. Not that she found it necessary to take pains, for she saw from the first minutes of encounter that his mind was far away from that part of their interests which she put first. Into her comments on the wonderful courage displayed by Mr. and Mrs. Masterman he broke, abruptly:

"They've arrested Fay."

What came next was as nearly of the nature of a vow as a man could venture on without melodramatic eloquence. All his energies, all his money, all his time, were to be dedicated to securing Fay's acquittal. For Claude's death one man, and one man only, was to blame. It was probable enough that Fay had actually struck the blow; it was probable, too, that he had done it not to avenge himself primarily on Claude, but on Claude's father. To Thor that was secondary, almost of no importance. Had he not allowed himself to become a prey to whatever was most ferocious and malignant in human nature, the crime would never have been committed. Granting that Fay would have lain in wait for Claude in any case, an agile young man would have been more than a match for so enfeebled an antagonist even when armed with a knife, had not some preceding struggle exhausted him.

To Thor it was so clear that he was beyond the reach of argument. He was likewise beyond the reach of anything that could be called a purpose or a wish but that of seeing that another man shouldn't suffer in his stead. From the region into which this absorption and consecration carried him Lois found herself and her claims on him thrust out. Whether he went back to her or whether he did not was, for the time being at any rate, of so little moment in his eyes that apparently no thought of this aspect of their situation had occurred to him. It was more stinging to her pride that he should not consider it than that he should consider it and refuse. She was fully aware that her irony was thrown away when she said, in a tone kept down to the matter-of-fact and colloquial:

"And, Thor dear, if they ask you to stay on at the other house, don't think of me. I've got papa and mamma again. They'll keep me company as long as"—she was obliged to think of an expression that would imply a term —"as long as I may need them."

In response to these words he merely nodded. "Very well." The assent was given as if, whatever the arrangement, it would be a matter of indifference to them both.

So he went his way and she went hers. Monstrous as it was, monstrous as she found him, as she found herself, she could hardly conceive of their doing anything else. If she was unhappy, her unhappiness lay too deep in subliminal abysses to struggle to the surface of her consciousness. That he should go to the one house and she to the other was as right as it had been ten years before. It was so right that she was stupefied by its rightness. It was so right that the rightness acted on her like an opiate. It was a minute in which sheer helplessness might have relaxed her hold on her substitute for love had she not had such pressing need to make use of it there and then.

She made use of it as, on occasions requiring a show of lavishness, people eke out a meager supply of silver with plenty of plausible electroplate. In installing her parents in their old rooms, in bidding them take their place as masters and forget that they were guests, she simulated the pleasure not only of a happy daughter but of a happy wife. While the circumstances of the home-coming tempered anything in the nature of exuberance, they couldn't forbid all joy, and of joy of just the right sparkle she was as prodigal as if her treasure-chest had been stocked with it. Moreover, she was sure that except for the protest, "If we take these rooms, what are you going to do with Thor?" the worthy couple didn't know the difference between what she placed before them and the sterling metal with the hall-mark.

If there was a suspicion in her mother's mind it reserved itself till, on kissing them good night, Lois fled to the room she had occupied as a girl. Though she closed the door behind her, the mother pushed it open. "Look here,

Lois," Bessie said, not quite with anxiety and yet not quite without it, "there's nothing between you and Thor, is there?"

Lois felt that the form of the question saved her. It enabled her to answer so much more truthfully than her mother knew. "No, mamma dear; there's nothing at all between us." She went so far as to make the declaration emphatic and indulge in a tone of faint bitterness: "*Absolutely* nothing at all—and I doubt if there ever will be—now."

Though the mother retired before she could catch the concluding syllable, Lois regretted the bitterness as soon as she felt it escape her. There was no bitterness in her substitute for love, for the substitute for love was . . . She had always admitted that she didn't know *what* it was. But there came back to her mind the words she had been acting upon for a fortnight and more: "The mission of Christ, me dear Mrs. Thor, was salvation." And there was no bitterness in that.

CHAPTER XXXVI

"FUNNY thing the way people talk about salvation," Uncle Sim observed to Lois, on an evening in the autumn when his legs were extended before her fire. "To hear 'em you'd think there was no salvation except for sin, and none even for that but what is post-mortem. Post-mortem salvation may be all very well, but if there's anything blessed I want it right now."

"Of course, with a good man like you—"

"Good? Good's got nothing to do with it—or not much. The man who is called the Saviour, above every one else, didn't wait for people to be good before He saved them. He saved them first and said 'Sin no more' to them afterward."

"Oh, but with His extraordinary means—"

"He had no means that you haven't got yourself—in essence. Difference between you and Him is not in kind, but in degree. If He could save all men, you and I can at least save one or two or a dozen—or do something toward it."

"You mean save them *here*."

"Saving 'em here is saving 'em anywhere, isn't it?"

"And you don't mean saving them only in the theological sense of saving their souls—"

"Mean saving 'em anyhow. Save a man from hanging, or a child from tumbling in the mud, or an old woman from having her best bonnet spoiled by rain—it's all salvation—it all meets the human need—it's all part of the same principle—it all works to the same end."

"And what is the end?"

382

"The same as the middle, and the same as the beginning, and the same as it is all through." He rose and stretched himself. "I leave you to find your own name for it. I call it by a word of four letters," he laughed, "and it begins with an *l*. You can't have too much of it, if you know what it is—which is just what many people don't know."

She stood before him, coloring, smiling a little, but with eyes lowered. "I wonder if *I* know what it is, Uncle Sim?"

"If you don't," he smiled down at her, "you're taking a good way to learn."

This view of the principle she was using as a guide was not new to her; it was only illuminating and corroborative. It was spectrum analysis where she had seen a star. It was the kingdom of heaven reduced from a noble phrase to such terms of simple, kindly living as she knew herself able to fulfil. It was the ideal become practical, and the present rendered one with the eternal, with the fruits of righteousness sown in peace of them that make peace beyond anything she had ever expected. On the winter afternoon when Jasper Fay was acquitted she could look back over the preceding seven or eight months and see how relatively easy all had been. She said relatively easy for the reason that much had of necessity been hard. The distinction she made was that what had been hard would have been overwhelming had she not taken the principle of immediate salvation, where it could be brought about, as law. By meeting each minute's need with the utmost of her strength she found the next minute's need less terrible. By allowing no one to suffer a shade more, or an instant longer, than she could help, she perceived a lessening of the strain all round. With the lessening of the strain it was easier to calm passions and disarm antipathies. If she could say nothing else for her substitute for love, she was obliged to admit that it worked.

She was thinking so with a great thankfulness when Thor came to tell her of the rendering of the verdict. Though he had telephoned the fact, he was eager to give her the details face to face. He did this while they stood in the tapestried square hall, avoiding each other's eyes.

It had not been picturesque, he explained to her; but it had been satisfactory. Though an hour had sufficed the jury to reach their decision, the farmers and market-gardeners who had formed the mass of the spectators had forestalled it and scattered to their homes. The dramatic interest was over; it was generally felt that no more than a formality remained. When for the last time Jasper Fay was led in to confront his peers it was before a comparatively empty court.

Because he had suddenly become self-conscious, Thor went on with his account stammeringly and with curious hesitations. Still wearing his fur motoring-coat, he held his cap in his hand, like a man in a hurry to get away.

"I couldn't see even then—at the very end—that the old fellow knew what it was all about. He looked round him with the same glassy stare that he's had ever since— ever since that morning when we gave him the coffee. Mind all gone, poor old chap—and perhaps it's just as well. He smiled a bit when it was all over and they pushed him from one group to another to shake his hand, but he didn't realize what he had escaped."

Lois, too, was self-conscious. In this lifting of the burden from Thor's mind something had changed in their mutual relation. It was as if a faculty arrested on the night Claude died had suddenly resumed its function, taking them by surprise. Not in this way had she expected the thing that seemed dead to come to life again, so that she was unprepared for the signs of its rebirth. Absorbed as she would otherwise have been in Thor's narration, she could now follow him but absently. "How did they get home from Colcord?"

She asked the question to keep him going, lest he should

say the thing she was so strangely afraid to hear. He answered like a man who talks about what isn't on his mind in order to conceal what is. "I drove them in. The old fellow sat in the tonneau with Rosie and Jim Breen. Matt Fay refused the lift and took the train to Marchfield."

A little crowd at the court-house door, he recounted further, had called, "Three cheers for Dr. Thor!" Another little crowd had greeted them with a similar welcome on their arrival in Susan Street. A third had gathered in the grounds of Thor's father's house, shouting, "Three cheers for Mr. Masterman!" till the object of this good will responded by coming out to the porch and making a brief, kindly speech. He was delivering it as Thor drove up, just as the winter twilight necessitated the turning on of the electric lights—his slender, well-dressed figure distinct in the illuminated doorway. Thor could hear the strains of "For he's a jolly good fellow" as, to avoid further demonstration, he backed his machine from the avenue and turned toward the other house.

She seized the opportunity to say something she had at heart, which would also help to tide over a minute she found so embarrassing. "Oh, Thor, I hope he'll not have to suffer any more. He's paid his penalty by this time."

"You mean—"

"I mean that I hope he'll never have to be any more definite with himself than he's been already. You can easily see how it is with him. It's as if he was two men, one accusing and the other defending. I don't want to have the defense break down altogether, or to see him driven to the wall. I couldn't bear it."

He waited a long minute before speaking. "If you're thinking of the real responsibility for Claude's death—"

She nodded. "Yes, I am."

Again he waited. "He puts that on me."

"He puts it on you so as not to take it on himself,"

she said, quickly, "because to take it on himself would be beyond human nature to bear. Don't you see, Thor? We know and he knows that if Jasper Fay did it, it was not to avenge himself on Claude, but on some one else. But now that the law says that Fay *didn't* do it—"

He interrupted, quietly: "I've talked it out with father, and we understand each other perfectly. You needn't be afraid on his account. I've taken everything on myself—as I ought to take it."

"Oh, Thor!"

"The only thing that matters about the law is that it shouldn't condemn any one but me. Now that that danger is out of the way, I can—begin."

She forgot her embarrassment in looking up at him with streaming eyes. "Begin how, Thor?"

"Begin doing what you told me from the first—begin to start again—to get it under my feet—to stand on it—to be that much higher up—and not be"—he fumbled with his cap, his head hung guiltily—"not be ridden by remorse—any more than—than I can help."

"You'll do it, Thor; you'll do it nobly—"

What she had to say, however, got no further, for the front door was flung open to allow of Mrs. Willoughby's excited entrance, with Len puffing heavily behind her.

"Oh, so you're here, Thor!" Bessie cried in the tone of a woman at the limit of her strength. "Well, I'm glad. You may as well know it first as last." Breathless, she dropped into one of the hall chairs, endeavoring to get air by agitating an enormous pillow-muff. "Len's been having— No, it's too extraordinary!—and I predicted it, didn't I? If you've kept my letters you've got it down in black and white! Len's been having— It's just as I said!—it's the shroud and the lighted candle! Len's been having the strangest, the very *strangest*, talk with Archie."

Lois crept near to her mother, bending down toward her. "But, mother dear, what about?"

Bessie answered, wildly: "Oh, I don't know what about. I wasn't there. I was in the drawing-room with Ena. I knew something was going on, from Ena's manner. What's come over Ena I can't imagine. I've heard of trial turning human beings into angels, but I never believed it and I can hardly believe it now. Archie began it himself—I mean with your father. He beckoned him into the library in the solemnest way. That was after he had finished his speech and the crowd had stopped cheering. If it *is* the shroud and the taper—well, all I can say is that he carries them off just in the way you would expect. No one could do it better, as far as *that* goes."

"As far as what goes, mother? I wish you'd tell us."

"It's exactly what I said when I wrote you from London last year. If you've kept my letters you've got it all down in black and white. He wants us, and Ena wants us, all to come to dinner. I'm not a bit surprised—not a bit—though I never counted on it—*never!*"

Thor also bent over her, standing before her, with his hand stretched out to the back of her chair. "Is it about money, Mrs. Willoughby?"

But she was too far beyond coherence to explain. "He says he wants to talk to us both after dinner—to Len and me. He's been going over the accounts again and he finds—he finds—" But she beat with her high heels on the floor and buried her face in her muff. "Oh, tell them, Len!—for goodness' sake, tell them! They'll never believe it—not any more than me."

But her emotion was too much for the big man's shattered nerves. As he stood just within the doorway, looking with his snowy beard and bushy white hair like some spectral, aureoled apostle, he began to cry.

CHAPTER XXXVII

THOR and Lois were glad of this interruption. They were glad of the new and exciting topic. They were glad of the family dinner at the other house, where they could be together and yet apart. Taking refuge from each other in any society they could find, they kept close to Mrs. Masterman when, after dinner, Thor's father retained his two old friends in the dining-room for the promised explanations. Later in the evening it was with an emotion like alarm that Lois heard that her parents had gone home without waiting to bear her company. Secretly she began to plan methods for stealing away alone. Her shyness of Thor was like nothing she had known in the days of courtship and marriage, or during the months in which they had been holding off from each other for scrutiny and reflection.

It was a shyness which, when they were at last side by side in the avenue, drove her to affect an over-elaboration of ease. She talked, not merely because there were so many things to say, but also for the sake of talking. She talked because he did not, because he towered above her in the moonlight, dumb, mysterious, waiting. It was that sense of his waiting that thrilled and terrified her most. It was a large waiting, patient and deep, the waiting for something predestined and inevitable that could take its time. It was like the waiting of the ocean for the streams, of sleep for the day's activities, or of death for all. It seemed to brood over her like the violet sky, and to quiver with radiance as the crisp air quivered with the moonlight. It was wide and restful

388

and bracing. She was walking toward it, she was walking into it, as she walked over this virginal carpet of snow.

She talked with a kind of desperation—of Thor's father and mother first of all, of how good they were, each with a special variety of goodness. It was wonderful what sorrow had done for Mrs. Masterman. "I never see her now, Thor dear, without thinking of that look in Claude's face that seemed to us like dawn. I see it in her. Don't you?" Without waiting for an answer she hurried on. "And your father, Thor. He *is* good. No one but a good man could have been so noble toward poor old Fay, when he knows—when *every one* knows—no matter what was proved or wasn't proved in court—when he *knows* the truth." She seemed to be answering some unspoken argument on his side as she continued: "Oh yes, I remember what mamma wrote about it—about the hoodoo or the voodoo—mamma's *so* amusing!—but you and I have nothing to do with that, have we, Thor? We can only take what we see, and judge by what is best. And so with this wonderful new thing for papa and mamma— that they're to have some of their money back—we *can't* go behind it, can we? If he says it was a mistake we must accept it as that, and never, never let any other thought come into our minds. I know that papa and mamma, dear, innocent things—they *are* dear and innocent, you know, in spite of everything!—I know they'll only be too glad to take it in the same way."

Except for an occasional word he had hardly spoken by the time he had reached the corner of Willoughby's Lane and County Street. Lois had a renewal of the terror from which her own conversation had distracted her. The crucial minute was at hand. The door was but a few yards away. He would either go in with her— or he would go back. She hardly knew which would be the more supportable—the joy or the dismay.

She caught at the first possibility of postponing both. "Oh, it's so lovely! Let us walk on a little farther. It isn't half-past nine yet. I looked at the clock as we were coming out. Papa and mamma ran off so early. Don't you adore these windless winter nights?—when the air is as if it had been distilled." She paused in the middle of the road and looked around. "What's that star, Thor—over there—the one like a great white diamond?" He told her it was Sirius, adding that its light took eight years to travel to the earth, and going on to trace with his finger the constellation of the Dog. The minute's return to the old habits took some of the feverishness from her sense of tension as they continued their walk up the hill.

Up the hill there were only two directions in which to go—along the prosaic road to Marchfield or into the quiet winter woods where masses of shadow lay interspersed with patches of white moonlight, while, on this soundless night there was not a murmur in the tree-tops. By instinct rather than intention they followed a faint, familiar path running under pines.

Lois was now speaking of the Fays. "Mrs. Fay *knows*. The others don't—not certainly. Rosie has brought herself round to thinking him innocent, and Matt and Jim only suspect what happened—but Mrs. Fay *knows*. It must be a tragic thing to spend your life with a man who's done a thing like that. Poor soul! We must do what we can to help her, mustn't we?"

She pursued the theme not for its interest alone, but for the sake of the objective point to which it was leading her. By speaking freely, first of Matt and then of Jim Breen, she came at last to Rosie. She spoke freely of her, too, at the risk of opening up old wounds, at the risk of lacerating that which was probably still sensitive. Her main purpose was to speak, and if possible to make him speak, so that this name should no longer be kept as an inviolable symbol between them. Since the day when it began to have significance for them both it had scarcely been pronounced by either otherwise than allusively or of necessity. She was resolute to make it as little to be shunned as his or her own.

Not that she was successful, for the minute at any rate. His responses continued to be brief, so brief that they were hardly responses at all. They were not grudged or ungracious; they were only like those first little flashes of lightning which hint that the heavens will soon be alive. As a frightened boy whistles from bravado, she talked to conceal her trembling at this coming of celestial wonders.

"Oh, Thor, there'll be so much now to do! It's really only beginning, isn't it? And it brings in so many elements of our life—I mean of our whole national life. I like that. I like getting out of our own little groove— so futile and narrow as it generally is—and being in touch with what is stronger, even if it's terrific. That's what I feel about Matt Fay—that he's terrific. He represents a terrific movement, doesn't he? and one we can't ignore. When I say terrific I don't mean that I'm afraid of it. I'm not. It seems to me too strengthening to be afraid of. With all you can say against it, it strikes me as a tonic in our rather flaccid life, like iron in the blood. I've sympathy with it, too, to some extent; I've sympathy with *him*. You know, I *do* belong to the people. I'm glad we know him, and that in a way we've a right to get near to him. It puts us in touch with our own national realities as perhaps otherwise we shouldn't be. Oh, Thor, there's so much to work out! Isn't it a splendid thing that we can help even to the slightest degree in doing it!"

To this there was no response whatever. She was not sure that he listened. Beside her the tall form strode on dumb and dark, crunching the frozen snow with a creaking sound that roused the winged and furry things of the wood and silenced her half-hysterical efforts to fight against that which awaited her like a glory or a doom. Growing suddenly aware of the uselessness of speaking, she said no more.

After an interval in which her mind seemed to stop working, that of which she became conscious next was a world of extraordinary purity. Nothing was ever so white as this snow or this moonlight; nothing was ever so like the ether beyond the atmosphere as this air; nothing was ever so golden as the stars in this purple sky, or so mystically solemn as these pines. As they climbed upward it was like mounting into some crystal sphere, where evil was not an element.

They came out on that spot in which all the wood-paths converged, that treeless ridge that rose like a great white altar. It was an end which neither had foreseen when a half-hour earlier they had prolonged their walk; otherwise they might have shrunk from it. As it was, the association of the past with the present startled them, startled them into pausing long enough to become conscious, to seeing each in the eyes of the other such things as could not pass into words, before renewing the ascent. As they continued the way upward it was as if in fulfilment of some symbolic ceremonial.

They had stood for some minutes silent on the summit, looking out over the wide, white radiance at their feet, when Thor spoke. "I'm not thinking about the things you've been talking of. I'm not primarily interested in them any more."

"You mean—?"

"I mean the helping of others—in the way I've tried it. I see the mistake in that."

She was faintly surprised. "Indeed?"

"Through the things that have been happening I've worked out—I may say I've stumbled out—to a great truth."

There was not only surprise in her tone, but curiosity. "Yes, Thor dear. What is it?"

"It's that a man's first occupation is not with others, but with himself. It's not to put them right; it's to be right on his own account." As for the moment she was too disconcerted to comment on this, he continued: "If reaching this conclusion seems to you like discovering the obvious, I can only say that it hasn't been obvious to me. It's just beginning to come to me that I was so busy casting out other people's devils that I'd forgotten all about my own."

"You've been so generous in all you've thought about other people, Thor—"

He interrupted with decision. "The most effective way in which to be generous to other people is to be strict with one's self; but it never occurred to me till lately. I've been so eager that my neighbor's garden should be trim and productive, that mine has been overrun with weeds."

Against this self-condemnation she felt it her duty to protest. "But Uncle Sim says you've always been on the side of the—"

"Yes, I know," he broke in, with what was nearly a laugh. "But it's just where the dear old fellow has been wrong about me. I've wanted every one else to be there, on the side of the good things—I admit that—but I was to have plenty of rope. Now I'm coming to understand—and it's taken all this trouble to drive it home to my stupidity—that if I want to see any one else on the side of the angels I must get there first. That's where the ax must go to the root of the tree. In the main other people will take care of *them*selves if I take care of *my*self—and I'm going to try."

She was hurt on his behalf. "Oh, Thor, please don't say such things when you're so—so noble."

"I'm only saying them, Lois, to show you that I see what's been wrong with me from the start. You've tried to say it yourself at times, only I couldn't take it in. Do you remember the day in my office when you came to tell me that"—he nerved himself to approach the subject with the simple directness he knew she desired—"that Rosie had—?"

She hastened to come to his aid. "Yes, but I didn't mean it in just that way."

"No; but I do. I mean it because I can look back and trace it as the cause of all our disasters from—"

"Oh, Thor!" she pleaded.

He went on, steadily: "From the way in which I asked you to marry me right up to what—to what happened about Claude." He was obliged to draw a long, hard breath before saying more. "I was so determined that every one else should be right that I didn't care how wrong *I* was—which is like handing out water from a poisoned well."

She wished she could touch him, or slip her hand into his, by way of comfort, but the distance between them was still too great. She could only say: "That's putting it unjustly to yourself, Thor. If you've made mistakes they've been splendid ones. They've been finer than the ways in which most of us have been right."

She thought he smiled.

"Oh, I don't ask to be defended or explained. I only want to say that from to-night onward I shall be starting on a new plan of life. I shall be working from the inside, and not from the outside. If I'm to do anything in this world, something must first be accomplished in me—and I've got to begin." He turned from his contemplation of the dim, white landscape to look down at her. "Will you help me? Will you show me how?"

It seemed to her that without having moved she was somehow nearer to his breast. She couldn't so much as glance up at him. She could hardly speak. The words only trembled out as she said, "If I can, Thor dear."

"You can," he said, simply, "because you know."

She barely lifted her eyes. "Oh, do you think I do?"

"You've got the secret of it. There *is* a secret. I see that now—a secret, just as there is to everything else that's worth learning."

"Oh, Thor, you make me afraid—".

"Through all these dreadful months," he pursued, tranquilly, "you've kept us straight, and led us out, and raised us higher, not because you're specially strong, Lois, or specially wise, but because—because you've got some other quality. I want you to show me what it is, so that I may have it, too. If I could get it—get just a little of it —it would seem as if Claude hadn't—hadn't died in vain." She was now so near his breast that he was obliged to bend his head in order to speak down to her. "You wrote me last year that you were looking for a substitute for love. Couldn't you find it in that?"

She was so close to him that her cheek brushed the fur collar of his coat, yet she managed to keep her mind clear and to control her voice so as to ask the thing she most vitally needed to know. "And if I did, Thor—if I *could*—what should you find it in?"

"In adoration—for one thing," he said, simply.

It was such happiness that she tore herself away from it. Advancing swiftly over the light snow to a higher point of the summit, she stood for a minute poised alone against the dark sky, crowned to his eyes with a diadem of stars. Very slowly he strode after her, but even when he reached her side it was only to slip his hand into hers and gaze outward with her into the far, dim, restful spaces.

It was she who spoke at last, timidly, and against rising tears. "Shall we go home, Thor?"

"I'm *at* home," he said, quietly. But the quietness gave way suddenly to fierceness, as little lightning flashes yield in a few seconds to the violent magnificence of storm. Seizing her in his arms with a clasp that would have been brutal if it had not been so sweet, he whispered, "You're home to me, Lois—you're home to me."

"And you're the whole wide world to me, Thor dear," she answered, drawing his face downward.

THE END